The Girl of His Dreams

Also by Amir Abrams

Crazy Love

Hollywood High series (with Ni-Ni Simone)
Hollywood High
Get Ready for War

Published by Kensington Publishing Corporation

The Girl of His Dreams

DISCARD

AMIR ABRAMS

Dafina KTeen Books
KENSINGTON PUBLISHING CORP.
http://www.kensingtonbooks.com

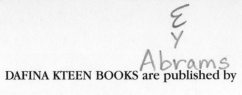

DAFINA KTEEN BOOKS are published by

Kensington Publishing Corp.
119 West 40th Street
New York, NY 10018

All Kensington titles, imprints, and distributed lines are available at special quantity discounts for bulk purchases for sales promotion, premiums, fund-raising, educational, or institutional use.

Special book excerpts or customized printings can also be created to fit specific needs. For details, write or phone the office of the Kensington Special Sales Manager: Attn.: Special Sales Department. Kensington Publishing Corp., 119 West 40th Street, New York, NY 10018. Phone: 1-800-221-2647.

KTeen Reg. US Pat. & TM Off.
Sunburst logo Reg. US Pat. & TM Off.

ISBN-13: 978-0-7582-7357-4
ISBN-10: 0-7582-7357-6

First Printing: July 2013

eISBN-13: 978-0-7582-7529-5
eISBN-10: 0-7582-7529-3

First Electronic Edition: July 2013

10 9 8 7 6 5 4 3 2 1

Printed in the United States of America

1

Antonio

No lie. Broads are good for only two things—well, three…good sex, good brain, and keepin' my sneaker, fitted-hat, and Polo game up—and not necessarily in that order. They can scratch all the extras. I'm not lookin' for love. I'm lookin' for a good time. And the only thing I'm *lookin'* to do is give 'em this good lovin'.

Who am I?

Oh, my bad. Thought you knew.

I'm that hot boy wit' the spinnin' waves.

Antonio Lopez.

Dominican and Black.

Six-four, rock-hard body.

Smooth, suave, pretty boy wit' that mad swag.

A chick magnet.

The most popular dude at McPherson High.

Voted best lookin', best dressed, and homecoming king three years in a row. All-star basketball champion.

Need I say more?

Not to pop my own collar or sound cocky wit' it or any-thing. But, real rap. I'm that dude, yo. Front if you want. Eight pack on deck. Nice chest, arms, legs, 'n' back. The chicks go crazy when they see this body. And I gotta mad assortment of colorful panties, text messages, photos, and phone numbers from thirsty broads who stay tryna get a piece of the kid to prove it.

Oh, you still don't know?

Let me put you on then.

I'm checkin' for them sexy dime-pieces who know how to handle a man like me. And oh yeah, I'll even holla at the ooga-booga as long as she gotta nice phatty, a whip, and a j-o-b. But I ain't ever gonna be seen wit' her out in public, givin' her no daytime airplay. Nah, them kinda broads gotta get it at night—*late* at night wit' the lights down real low. Better yet, they get the black light special. Once I'm bored wit' 'em, *chop!* It's on to the next.

So the moral of the story is, proceed wit' caution. And don't ever catch feelin's. And don't get too comfy, either, 'cause all good things gotta come to an end. And just like with tires and oil changes, chicks gotta be rotated and changed every three thousand miles—or in my case, every three weeks, otherwise they start gettin' real nutty, actin' like they own you. And after seein' the latest Facebook sta-tus I've been tagged on To all you birds cluckin' 'round Tone. Back up or get ya feathers plucked! Get ya own man and leave mine alone or i'm snatchin lace fronts n slashin faces!, I'm more convinced than ever before that most of 'em are straight-up psycho, like this chick Quandaleesha. My stalker. My worst nightmare.

I sigh, shakin' my head when I peep she has ninety-two

likes to her ignorant post and seventy-eight comments. All birds, I bet.

My pops peeped how triflin' Quanda was the minute he met her. And although he's never told me who to rock wit' 'cause he believes some things a man needs to learn on his own, he warned me about her. He said, "Tone, that girl's trouble. Don't give her too much of that Lopez lovin', boy. You hear? She ain't ready for it. Her mind's too weak. Give her one round, then get rid of her. And make sure you double-wrap."

"I got you, Pops," I assured him. "I'ma beat it down, then give 'er the boot."

He laughed. "Just like your pops. Give 'er just enough so that she'll never forget ya. But not enough for her to get crazy."

"No doubt," I said, givin' him a pound. See, Pops is mad chill like that. He stays schoolin' me 'bout life 'n' the honeys. So he's cool wit' me sexin' chicks and havin' 'em over as long as they bounce up outta here before eleven on weeknights, and by 1 AM on weekends. And for the most part, he's hardly ever home 'cause he's a contracted truck driver—he owns his own truck company—and spends most of his time on the road, goin' 'cross the country. And when he's not on the road, he's usually gettin' it in over at his main chick's crib or at one of his jump-offs' cribs puttin' in that work. Or he's here locked up in his room goin' at it.

I've had mad chicks up in here, over forty, and I've been havin' sex since I was thirteen. Pops made sure to it. It was the night before my thirteenth birthday. Pops walked up in my room and flat-out said, "Get showered and dressed. Tonight you become a man." I had no idea what to expect. The only thing I knew is, it was goin' to be my rite of passage into manhood. And that, no matter what happened, nothin' would ever be the same for me.

An hour later, we were at his flavor-of-the-moment's crib—this thick-in-the-hips Dominican mami wit' big boobs and a real big booty. They were upstairs, doin' what they do. And I was down in the basement wit' her nineteen-year-old daughter, who was mad sexy, bein' welcomed into manhood. I smoked my first blunt, tossed back the yak, and then...she did all kinds of things to me that had my toes curlin', my eyes crossin', and my heart racin' so hard I thought I was gonna die. I was mad nervous as I fumbled around tryna find my groove, but that night I learned e'erything I needed to know about handlin' my business as a man. Then on our way home, Pops looked over at me as he drove, and said, "You a man now. You hear me? And a real man ain't meant to be chained to the hip of one woman. Men need variety. And it's in a man's nature to have lots of sex. And lots of women. That's what they're put here on earth for, to keep a man sexed and satisfied. They're not good for nothin' else. You understand me?"

I nodded, still floatin' from the weed, the drinks, and the memory of losin' my virginity to an older chick. But I was well aware of e'erything Pops was sayin' to me. That chicks are strictly for hit 'n' runs.

Now, I'm standin' here kickin' myself for not gettin' rid of Quanda sooner than later. Like I said, Pops had warned me. After all, he's had more than his share of nutty broads. So the one thing Pops knows is females. He's Mr. Playa-Playa, the original don. The Dominican panty dropper. And the egg donor—well, for a lack of a better title, the broad who gave birth to me—is Black. And ghost! But whatever! It is what it is. Anyway, back to Pops.

Truth is, Pops's a real smooth dude when it comes to the ladies. And he's been schoolin' me since I was seven years old, preparin' me for manhood. E'erything I know about broads—that they can't be trusted, that you can't give 'em too much of ya time, that you can't ever let 'em into ya heart, and the list goes on—I've learned from him. "I'ma give you what you need to be a man," Pops always told me. "And hopefully protect you from a buncha heartache 'n' disappointment. But there are some things you gonna hafta go through and learn for ya'self."

Like this ish wit' Quanda. Ever since I hit her wit' them discharge papers, like, just before the end of the summer, she's been runnin' around actin' like she's stuck on psycho. No lie, I dumped this broad three weeks ago and here it is the first week of September and this cuckoo bird is still cluckin' all up in my space, tryna block my flow. Talkin' 'bout I'm hers and she ain't lettin' me go. Real talk, she's outta control!

I get another Facebook alert. Now Quanda's tagged me wit' some more of her craziness. I click back onto my page, shakin' my head. It's a picture of her blowin' a kiss into the camera. Stop playin, boo. u know u miss these sweet kisses! can't wait to see u in school!

It's really too early in the mornin' for this nuttiness. I scroll through my FB settings and finally do what I shoulda done three weeks ago—I block her!

2

Antonio

"Yo, Tone," someone calls out in back of me as I snake my way through the crowded halls while clickin' on the HOME link, then scrollin' through the Facebook news-feed on my iPhone and tryin' not to get caught havin' my phone out. I look up from my phone and glance over my shoulder. It's my boy, Lil Cease. Even though e'eryone calls him Lil Cease, at six-five, two-hundred plus pounds, there ain't nothin' little 'bout the center guard on McPher-son High's basketball team. Dude wrecks shop on the court, makin' him second-in-command mack daddy to the hottest shorties on the yard. Umm, if you ain't know... I'm first in command; straight like that.

I stop walkin' and wait for my boy to catch up to me. He's named after his pops, Ceasar, hence the name. A name he hates. But whatever; it is what it is. Me and Lil Cease been mad tight since third grade. He's like the brother I never had. And he's my dawg to the end, real talk. You got beef wit' him, you got beef wit' me. That's how we get down. We rock 'em 'n' drop 'em; no questions asked.

"Yo, what's good, playboy?" I say, as we give each other dap while bumpin' shoulders. "You glad to be back up in this dip, yo?"

He steps back from me, scowlin'. "Hell naw, son. I'm real heated summer's over, man. You already know. The end of summer means the end of bikinis and thick juicy booty cheeks peekin' outta them sexy lil booty shorts. And no more smokin', son. Yo, fam. I got smoked out last night. Now it's a wrap. And I know I'ma be goin' through mad withdrawals real soon, yo."

I laugh. Like Cease, I dig gettin' my smoke on too. But, dude gets it in, hard. He blazes e'ery day durin' the summer, then stops as soon as the school year starts so he can get his mind and body right for basketball season. But come summertime, forget it. He'll take his whole paycheck from workin' at his pops's landscapin' business and blow it on bud. Not me, yo. I'll blaze on the weekends, and maybe one or two nights outta the week if I'm chillin' wit' a shorty who likes to roll. But I ain't a fiend like my boy. Trickin' up all ya paper on bud is crazy to me, but that's what he does.

"Right, right," I say, shoulderin' my book bag.

"Yo, watch where you goin'," Cease says as he's bumped by the backpack of some lil dude who clearly has to be a freshman. The halls are mad crowded wit' heads yellin' out to their peeps, runnin' up givin' 'em hugs 'n' daps while stoppin' in the middle of the hallways to get caught up from the summer. Lockers are bangin' shut, peeps are pushin' to get through the halls, newbies are lookin' 'round all lost 'n' whatnot tryna maneuver their way 'round, chicks are profilin' tryna snag up some atten-tion or talk 'bout what some other chick's rockin', dudes are posted up against lockers stylin' in their fresh kicks 'n' wears. Yo, McPherson is live 'n' poppin' this mornin'.

I bump into this cutie who's lookin' all lost. She has her schedule in her hand, lookin' from the paper to each doorway. "Yo, what's good, ma...you lost?"

She looks up from her schedule, sighin'. "A little. I'm tryna find my homeroom. Room one-twenty-one." I tell her where she needs to go. She smiles. "Thank you."

"Yo, what's ya name, shorty?" Cease calls out.

"Courtney," she says over her shoulder.

"A'ight, ma; that's wassup wit' ya sexy self. I'ma check for you a lil later." She starts grinnin' mad hard, almost walkin' into a wall.

"Yo, you got broads stumblin' into walls already," I say, chucklin'.

"Anyway, like I was sayin', fam, it's a new school year. And a new school year always means fresh sweet meat, ready to be eaten alive, like that lil hottie right there." He points at a dark chocolate, dimpled cutie standin' by the attendance office.

"Yeah, maaaaan," I say, noddin'. "There's only one thing better than old booty, and that's new booty!"

He laughs, givin' me a pound. "Word is bond, son. And I'ma be wrappin' it 'n' tappin' it e'ey which way. I better reup my Trojan collection."

"Yo, you already know," I say, laughin' wit' him.

"Speakin' of which," he says, slingin' his backpack up over his broad shoulder, "you peep some of them fresh-men, yo? Word is bond, son, it's somethin' in the water.

Some of them biscuits got cakes stacked like whoa, son. I ain't even gonna front, yo. I'm tryna snatch me up a few of them young tender chickens real quick before the vultures swoop down on 'em."

I laugh. "Yo, ninja. You a damn fool, yo. You know I ain't thinkin' 'bout them freshman broads. Them chicks mad young. I ain't got time tryna train no young head how'ta get wit' the program. You know I like 'em already broken in. Sophomores and up."

He laughs. "Yeah, but some of 'em are young hoes who been in trainin' since middle school so they already know what it is, feel me? They mad hot in the drawers, fam."

"No doubt," I say as my eyes zoom in on all the new faces walkin' through the halls. So far, nothin' worth hollerin' at. Several chicks walk in our direction. Two of 'em are junior hoodrats. Broads I ran through either last school year or two summers ago. They walk by, rollin' their eyes at Cease and me. I ig 'em, but he laughs at 'em. Three more chicks walkin' in our direction are sophomores. "Heeeey, Tone," they sing in unison, wavin', smilin' and stickin' out their chests to make their twins pop out at me.

I eye 'em all, lickin' my lips. It ain't no mystery. I'ma breast 'n' booty man. I love the shorties, and the shorties love me. And they'll do almost anything to get my attention *and* my lovin'. Heck, it ain't no secret. I've smashed most of the broads here. And the ones I haven't gotten it in wit', it's because they're either a) dog-faced ugly and broke, b) freshmen, or c) campaignin' to be nuns. Yo, eff what ya heard. I might be a panty hound, but I ain't humpin' nothin' that looks like it should be caged or on a chain. And I'm not beat for tryna convert a buncha uptight, stingy chicks tryna hold on to their V-cards 'til they turn eighteen or the world comes to an end to get them to loosen up the buckles to them chastity belts.

"Oh, word?" Cease says, stoppin' in the middle of the hall and openin' his arms in mock hurt. "Y'all just gonna dis me. Big Daddy can't get no love? Tone the only dude y'all see? I know y'all see all this fineness starin' you in the face."

"Hey, Ceeeease," they say at once, gigglin'.

He flashes 'em a smile. "Now, that's more like it." He reaches for LuAnna. This half-Filipino, half-Black shorty wit' a short bob cut, slanted grey eyes, and a double-D rack. I glance at the words JUICY FRUIT stretched across her chest in hot pink letters. "When you gonna stop frontin', LuLu baby, and let me be ya man?"

LuAnna playfully pushes him off of her, eyein' me on the sly. "I'm already taken."

He smirks. "Yeah, right. But whatever. What that got to do wit' me and you? I bet he can't do you like I can."

She waves him on. "Oh, puhleeze. Whatever."

"Whatever nothin', yo . . ."

"Wassup, Chantel?" I say, eyein' the one in the middle. A caramel-coated cutie wit' big round eyes, thick lashes, and a set of juicy, red-painted lips. Her body ain't really hittin' on much, and she's kinda flat in the back. But what she lacks in booty, she makes up in boobs.

She grins, flashin' a set of pearly whites. "You already know what's up, Tone. But you stay playin' games."

"Nah, baby. I'm too grown for games. I'm sayin' . . . you the one frontin', ma. Holla at ya boy and I'll show you what's really good."

She smacks her big lollipop lickers together, then licks
'em real slow and sexy like. "Okay. I'ma see."

"Oh, word? How 'bout if you stop frontin' and let me
let you *feel* it, too?"

"Ugh," the nondescript chick on the left of her says.
She's the color of dark chocolate and has deep dark
brown eyes. Her hair is in locks, pulled up in a twist. She
isn't busted in the face, but she ain't somethin' I'd wanna
rock the springs wit' either. "Why don't the two of you go
at it already?"

She must be pissed she can't get no rhythm.

"I'm out," she huffs, stormin' off. Chantel laughs at her,
wavin' her on as she tells 'em she's goin' to her homeroom. I watch her tryna shake what ain't there down the
hall, then glance at my watch. We have less than fifteen
minutes to get to our respective homerooms. Mad heads
go by givin' Cease 'n' me dap as they head to homeroom.
Chantel and I flirt back and forth for a few seconds more
while Cease pushes up on LuAnna before we roll out.

"I gotta get to homeroom," LuAnna finally tells Cease,
still eyein' me on the low. "But I'ma see you around."

Cease scoops her up in his arms and gives her a hug.
"That's wassup, ma." They go back and forth for a few
minutes more while Chantel and I kick it.

I step up on her, lean up into her ear, then say real low,
"So what's good? When you gonna let me get that goody?"

She grins, twirlin' a curl from her weave, then tuckin' it
behind her ear. "I don't know. I thought you had a girl."

"Nah. I don't. Not anymore."

"Well, what about that crazy chick I saw you with over

the summer? I can't think of her name, but she goes here too."

Of course she's talkin' 'bout Quanda since that's who she saw me wit' at the mall when she was coppin' me them new Jordans and a fitted to match. "Ain't nuthin'. I got rid of that problem. I'm single, baby."

She smirks. "Oh, for real?"

I stroke her cheek. "Yeah. Now I'm tryna see what's really good wit' you. I'm tryna make you mine."

She laughs, playfully swattin' my arm. "Whatever, Tone. Trust me. I've already heard all about them nasty things you do."

I rub my chin and grin. Chicks stay runnin' their mouths so I already know she got the scoop on my sex game. And, I know she wanna find out if what she's heard is all true. "Well, uh, don't believe e'erything you hear," I tease. "Some things you need to find out for ya'self, feel me?"

She rolls her eyes. "Whatever. I bet nasty stuff's all you think about, too."

"Nah. That's not *all* I think about. But, yeah, I ain't gonna front. It ain't no secret I likes to get it in. And right now, I'm tryna set things up so I can get it in wit' you."

She waves me on, shakin' her head, tellin' me how crazy I am. Then hits me wit' some BS 'bout not bein' that kinda girl. That she doesn't have sex just to be havin' it; that she only gets it in wit' her man, *after* they've been chillin' for a minute.

I laugh at how retarded she sounds, tryna play like she's a Miss Goody Two-shoes. "Yo, sounds like you be watchin' too much Oprah, boo."

She sucks her teeth, playfully rollin' her eyes. I already know she's only talkin' that dumb ish 'cause LuAnna's standin' there, practically tryna ear hustle in on our convo.

I lean into her ear and whisper, "You got me goin' through it, ma."

She steps back from me, grinnin'. "You're such a flirt. And a sex hound."

I slip my hand to her waist, then her hip, where it stays. "Nah, I'm keepin' it a hunnid, ma. I'm tryna be your hound. I want you."

She smiles. "I bet you say—"

LuAnna shoots a look over at us, squintin' her eyes. "C'mon, girl," she says, cuttin' Chantel off while walkin' over and pullin' her by the arm. I smirk. I know what it is. She's tryna block. She ain't beat to let Chantel get what she wants, first. "We need to go. I'm not tryna hear Ms. Dayton's mouth first thing this morning for being late to homeroom on the first day of school. You know how she is."

Chantel agrees, glancin' at me. "Yeah, you're right. We need to get going. I'll see you later."

"Yo, hol' up. Before you bounce, let me get ya digits." I pull out my iPhone and hand it to her so she can put her number in. She doesn't hesitate grabbin' my phone, and hittin' me wit' them digits, like I knew she would. "A'ight, bet. I'ma holla."

They say their good-byes, then step. Cease and I crane our necks as they swish their hips off toward their lockers. "That Chantel chick's feelin' you hard, fam. I peeped the way she was checkin' you, lettin' you feel all up on her body. Yo, she's real ripe 'n' ready for a good pluckin'."

"I already know. And I'ma give it to her real good, too. But she mad flat in the back, though." I shake my head.

Cease laughs, then starts whinin' as we climb up three flights of stairs toward our lockers. "Man, this don't make no sense," he complains as we climb the steps. "Who in the heck puts lockers up on the fourth floor when most of our classes are on the second and third floors?"

"Uh, correction, yo. All *your* classes are down on the second and third floors. All *my* classes are up on the fourth." The fourth floor is mostly honors and advanced placement classes.

"Whatever, man. We all know you're an undercover nerd."

I laugh. "Whatever, yo. Don't hate, bruh." He starts goin' in 'bout havin' to walk so far. I tell 'im to stop complainin'. "After all the bud you done smoked over the summer, you need the exercise. It'll clear ya lungs. Besides, it's a good warm-up to preseason conditionin'."

He groans. "I'm sure Coach is gonna kill us in practices. Oh, snap. I meant to ask you. What's good wit' that lil biscuit you snatched up last week at the mall, yo? She was lookin' right. She let you beat that thing-thing up, yet?"

"Nah, son. I told her I'm not tryna marry her, just test-drive that booty."

He keeps laughin'. "Yo, I heard that. So what she say after that?"

"What *who* said after *what*?" I hear as I step up to my locker and start twirlin' the combination to my lock. It's Quanda, wearin' this tight-fittin', low-cut white shirt, a short plaid skirt, white knee-high stockin's and black heels, lookin' like a fake Catholic school girl. Her long weave, with short bangs, is hangin' down her back, brushin' the top of her butt cheeks. This broad stay frontin' like she's Indian.

"Yo, what's good, Quanda?" Cease says, pullin' open his locker. "How was ya summer?"

She rolls her eyes at him. "Don't speak to me, boy." She turns her back to him, placin' a hand up on her hip as she leans her fine frame up against the bank of lockers.

Cease laughs, shakin' his head.

She shoots him a look. "Annnnyway, beat it!" Oh, and did I mention this broad's a loudmouth headache. And she loves drama—lots of it. But wit' a name like Quandaleesha why would I, or anyone else, expect anything less?

"A'ight, yo," I say to Cease, stuffin' my book bag in my locker, then shuttin' the door. "I'll get at you durin' lunch period."

"A'ight, bet," he says, walkin' off.

Quanda's starin' at me, lookin' mad tight. "Why you unfriend and block me on Facebook?"

I sigh. " 'Cause you be buggin', yo."

She puts a hand up on her hip. "Oh, puhleeze. How am I buggin', boy? You the one buggin' for breakin' up with *me*."

I suck my teeth, walkin' off toward my homeroom. "Yo, you can stand here and play stupid if you want, but I don't have time for this."

"Well, you better make time, boo-boo," she says, walkin' up behind me wit' a hand up on her hip, " 'cause if you think you're gonna dump me and move on to the next chick, you got another think comin'. I already beat up one of your lil hoes at the rink last weekend. And you already know I have no problem doin' it again. Now that we back in school, you are not gonna be tryna play me with none of these hoes up in here. So go 'head and be up in some other chick's face and see what happens. You've been warned."

"Yo, whatever," I say, walkin' into homeroom just as the bell rings.

3

Antonio

By fourth-period lunch, mad heads are talkin' 'bout this new biscuit, wit' the stacked cakes and light brown eyes, floatin' 'round the buildin'. They're goin' on and on 'bout her small waist and long, sexy legs, and monster booty, talkin' 'bout she's supermodel fine. I mean, these thirsty mofos are pumpin' her up to be some real live dime-piece that I have yet to lay my eyes on. So until I see it for myself, I ain't beat to believe the hype. I pull out my phone and hit Chantel real quick wit' a text tellin' her I wanna get at her after school. I slide my phone back down into my pocket.

"Yo, fam, word is bond," Cease says, tryna convince me how bad she is as he's chompin' on sunflower seeds. "I'm tellin' you, yo. I don't know who she is, or where she came from, but I'm tryna find out, fast, ya heard?" He tells me she's in his third-period biology class. "Man, listen. Nobody could stop eyein' her. Even Mr. Greene wit' his old azz kept starin' at 'er."

I laugh. Mr. Greene is like a hunnid years old. Well, not really. But he looks it. And his wife is mad young, like in her thirties or somethin'. She's like his fourth or fifth wife. And he already has three kids wit' her. But like eight or nine other kids wit' his other wives. Cease and I joke 'bout how he's old as dirt, and how he's old enough to be most of his kids' grandfather.

"That old dude stays snatchin' up chicks."

"Yeah, man; even in them old-azzzz suits he stays rockin'. Mr. Greene's one of them old-school players for real, yo."

It's just me 'n' Cease sittin' at the table right in the middle of the cafeteria so we can see who's comin' 'n' goin' and what's 'bout to pop off. By the end of the week, our table will be packed wit' all the popular heads at the school. And e'eryone else who wants to be in our space will be at the tables closest to ours. That's just how it is. The first two days of school peeps are just tryna get back into the groove, then it's block-party central up in this piece.

"Anyway, yo. Back to shorty. I'm tellin' you, fam, she's bad as hell." He shakes his head, leanin' up in his seat. "Wait 'til you see her, fam."

"She's probably hidin' what she really looks like under two coats of face paint. Chicks stay ODin' on makeup. They be havin' their faces three shades lighter than the rest of their bodies."

He laughs. "Yo, you stupid, fam. You right, yo 'bout chicks packin' on all that face paste, but you dead wrong 'bout this one, son."

"Nah, real rap, bruh. She's prolly some insecure, butt-ugly broad wit' crooked teeth who gotta wear a buncha war paint to cover up her battle scars."

"Nah, fam. No makeup. No crooked teeth, from what I could tell. No nothin', just straight-up all natural. Real talk, son. She's hot like fire. I'm tellin' you, yo. Wait 'til you see her. Twenty bucks says you're gonna drool."

"Oh, word? Ya cheap azz bettin', then I def gotta check for this broad 'cause we both know how tight you try holdin' on to ya paper."

He starts laughin'. "Word up, fam. She's hot like that. First chance I get to holla at her, I'm goin' in for the kill. So, fall back, son. I got first dibs on that."

"Yo, whatever, man. You already know what it is. If she's as fine as you say, it's e'ery playboy for himself."

"Yo, that's what it is, then."

"Well, she must be a freshman or sophomore," I say, eyein' Quanda as she heads toward our table, " 'cause she's not in this lunch period wit' us." I shake my head, sighin'. "This broad," I mumble under my breath, but Cease catches it.

"Who?" he asks, lookin' over his shoulder in her direction. "Aah, say no more. All I can say is I'm glad she's your headache and not mine. That girl's nuts, man. My peeps told me how she stalked the last dude she was effen wit'."

I frown. "Mofo, fine time for you to tell me—*after* the fact."

He laughs. "Yo, I ain't know, man. Word is bond. You said ya pops told you not to eff wit' her from the rip. But you did anyway." He shrugs. "So I guess that's what you get for not listenin'."

I cringe as she stops at one of the tables where six girls are sittin'—three of 'em are seniors; the other three are juniors. Only two of 'em are worth givin' second glances to. And of one 'em, I've already tapped up. So she's a no-go. I don't do repeats. Once I smash it, then dismiss it, there are no second chances. Goin' back, tryin' it again, ain't what I do. Quanda leans in, says somethin' to 'em, then points over in my direction. They all shift their gazes at me. I act like I don't peep it, shiftin' in my seat.

"Don't remind me, yo. Did you see that craziness she posted on my wall this mornin'?"

"Nah, man. I missed it. You know I ain't on the Book like that anymore. What she post this time?" I tell 'im, then tell 'im about this mornin' in the hall. He shakes his head. "Damn, son, you got that girl hooked."

"Yeah, on stupid," I say, feelin' myself gettin' heated. "She needs to get a life, quick. I hope she finds a hobby or somethin' 'cause, man, I ain't beat for her craziness all school year."

He laughs, twistin' off the cap of his Sprite. "Yo, she already gotta hobby, son—*you!*" He places the bottle to his lips and gulps it down, then lets out a loud burp.

I frown, reachin' for his bag of sunflower seeds. "Whatever, yo. She needs to find another one, word is bond. I ain't beat. It's a wrap. First day of school and she's already at it tryna get some mess started. I swear she's a real bit..." My voice trails off as I spot this mad sexy shorty strut through the cafeteria doors, lookin' like she stepped off a video or magazine shoot. "Daaaaayum, who is that right there?"

Damn...she's fiiiiyah!

Cease cranes his neck, then hops up, gettin' all amped. "Yo, son, that's the shorty I was tellin' you about. What I tell you, yo? She's hot to death. Check out that body, yo."

I keep my eyes on her as she walks over toward the

salad bar. She's this caramel-skinned cutie, rockin' some lil slinky black dress thingy that's wrapped 'round her body. She's definitely not from around here dressin' like that. Real rap. She's takin' hood fly to another level. I lick my lips. *Damn!* From what I can see, she got killer curves. The kind of body I wanna get up on and run my hands all over. My eyes zoom in on her juicy-apple bottom, and, no lie, I feel myself gettin' lightheaded. She's the truth! But I peep I ain't the only one checkin' this fine honey out. They all see what I see. She's that chick! Hands down, she got the whole cafeteria on pause. Kats are snappin' their necks to get a second look at her. Chicks are eyein' her, hard. Even Quanda does a double-take as she walks by, then gives her the evil eye. Oh yeah. Whoever she is, she's gonna be a real problem, fo' sho!

I keep my eyes on her as she struts her sexiness over to the cashier, her hair bouncin' 'n' swingin' past her shoulder blades. She tucks her hair behind her ears, then reaches into her bag and pays for her salad. As quickly as she appeared, she disappears out the cafeteria doors.

I almost wanna get up and run after her, but I'm not about to play myself like some thirsty mofo, especially when I can have any girl I want. Besides, I can already tell she's used to kats gettin' all up in her ear. I'ma just chill, and when the time is right, she'll be tryna holla at me. Just like the rest of 'em.

And if she is a freshman, as fine as she is, I just might have to break my no-freshman rule and make her an exception.

Cease has a big smirk on his face.

"What?" I say, frownin' at him.

He laughs, tossin' me two napkins. "I'm waitin' for you to wipe up the drool from ya lip 'n' chin, fam."

I wave him on, shiftin' in my seat. "Man, go 'head wit' that dumbness. Ain't nobody droolin' over that broad. I mean. She's a'ight-lookin'. But she ain't nothin' to be gettin' all nutty over. You fiends were goin' in like she was a ten or somethin'."

"Tone, man, cut it out, yo. You stylin' for real, son. That biscuit is fine so stop frontin'. She *is* a ten. Wait 'til you see her up close 'n' personal."

I shrug. "From here, that body's right. But I couldn't really see her face."

He keeps laughin'. "Yo, whatever. Save that bull. I peeped how your eyes almost popped outta ya skull the minute you spotted her. So you can front if you want. But I already know what it is."

My boy was right. I was frontin', like crazy. He knows I can spot a beauty a mile away. And that lil sexy mama is the truth. I open the cap of my Vitaminwater, then take a swig. "Man, whatever," I say, wipin' my mouth wit' the back of my hand. "Ain't nobody even thinkin' 'bout that broad like that."

"Good," he says, bitin' into his cheeseburger. He looks up at me and shakes his head as I guzzle down my drink. He talks 'n' chews. "Yo, you stay drinkin' that sugar water. You do know there's nuthin' healthy 'bout that drink, right? You keep drinkin' that mess and I'ma start callin' you Sweet T."

"Yeah, a'ight, Meathead. And get ya chin checked. Ain't nuthin' sweet 'bout me, yo."

He starts laughin'. "Ninja, you soft as cotton." He lifts

his right arm up and flexes his bicep. "You see this, son? Rock solid, bruh. And I hit hard."

"Hahahaha. You mad funny, yo. But you already know what it is." I pull out my phone as it vibrates. I glance at the screen. I have a new text. "Yo, Chantel just hit me up," I say as I open her text message.

"Oh, word? What she talkin' 'bout?"

I laugh. "What you think, fool? She comin' through later."

"Yo, what I tell you, son?" he says, givin' me dap. "I told you she was checkin' for you."

"Man, she ain't really my flavor, but I'ma give her a mouthful of this log."

He cracks up laughin'. "Yo, fam, you wild. That broad's mad freaky, bruh."

"Man, listen. I'm only givin' her what she wants. And I always aim to please."

I text back: come 2 my crib after skool

Five minutes later, she texts back: wat x?

I shake my head. *That dumb broad.* I text: wtf, yo?! Don't play. Wat time u think? RIGHT after skool, yo!!!

I slip my phone back into my pocket. These broads stay playin' stupid.

4

Miesha

Ooh, the haterade is on full-blast! All around me, hoes whisper as I strut by in my wears—a black knit jersey dress and black, six-inch strappy heels. And so what if my booty is bouncing real lovely as I click my way through the halls, causing all the boys to snap their necks. Point is, I'm not here for any of these tricks. And I'm definitely not thinking about any of these little boys. Chicks are phony. And, most boys are straight-up dogs. I'm not beat for either. Matter of fact, I don't even wanna be at this dumb, ghetto school. But I am. Already I can tell I'ma have problems. And ninety-nine reasons to go upside a ho's head.

"Look at her. That stuck-up ho thinks she cute."

"Oooh, who died? She's dressed like she's goin' to a funeral."

"I don't like that trick."

"Video ho on deck!"

"Hooker heels in school? Where they do that at?"

"Where she from?"

"I bet those aren't even her *real* eyes."

"Her weave's cute though."

"All I know, that skank better not even think about lookin' at my man!" And then Drama—with a capital D—steps right in front of me, wearing some imitation Catholic schoolgirl getup and a long weave that hangs down to her butt.

All I'm tryna do is go out to my car, FaceTime it up with my girls back in Brooklyn, eat my Caesar salad, then get to my next class—World History, I think. No, Afro History—in peace. But noooo, here stands this ghetto ho blocking my way, tryna set it off. First day of school, no less. She steps up in my face, and says, "Listen, boo. I don't know who you are. But hoes aren't welcome here. So you need to go back to wherever you came from."

I flat-out laugh in her face.

She blinks, clearly taken aback. But she quickly regroups. "Oh, you think this is funny? Well, let's see how funny it is when I punch you in your mouth."

"Oh, really?"

Now I don't know why chicks stay testing me. I swear I think it's something in the air. Oh wait. Maybe it's this pretty face. Or these light brown eyes that almost look hazel when the sun hits them. Oh, no. That's not it. It's gotta be the silky hair that stays fly—thanks to the Dominican spot I go to over on One Hundred and Forty-ninth and Amsterdam Avenue in New York. Uh, maybe, it's this small waist that has 'em all gaggin' on hater juice. Whatever! All I know is, where I'm from, you don't step up in a chick's face and pop noise. You got beef, you swing and take her face off. Period, point blank. I'ma feel real sorry for her if she's dumb enough to let these nondescript chicks gas her into gettin' a beatdown. She's real lucky. 'Cause if this was last year, I swear she wouldn't still be standing. She'd be dropped to the ground and I'd be standing up over her body stomping her lights out. But I'm tryna change. Tryna be the better person. New school, new beginnings...whatever!

Point is, I miss Brooklyn!

I miss Flatbush Avenue.

I miss Fulton Street.

I miss Fort Greene Park.

I miss my old high school.

I miss my girls, Stacy, Jalanda, and Tre.

I miss the hustle 'n' bustle of the streets. Brooklyn at night is live 'n' poppin'.

At my old school, I was *that* hot chick on deck. I *still* am. But these hookers and hoes here don't know that, *yet*. They too busy hatin' and throwin' shade. But trust. They'll get the memo. And when they do, they'll know, like they did at Fashion High, that I'm that mad sexy chick—the fly girl who stays dipped in all the fly wears. The one who keeps all the boys following behind her like lost puppies, eating outta the palm of her hands. Yeah, *that* chick.

At my old school, chicks *wanted* to be me!

And all the dudes *wanted* to have me!

And I had 'em all running around in circles.

Now look at me. My life is ruined.

Over!

I'm so pissed. Why my mom felt the need to move across the river will never, ever, make sense to me. If she wanted to get away from my father, she coulda moved up-town somewhere. Heck, she coulda even moved *waaaay* out to Queens, or out on Long Island. She had a choice of *five* boroughs. And all she had to do is pick one. Then I'd still be in New York. But, nooooo. She wanted out. Out of her life with my father. Out of New York. And she just had to drag me across the bridge—well, through the tunnel—with her. Just had to disrupt my whole life...scratch that, my whole world, and move to corny Jersey.

Now here I am...!

First day of school with chicks slick talking when I walk by. Guys either tryna holla or eyeballing me all reckless and whatnot. And now I gotta deal with this chick standing here practically begging for these hands upside her head. I look her up and down, then dead in her face, letting her know ain't no punk standing here. Still, I'm not gonna toss shade and say she's ugly 'cause she's not. I mean, she's *not* as fine or as fly as *me*, but she's still kinda cute. I guess. And I'm not gonna hate on her shape 'cause she's definitely holding her own. But her body isn't bangin' like mine. And her hair...mmmph. Well, mine is real. Hers, a straight-up nightmare! Horrid!

"Yes, really," she snaps, narrowing her eyes. "You'd better buy a vowel and get a clue, sweetie."

I tilt my head. "Excuse you? Have we met?"

She twists her lips up. "No, we haven't met, trick. I'm the Welcome Committee. Here to warn you that if you even think about going after my man, I'm gonna welcome you to a beatdown, boo."

Two of the girls in her fan club start laughing. I cut my eyes over at them, then back at Miss Ghetto. "Okay, so I've been warned. You done?"

She gets real up close and personal, ramming her face

close to mine. I can smell the watermelon Jolly Rancher she's eaten on her breath.

"No I ain't done, trick. Do I *look* done to you? You'll know I'm done when I say I'm done."

Now trust me. I already told you that I ain't scared to fight. And I have no problems taking it to a chick's face when it's warranted. But, the truth is, I'd fight a boy quicker than I would another female 'cause all most of 'em ever wanna do is scratch and pull you hair instead of bringing it to you knuckle up. I mean, really. Who has time to be all clawed up? I know I don't. Punch me, boo. Slap me, even. But don't go digging your nails in my face or tryna yank my hair outta my scalp. If we gonna fight, then let's fight. Fist to fist, toe to toe. But that ain't how most chicks tryna bring it. So I really try to avoid confrontations with 'em whenever possible, like right now. This ghetto trash is really, really pushing her luck with me. But I'm still tryna keep my cool.

I back up a bit, just in case I gotta hook off on her. Count to ten in my head. Then politely say, "Look, don't let the pretty face and silky hair fool you, sweetie. Step outta my face. You don't know me. And I *really* don't think you want it with me."

"No, you don't want it with *me*. But you'll get it if you don't watch yourself. So consider yourself on notice."

I take a deep breath. Assess the situation. Truth is, I'm really not dressed for the occasion. I'm not tryna drop my handbag and have her little sea creatures scooping it up. But I will step outta these heels and rock her to sleep if I have to. Still, I have to ask myself: Do I beat this chick down and get suspended on the first day of school? Do I slam her face into the wall and then, have to fight her little pep squad? Or do I bow out gracefully and let her *think* she's played me?

I hear my mom's voice in my head telling me to ignore this girl, warning me not to get into any trouble here, threatening to take my car from me. Telling me that this chick really isn't worth it. And maybe she's right. But I already know if this ho puts her hands on me, I'm gonna mop the floor up with her face.

I smirk. "Sweetie, *boom!* You're a real clown. Save your notices. Say what you gotta say, then step."

"Trick," she snaps, pointing a finger in my face. *Strike one!* "I already said it. We don't do hoes here. So if you even think about tryna ho it up with any of our boyfriends, be ready to fight."

I shift my handbag from one hand to the other, then sweep my bang across my forehead. I fake a yawn, then flick imaginary dirt from my fingernail. "The name's Miesha, hun. And trust me. I *stay* ready for a good fight, so back—"

"Okay, ladies," a tall, brown-skinned woman says, walking over to us. "Shouldn't you young ladies be in the cafeteria or outside in the commons area?" She eyes Drama. "Quandaleesha, you know we don't allow loitering in the halls. Is there a problem over here?"

Quandaleesha? I keep from laughing in her face. "It's Quanda," she snaps. "And, no, there's no problem, Mrs. Dean. It's bein' solved."

She narrows her eyes. "Then let's break this party up, *Quanda.*" She turns to Drama's fan club. "Same thing with you, young ladies."

"We're going now, Mrs. Dean," they say in unison.

"Good," she says, locking her stare back on Drama. "And, Quanda, I want you to go have a seat in my office."

"Whaaat?! Why? What I do?"

"Nothing that I'm aware of, which is why I think we should have a chat, now."

"But this is my lunch period."

"Well, since you're standing out here in the hall that says to me that you've either already eaten or you're not hungry. So go have a seat in my office. I'll be there in a few. I'll only take a minute of your time. I'll write you a pass when I'm done."

"Can't this wait until after classes?"

Mrs. Dean narrows her eyes. "Quandaleesha, this is *not* up for debate. My office. Now."

Drama huffs, shooting me a dirty look. I shake my head as she stomps off, holding in my laugh. *Quandaleesha. Hahahaha! What a ghetto joke!*

"Hi. I'm Mrs. Dean. The vice principal." She extends her hand. "And you are?"

"Hi," I say, shaking her hand. "I'm Miesha. Miesha Wilson."

"Oh, yes. The transfer from Fashion High." She takes me in. "And I see you dress the part. But as you can see, it's a little more relaxed here at McPherson. And some of the kids here might not be, um…" She pauses, then smiles. "Let's say they might not be ready for you."

I shrug. "Yeah, I see. Well, they had better get ready 'cause I'm not changing who I am to fit in."

Her smile widens. "And so you shouldn't. Always be you. It'll take some getting used to, but I'm sure you'll fit right in just fine here. Don't let those girls get to you."

I run my hand through my hair. "Oh, trust. They're lightweights compared to what I'm used to."

"I'm sure." She glances down at her watch, then at the

lunch in my hand and says, "Well, I'd better let you go have your lunch. Welcome to McPherson High." She smiles again.

"Yeah, thanks."

She starts to walk off, then turns back around. "Oh. One more thing. We have a zero-tolerance bullying policy here. If you have any problems with *anyone,* come see me. And it will be addressed immediately. I have an open door, no matter what the issue is."

Sweetie boom! I have my own policy for bullies. Beat. Them. Down! "Okay, thanks," I say. "I'll keep that in mind." I head toward the door that leads out into the parking lot. Pissed that I have only ten minutes left before the bell rings for my next class.

I hate this school!

5

Antonio

Sixth period, I'm sittin' in my Advanced French class. Mrs. Duvet is my teacher for the second year in a row. She's mad strict, but I like her. And I actually dig French. But I ain't 'bout to tell my boys this. Still I enjoy it. It's a mad sexy language; real rap. And, between you and me, anytime I'm in class or I hear it bein' spoken, it always reminds me of my French teacher from freshman year, Miss Singleton. Whew! I get mad excited e'erytime I think 'bout her. She was...uh, the one who got me interested in wantin' to speak the language. She made e'erything about the language sexy. I'm not gonna front. At first I wasn't really beat for takin' French or any other language, but it's required that e'eryone takes at least two years of a language so I chose French 'cause I already know Spanish and I wasn't beat for Italian or Latin. Plus, the French teacher at the time, Miss Singleton, was, like twenty-eight, mad sexy, and always gave her male students and even some of the chicks somethin' nice to look at in class whenever she wore short skirts and too-tight blouses. So I figured I could kill two birds wit' one stone. Handle my requirements *and* check out the hot new teacher e'ery day. For me, it was a straight-up win-win situation.

All I did in class was daydream about seein' her wit' out clothes on, then go home and fantasize about gettin' it in wit' her. Then, finally, I got my wish. At first, it was just her bendin' over and lettin' me get sneak peeks of her kitty anytime she thought no one else was lookin'. Then it went to me stayin' after school for extra credit and her always insistin' I sit up in the front row while she sat up on the edge of her desk wit' her skirt hiked up and her legs opened. Sometimes she would touch herself; other times, she would let me touch her. But most times she just wanted me to look at it. It was torture. Real talk, she was playin' head games and it was killin' me. I had to have her. I wanted her, bad! And, after almost three months of torture, ish escalated to me finally knockin' it down. We was goin' at it hard. I'd either sneak over to her crib and we'd get it in. Or she'd scoop me up on the corner somewhere, drive to one of the parks in the area, and we'd rock it out in the backseat of her whip.

We was sexin' it up almost e'ery night for months before some hater found out 'bout us and reported it. Two weeks before the end of the school year and it was lights out—for the both of us. Even though I denied gettin it in wit' her to the police and school officials, she was still arrested and charged wit' sex abuse—and eventually fired— 'cause two other dudes ratted her out and admitted that she had let them smash too. So basically, I wasn't her first. Still, by that time, I had already started diggin' the language and wanted to learn more.

The only person I kept it a hunnid wit' was my pops. One night, I came home and told him e'erything. He rubbed his chin the whole time I was tellin' him, noddin' as he took it all in. When I finished, he just stared at me, long 'n' hard for a few seconds, broke out in a wide grin, and said, "You're becomin' a Casanova like your pops." Then he wanted to know if I had handled my business in the sheets right.

"No doubt, Pops," I said, puffin' my chest out wit' a buncha pride 'cause I was livin' out e'ery guy's ultimate fantasy. "I destroyed it."

His grin widened as he patted me on the back. "You've done me proud, son."

"Okay, class," Mrs. Duvet says, clappin' her hands and gettin' up from her seat. E'eryone stops talkin' or whatever else they mighta been doin' and brings their attention to the front of the class where she stands. "Let's get started. Shall we? Welcome to French Five. I trust everyone has had a great summer. If you are in this class, it is because you have mastered the first four levels of the language and are now ready for more advanced study. With that being said, *Vous lirez, écrire et parler le francais seulement.*"

She tells us we will read, write, and speak in French only.

I pull my phone out on the sly and hit Chantel up real quick. You still comin thru, right?

It doesn't take her long to hit me back wit' her reply. yes

I grin, slidin' my phone back into my pocket. *I'ma tear that up!*

*   *   *

By the end of the day, I say wassup to a few peeps, shoot the breeze wit' a few cuties, then grab my things from outta my locker, and dip. I hit up one of my standbys just in case Chantel decides to front and not come through.

"Hey, boo," Shania coos into the phone the minute she answers. She's this thick-hipped seventeen-year-old hottie from Brick City—Newark, that is—who I been kickin' it wit' off 'n' on for a minute. Pops says a man should always have some backup booty on hand, and on call. And she happens to be one of many I keep tucked on the low for those late-night emergencies.

"What's good, ma? How you?"

"Missin' you, boy. But other than that, I'm good. Just walkin' up outta school. I'm so glad this day is over. I can't wait to get home and chill. Wassup with you, boy? I haven't heard from you in a minute. And why haven't you hit me back on the Book, yet? I don't know why you gotta play me."

I suck my teeth. "Girl, ain't nobody tryna play you. You already know what it is wit' us." I lower my voice. "Who you got beatin' that up?"

She sucks her teeth. "Nobody. That's the problem. You stay frontin' on all'a this goodness."

I laugh. "Nah, never that. But, I'm sayin', yo. Don't let me find out you lettin' some other mofo tap that out. It's gonna be some major consequences 'n' repercussions."

"Whatever, boy. All I know is I haven't seen you in weeks. You could be gettin' this goody on the regular. But you wanna front. And I know you got that message I sent in your inbox."

"Nah, I ain't get it," I tell 'er, walkin' up outta the buildin' toward the parkin' lot. Truth is, I have over thirty-five hundred friends and most of 'em are broads who stay floodin' my Facebook inbox wit' all kinda messages 'n' half-naked flicks and sometimes I just ain't beat to respond back. "Well, maybe I did, but I haven't gone through all my messages, yet."

She grunts. "Mmmph. Well, that was like three weeks ago anyway. So whatever."

I blink. *WTH?!* Quanda's sittin' up on the hood of my whip. My pops hit me wit' his '07 Acura when he copped him that new Benz over the summer. I got it piped out, sittin' on twenty-twos wit' the knockin' beats. I shake my head, ice-grillin' her.

"Yo, check it," I say to Shania when I step up to my whip. "Let me hit you back in a few."

"Don't front, boy," she says, soundin' like she's feelin' some kinda way 'bout me endin' the convo. "Make sure you hit me back, *today*."

"I got you, mama," I say. "Make sure you pick up. I wanna see you." I ain't surprised when she says she wants to see me, too. I grin. "A'ight bet. That's what it is." I disconnect, scowlin'. "Yo, what is you doin'?"

Quanda folds her arms, smacks her lips. "Uhhh, what does it look like I'm doin'? I'm waitin' for *you.* It took you long enough."

I feel myself 'bout to scream on her. I take a deep breath. "Chill wit' all that boo shit, yo. You already know what it is wit' us. So stop playin', yo. Now whaddaya want?"

She steps up into my space. I pull away as she reaches for my arm. "I'm not playin', Tone. Whether you wanna believe it or not, you always gonna be my boo. And there's nothin' you gonna do or say to change that. You're not gonna get rid of me that easy, so get used to me being around 'cause I'm not goin' anywhere."

I stare at her, hard. "You effen crazy, yo. You need treatment or somethin'."

"No. What I *need* is *you*."

"Well, you can't have me. The meat shop is closed."

She rolls her eyes. "Boy, please. That's not all I want from you."

"Yo, I don't know what else to tell ya. I ain't got nothin' for ya. It's a wrap, yo."

"Then you need to unwrap it 'cause I'm not lettin' you go, Tone. I love you."

I let out a disgusted sigh. This chick sounds nuts! "Yo, real rap, you need to focus on lovin' ya'self, yo."

"But we're so good together. I'm not givin' up on us."

"How many times I gotta tell you, yo. There is no *us*. Get yo' life back 'cause you sound mad nutty right now, fa real fa real."

"Why you'd break up with me?"

"I'm not beat for you, yo."

"Why not?"

I take a deep breath. "Real ish, Quanda, you stay on ten, always lookin' to set it off. And, keepin' it gee wit' you, the only thing you was really ever good for is sex."

For a split second, I swear it looks like I see hurt in her eyes, but whatever sadness that mighta been there is quickly replaced wit' 'tude the minute she sees me eyein' the new hottie that catches my eye as she glides by us. She tosses her hair, then shakes her hips toward her whip, her booty bouncin' wit' each step. *Damn, she fine!*

Quanda snaps, gettin' mad loud. "Boy, I know you not

gonna stand here and disrespect me, lookin' all up in some trick's face while I'm standin' here! I should punch you in your face!" She has her hands up in my face. I step back, puttin' some distance between us just in case she tries to hook off. She's talkin' mad reckless now, and I already know where this is gonna go if I don't dip, now. "This is my man. So make sure you stay in your lane!" she shouts over at Cutie.

"Yo, will you stop all the rah-rah. I don't know how many times I gotta keep sayin' this. I ain't ya man, yo!"

I peep shorty shakin' her head as she disarms her alarm, opens her door, then slides behind the wheel of a silver Mazda. A few seconds later, she pulls outta her parkin' space, then peels off, leavin' the image of her bouncin' booty stamped in my head. I bring my attention back to Loudmouth.

"...I don't know why you gotta play me, Tone. Ain't no other girl gonna ever love you the way I do."

I feel myself gettin' a poundin' headache as I stare at Quanda. She's standin' here lookin' mad pitiful. I shake my head, decidin' not to go in on her too hard. "Ain't nobody playin' you, yo," I say, walkin' over to the driver's side door. "You standin' here playin' ya self. I'm tellin' you it's curtains, a wrap, lights out! Damn. Let it go, yo! We can still be friends if you just chill."

She frowns. "*Friends?* I don't wanna be *friends*. I wanna be your girl. I mean, if you wanna see other girls, okay. I'll let you."

"Yo, you not 'bout to *let* me do nothin'. I don't answer to you."

I pull out my phone as it vibrates. I have a new text from Chantel, tellin' me she's on her way over to my crib.

I text her back, tellin' her I'll be there in ten minutes, then look over at Quanda as I open the door. "Look, I gotta bounce. I don't wanna beef wit' you, Quanda. All I wanna do is have a peaceful school year."

She narrows her eyes. Once again, flippin' the nut switch. "Well, you damn sure won't be gettin' any peace if you think you're gonna be with some other chick! I promise you that, Antonio Lopez. I'm gonna make your life a livin' hell!"

"Whatever, Quanda. Do what you gotta do. My life was already hell the minute I got wit' you," I say, hoppin' into my whip and slammin' the door. I crank the engine, then back outta my parkin' space mad fast.

She throws her backpack at my windshield, spazzin' out. "It ain't ever gonna be over between us, so you better buckle up 'cause you in for the ride of your life, asshole!"

I rip the pavement, leavin' her standin' in my tire tracks wit' a trail of fumes lingerin' behind. I wanna get as far away from her as I can. *I shoulda never effed wit' that broad!* I speed home wit' thoughts of gettin' hot 'n' sweaty wit' Chantel to take my mind off Quanda and all'a her craziness.

6

Miesha

"**O**kay, girl, spill it," my cousin Mariah says, standin' inside the doorway of my bedroom. I am lying across my bed—glad to be outta that school, listening to the radio and reading this book *No Boyz Allowed* by this chick Ni-Ni Simone. Oooh, it's sooo good. I peel my eyes from the pages and look over at her, annoyed that she's disrupting me right when the book is starting to get juicy. "Save the attitude, boo. You can go back to reading your little fantasy book after you give me the scoop."

I roll my eyes, sitting up.

Mariah's a year older than me. Well, actually, we're like ten months apart, but whatever. Like me, she's the only child. Well, not really. Her dad has kids by some other woman, two boys that are around the same age as her. So technically, she has two brothers. Our moms are sisters. And they both married cheating men. Go figure! I guess it runs in the blood. Anyway, Mariah is a freshman at the

Fashion Institute of Technology in Manhattan, majoring in fashion merchandising management. She's wearing a short faded-jean skirt with a fringed hem and a pair of white leggings. She has on a cute little sleeveless denim jacket that she wears over a white midriff shirt, showing off her flat stomach and pierced navel. "Now how was your first day at McPherson?" She taps her foot, waiting.

"Umm, let's see. Hatin' chicks eyein' me all sideways and slick talkin' me. Mad thirsty dudes gawkin' me like they ain't never seen a hot chick in their life. And a buncha wannabe playboys, thugs, and pretty boys all tryna holla. I'd say, it was a day from hell."

She laughs. "Oh, how you love the attention."

I laugh with her. "Basically. Still, I hate it there. And hate you for graduating. Why couldn't you get left back so we could be seniors together?"

I eye her as she slinks her way over toward my dresser, then hops her basketball butt up on it. My eyes drop to her red, knee-high boots with the pointy toe and pencil heel. *Oooh, those are sexy! I'ma have to run her closet and rock them to school with my grey pleated mini.* One thing about Mariah, the girl can dress her butt off. Like me, she has an eye for fashion.

"Hahaha...no thank you," she says, tossing her short layered cut. I love this haircut so much better than those micro braids she rocked over the summer. This cut is fly on her, and fits her oval face to a T. She kinda reminds me of a younger, browner version of Halle Berry. "My days at McPherson are over, boo. And yours are just beginning."

I flash her an *oh, please* look.

She crosses her long legs. "You'll survive. Trust. You'll

have every boy eating outta the palm of your hand, and every chick hating you—just like at your old school. Then next year we can be at F.I.T. together."

I shrug. "Yeah, I guess."

She eyes. "What do you mean, 'I guess'? You are still coming to F.I.T. in the fall, right?"

Ever since we were like in fourth and fifth grades, Mariah and I have dreamed about being rich and famous and have wanted to pursue careers in the fashion industry, her in merchandising, me in designing. We said that once we graduated high school we'd both go to the same college. And, once we both got into middle school, we'd both set our sights and our minds on going to F.I.T. But now that I'm all caught up in watching *Project Runway*, I'm kinda thinking about applying to the Parsons School of Design. I tell her this.

She rolls her eyes. "Oh, whatever, traitor. Go on over to the other side."

I laugh. "Girl, you act like I'm gonna be hundreds of miles away. I mean, I'm gonna apply to both. But if I get accepted to Parsons, then that's where I'll probably end up going. I'll be only a few blocks away from you."

She sucks her teeth. "It's not the same, hooker. But whatever. Go on over to Fifth Avenue, Sweetie. I'll be fine without you." She hops off my dresser, walking over and plopping down on my bed. "I'll stay over on Twenty-seventh."

"And you'll continue to do fine there, I'm sure."

"Of course I will. Anyway...so back to you, Miss Divalicious. You mean to tell me you didn't see one cute boy at school today?"

I shrug. "I wasn't looking. I mean, there were a few that

I did briefly cut my eyes at, but when I glanced down at the footwear I was like, 'no thank you.'"

She laughs. "You and your foot fetish. Girl, please. You can't judge a boy by that."

I raise my brow. "Uh, yes, I can. And you *know* that's the first thing I look at. What's on a guy's feet says a lot about who he is, in my opinion."

"Mmm. Okay, Miss Material Girl. Everyone can't afford to rock expensive kicks."

I shrug. "Oh well."

"'Oh well' nothing. Don't judge 'em too hard based on what's on their feet. Trust me, there are a few cuties still there I woulda snatched up if I hadn't been all in love with my boo."

I laugh. "Girl, and you still in love."

She grins. "I know, right. And I wouldn't have it any other way." Mariah and her boo, Brian, have been together since her freshman year of high school. And I gotta admit, whew, sweet jeezus...he is F-I-N-E! Think Trey Songz fine with big, round brown eyes and dimples. He's even tatted up like him. Anyway, he's one of the star players on the Rutgers basketball team. "But it never hurts to look," she adds, winking at me. "A girl can *always* look as long as she's not touching. Believe it or not, McPherson has some real cutie-boos, especially that Antonio Lopez and his boy, Cease. Girl, I'm surprised you didn't see either of them." She starts describing them both to me. "But Antonio has them all beat. When I tell you he's super-duper extra-sexy and fine, girl, I mean it. That boy is too fine for his own good. And he knows it, too."

"Ugh, no thank you. He sounds like trouble."

She laughs. "Uh-huh. Good trouble, boo. And everyone

wants a piece of him. Problem is, he's slept with almost every girl there." She leans in like she's about to tell me something top secret. "And rumor has it he's packing enough meat to feed the needy."

I frown. "Ugh. I'm not interested. There's nothing that boy, or his third leg, can do for me."

She grins, twirling her finger in the air. "Yeah, yeah, yeah, blah, blah, blah. Maybe if you got the dust knocked off that box you wouldn't be so uptight. I'm tellin' you, word on the street is that boy is just the guy to deliver."

I roll my eyes. "I don't care what the streets are saying. He sounds like a manwhore to me. And I'm not interested. Now let me tell you about this loudmouth broad who tried to bring it to me at lunch." I describe her to her, then tell her what happened. "And that ghetto-hoodrat trash got the nerve to be named..."

"Quandaleesha," she finishes. We bust out laughing. "Girl, you think that's bad. Her sister's name is worse." She tells me her name is Hennessey and I roll off the bed, hollering. I'm laughing so hard my sides hurt and I have tears rolling down my face. "Now how you gonna name your child after a drink? Their mother was just wrong for that."

"She probably was drunk when she named 'em," I say, still cracking up.

"Ain't no way a sober, sane woman would ever do that to her child. Anyway, you think Quanda is a ghetto mess, you shoulda been there last year with her sister. She had the gold fronts, the colored yarn braided all up in her hair, and always wore a buncha bright, multicolored fingernails. And chick loved to fight. Trust, Quanda is just like her sister. Trouble. But all you gotta do is run your fist in her mouth one good time and she'll step real quick. Oh, Miss Henney thought she was gonna bring it to me, too, freshman year, until I brought it to her face. After that, she stayed away from me. But them two together..." She shakes her head. "They are a hot mess. From the time Quanda got to high school, those two hood hoes were in some kinda fight almost every week, either at school, the mall, or somewhere else. And it was always over a boy. Or with some chick they didn't like for no other reason than her looking better than them. She probably thinks *you* think you're hot stuff."

"Mmmph. Well, I *am* hot! Can't argue fact. So that trick needs to get over herself."

Mariah laughs. "Good luck with that. She's gonna keep testing you."

"And she's gonna get a chin check. Bad enough she called herself stepping to me about some boy I don't even know exists, telling me to stay away from her man. Like really, who does that? I wanted to tell her, 'Sweetie, any boy who likes digging in trash isn't who I'm interested in so no worries, boo-boo. I don't want him.' That chick's lucky I don't like fighting little girls or I woulda smacked her face off."

Mariah shakes her head. "I'm telling you, hun, she's just like her sister. She's not gonna back down 'til you knock her snot-box in."

"Then so be it. You already know how I do mine. I have no problem beating her face in if I have to. But that's not how I wanna get down. So I'ma let her keep running her trap. As long as she doesn't put her hands up, we good. But, trust, the first time she lifts an arm like she's tryna bring some work my way, I'ma stomp her lights. I'ma give it to her Brooklyn-style. Real raw 'n' gritty. And then she better hope I don't slash her damn face with my box cutter when I'm done punching her grill up."

Mariah laughs. "Ooh, I love it when you get all gritty 'n' hood, boo."

I laugh with her. "You know I'm not tryna take it there, but that chick is about to bring it outta me."

Mariah shrugs. "Oh, well. That'll learn her."

I laugh, eyeing Mariah as she gets up from the bed and walks over to the mirror hanging on my closet door. She stares at herself, swiping a finger over her neatly arched brows, then blowing herself a kiss.

"Oh my god, you're so conceited."

She shoots me a look over her shoulder. "No. I'm fine. And you are?"

I give her the finger. "Finer than you."

She laughs. "Lies. You're extra ugly, boo." She turns sideways, looks at her booty, then slaps it. "Brian calls all this Big Juicy."

"Ugh. I think I just threw up in the back of my mouth."

She turns to face me. "Oh, whatever. You should really turn in your hater card. Green is so not you."

I laugh, tossing a pillow at her. "Sweetie, *me* jealous? Ha! Never that."

"Whatever, ugly. Get your lazy butt up and let's go over to Newport Mall so I can go to Charley's and get me a grilled sub."

I slip into a pair of ripped low-riders, throw on a cute black V-neck tee with the word HOT scrawled across my chest in red letters, then slip my feet into a pair of red heels. I grab my bag, following her outta my room. I laugh as she shakes her butt real fast 'n' nasty-like as she walks toward the stairs. I love my cousin. Truth is, I'd probably go crazy if I didn't have her here to talk to. God, how I hate Jersey!

Just as we get to the bottom of the steps, the front door opens and in walks my mother. She's on the phone yip-yappin' it up, grinning and talking all light 'n' fluffy, like she's floating on clouds. I roll my eyes up in my head at her 'cause I know she's on the phone with my father, believing more of his lies. *God, she's so stupid!*

"Oh hey, Aunt Rhonda," Mariah says, walking toward the door.

"Hold on a minute," she says, bringing the phone from her ear. "Hey. Where you girls off to?"

"The mall," Mariah tells her.

Mom looks over at me. "You can't speak?"

I give her a dry "hey."

"You need money?" she asks me. I think for a moment. I start to tell her no since I still have two-hundred-and-fifty bucks left over from my summer camp job and birthday money. But why spend my money when I can spend hers? After all, she owes me for dragging me waaaay out here.

"Yeah," I tell her. She reaches into her purse, digs out her wallet, then hands me forty bucks. She tells me to not spend it all. I suck my teeth. How far does she think forty dollars is gonna stretch at the mall? I mean, really. "Thanks," I tell her, stuffing the money into my bag.

"Oh, by the way, how was your first day at school?"

I huff, walking toward the door. "How you think? Miserable. I wanna go back to Brooklyn."

She frowns. "Well, you can't. So you're going to have to figure out a way to make it work."

"Whatever," I say as I go out the door. The last thing I

hear the minute the door shuts behind me is her giggling like she's stuck on silly. Truth is, she is!

I slide in the passenger seat of Mariah's black Camry, and fasten my seat belt.

"How much you wanna bet," she says, glancing over at me as she backs out of the driveway, "that was your father your mom was on the phone talking to?"

I roll my eyes.

I shoulda known she wasn't gonna be strong enough to stay away from him. She never is. I mean, why pack up and leave him when you're only gonna end up going right back to him? She always does. It's crazy! Last time she left him, when she found him in a motel room again—because she goes out looking for him—with another woman, we stayed gone for three weeks. But we were *still* in Brooklyn. So I didn't care that we bounced. The time before that, she caught him with yet another woman—she put him out that time. But after a week of him begging and making promises—they both knew he wasn't gonna keep, like he *never* does—she let him back in. Like she *always* does.

"Of course," I say, utterly disgusted.

"Do you think she's going to take him back? I mean, I know that's your dad and all, but I swear I hope she doesn't. I don't want you to have to move."

I know Mariah means well, but I'm honestly not beat to do this with her. Not today, not ever. Talking about my parents makes me nauseous to my stomach. I swear. It's like a never-ending roller-coaster ride with the two of them.

Nonstop dumbness if you ask me. Fact is, my dad's been cheating on my mom for as long as I can remember, and she continues to put up with it. I hate to say this, but I have no respect for my mother, either. Not when it comes to my father. He's such a dog! And she keeps letting him crap all over her. I sigh, looking over at Mariah. "It'll be no surprise if she does."

She shakes her head, knowingly. She's been through what I've been through, so she understands what it is I am going through. And what it is I'm feeling since she's felt it too. Pissed. Hurt. Confused. Torn. I love my father, but I hate him, too.

A part of me feels like I really shouldn't be mad at him for doing what *she* keeps allowing him to do. But I am. Because the truth of the matter is, he needs to learn to keep his thing in his pants, and stop sleeping around with a buncha women, disrespecting my mom like that. And she needs to stop letting him. Or they both need to let each other go and be done with it. I swear. I don't ever wanna end up like my mom—weak.

7

Antonio

"Come on, ma...stop playin'," I whisper in Chantel's ear. "You know you want it."

We're both breathing hot 'n' heavy. "Please," she says in between kisses. "You're making me crazy."

"Then let me make you feel crazy good," I say, kissin' her neck, her shoulders, as my hands roam her body.

"It's...gonna...hurt."

"I'll be gentle," I say, kissin' her lips again, as I start inchin' my hands back over her hips, to the band of her underwear. She grabs my hand.

Mad frustrated, I roll off her, climb outta bed. I walk over to my window and snatch open the curtains, floodin' my bedroom with light. "Yo, get up and get out," I say, walkin' back over toward the bed, pickin' up her bra from off the floor and tossin' it at her.

She gives me a shocked look as it hits her in the face. "W-w-what, you're putting me *out?*"

"Yeah," I say, slippin' back into my boxers. "Bounce. I ain't wit' these games, yo."

"I'm not playing games. I wanna be here with you. I said I'd give you oral again."

I frown. "Yo, what I look like? I can get topped off anytime I want. I want more than that. You already know what it is. You got me mad excited." I step back so she can get a good look at my nakedness. "You see all this? You did this, ma. But you wanna be on some ol' other bull. So step."

I walk over and swing open my bedroom door. She's lucky I ain't the type of dude to straight-up dis her and toss her out in just her drawers.

"Oh my god! I can't believe you're gonna throw me out because I don't wanna go all the way with you."

"Believe it, yo."

She gets outta bed and starts throwin' on her clothes. "This is so messed up."

"Nah, what's messed up is you wastin' my time wit' these silly games, lil girl."

She sucks her teeth. "Whatever, Tone. I knew I shoulda listened to LuAnna and not come over here."

I laugh. "Yo, you straight-up dizzy for runnin' ya trap in the first place. That broad had no business knowin' what we were gonna be gettin' into. But let me tell you somethin' 'bout ya girl LuAnna. She wanna get up on this, too. And you know what? If I woulda known you was nothin' but a trick-tease I woulda got wit' her instead of wastin' my time wit' you."

"You're such a dog!"

"Yo, stop wit' all the talk, get dressed, and bounce before I throw you up outta here in ya drawers."

I walk over to my dresser and scoop up my phone, scroll through my history 'til I get to Shania's number. I hit the call button, then wait for her to pick up.

"Hey, boo," she answers. "I see you ain't front."

"Nah, ma. I already told you what it was. So, wassup?"

"You," she coos into the phone.

I cut my eye over at Chantel. She got the nerve to be ice-grillin' me like she wanna pop off. I stare her down.

"Yo, that's wassup. You feel like chillin' tonight?"

"It's been mad long so you already know, boy. Just let me know when."

"A'ight, bet. I'ma swing through as soon as I toss out this trash."

Chantel slams a hand up on her wide hip. "Boy, I know you not even standin' here tryna call *me* trash when that's all you'll ever be. You ain't..."

"Who's that in the background?" Shania asks.

"Nobody important," I say, eyein' Chantel as she sits on the edge of my bed and puts on her shoes.

Shania grunts. "Sounds like a buncha drama to me."

"Nah, ain't nothin' major. I'ma hit you up when I'm 'bout to head out."

"Okay—" I disconnect before she finishes her sentence.

"You real foul, Tone, for real. But it's all good. I'm not ever gonna be pressed for no boy, especially one like you."

I laugh. "Yeah, right. You mad thirsty, yo. Front if you want. You been eyein' me from the rip. You been wantin' a taste of all'a this."

"Screw you, Tone!" she yells, snatchin' her bag and stormin' outta my room. I follow behind her as she stomps down the steps, talkin' mad reckless. "You lucky I don't get my uncles to beat you down."

I keep laughin', openin' the front door. "Yo, get the eff
outta here wit' that. And what you want me to tell 'em
when they come through? That their niece is mad freaky
wit' the lip work?"

She gives me the finger, then slams the front door behind 'er. I shake my head. Real rap, yo. I'm glad my pops is
on the road this week and wasn't posted up here seein' or
hearin' all'a this craziness. He's already warned me mad
times 'bout bringin' drama to up in here. If he had walked
up in here and peeped this, he'd be snappin' for sure, especially after what popped off last summer when he let
one of my lil thing-things from last summer in the house
and didn't know I was already up in my room gettin' it in
wit' another chick. Stupid me forgot to lock my bedroom
door so she walked in on us rockin' the springs. She
flipped her lid, snatchin' the girl off of me by her hair, then
swingin' her 'round my room. They tore my bedroom up.
Broke my laptop, cracked my flat-screen, and even put a
hole in my wall. Yo, tryna break up two broads goin' at it
extra hard was mad hectic, especially while bein' naked.
And it def wasn't a good look when Pops had to see it.

Then to top it off, that nutty broad came back later that
night and smeared dog poop on my Pops's whip, then
threw a brick through our living room window. Pops was
heated, yo. He had me on shutdown for weeks after that.
And I had to work the rest of the summer wit' him *wit' out*
gettin' paid. He said that was how I was gonna pay for all
the damages. Havin' to spend the rest of my summer on
the road wit' no paper in my pockets sucked!

I shake my head, sighin' as I take the stairs two at a
time, goin' up to the bathroom to brush my teeth and
wash up. I smell Chantel's perfume on me and decide to

hit the shower real quick. Ain't no sense in goin' over to a
shorty's crib smellin' like another broad. I head back into
my bedroom and slip on a pair of black sweats and a red
long-sleeved Hollister tee. I grab my cell and my keys,
then bounce.

As I'm walkin' outta the crib, my phone rings. I pull it
outta my pocket and glance at the screen. It's Pops. "Wass-
sup, man?" I say, gettin' in my whip, then crankin' the engine.

"Chillin', son. Makin' that money. You know how ya old
man does it. And how you'd better do it."

I smile. Pops may not always be home, but he's always
held it down. And I ain't ever hafta rock hand-me-downs
or some kicks leanin' to the side. Nah, Pops always made
sure I stayed laced. And we've always had a nice spot to
rest at. "Yeah, no doubt," I say, backin' outta the driveway,
then peelin' off. "You good?"

"Yeah. You?"

"No doubt. I'm good."

"Listen. I'm gonna be out on the road for the next three
days so make sure you handle your business right." Code
for: *Don't let me come home and find the crib wrecked*.

"I got you, Pops. Where you off to?" He tells me Boston,
then Rhode Island. "How was your first day at school?"

I make a right onto Central Avenue, then stop at the
light. "It was a'ight. You know. Same crap, different year."

He chuckles. "And how them lil honeys lookin'?"

"Man, slim pickin's so far. But a lil thing-thing did catch
my eye. Man, she's stacked in the back real right." He
laughs. Tells me to make sure I keep it strapped up. Reminds me that he's not beat for grandkids. "Don't worry,
Pops. I keeps it wrapped. You already know."

"Yeah, I know how it is. But some'a them fast-behind girls out there will try'ta trap you if you don't keep your mind right."

"I got you, Pops. I'm definitely not tryna have kids, man. I'm still tryna have fun."

"Yeah, well, you just make sure you keep all that fun of yours in a condom."

I shake my head. Pops be buggin' hard 'bout me gettin' some chick knocked. He should know that ain't how I get down. No matter how many times I tell 'im I've never even had sex wit' out a condom, he still ain't tryna hear it. "By the way," he continues as I head toward Shania's crib. "You not still messin' wit' that lil loudmouthed hoodrat, are you?" He's talkin' 'bout Quanda. "I don't want her up in that house, you hear me?"

"I got you, Pops. Nah. I deaded that a minute ago. I thought I told you. But, man, she's still sweatin' the kid, hard, yo. She was all up in school today startin', then was out sittin' on the hood of my whip waitin' for me this afternoon."

I can almost see him shakin' his head at me, lookin' at me like I'm mad stupid for not listenin' to 'im in the first place. But Pops ain't gonna ever say it, even if he is thinkin' it. "You just make sure you don't let her up in that house," he warns. "I don't wanna repeat of what happened last summer. You hear me?"

"I got you, Pops," I say, pullin' up to Shania's. She's out on her porch wit' her thick, chocolate hips stuffed in a pair of skimpy lil short-shorts. She's rockin' this low-cut tee that has her boobs practically bustin' out. She grins, eyein' me as I hop outta my whip. Pops and I kick it for a few extra seconds, then I tell 'im I gotta bounce.

"Yo, wassup, cutie?" I say, walkin' up on the porch.

She stands up. And the way she's lookin' me up 'n' down lets me know what's really poppin'. She's ready to get that back cracked. "What you think's up, boy?" she replies, grabbin' me by the hand, then pullin' me toward the door. She tells me her moms won't be home 'til after ten and her sister's at work so she has the spot all to herself. "So you know what that means, right?"

I smirk, followin' her into her bedroom. "Nah. What it mean, yo?"

She shuts her door, pulls her shirt off, then walks up on me. "It means you got work to do. And I hope you ready to deliver."

"Yo, I stay ready," I say, pullin' her into my arms.

8

Miesha

As horrible as yesterday was being at this dumb school, I only hoped today wouldn't be as miserable. But, considering how the morning popped off, I was doubtful the rest of the day, let alone the rest of the week, would be any better. Last night, when Mariah and I returned from the mall, my mom came into my room, trying to convince me to be more open to "having a fresh, new start," as she called it. And yeah, I rolled my eyes at her. Because the only thing I wanted to know was who was this *fresh, new start* really for?

"For both of us," she had the nerve to say, sitting at the foot of my bed.

"No," I huffed. "This is what's best for *you*, definitely not me. Not once did you ask me what I wanted. And yeah...I know you're the parent. But this is my life, too, and I shoulda had a say in where we moved."

She reached for my hand, but I pulled away. "Listen, sweetheart. I know you miss Brooklyn. I miss it, too. It

was our home. And I know we've left behind a lot of memories by moving out here to Jersey. But one day I hope
you'll understand that this was the best thing for us."

"I will never understand so don't hold your breath waiting on a miracle. What you did was selfish."

She huffed. "*Selfish?* Oh, you've got to be kidding me.
I've done nothing but put *you* and your father's needs be-
fore my own. Now it's time I start looking out for my own.
Starting with this move."

"Oh, please. It's *always* been about you. Anytime you've
left Daddy or put him out, it was about *you*. And if it wasn't
about you, then you sure picked a fine time to wanna start
thinking about *you* now. What about *me,* huh? How and
when did you ever put me before your needs? Please refresh my memory on that 'cause I musta missed it. The
only thing you've ever cared about is keeping track of a
man who spent more time in the streets than he did at
home with his family."

She yanked me by the arm. "I'm warning you, Miesha.
Don't you dare talk about your father like that, or use that
tone with *me*."

"Well, it's the truth!" I shouted. "And all you wanna do
is act like it's not. So then why'd you—no excuse me,
we—leave him, *this* time?"

She narrowed her eyes at me. "*I'm* the parent here. Not
you. What your father and I go through is not your concern."

I let out a sarcastic laugh. "Oh really? And you still
haven't answered the question. Well, newsflash, *mommy
dear*"—she hates when I call her that—"it *is* my concern!
You made it my business *and* my concern when *you*
dragged me into it!"

"Oh, Miesha, stop. Now you're being melodramatic. I did—"

I cut her off. "I am not *being* dramatic. I'm being real."

"I said you were being *melo*dramatic...."

I huff. "Same difference. The point is—"

"You keep cutting me off. And yelling at me. Now if you'd just shut your mouth and stop trying to talk over me maybe you'd..."

I threw my hands up over my ears. "I'm not hearing you!" Her lips were still moving, but I kept yelling over and over, "I'm not hearing you! I'm not hearing you...!" Finally she got the hint and walked outta my room.

Then this morning while I was getting ready for school, Mariah's mom came in my room tryna check me for coming at my mother sideways the night before. "Miesha," she started, leaning up against the frame of my door as I stood at the mirror and combed out my wrap. "I heard you yelling at your mother last night."

I glanced over at her and gave her an *Okay, and?* look, then went back to staring at my reflection in the mirror. I have my mother's doe-shaped eyes framed by long, thick lashes and her narrow nose and pouty lips. But I have my father's forehead, his caramel complexion and his bright smile. As much as I don't like her and can't stand him— okay, okay, I'm lying...I love him. But, whatever! I am both of them—neatly wrapped into one big ball of mess.

"I know this move is hard for you," she continued as she eyed me. "But no matter how you feel about being here, that doesn't give you the right to be disrespectful to your mother."

I frowned. I hated when adults—who didn't know jack about what *I* was going through or had been through—felt it was their right to tell *me* what I had to do. Sorry, boo-boo . . . respect isn't given! You either earn it or you take it. My mother has done neither. I remember asking my father two years ago—after she caught him in another motel room—why he kept cheating on her. I was crying and pissed and all emotional because they were going through it, *again*. And you wanna know what he said to me? He said, "Because ya mom keeps lettin' me. I don't mean to hurt her. I love her. But I don't think I love her enough to stop doin' what I do. And as long as she keeps allowin' me to do it, I ain't gonna ever have a reason to wanna try 'n' stop."

Ouch! As effed up as that was for him to say, to *me*—his daughter, I had to respect it because it was real. So, no. I'm not gonna respect her until *she* starts respecting herself. And instead of telling my aunt Linda this, I let her beat me in the head. But I was lookin' at her kinda sideways, too, since she really isn't no different from my mom when it comes to men. But I knew enough to stay in my lane. See. If I brought it to Aunt Linda like that, she'd jump up on my back and stomp me down. So, nope, I didn't say a word. But I thought it. Then I walked over and gave her a kiss on the cheek. "Aunt Linda, I appreciate you letting me and my mom stay here, but this is *not* where I wanna be, period."

Yeah, she has a nice four-bedroom, two-and-a-half bath-room spot in the Jersey City heights section of Jersey City. And yeah, it's extra close to the city and all. But it's still not *my* home. And it's *still* not Brooklyn! I slipped into my heels, and grabbed my bag. "Aunt Linda, I won't yell at her again in your home, okay? But I am *not* going to respect her. I'm not respecting a woman who lets a man walk all over her."

"Sweetie, you got a lot to learn about life and love. But I'ma let you figure it all out on your own since you seem to already have all the answers. That's the problem with you young girls—you think you know everything." This time, I gave her a hug, told her I loved her, then walked out.

"Umm, why don't you watch where you're goin', trick!" someone snaps, banging her shoulder into me, shaking me outta my thoughts.

I blink. I know I wasn't that caught up in my head that I wasn't aware of where I was walking. And I know for certain I didn't walk into this chick. No. Judging by the smirk on her face, she purposefully bumped into me. And that's a no-no, boo!

"Uh, no, hun," I snap back. "Why don't *you* watch where the hell *you're* going? You bumped into *me*, you buffalo. Get it right."

"And? What you gonna do about it? Trick, *you* a buffalo."

I take a deep breath. Size this dark chocolate chick up. She's a thick, ham-hock-and-biscuit-eating ho with humongous boobs and extra-big hands, which means I would have to punch her in her neck real hard to drop 'er. She has on a pair of ripped blue jeans and her double-D watermelons are stuffed into a pink tee with the words DON'T HATE stretched across the front of them in silver glitter. *This broad is delusional*, I think, frowning, *if she thinks someone is gonna be hating on her.* She has the nerve to have extra-long lashes on and pink lipstick painted over her big lips. She's a cosmetologist's nightmare!

I blink. *Oh my god...this broad looks like that chick from Barney. Baby Bop!*

Wait! Is that a mustache I see?

"I should punch you in your face," she growls. She's about two, three, inches taller than my five-foot-six frame. Luckily for these six-inch heels on my feet, I'm hovering slightly over her as she stands here in her crispy white Nikes with the pink *swoosh* on the side.

I swear I'm really not in the mood for this ish! Two days of hoes comin' at me all slick is really more than I can take. I feel myself about to snap. Outta the corner of my eye, I see the queen of ghetto standing by the girls' bathroom with her arms folded, taking it all in. I'm sure some kinda way her hatin' azz is behind this zoo creature being all up in my grill.

I hear Mariah's voice in my head saying, "I'm telling you, girl. You're gonna have to drag one of them hoes real good for them to know you ain't the one." I sigh. It's too early in the morning for this craziness. The only thing I wanna do is get to homeroom.

I tilt my head. Keep my voice calm and steady 'cause unlike this half-man, half dinosaur, who's loud-talking and going with the hands in my face, I'm not interested in a show. And I'm not about to hook off on her first. No, ma'am. I want this beast to swing first so I can claim self-defense when I take it to her gut. I keep my eyes on her hands.

"You know what, buffalo? I see why you're miserable. You're ugly, boo. You know it. I know it. And the world knows it. And if I had to wake up every morning looking like you, I'd be miserable too. Everything about you is dead wrong. From them whiskers around your face to them big-azz hands of yours, you're a tragic waste. But I tell you what. Press me if you want. I'ma help put you outta your misery."

She blinks. I can tell she's kinda shocked I brought it to her like that. And embarrassed since a few heads in back of her start snickering and saying stuff like, "Oh snap... she went in on her beard....Dang, she callin' Samantha out....Hahaha, she called her a buffalo...." Of course, the comments get her all amped and she starts yelling and cursing, but hasn't swung off yet so I already know what it is with this one, too. She's another loudmouth broad who's all talk and no action. But I'm done.

Just as I'm about to step outta my heels, a golden-brown cutie steps in between us. "Yo, Sammie, baby," he says, wrapping his arm around her/it, but eyeing me. "Why you effen wit' the newbie? Let her live, ma."

I twist my lips up. *Sammie?* Hmmph. Whatever.

She shifts her glare from me and goes all starry-eyed looking up at Mr. Fine, like she's snagged the jackpot. "You know what, Cease, you right, boo. I'ma let the trick live."

I laugh. *"Trick?* Sweetie, *boom!* I'm everything you'll never be. Fly. Fabulous. Flawless. So before you bring it to me, go shed a hundred pounds, shave them whiskers and that mustache, get those hands and feet right, then come check for me. 'Cause the *next* time you do, Sam the Man with the big hands, I'ma set it off on your face!"

She tries to lunge at me, but Mr. Fine holds her back.

I'm tired of talking. I wanna fight! "Bring it, baby. Punch me, ho."

Everyone starts scattering when security comes down the hall, telling everyone to clear the halls and get to their homerooms. Mr. Cutie pulls Baby Bop down the hall in the opposite direction. I peep that Quanda broad—with her ugly, trifling self—dipping into the bathroom solo. My first thought is to creep up on her while she's in the stall and do her face in lovely. But, then I decide against it.

I strut off down the hall, my mind made up. The next ho who steps to me outta pocket is gonna get her sockets rocked—period, point blank!

9

Antonio

Seconds before the second-period bell rings, I drop my backpack to the floor and slide into one of the chairs closest to the door, in back of AP English class. I decide this will be my seat for the rest of the school year. I ain't ever beat to sit any closer to the board than I have to. And, yeah, I get mostly A's—some B's. Still, I prefer to sit in the back of the class wit' my peeps. But don't get it twisted, yo. Even when it looks like I'm not listenin', I'm still payin' attention. I just don't like to let peeps know that I am, so I front like I'm kinda slow, even though I'm in mostly advanced placement classes. Still, for me, sittin' up front is whack. It's reserved for the nerds and teachers' pets.

"Okay, class," Mrs. Sheldon says, getting up from her desk, then writing on the chalkboard. "Let's get started. For those of you who had me last year, you already know what to expect...." *Yeah, mad readin' assignments, essays, and twenty-page tests!* Mrs. Sheldon's a beast, real rap. But it's all good 'cause I dig readin' all kinda books and poems, then pickin' 'em apart. She makes us read books written by some of the greatest authors and poets in the world, then forces us to think about the themes and the characters in each book. She challenges us. And I dig that. I dig a challenge. That's what keeps me comin' back for more.

"So, Mr. Lopez," she says, turning around from the board and eyeing me. "I guess it would be too much to ask for you to step outside of your comfort zone this year and sit in one of the seats up front where I can keep my eye on you."

I grin. Last year, I had her class last period and a few times I would slip outta class before the bell rang. She never wrote me up for it 'cause—aside from the fact that I'm one of her favorites, even though she'll never admit it—I always had my assignments turned in on time and I always got one of the highest grades on tests. "Nah, Mrs. Sheldon," I say, smilin' at her. "I'm good."

She raises a brow. "Well, you had better be 'cause I expect much more from you this year than I did last year, so slipping out of class will *not* be tolerated unless you're looking to fail for the year. Are we clear?"

"I got you, Mrs. Sheldon."

"Good. You make sure you do. Now let's…" She stops herself when the classroom door flies open, and in struts the hottest chick in the game—my future wifey. Real rap. E'eryone's head spins in the direction of the door as she glides her sexy self up to the front of the classroom, wearin' a pair of black designer shorts that hug her curves like a glove and a white gauzy-type blouse over some kinda black tube thingy. Her smooth, toned legs look mad sexy in what I can tell are expensive heels. *Damn, she's fine!* I've never bagged a chick who rocked heels to school. But, I could most def get used to havin' a sexy chick like this hottie on my arm e'eryday.

"And *you* are late," Mrs. Sheldon says, clearly annoyed that her class is bein' disrupted even if the bell only rang five minutes ago. It doesn't matter that the hottie is new to the school either. Mrs. Sheldon doesn't play that steppin' up in her class late mess. She expects e'eryone to be in their seats before the bell rings.

All you hear as she walks by is, "Yo, she's hot like fire, son....Damn, she gotta phatty, yo....Yo, you see her body....Whoa, she's bangin' for real, yo!"

I wonder why she wasn't in class yesterday.

"I apologize," Sexy says, handin' Mrs. Sheldon a hall pass. "I had to speak to my guidance counselor about changing one of my classes."

"How special." Mrs. Sheldon eyes her as she says this and I'm kinda shocked that her voice is drippin' wit' sarcasm. *Oh snap! Let me find out Mrs. Sheldon's a hater on the low!* "Well, take a seat, Miss..." She glances down at the pass. "Miesha Wilson. You've already taken up five minutes of the class's time."

Miesha? Nice!

Dudes are mad hyped wit' this hottie up in the classroom. Some of 'em even talkin' mad reckless 'bout how they'd beat it down. But this sexy babe doesn't seem pressed that she's the cause of all the commotion. In fact, except for Mrs. Sheldon, she hasn't given anyone in here any eye contact.

"Okay, class...settle down," Mrs. Sheldon says, givin' Miesha a stern look. I wanna tell 'er to ease up off her since she's new, but decide to stay in my lane and let Mrs.

Sheldon do what she does. Nitpick over stupidness. "In less time than it takes to get to class on time, you have singlehandedly managed to shake my classroom up with your presence."

I laugh to myself. Mrs. Sheldon's gonna ride her e'ery chance she gets now that she's disrupted her class.

"Please...take a seat, Miss Wilson." She eyes her closely.

Miesha shrugs. I grin, watchin' her take a seat in the front of the class. She slides her sexy frame onto her chair, shifts her body some, then crosses her legs. I peep all the kats in class eyein' her smooth, shiny legs. I hear a few chicks suckin' their teeth. *Yeah she's def gonna be a problem*, I think, smirkin'.

Mrs. Sheldon clears her throat, her eyes sweepin' around the room until e'eryone finally gets quiet. "Ohhhkay. Now that we're all back to reality, let's get started. Shall we?" She walks back over to the board and starts writin'. She tells us that our first readin' assignment will be James Baldwin's *Go Tell It on the Mountain*. Some peeps start to groan. She faces the class. "Groan if you will. But James Baldwin was one of the twentieth century's most extraordinary men of letters. And through his classic volumes of fiction and nonfiction, he boldly explored race and sexual relations."

"Oh, yeah, that's what I'm talkin' 'bout," this dude Kent says, clownin'. "I dig me some good sexual relations."

A few heads laugh.

"And you're going to *dig* yourself into two days of detention," Mrs. Sheldon shoots over her shoulder, "if you don't watch your step, Mr. Lyons." She turns to face him. "Now *dig* that," she adds. E'eryone laughs, except him.

For the rest of the period, we listen to Mrs. Sheldon go on about how wonderful this Baldwin dude is. E'eryone hops up outta their seats the minute the bell rings, scattering for the door. I try to hang back and wait for the hot chick to walk outta class so I can check for her, but Quanda peeps me as she walks by the classroom and stops in her tracks.

I grab my backpack and walk out the door, eyein' her. I already know iggin' Quanda is only gonna make her turn it up more so I decide to kill 'er wit' kindness. "Yo, wassup?"

"You," she says, grinnin' as she walks alongside me. "I'm glad you finally startin' to come to your senses."

This broad makes me effen sick! "Yo, that was real foul what you did yesterday," I say, lettin' her comment go over my head, "throwin' ya bag at my car window like that."

"Oh, well. It was real foul how you tried to play me, too. But today's a new day and all is forgiven, boo."

I let out a sarcastic laugh. "I'm not lookin' for ya forgiveness, yo." *I'm lookin' for you to leave me the hell alone!*

"Oh, well. That's your choice. But you know how my feelings are for you, Tone."

I shake my head. "And I keep tellin' you I don't feel the same way 'bout you, but you ain't tryna accept it. I keep tellin' you it's over and you still buggin'."

"Because it's not over for me, Tone. And no. I ain't acceptin' it. I love you. I know things between us could work if you just gave us another try."

I tell 'er it's not gonna happen. That there are no second chances.

"Tone, please. I mean what do you think you gonna get from these other chicks that you weren't already getting from me? Sex? Money? You know I always sexed you real good and I don't ever have a problem spending money on you. So what is it?"

She leans up against the wall of lockers as I open mine to get out my books for my next three periods. I glance over at her. She's standin' there lookin' all sad and crazy. "Quanda, I don't know how many times I gotta say it, yo. It's over between us."

"Didn't I keep you satisfied, Tone? Didn't I let you get it any way you wanted it, any time you wanted it?"

I sigh. *How many times are we gonna go through this?* "Yeah, I ain't gonna front. You kept ya sex game tight. And you def kept me laced. But you also keep a lotta drama goin' and I ain't wit' the extras."

"You didn't have to keep cheatin' on me with them other girls, either."

"Yo, you buggin' for real. I ain't never cheat on you, yo. I told you what it was. It's only cheatin' if I didn't tell you."

"Say what you want. You *still* cheated."

I blink. Word is bond, yo. This broad has a screw loose for real. A'ight, I told her she could be my girl. But I also told her from the rip that e'ery now and then I'ma wanna tap somethin' else, too. And she said she was good wit' it as long as I didn't rock wit' anyone *she* knew. So I didn't. I respected that and went 'cross town and rocked wit' a few shorties from Synder High. Or I dipped over to Brick City and chilled. And, whenever she asked me 'bout doin' my thing, I told her. I kept it on the up 'n' up.

She rolls her eyes. "But I told you I didn't like it and you kept on doin' it anyway."

"And you kept doin' dumbness. But whatever, yo. It's over, so it don't matter."

"Whatever, boy. I don't care what you say. I'm not givin' up on us. So you can say whatever you want. All that you talking I'm not tryna hear. So go run off and sleep with whoever you want. But, trust and believe, boo. If I can't be with you, no one else will either."

"Yo, go 'head wit' that, girl. You soundin' mad nutty, yo." I step off.

Quanda catches up to me, grabbin' me by the arm.

"Nutty or not, I mean it, Tone. You just watch and see. It's not over until *I* say it's over. And I'm not gonna let *anyone* come between us."

I yank my arm away. "Yo, Quanda, for real. Do what you gotta do. I'm done."

I'm mad relieved when she doesn't follow behind me this time tryna crank up the rah-rah. Instead, she walks off, turnin' down another hall.

Two periods later, I'm walkin' outta my economics class wit' my boy Luke—the center for our basketball team—laughin' 'bout this chick passin' gas in class mad loud 'n' nasty just as the bell rang. She bust off like it wasn't nothin', then had the nerve to start poppin' ish when we started gunnin' her for smellin' like a sewer and bein' so triflin'. Even Mr. Dangerfield, our econ teacher, was lookin' at her crazy after she let loose.

"Yo, word is bond," Luke says, still crackin' up. "Maribel tore a hole in her drawers, man."

"Yeah," I agree, pullin' out my phone to see who hit me up. I grin when I see text messages from two of my jump-offs. And they both wanna let me smash tonight. "She walkin' 'round wit' chocolate tracks in her drawers."

"Hahaha . . . that's if her nasty, stank-butt had any on."

"Right, right." I shake my head. "That broad's a walkin' sewer, yo."

We gun on her a few more rounds as we head toward our lockers, then start talkin' 'bout our upcomin' basketball drills and how neither of us is really lookin' forward to them. Luke blazes almost as much as Cease durin' the summer, but he also likes to toss back the yak mad heavy, too. So I already know what it's gonna be like for him out on the court. As we round the corner to where our lockers are, I spot her. And, of course, some corny mofo from the lacrosse team is all up in her face tryna holla at 'er. "Yo, word is bond, son," Luke says, practically droolin' as he taps me on the arm. "You see that honey right there, yo? She's straight fire, man. Hands down, fam. She's one'a the hottest hoes I've seen in a minute, for real for real. And I thought Fiona was fine. But that cutie right there. She's smokin' hot, yo." I gotta agree. She is. But I keep it to myself. "I can already tell she's one'a them stuck-up ho-types. But I'd still beat it down."

I nod in agreement. "Yeah, she prolly is."

"I know she is, yo. And them stuck-up ones be the mad nasty ones, man."

I keep my eyes on 'er as she plays cat to the left. I can tell dude's game's mad whack just how she's lookin' at him. I peep how she dismisses him. He says somethin' else, then walks off. She catches me lookin' at her. And I swear I think I see her lick her lips at me. At least that's what I see in my head.

At lunch, Cease, Luke, and Justin—another one of my boys and our team's power forward—are sittin' at our usual spot eatin' mad junk. Sweet potato fries, a buncha hot wings loaded wit' blue cheese, cheeseburgers, and chips. The only healthy thing on our table is the cartons of milk we drink to wash e'erything down. Cease and Luke burp at the same time, then start laughin'. I frown. Tell 'em both they should learn some table manners for real. But they ain't beat. They just keep on burpin' like wild animals wit' no home trainin', laughin' at that nastiness. Afer a while, like we always do, we start poppin' mad ish 'bout chicks and some of the stuff we did over the past summer in between makin' paper to stack for the school year.

"Yo, man," Cease says, glancin' over at me, while stuffin' the rest of his fries in his face, "how you make out wit' Chantel yesterday?"

"Man, nah. She started frontin' on them panties, yo. So I threw her out."

They laugh, givin' me daps.

"That's what I'm talkin' 'bout," Justin says, dustin' off the rest of his wings. "If a broad don't wanna put out, then put *her* out." He licks sauce from his fingers.

"Man, listen," I say, pullin' out my phone. "There's mad booty out here to bounce up on for me to be beat for some bird who ain't 'bout puttin' in no real work. Sweatin' some chick who wanna play tricks ain't it. I called one'a my other pieces over in the Brick, then went to her spot and gave her the business real right." They give me more dap.

Justin says, glancin' over toward the door, "I wanna try that hottie right there out." We all follow the direction of his gaze. And there she is again. Mad sexy as ever!

Luke laughs. "Yo, dawg. I don't mean to burst ya lil air bubble, but that broad's waaay outta ya league, son."

Justin frowns, shootin' him a look. "Whatchu mean she's outta my league, dawg?"

Luke shrugs. "I'm just sayin', man. Look at 'er. She's mad fly. All labeled up. Real classy type. Chicks like her ain't checkin' for no dudes like you"—he points at Justin, then over at Cease—"or you"—then points at me—"or *you*."

I shake my head, eyein' 'er on the low. She is over by the salad bar. Two of the older cats who work back in the kitchen peep 'er from behind swingin' doors. One of 'em steps out into the open—he's like twenty-somethin'—and tries extra hard to get her attention. But she ain't payin' him no mind. She tosses her hair to one side, walkin' over toward the cashier.

"Oh, word?" Cease says. "Then who's she checkin' for if it ain't one'a us?"

"Who you think, ninja?" Luke thumbs himself in the chest, laughin'. "Me! I got the kinda swag chicks like her check for, yo. Watch what I tell you when I finally press up on 'er and get them digits. I'ma have her booed up by homecomin', watch."

"Yeah, whatever," Justin says, wavin' him on. "I'ma be poundin' that out before you."

The three of us start laughin' at 'im. "Yo, you delusional. The only thing you poundin' out, son," Cease says in between laughin', "is ya hands."

"Eff y'all, mofos," he says, soundin' like he's gettin' mad tight. "Don't sleep on my skills, fam. Trust me, dawg. I can bag that."

"Keep dreamin', ninja. The only thing you baggin' is a buncha lies," Luke says, reachin' for another carton of milk. He opens it, puts it up to his lips, then tosses his head back and guzzles it down.

"Lies nothin', yo," Justin snaps, leanin' forward in his chair, restin' his arms up on the table. "Man, I ain't gotta lie 'bout jack, yo."

I laugh. "Man, go 'head wit' that. You stay frontin' on ya woodwork, bruh."

Cease and Luke crack up.

"Yo, eff y'all," he snaps, hoppin' up from his seat and grabbin' his tray. "I'm out, yo. You clown mofos not about to stunt me."

Cease and Luke keep laughin' as he walks off. I can tell I got my boy feelin' some kinda way, but oh well. He'll get over it. But the last laugh is on us when we look over and peep him holdin' the cafeteria door open for the new hottie, then walkin' out wit' her, leavin' the three of us wit' our jaws dropped.

10

Miesha

"So how you like the school so far?" this brown-skinned dude rocking the new Lebrons asks as he holds open the cafeteria door for me. At first, I felt like dissin' dude and paying him dust, but when I peep Miss Ghetto and her hooker crew giving me the screw face, I decide to give this boy some rhythm. If for nothing else, just to piss 'em off.

I eye dude on the sly. He's extra tall, the way I like 'em, and he's...*cute!* But he's kinda nerdy-looking in his rim-framed glasses and Hollister tee and a pair of faded skinny jeans that hang off his hips, but not too over-the-top that it looks nasty. He kinda reminds me of a skater boy. I eye him long and hard, then decide he's harmless enough.

"I don't," I tell 'im as he walks alongside of me as I make my way outside toward the parking lot. With no friends here—not that I want any—I'm not beat bein' the new chick sitting in a cafeteria full of fakes, flakes, and wannabe-gangsta boos. So I'm taking it to my car where I can eat my salad and talk and text in peace. Well, that was the plan up until this very second.

"Oh, word? I can dig it."

"Can you really?"

"Yeah. No doubt. I transferred here in the middle of my freshman year from San Diego." *Mmmm, a surfer boy. It figures!* "I can't lie. I hated it at first. But then I made a few friends and things got better. It's really not that bad here once you get used to it. I mean, we got our share of trou-blemakers just like any other school. But there are some real cool kids here, too."

I look up at him. He has nice skin for a guy. And his waves are sick. He has 'em spinning all around his head. I shrug. "I guess. But I'll never get used to it because I don't wanna be here." He wants to know where I'm from. "Brooklyn."

"Ah, *Brooklyn*," he says tryna mock my accent. "That's wassup. What part?"

Although I'm really from Do-or-Die Bed-Stuy, I tell him Park Slope since that's where we moved to, like three years ago. "Why?"

"Oh, nah. One of my boys is from Brooklyn, too. Crown something."

"Crown Heights," I tell 'im.

"Oh, a'ight. Yeah, that's it. So what's your name?"

I frown. "Umm, who you working for, Secret Service? What's up with all the questions?"

"Oh, my bad," he says, kinda chuckling, putting his hands up. "I didn't know askin' you ya name was a crime."

Girl, stop. Check ya 'tude. He's only tryna be nice. I

reel in my 'tude, just a pinch. "It's not. And I didn't mean to come at you like that. It's just that"—I shake my head— "I'm not here tryna make friends."

He laughs. "Whoa, who said I was tryna be *friends*? I'm being *friendly*. Big difference. So unless you plan on going back to *Brooklyn* real soon, you might wanna *try* being friendly back. Otherwise, it's going to get real lonely around here with you giving everyone the stink-face all the time."

"Lies," I say, acting like I'm offended. "I'm not walking around doing that."

He starts laughing. "Yeah, okay. Yes, you do. This is you all day." He makes a face, twisting his lips up real tight and scrunching his nose up, squinting his eyes.

"Oh my god," I say, trying not to laugh at his impression of me. "That's so not true."

He chuckles. "Okay, if you say so. But I know better. Me and my boys peeped you when you walked into the cafeteria earlier. And I see you in the halls. You stay with the skunk face on."

"The what?"

"Skunk face. You know, your face was all twisted up tight like someone squirted skunk juice on you or something."

I laugh. "Okay, okay. You got me. But, ewwww...that's so nasty. That's not how I really am."

"Maybe not, ma. But that's what you show us. Everyone here thinks you're stuck on yourself."

"Well, I'm not," I say, defensively. Truth is, I'm far from conceited. I'm convinced. Big difference.

"Then show it. Let us see that you're not."

I frown. "Wrong answer, boo-boo. That's not what I do.

I don't care what these crab-cake hoes and corny busters around here think about me, so it is what it is. They can eat dust for all I care. I don't worry myself about stuff like that. So they can think what they like."

"True. Still, someone asking you what your name is doesn't have to become a big production, feel me? All it is is someone tryna be nice, maybe get to know you, like me."

"You know what?" I say, disarming my car alarm. "You're right. My bad. It's Miesha."

He grins. "See. Was that so hard, Miesha? That's a pretty name. It fits you."

I smile. And it's the first time I've smiled since stepping foot in this school. "Thanks," I say, opening my car door. "And thanks for walking with me to my car." I mean it, too. Truth is, it's nice to finally talk to someone. And, corny or not, he's a *cutie.* He seems really nice, although looks can be deceiving. Still, it really feels good to laugh with someone, a boy.

"No sweat. It was my pleasure. By the way, I'm Justin."

"Cool," I say, staring at his hands. He has nice hands with long fingers and his nails are neatly trimmed. He tells me he plays basketball. That he's their something *forward.* Whatever that is. Yeah, I like watching the boys hooping it up. But I can't tell you jack about who plays what position. That's not what I'm there for. When I go to the courts, I watch basketball for one thing, and one thing only. To get my peep show on, watching them hard, sweaty bodies run the ball up and down the court.

"Maybe you'll come check out some'a my moves when the season starts."

I run my hands through my hair, then twirl a strand of hair through my fingers. "Maybe."

He grins. "That's wassup." I'm surprised when he holds my car door open while I get in and slide behind the wheel. I crank the engine and roll down the window after he shuts my door. Most boys wouldn't have done that much.

I smirk. "Uh, don't get gassed. If I come check for you, it won't be to make goo-goo eyes over you."

"That's cool," he says, laughing as he leans into my car. "So what class you have next period?"

I tell 'im Afro Studies.

"Oh, word? With Mr. Nandi?" I nod. "Cool-cool. I'm in that class, too. Wait. I didn't see you there yesterday." I tell him I didn't go. That right after lunch period I left. Yup. First day of school and I cut classes. Puhleeze. After that booga bear, what's-her-face—Miss Ghettolicious—stepped to me, I was in no mood to go back up in that school. So, I dipped. He tells me all about the class, and what's to be expected. I thank him again.

"So, you not rollin' out, are you?"

I shake my head. "No, not today."

He smiles. "Good. I'll see you in class, then."

I smile back at him. "Yup. I guess you will." He walks off and I eye him through my rearview mirror as he zigzags his way in between parked cars back into the school. *He isn't my type, but it'll be nice to have at least one person I'm cool with. And it doesn't hurt that he's on the basketball team. And he's kinda cute, too.* When he is no longer in my sight, I pull out my phone, and start texting Mariah while I eat my salad. We go back and forth for about ten minutes before she has to go to her next class. I glance at my watch. It's eleven-twenty. My lunch period is over in ten minutes. I sigh, flipping down the sun visor, then fishing through my bag for my cherry-flavored lip gloss. I glide some over my lips, then press my 'em together while brushing down my bangs. *Boo, you just too cute for this whack-azz school!*

By the time I get to last period, there's a rumor spreading around the school like a wildfire that I had sex out in the parking lot with three boys from the basketball team. *Are you effen kidding me?*

"I told you that trick was nasty."

"They said she gave it up like a porn star in the backseat of her car."

How could that boy go back and spread those lies about me? Corny-azz mofo!

Maybe it wasn't him.

Then who else woulda did some foul ish like that?

He was the only one I was outside with. *I knew I shoulda igged him.* Whatever.

Now I'm sitting in my Algebra III class smoking-pissed. I'm so heated right now I can barely see straight. Someone in back of me disguises their voice and says, "Smut on deck." Then there's laughter. It's a dude's voice. I glance over my shoulder. There are a few dudes—all rocking dreds—huddled in a corner on the right side of the room, looking over at me. One of them—a dark-skinned boy with juicy red lips—flicks his tongue out and that's all it takes for me to go off.

"Boy, don't you ever disrespect me, sticking your nasty

tongue out at me!" I snap, jumping up from my seat and throwing my Algebra book across the room at him. "I will beat the black off you!"

Mr. Evans, this old rickety-crickety dude with a buncha wrinkles and a shiny bald head, quickly turns from the chalkboard. "What's going on? Mr. Richardson, get back in your seat this instant. Or see yourself down to the vice principal's office. Outbursts are not allowed in this class."

"Well, tell that ho over there that," he answers, pointing over at me. "She's the one throwing books across the room. And she'd better be glad she missed."

"No, *you'd* better be glad I missed," I say, sitting back in my seat. " 'Cause the next time I won't. And, trust me, little boy, the *only* ho in the room is *you* with ya crusty looking self. Effen critter. You don't know me. None of you do. So keep my name outta ya mutha-effen mouths. Period."

There are a few ooohs and aaahs floating around the room. He starts going in on me, and I give it right back. I call him all kinda nasty names. "Now eat the back of my—"

"Miss Wilson, enough," Mr. Evans snaps, slamming his hand on the desk. "Your vulgar mouth is unacceptable. I will not have this filthy talk in my classroom. And, Mr. Richardson, you know better. Do I need to throw the both of you out of here?"

The boy stares me down. And I give it back. "Nah, I'm good," he says, shifting in his seat. "My bad, Mr. Evans."

"Now, let's get back to work. Mr. Richardson, give me the definition of the Pythagorean theorem."

"C'mon, Mr. Evans, it's only the second day back in school. Let me get back to you on that. My brain is still on vacation."

Mr. Evans eyes him. "Vacation or not, you should *know* this. It was learned in Algebra One, young man. So you *and* your brain had better be here tomorrow, or you'll be spending your time in detention."

"A'ight, a'ight, I got you. It's A-square plus B-square equal C-square."

Oh my god! What a coconut head. I roll my eyes up in my head.

"Mr. Richardson, that is an example. *Not* the definition. Someone else? You"—he points at me—"Miss Wilson. Give me the definition."

Ugh! Old stank buzzard just had to call on me! Mmmph. I shift in my chair. I'm soooo not interested.

"She prolly don't even know herself," some idiot remarks.

I shoot another look over at Critter and his cornball crew, then bring my attention to the front of the room. "Pythagorean theorem is the square of the hypotenuse—C—of a right triangle is equal to the sum of the square of the legs—A and B. The example: C-square equals A-square plus B-square."

Mr. Evans nods. "Very good. Now go pick up that book you threw across the room. And don't let it happen again."

"I got her," one of Crispy Critter's crew members says, getting up from his seat and picking up my book over in the corner. He's a short, stocky dude with shoulder-length dreds. He has a thick neck and is built like a wrestler. *Mmmph, he'll probably be a fat, pudgy cow in two years.* Mr. Evans keeps his eyes on him—eyeing him over the rim of his glasses—as he walks over toward me with a smirk on his shiny face. *Ol' ugly grease monkey!* Now the street chick in me tells me to get up and face off just in case he tries to molly-whop me upside the head with that thick-azz book. But I sit and am still.

Mr. Evans must have read my thoughts. "No. Bring *me* her book, Mr. Sweeney, and go back to your seat. And, Mr. Richardson," he says, eyeing Critter, "not another word out of you. Now, the rest of you open your books to Chapter One. Equations and Functions review." Thick Neck hands Mr. Evans my book, then glances over and winks at me. I roll my eyes, turning my head.

I swear. Boys make me sick! And that's exactly why I dog 'em!

As soon as the bell rings, Mr. Evans calls me up to his desk and hands me my book. "Miss Wilson, I understand you are new to this school and might be having some difficulty adjusting to being here. If that is the case, I recommend you speak to your guidance counselor or the vice principal. Lashing out at other students isn't going to solve anything. In fact, all it's going to do is get you into trouble. Do I make myself clear?"

"Listen, Mr. Evans. No disrespect, sir. But don't do me." He raises his left brow, gives me a confused look. Whatever. "I don't know how y'all do it here, but I'm not having it. That boy came outta his face and disrespected me. And where I come from, that's a no-no. Then to top it off, you didn't check him. And then someone else said something slick on the sly and you didn't get at him, either. But you wanna lecture me. Oh, no thank you. Save the speech, sir. I'm here to do what I gotta do, that's it. So from here on out, I'ma ignore the ignorance in the room. But the one thing I won't do is go running off to some principal's office tattling. That's not what I do. I handle it my way."

11

Antonio

"Yo, son, what's goodie?" Luke asks the minute I answer my cell.

"*De nada*, yo. Just gettin' in from this shorty's crib."

"Oh, word? You hit?" He starts laughin'. "Never mind. I already know."

"Then why you ask, fool? You know how I do. Player for life, ninja."

"I heard that, yo. So wassup for the rest of the night? I got some Peach Ciroc 'n' a bag of sour. Let's get lit, yo."

I crack up laughin'. This mofo is really tryna see if you can overdose on smokin' weed. He's been tryin' it all summer long and it still ain't happened yet. But his dumb butt's determined.

"Yo, where ya parents at?" He tells me his pops is on a business trip. He's like some kinda pharmaceutical rep and travels mad places e'ery month. He says his moms went back to Atlanta again to help wit' his sister's babies. I shake my head. I thought my pops stayed gone, but geesh...his par-

ents ain't hardly ever home. I can understand why his
pops be out, but his moms…yo, she be actin' like she
straight-up ain't beat to spend time wit' him. Seems like all
she care 'bout is his sister and them twin babies. He ain't
ever say nothin' to me 'bout it. But sometimes I can hear it
in his voice, that he's feelin' some kinda way 'bout it.
"Man, it's a school night. I ain't smokin' or drinkin' tonight. And you shouldn't either, yo. You know we startin'
preseason trainin' next week."

"Yeah, I know. That's why I'ma smoke the rest of this
bag up tonight. But I'm sayin'…you ain't gotta smoke,
just come through. I got these two honeys from Bayonne
comin' over to chill. And you know they gonna wanna get
it in after we pop this bottle."

I laugh. Ask him what two chicks he's talkin' 'bout. He
tells me Rosa and Carmela. I tell him I don't know who
them broads are.

"Yeah you do, yo. They the two Spanish chicks we got at
over the summer. We peeped 'em at the beach, then
snatched 'em up 'n' chilled the whole day.…"

I grin, rememberin'. One was dark complexioned, and
looked more Dominican than Puerto Rican. The other was
fair skinned. Although one had more booty than the other,
they were both mad sexy 'n' had bangin' bodies. I bagged
the darker one 'cause she had the extra junk in the trunk
and knew how'ta shake it. But, by the end of the night, me
'n' Luke ended up takin' turns wit' both of 'em. "Oh, right-
right. I don't know how I forgot 'bout them two freaks.
But, nah, yo. I ain't effen wit' them broads tonight."

"Say what? *You* turnin' down some easy play, son? Yo,
you a'ight?"

"Yeah, I'm good, yo. Just kinda beat. I'ma take a

shower, kick back 'n' watch *Dance Flick* on DVD, then hit the sheets, yo."

He tells me to stop through in the mornin' to scoop him up 'cause his pops took the keys to his whip 'n' took the plates off 'cause he got two speeding tickets that he didn't pay, or tell them about.

"Damn, that's cold, yo. How long ya pops got you on foot?"

"Prolly 'til my feet blister. Who knows, yo? He stays doin' dumb shit to make my life miserable. He let Maurice 'n' Amber do whatever they wanted when they were home. But now I'm tryna live 'n' do me and he won't let me. It sucks, man. He can take his whip 'n' shove it, though. I ain't beat."

I shake my head. This dude got parents who got mad cheddar. They give 'im anything he wants. Let 'im practically do whatever he wants. And the mofo complainin' like he's stuck on death row or somethin'. I sigh. "Man, go 'head wit' that dumbness. Nobody told you to be doin' sixty in a school zone, yo. So chill wit' all that. You did this to ya'self, bruh."

"Man, let me bounce. I ain't tryna hear that. Make sure you come through in the mornin', yo."

I laugh. "Yeah, a'ight. Whatever, yo. Go take ya block-head on." We BS a few secs more, then disconnect. Five minutes later, my cell rings, again. It's Pops hittin' me up to check in. He wants to know what's good on this end. I tell 'im what it is, then ask him where he is. He tells me he's down in Norfolk, Virginia, 'til tomorrow night.

"Oh, a'ight. Be safe, man."

"No doubt. You good?"

"No doubt."

"Cool. That's what I wanna hear. Listen. I'ma be home for a few days in between runs and I was thinkin' we could do somethin', just the two of us."

I grin. "That's wassup, yo. No doubt."

"A'ight. We'll figure somethin' out when I get back. Make sure you handle ya business while I'm gone."

"I got you, Pops."

"If you need money, you know where it is."

"True that."

"A'ight. Let me go. Ya old man's gettin' ready to go handle this lil thing-thing I got down here. And she gotta daughter I'ma put you on to. She's sexy just like 'er momma. I already tol' 'er you a smooth cat, just like ya pops."

"Oh, word? That's wassup. How old is she?"

"Twenty, and she hotter than a furnace. She need some'a that Lopez lovin' to hose her flames out."

I laugh. "Yo, Pops, you shot out, for real for real. That's wassup, though. If she mad sexy like that, tell 'er to hit me up on the Book 'n' we can take it from there."

He tells me he's on it. I end the call, toss my cell on my bed, then head for the shower, shakin' my head. One time I asked Pops if he was gonna ever slow down from all the women 'n' he said, "Yeah. When I'm dead. Until then, I'ma keep plowin' the fields 'n' plantin' these seeds."

I stop for a sec to grab some clean boxers and a T-shirt outta my dresser, then walk into the bathroom, and turn on the shower. I hop in 'n' handle my handle, thinkin' maybe I should go on over to Luke's 'n' get at them freaks. Thinkin' 'bout what we could be doin' starts gettin' me all excited 'n' I start tryna convince myself that I need'a go on 'n' get me a taste of them goodies, but then outta nowhere I lose my excitement. The shower's still hot, but I'm all cold. I lean against the wet tiles as the water cascades over me, tryna blink back memories—what lil I have—of my moms. Most of who she is or was to me is a big blur. I don't know if it's 'cause I've blocked that part'a my life out, or if the memories have faded away. All I know is, I hate when bits 'n' pieces of her flash in my head. I blink. I can't see 'er face, but I can hear 'er voice 'n' I can feel her hugs. How she'd kiss me e'ery night before tuckin' me in 'n' tell me she loved me, then read to me 'til I fell asleep. I 'member one time wakin' up from a bad dream—monsters wit' fangs were chasin' me 'n' tryna eat me—'n' she came into my room, climbed into the bed wit' me and said, "Everything's gonna be okay. Mommy's not goin' anywhere, my handsome little prince. Your mommy's gonna keep her sweet pumpkin safe." And I 'member her holdin' me real tight 'n' she was cryin'. When I asked her why she was cryin' she said, "Because I love you so much. You're my whole world. Please, don't ever forget how much I love you. How much I will always love you..."

Two days later, she was gone. Who does that? Just bounces on their kid like that? I hate havin' to remember, then havin' to try 'n' forget, how she effen left me. I hate rememberin' how it felt, knowin' she wasn't comin' back. How I cried 'n' couldn't eat or sleep. How I sat up, lookin' outta the front window e'eryday for a week waitin' for her to come back. But she never did!

"*Daddy, when's mommy gonna come back?*"

"*She's not. Now stop all that cryin', son. Tears ain't gonna bring her home. She's never comin' back.*"

"*Why not?*"

"*'Cause she stopped lovin' us! That's what no-good women do. Love you, then leave you.*"

"But she said she was gonna always love me; no mat-
ter what, Daddy. She promised!"

"She promised me a buncha shit, too. But she still left.
We on our own now. It's you and me. So you gonna hafta
forget about 'er, son. She don't love you, or me. If she did,
she woulda never left. She's gone. Dead. Buried. And
that's the way it's gotta be."

Three months later, we were movin' up outta our crib
in Crown Heights, Brooklyn, to Jersey City. Pops thought
we both needed change. To move on 'n' get on wit' our
lives wit' out her. He told me real men don't cry over a
woman, they go out 'n' find themselves two more to help
'em get over the one they lost. Still, it hurt. But I couldn't
show it 'cause Pops said I had'a get over it, like he did. And
he wasn't tryna hear nothin' else 'bout it. But I couldn't
just let it go. It was hard. I missed her. And loved her. And
wanted her to come back. I waited for her. Watched for
her. I prayed and prayed, waitin' 'n' hopin', but nothin'.
She was ghost. I was eight years old when I finally accepted—after gettin' into mad fights at school 'n' suspen-
sions 'n' havin' to go to counselin'—that Pops was right.
She was never comin' back. That she effed up my life. So I
did e'erything I could to block 'er outta my mind...and
heart. Wit' each passin' day, it got a lil easier, and the memories of 'er slowly started to fade 'til they were long gone,
like her. Real rap, I don't know what hurt most, her leavin'
or her lyin'. All I know, she did both!

You see what happens when you let a woman into
your heart? She hurts you. I take a deep breath. *Screw this*
crap! Pops is right. She ain't ever love me! If you can't
trust ya own moms to love you, then who can you trust?
Twenty minutes later, I turn off the shower, dry off 'n'

throw on my boxers, then head down the stairs into the kitchen. Real ish, I wanna roll a phatty 'n' get lifted, but I know that ain't what I need'a be doin'. I open the fridge. There's leftover spaghetti from two nights ago 'n' three slices of pizza. I ain't beat for the spaghetti so I pull out the slices 'n' nuke 'em in the microwave for a few secs. I take a handful of Cheez-It crackers outta their box, then chomp on 'em, pourin' myself a glass of apple juice. When the microwave dings, I pull out my slices and tear into 'em, washin' 'em down wit' two glasses of juice. I wash my dishes, then head back upstairs, decidin' to stick to my original plan 'n' stay home. *I'll get at them freaks some other time*, I think, poppin' in my DVD, then lyin' 'cross my bed. I'm not sure when I dozed off, but when I wake up, it's five o'clock in the mornin'.

12

Miesha

"Hey there. Welcome to McPherson. I've been meaning to introduce myself to you, but kept getting sidetracked with other things. You're the new girl from New York, right?"

What the heck? I've been at this school for over two weeks and now someone wants to roll out the welcome mat. Puhleeze! I take my slow sweet time before I actually peer around the door of my locker to see whom the sweet, sappy voice belongs to. I blink. Standing here is this light-bright chick with a blond ring of curls and sparkling green eyes, staring at me with a wide smile. Her face looks like it should be on the cover of one of those teen magazines, like *J-14* or *Teen Vogue*. Now, I'ma just put it out there. I'm not the kinda female who makes nicey-nice with a buncha chicks. Outside of my girls back home, chicks are not to be trusted. Every now and then, I stumble up on a cool chick—outside of my clique—who I *think* might be worthy of my time until she crosses me.

I look chickie up and down, taking in her wears. *Oh, she's serving it up lovely in white*. She has on a pair of white stretch jeans and white linen blouse with a white Gucci belt pinched around her ultra-small waist. I glance down at her footwork. A banging pair of gladiator sandals are on her feet. *Oooh, cute!*

"And *you* are?" I ask, shutting my locker door, then tossing my sleek wrap. It's full of bounce and shine and hangs to my shoulders.

"I'm Fiona." She extends her manicured hand to me. I eye it. She eases it back down. After how some'a these chicks came at me yesterday, I'm simply not taking any chances. So, *yes*, I'm guarded and on high alert.

"Well, all righty then," she says, raising a brow. "I see you're not too friendly. If you wanna be a snot, be one. I just wanted to say hi and welcome you to the school."

Now any other day I would give her the business, then spin off, but I don't know. My mom always says you can catch more flies with honey than you can with vinegar. So, I'ma drip outta little sweet-goo and see what it do. "Hey, wait. Thanks for the welcome. I didn't mean to come off rude...."

Her green eyes become narrow slits, then relax. "Girl, please. Yes, you did." She starts laughing. And I can't help but laugh too because it's true.

"My bad," I say, deciding to try to play nice with at least one of these chicks here. And since she's the only one who's actually introduced herself to me instead of tryna come at me sideways, the least I can do is "color within the lines," as my granny would say. God how I miss her. She died last spring from a stroke.

"Don't sweat it," she says, shouldering her black Gucci

knapsack. "Which way are you headed?" This school is so dang huge. It has four floors and four sets of wings. The seniors' lockers and most of their classes are all up on the fourth floor. I tell her I'm going to the west wing for homeroom. "Okay. I'll walk with you, if that's okay." She smirks.

"No, it's cool."

"By the way, what's your name?"

"It's Miesha."

"Oh, nice. Pretty name." She eyes me. "Do you model?" I tell her no. "Well, you should. You look like you could work a runway. You're so graceful when you walk." She giggles. "No, sashay. Yeah, that's what you do."

I laugh. Tell her that I do know how to work a runway, but that that's not my interest.

"Oh. Well, you should give it some thought. Sooo, what school were you going to before you got here?" she asks as we move through the crowded hall. And, yeah, I'm kinda looking at this chick sideways, tryna figure out why she's tryna be so chummy. If she thinks I'ma be fallin' for the okey-doke, she got another think coming. She won't be setting me up for a beatdown. Oh, no, sweetie. These hoes here ain't gonna catch me slippin'.

A few boys holla at her, then whistle as we walk by. She shakes her head. "Let me tell you. Most of the boys here are a buncha horny man-tramps." She starts pointing them out. "See that one right there...?" She points to a medium built, brown-skinned guy with dreds flowing down his back. "That's Keyshawn. Stay far away from him. Don't even let that boy breathe on you. He has three baby mommas and two other tricks over at Synder High knocked up...."

I frown. "Ugh! How old is he?"

"Seventeen, girl. And that one over there..." She points

to a tall, jet-black boy with cornrows and a neck full of gold. He flashes her a bright white smile as we walk by. She waves at him. "That's Marcellus. He keeps a nasty drip, girl."

"Yuck."

"Exactly. The boy spends more time down at the clinic than he does in school. He doesn't know what a condom looks like. Probably can't even spell it."

"Yo, Fiona," this cocoa-brown guy rocking a low-fade says as we walk by. "When we gonna chill, girl?"

"When you stop being all busted and broke and get a car and a job," she says, shaking her head.

He laughs. "Ouch, that hurt. You killin' me, baby."

"Drop dead, boo." She glances over at me. "That's Christian. Resident bum. He likes to sleep with girls for money. Like really? Who'd pay for that broke-down boy? Some of these girls have, especially them real fat ones with the double chins. But whatever. Jabberjaws can yabba-dabba-do him all they want."

I can't help but laugh at this chick, shaking my head. She gives me the run-down on almost everyone she sees in the halls. I watch her outta the side of my eyes. I can already tell she's real messy. And definitely not someone I'd wanna chill with 'cause she stay running her mouth.

"Yo, Fiona, who's that you with?" this cute white boy rocking cornrows, sagging jeans, and Timbs says. He kinda reminds me of that actor Channing Tatum, but thicker. "She's mad sexy, yo. Let me holla at 'er for a sec."

"Boy, beat it," she tells him. "She don't want ya con-fused butt.... That's Pauley. Everyone calls him P-Money. But if you ask me, someone needs to call that boy a shrink. He really thinks he's Black. Mmmph. And he loves him some black booty, girl. He's hanging heavy, too. I had to shake a few rounds off that vanilla stick to see for myself, girl."

I frown. I don't respond.

"Yo, Fiona. What's good, ma?" another guy calls out, slamming his locker shut. He's wearing a muscle shirt that shows off a chiseled chest and bulging biceps. "When we gonna link up, girl?"

"I'll call you," she says, holding her hand up to her ear as if she's making a call.

"Yeah, a'ight, yo. You stay frontin' with ya ugly-azz."

"Middle finger up," she says back, throwing her left arm and middle finger up. He laughs. "That's David. He used to be on the baseball team until he got kicked off the squad for punching his ex out in the lunchroom last year. Anyway, he's into all kinda kinky stuff, too. Like putting dog collars around chicks' necks and making them crawl around on their knees blindfolded. I had blisters on my knees for weeks behind that."

Oh my god, this chick's a damn trampazoid.

"Oooh, wait. Girrrrrrl, I heard you done already got into it with Quanda and Samantha." She shakes her head. "They love trouble, boo. Both of them whores are bullies. Don't let them punk you, girl." She looks over at me. I nod. But I keep my lips sealed. Not. A. Word. Okay? I learned a long time ago to never, ever, share what your real thoughts or intentions are, especially to a messy chick like this. We round the corner of the fourth floor toward my wing and there are three guys hanging out in the hallway, laughing and joking. One of them is Crispy Critter from my algebra class.

I frown.

"Yo, Fiona, what's goodie, baby?" he says, walking up

and giving her a hug. He eyes me, smirking. I roll my eyes as she hugs him back.

"Boy, where's my money at?"

"I got you, yo. You know I'm good for it."

"Yeah, you good all right. A good dang lie."

He laughs. "Yo, I'ma hit you wit' that later on tonight. You still coming through, right?"

"You better. And, yeah, I'll be there around eight."

"A'ight, bet."

As soon as we get outta earshot, she says, "That's Travis Richardson. One of my ex-boos..." *Ill, she messed with him? Yuck! This chick's standards are way down in the basement.* "He has a nice body, but"—she sticks out her pinky finger—"he's *all* body and no beef, girl. If you know what I mean."

Oh my god, this chick's a slore!

When we get to Room 418, I let out a sigh of relief to finally get away from this messy chatterbox. "Here's my homeroom," I say. "Thanks for the newsfeed update. It was quite...interesting."

She waves me on. "It's nothing, girl. I'm always happy to help a fellow fly girl out. By the way, I'm loving them shoes, boo. I meant to tell you that earlier. I'ma shoe whore myself."

Girl, boom! That ain't the only thing you whoring for. I smile. "Thanks."

"Hey, if you want, come sit at my table during lunch period. I sit with the cheerleaders. I can introduce you to my girls, and finish giving you the lowdown on the rest of these boys here."

"Oh, thanks. But I can't. I have to go out to my car and make some phone calls today." Of course it's a lie, but I'm not interested. I've had enough of her for one day. "Maybe some other time."

She shrugs. "Okay. But if you change your mind, you'll know where to find me. Toodles." And with that said, she spins off on her heels, shaking her hips down the hall. And I step through the door of my homeroom just as the bell rings.

"Soooooo, a group of us are going out to the mall after school today. You wanna chill with us? I personally don't really care for Newport Mall 'cause they don't have any of the high-end stores I like. But whatever. I go to hang out."

I roll my eyes up in my head, shutting my locker door. *Oh my god, not this messy broad, again!* Of all the chicks this broad can cling to, why-oh-why is she tryna cling on to me? "No. I can't," I lie. Truth is, I *don't* want to. But I don't really have the heart to come outta my face and tell her this. "Maybe some other time. I have a lot of homework to do. And a test I have to study for."

She pops her eyes open. "Study? Aren't you a senior? Girl, who does that? You study the first three years of high school, boo. I have two study halls and all easy classes. Senior year is supposed to be fun. Not full of stress."

I eye her. "Says who? I don't know about you, but I'm tryna get into college. And failing classes or tests in my last year isn't what I do."

"Well, come out to the mall with us for a few hours, bug out, then go home and study. All work and no play makes for a very boring life."

"Thanks, but no thanks. I'll pass."

"Oh, c'mon. It'll be fun. I know you gotta be bored

outta your mind just sitting up in your house all by your-self. Do you have brothers and sisters?"

I sigh. "Look, hun. Keep it real. Why are you so pressed to be friends with me, huh?"

She shrugs. "Well, for starters, you seem like a cool girl. And since no one else seems to like you—from what the other girls say about you—"

I blink. "Listen. These hookers here can think what they like about me. I'm not pressed. Trust."

"Girl, don't worry about it. They're just haters; that's all. They used to hate on me, too, until I sliced this girl in her face with a razor in seventh grade. I mean, yeah. I got locked up and had to go to juvie behind it. And I was kicked outta school for the rest of the year, but so what? I did her face real dirty and she left me alone after that. And I won't even tell you about the girl I stabbed in the forehead with a fork because she kept trying me. Anyway, the point is, these chicks think I'm a little crazy so they don't screw with me, unless I screw one of their boyfriends." She laughs.

A little crazy? You think? I blink. She talks a mile a minute as we walk through the fourth floor halls down to-ward the stairwell.

"Anyway, girl, I'm not one to gossip. And you didn't hear this from me. But Samantha's mother's a drunk and her father is locked up for drugs and robbery or something like that. That's why she's so miserable. And, Quanda"— she shakes her head—"is just plain ol' stuck on boy crazy. And I do mean *craaaazeeeee*. She stalks all her boy-friends. Her latest stalker-fixation is Antonio Lopez."

"Really? Why?"

"Girl, have you seen him? Of course you have. He puts the f-i-n-e in *fine*, girl. And since I don't believe in spreadin' gossip, I'm not even gonna tell you just how many girls' beds he's been in. Too many. But they all stay talking about *it* and him. My advice: Stay far away from him unless you're ready to battle it out."

My gawd... this girl's a motor mouth. Her jaws just keep going and going. I wish she'd just shut. Up!

"Well, she can have him. I don't know him and don't wanna know him. So I'm not interested. And I'm definitely not about to fight some girl over a boy. That's not what I do."

As we turn the corner, walking past the multi-purpose area, I see that boy Justin coming down the hall. He's heading in our direction, wearing a pair of blue shorts and a white cut-off with the words McPHERSON HIGH across his chest. He's all sweaty, like he's been working out or something. "Oooh, and this one here," she says, lowering her voice. "He can get it, girl. He's such a stud muffin. Gobble, gobble. Ooh, I just wanna eat him up."

"Yo, wassup, Fiona?" he says, stepping in front of us. "What's good, Miesha?"

"Nothing much," I say, trying not to stare at the sweat rolling down his face. He takes his towel from around his neck and wipes it dry.

The Fiona chick licks her lips. "Hey, boo. Where's ya muscle-head friend at?"

He laughs. "Who? Tone?"

"Yeah."

"He should be out here soon. We just finished lifting, why?"

"Ohhh, nothing," she coos. "Just asking." She turns to me, pulling out a Coach wallet. "Well, look. I gotta get going. But if you change your mind and wanna meet up"—she pulls out a card and hands it to me—"call me."

"Okay, cool." She walks off down the hall, swinging her hips.

Justin chuckles. "I see you've finally made a friend."

"I wouldn't say all that."

He laughs. "Oh, right-right. I forgot. That's not what you're here for."

I grin. "Exactly."

"Yo, where you headed?" I tell him out to my car. "Cool, I'll walk you."

"And I wonder what dumb mess somebody's gonna make up this time," I say, referring to the lie about him having sex with me out in the parking lot. When I confronted him about the gossip, he denied starting it. He might've just been a good liar, but his facial expression told me he didn't do it. So I let it go.

He shrugs. "So what. Let 'em say whatever they want. You know what's really good; that's all that matters. You know how haters are."

"Yeah, I do," I say as we approach my car. I pull out my keys and disarm the alarm. He wants to know if I have any plans for tonight. I tell him no. He asks what time's my curfew on school nights. "Eleven, why?"

"I thought maybe you'd wanna go for a ride into the city or something."

New York! Oooh, this boy's talking my talk. I grin. "Tonight?"

"Yeah, like around"—he glances at his watch—"six-thirty, seven? I can scoop you up, and we can head over. It's real nice outside, and it's supposed to be nice out tonight, too. I just need to go home and take a shower and make sure my parents don't need me to do anything."

I open the back door and toss my book bag onto the backseat, then open the driver's side door. "Mmmm... and where you tryna take me?" He tells me he has a twenty-four-hour spot he wants to take me to over on Seventh Avenue, down in the Chelsea section of New York, called The Cafeteria. He says they have good food. And they might. But when I think of New York, the *only* thing I hear is Brooklyn, baby! And I do have a taste for a chicken patty and cocoa bread. "I have a better idea. Let's go into Brooklyn instead. There's a spot on Fulton Street that serves the best Jamaican food. You do like West Indian food, right?"

"Yeah, no doubt. Let me get ya number." He pulls out the new iPhone and hands it to me. I plug in my digits, then call it, handing his cell back to him. "Cool. Now you have my number as well." As before, he holds open my door and waits for me to slide in behind the wheel, then shuts it as I let the window down. "A'ight, I'ma hit you up 'round six to get directions to ya crib. Get home safe."

"Thanks." I slowly back outta my parking space. "And don't even think you getting some, either."

He laughs. "Nah. I'm not even on it like that. I just wanna chill with you."

"Unh-huh. I bet you do." I pull off just as Antonio is walking through the parking lot toward where Justin is standing, carrying a gym bag in one hand and his book bag in the other. He looks at me, but I act like I don't see him, speeding right by.

13

Antonio

It's six o'clock in the evening and I'm up in my room, chillin'—kicked back in my boxers, blazin' a blunt and listenin' to that old school Jay-Z joint, "Can I Live" as it pumps outta my stereo while tryna finish up my Calculus homework in between tryna read this James Baldwin book for AP English. Real rap. I can't get into it. Can't relate to it. It's s'posed to be a story 'bout this fourteen-year-old dude, but there's a buncha other stories told within his story from his moms, pops, and aunt through a buncha flashbacks and whatnot. At first, I was kinda lookin' forward to readin' this book 'cause I thought it was gonna be like that joint *Manchild in the Promised Land,* by Claude Brown. Now that was a deep book. But this right here… *no bueno!* Well, uh, maybe it is good. But right now, I ain't feelin' it. It's whack! I take two pulls from my blunt, then shut the book, holdin' smoke in my lungs. I slowly blow it out, then go back to studyin' formulas.

I know I shouldn't even be blazin' right now since we

'bout to start preconditionin' in the next week or so and Coach is gonna slay us. Plus, I'ma hafta flush out my system 'cause they stay drug testin' us. But it is what it is. I'ma finish up these two blunts I have stashed, then be done 'til next summer, for real for real. Pops'll be real pissed if I get benched for some BS like burnin' trees. Especially when he allows me to blaze all summer if I want wit' out problems as long as I don't screw up my basketball career. His thing is, I should know how'ta move at all times. And he's right. But right now, I'm in the mood to smoke. So I am.

I open my notebook and start scribblin' out formulas. Then I solve the word problems. I'm finishin' up the third problem when there's a knock on my bedroom door. Thinkin' it's Pops, I put out the blunt and get up to open the door. Although Pops is cool 'bout me sparkin' up in the crib, outta respect I don't do it 'round 'im. I swing open the door, and almost pass the eff out.

I don't effen believe this ish! It's this broad Tiffany, a brown-skinned chick wit' big, round brown eyes and thin lips who I used to rock the springs wit' before I got wit' Quanda. I met 'er, like a few months after basketball season, while I was up at the food court in the mall tryna get my grub on. She was workin' at Burger King, and was lookin' kinda sexy scoopin' up them fries, so I slid her my digits. And that same night she hit me up and we started kickin' it. She's one a them easy, breezy chicks, so it ain't take long for things between us to get hot 'n' heavy 'cause she was diggin' the swag and I was whisperin' all that good stuff up in her ear. Real rap. It only took me three days to get her to drop them Vickies and let me hit it. After that, it was a wrap. E'ery chance she got, she was sneakin' up over here—'cause her parents were mad strict and all wrapped up in church—to get her eagle on. And it was all gravy 'til she started trippin', wantin' to be up in my face all the time, and textin' me mad crazy. Yo, real ish. She started becomin' a real fruit loop so I had to *chop*...give her the ax!

And now here she is. Still lookin' sexy. And *still* actin' crazy. I haven't seen her in a minute, though. Not since the night I deaded our lil fling. And, yeah, it was right after I let her top me off that I told her that it was a wrap. Like for real. All she wanted to do was lay up 'n' kiss and ask me a buncha dizzy-azz questions. First off, I don't do a buncha kissin', especially when I know a broad's a guzzler. And I ain't beat for havin' to always stroke some chick's fragile ego. And I ain't into handin' out bottles of self-esteem. That's what they have counselors for. Yo, real rap, this chick had to go.

I blink, hopin' that the bud I just smoked got me seein' things. But when I blink again, I realize she's really standin' on the other side of my door wit' her grill all twisted up. *How the hell did she get in here? I'm the only one up in this piece, so I know Pops ain't let her in. Or did he?*

Nah, dude wouldna let her come upstairs like that. Besides, he's out on the road 'til tomorrow night. I start buggin' and thinkin' this crazy broad done broke in or somethin'. That's the last thing I need. Word is bond. "What the fu—"

"Oh, what, you thought it was one of ya other hoes? Well, surprise, surprise, mofo. It ain't."

"Yo, how'd you get up in here?"

"Don't worry about all that," she snaps, foldin' her arms 'cross her juicy double-D's. Images of my face all pressed up in between them ta-tas pop in my head, and I feel my-self startin' to get excited. I quickly shake the thoughts outta my head before I forget the reason I stopped bangin' her out in the first place. "Instead, how about you tell me why you blocked me off ya Facebook page and stopped taking my calls. How about you do that, Tone. Now are you gonna let me in, or what?"

I clench my jaw, keepin' my body between her and the door. "I wanna know how you got in here, first."

She rolls her eyes, suckin' her teeth. "No, stupid. I didn't break in if that's what you're thinkin'. I'm not *that* crazy, boy." I give her an "oh, really?" look. "Boy, get over ya'self. I rang your doorbell, and knocked on the door. And when you didn't answer, I walked in."

I frown. "What? How you just gonna walk up in some-body's crib, yo?"

"Easy. The door wasn't locked. And we need to talk. Next time make sure the door's locked if you don't want anyone walking up in your house."

"Yo, you buggin' for real. You need to bounce."

"I'm not going anywhere. I told you. We need to talk."

"About what, yo?"

"About us."

I look at her like she's crazy. And she is. A real live nut-case. "Yo, Tiffany, for real. What we gotta talk about?" She stares at my bare chest, then glances down at my boxers. I frown. "Yo, what you want?"

"Are you gonna let me in?"

"Hell, no. You need to bounce, yo."

"I'm not leaving, Tone. You avoided my calls all through the summer, and I wanna know why. I opened myself up to you, *Antonio*. You knew you was the only boy I wanted to be with. I let you into my heart, then you just effen dogged me. And the least you can do is tell me why."

I sigh, starin' at her. I already know there's no effen way I'ma let her up in my room. I'll never get her outta here unless I knock her back out, and that ain't 'bout to happen since I ain't beat for her. Still, I gotta figure out a way to get this chick up outta here wit' out her bustin' up shit or tryna claw me up. Some chicks can't handle rejection, and she's definitely one of 'em.

"Hol' up, let me put some clothes on," I tell her, shuttin' the door in her face, then lockin' it. She bangs on it.

"I'm not going anywhere until we talk, so you might as well open up this door, Antonio Lopez. Otherwise, I'ma keep banging until you do. We need to talk, boy."

"A'ight, damn!" I snap, slippin' on a pair of Rutgers basketball shorts, then a white T-shirt. "Ease up off the damn door, yo. I said I'll be out in a minute."

"Well, hurry up."

Damn, this broad done jacked up my whole groove. I snatch up the half-smoked blunt in the ashtray, and spark up. I finish gettin' my smoke on. Then when I'm done, I grab my house keys and cell, and open the door. This bird's still standin' in the same spot wit' her arms folded.

"It's about time," she huffs.

I lock the door, then shut it behind me. "A'ight, let's talk, yo," I say to her, brushin' past her goin' toward the stairs. She follows behind me. Now, had I been thinkin' I woulda had her go down the stairs first, just in case she had a blade and tried to stab or slice me, feel me? But I'm so pressed to get this broad up outta my crib in case she goes off and starts tryna set it off up in here that I jump dead in front of her and race down the stairs.

I open the front door. "Yo, let's sit outside and talk."

She got the nerve to wanna know why we can't chill inside and talk. She has her hand up on her hip, standin' in the middle of the livin' room.

'Cause you effen crazy, yo. And I don't want you effen up my crib, I think. Instead, I tell her, "'Cause I need some fresh air." I stand wit' the door open, waitin' for her to walk out. I'm mad relieved when she does.

I step down from off the porch, then take a seat. She decides to stand in front of me wit' her arms folded tight 'round her chest. "Okay, so talk," I say, ice-grillin' her.

"I wanna know why you stopped callin' and returnin' my calls."

Umm, let's see. You mad dizzy. And ya sex game is mad whack. I sigh. "It wasn't workin' out, yo."

"So you just stop talkin' to me instead of tryna work it out?"

I tilt my head. Stare at this dumb broad long 'n' hard. "Are you serious, yo? Talk what out? You already knew what it was, Tiff, so why you wanna stand here 'n' front? I told you all I wanted was sex, didn't I?"

"Well, yeah. But..."

"'But' nothin', yo. We sexed and that's that. There's nothin' else to talk about. It's over, yo." I feel my phone vibratin' in my pocket and pull it out. Shania texts me: come thru and hit this.

"Yeah, but you didn't have to block me from your Facebook and Twitter."

I shrug. "And you didn't have to keep blowin' up my inbox wit' craziness." I text Shania back: yo, u don't really want it.

"I can't believe you'd pull out your phone and start texting while I'm standing here trying to talk to you. How jacked up is that?"

Shania texts: Whatever punk. U comin' 2 beat this up or wat?

"Yo, you standin' here, but you ain't talkin'. All you doin' is actin' like a desperate housewife, huntin' a mofo down 'n' whatnot. So whaddya want, yo? Say what you gotta say and dip, how 'bout that?"

I text Shania back: yeah, I got ya punk. I'ma hit u in a minute.

"You know what?" she snaps. "Screw you, boy! I don't need you, and I definitely don't need your no-good, lying azz to take care of my baby. Me and my parents will. And my baby will be just fine without you!"

I almost drop my phone. *What did this broad just say?* "Yo, run that by me again."

She twists her face up. "You heard me, boy. I said, *baby*. I'm pregnant."

I blink. Real rap. I might be many things, but a sucka ain't one of 'em. This broad is mad nutty if she thinks I'ma let her clown me into thinkin' she's carryin' my seed. "Okay, so you knocked up. What that got to do wit' me, yo?"

"It's yours."

I bust out laughin'. "Yo, ya desperate-azz mad funny, yo. Unless you preggo from swallowin', you better go back to the lab and find the real donor, yo, 'cause it ain't me; for real for real."

"Oh, laugh now, little boy, but I am pregnant. And it's yours. Believe that."

"Yo, Tiff, for real yo, you delusional. I stayed strapped up in that. And you know it."

"Yeah, and I know you was dumb enough to let me take the condoms off of you, too. And why you think I'd go straight into the bathroom? So I could handle my business." She rubs her stomach and I blink, noticin' how her once-flat stomach is kinda puffy now. She smirks. "All it takes is a turkey baster, and a few drops in the right spot… and *bam!*"

I jump up from off the porch. "Say what, yo? Tell me you didn't do no grimy ish like that, yo."

"Oh, believe it, baby daddy. Every condom you used, I used too. And, yeah, it took six tries to get it right. But it worked. I'm carrying *your* baby, Antonio Lopez. And I'm keeping it. So you might as well kiss your little basketball scholarship good-bye, 'cause we're having a baby."

I'm so heated right now, I'm seein' red. And real ish, this broad better be glad I don't beat up on chicks or I'd rock her jaw sideways for comin' at me wit' this. Who the hell does that kinda nastiness? I mush her in the head. "Yo, get the eff up outta here. I ain't havin' jack, yo."

"Yeah, okay," she says, rubbin' her stomach again, "we'll see in about six more months. If it's a boy, I'm namin' him after you."

I clench my fist. Yo, I'm ready to bring it to her chin, but I check myself. "You a straight savage, yo. If you are knocked up, yo, it ain't mine. So go find ya'self another sucka to pin it on."

"Whatever, Tone. It is yours. So you might as well buckle up and get ready 'cause you gonna be bouncin' a baby carriage instead of a basketball real soon."

I feel effen sick to my stomach. My head is poundin'. Word is bond, yo. My pops will flip his noodle for sure if this broad's really knocked up—by *me*. That's all he's

been beatin' me in the head 'bout. Not to get caught slippin'. To stay strapped. And real rap. I always stayed on
point. Or so I thought. Pops has stayed schoolin' me on
handlin' my business. Stayed preppin' me on the ways of
broads. He told me how slimy chicks get down when they
wanna trap a mofo.

"Don't serve none of them lil fast girls no raw meat,"
he's reminded me countless times. And I haven't. Never.
And, yeah, a few times I wanted to feel how good the sex
was wit' out a condom, but I ain't wanna chance it. So I
keep it wrapped when I'm tappin' it up. "Get your educa-
tion, boy. Graduate. Go away to college somewhere. And
do something wit' your life. Don't let a pretty face or good
sex get you all jacked up in the game." And now I got this
broad standin' here tryna get me all hemmed up.

I take a deep breath. Yo, real ish, this chick seemed like
one of them good girls who just liked to get her freak on.
And I liked freakin' her. But now this slimy trick's standin'
here comin' at me wit' this craziness. I shake my head. I
know there's some real grimy broads out there, but I ain't
really think this chick would be one of 'em. I mean, damn.
She's s'posed to be a church girl 'n' all. Yeah, I know, I
know...they the worst kind. But still...her pops is some
kinda deacon up in some church over in Newark. And
she's s'posed to be all into the choir 'n' whatnot. Yet, she
pullin' some triflin' stunt like this.

"Word is bond. Whosever seed you carryin', good for
you. But this ain't sucka-ville, yo. So stay the eff away from
me wit' ya dumbness 'cause I ain't beat."

"Well, we'll just wait and see about that, Antonio Lopez.
So you'd better get your dollars up 'cause our baby is
gonna need diapers and milk."

This skank is nutz!

She rubs her stomach, again. "We're havin' a baby, Antonio Lopez, so you'd better get used to…"

I'm not claimin' jack. And I'm not hearin' jack else she's sayin'. I bite down on my bottom lip to keep from comin' outta my face reckless at her. But…word is bond, yo. I wanna rip into her real good. Instead, I spin off—walkin' up the steps and back into the crib, before I snap on 'er—slammin' the door behind me.

14

Miesha

"I want you to catch the train over to the city," my dad says to me, "so we can go shopping on Saturday. A'ight, baby girl?"

I'm in my room, lying across my bed, flipping through the pages of *Go Tell It on the Mountain* for my English assignment. I can't get into it. It's *soooooo* slow. I need me a hood read. Something hot 'n' poppin'. But whatever. I'ma still ace the assignment we have to do on it. I sigh, shutting the book and tossing it on the other side of the bed. Anyway, I haven't talked to him—not because he hasn't been tryna talk to *me*, but 'cause I haven't been beat for him—in over a month. Not since Mom packed up and left him, exactly four weeks, four days, twelve hours, and twenty-seven minutes ago—dragging me with her. And even though I'm not really *that* pissed at him now, I'm still dragging him with my 'tude because he shoulda just kept his thing in his pants.

"I'll pick you up at Penn Station; then we can head up to Woodbury Commons. How's that sound?"

Like a buncha bull! I roll my eyes up in my head, sitting up. Now Daddy knows how much I love, love, love to shop. And usually he doesn't have to ask me twice to spend his paper. But tonight, I'm not feeling it. I curl my pink painted toes, gripping the carpet beneath my feet. For the last ten minutes, he's been sweating me extra hard to come to Brooklyn. It's his way of tryna use me to win cool points with my mom. Well, that's not entirely true. He always hits me up when he and my mom are all lovey-dovey too. But when he's tryna take me shopping *without* me hitting him up to run his pockets, then I know what it is. A bribe.

I guess all those giggly phone sessions he's been having with her haven't worked out the way he hoped this time 'cause surprisingly she hasn't packed us up to move back home, *yet*. Not that I'm opposed to moving back home 'cause at least I'd be back in Brooklyn—where I belong. But, I'm not with all this back and forth. And I'm not gonna help him convince her that he's tryna change. No, not this time. He needs to stop *trying* to change. And change, period!

"Mmmph. What it sounds like is you want me to get up in Mom's ear for you—*again*." I sigh.

"C'mon, sweetheart. Help ya old man out here. You know you and your mom are my world. I miss my family. I messed up."

"Like you always do," I snap. "Again and again and again. Over and over and over, Daddy, you keep doing the same thing. And it's not fair to me. *I'm* the one who has to suffer."

"You're right, baby...."

"Don't call me *that*. I'm not a baby, anymore. And you can't buy me things and think that's gonna make up for what you've done. I'm not for sale, Daddy."

"I know you're not for sale, baby cakes. And I'm not tryna buy you. You're my daughter and I wanna take you shopping. Is that such a bad thing?"

"It is *if* you think I'm gonna side with you. I'm smart enough to know what's going on here."

"Listen, baby cakes. I don't want you to side with me, Mi. I know I screwed up. It's all on me. You're my heart. I'd take a bullet to the head before I ever hurt you or let someone else hurt you."

"But *you* hurt me, Daddy. And you hurt Mom, too. And I'm sick of being caught up in the middle of y'all's drama. I have my own stuff to deal with. We shoulda never had to move. I should still be in Brooklyn with my friends, enjoying my life. But, nooooo, thanks to you, I'm waaay out here in Jersey—miserable."

"I know. And I'm sorry. I promise, I'ma make it up to you. Give me a minute to get it right, okay?"

I huff. *What. Ever!* I'm sick of him with his lies and broken promises to change.

And when I listen to my parents talking on the phone, I'm convinced it's only a matter of time before she starts packing up and I'm back in Brooklyn, where I should be in the first place. But I was too through when I heard Mom say, "I'll stay the night tomorrow night. We can talk more then....I'm not making any promises, Roland....I need you too....Don't worry about that. I'll tell Miesha that I'm staying in the city with Shelia because we have an early morning training...."

Miss Sheila's my mom's bestie. They both work in the same building. My mom's an investigator for child welfare for the city of New York. And Miss Sheila's a caseworker. Anyway, the point is, Mom's lying and sneaking to see Daddy, then looking me in my face like she's not beat. It's a hot mess! All I know is, the *next* time she catches him with another chick and she calls herself leaving him or having a mini-breakdown, she's on her own. I'm. Not. Doing. Jack! And I mean it. I'm tired of having my life turned upside down because the two of them can't make their minds up and get it together.

"Come stay the weekend here," Daddy says, "in your own home, in your own bed. It'll be just the two of us." He starts sniffling, and it sounds like he's crying. But I know better. It's just another part of the game. I close my eyes and think back to my last playdate with Daddy. It was three months ago. Daddy took me into the city to see the Broadway musical *The Lion King*; then we had dinner at Carmine's over on Forty-fourth Street. We were sitting at a table for two. After we placed our orders, I waited for the waiter to leave, then flat-out asked my father, "Do you love Mom?"

He looked me in the eyes and said, "Yes. I love your mom very much."

"Then why do you cheat on her?"

"Baby girl," he started, reaching over and grabbing my hands in his. "My love has nothing to do with my cheating on ya mom. Ya mom's the only woman who has my heart. Most men are gonna cheat. It's what we do. And most women, whether they accept it or not, already know this. It's in our DNA. I'm not sayin' all men cheat. But the majority of us do. And we will if the opportunity presents itself."

"Then why say you're not gonna do it, again, when you know you will?"

"Because it's what women wanna hear. They wanna believe that their man is gonna stay true to 'em, even if they know in the back of their minds that it's a lie."

Funny thing, I'd been cheated on a few times, too. But it really didn't matter because I was cheating on them, too. At the end of the day, most of 'em I was using anyway. So I didn't lose any sleep over it when I caught them out there. I already knew boys were no good.

That they can't be trusted.

That they're all liars and cheaters.

Daddy had already taught me that.

And my mom was teaching me that girls take back their cheating, lying boyfriends because that's what women do. Take back their cheating men. Like she does. Over and over and over.

The crazy thing is, Daddy would tell me (he still does) not to be one of those silly chicks who puts up with cheating or lying. He tells me to dump 'im. Tells me that if a boy can't respect me, or our relationship, then he doesn't deserve to be with me. Yet, he doesn't ever follow his own advice.

"It's not that I go out looking to cheat on your mom, baby girl," he continued. "It just happens. Temptation, baby girl, finds me." He paused when the waiter returned to our table with our appetizers, then continued when the waiter walked off. "Just because a man cheats on his woman, Mi, that doesn't make him a bad man. Even a good man has flaws. And his cheating doesn't mean he loves his family any less."

I shrugged. "But if what he's doing is hurting his wife or girl, why wouldn't he just love them enough to stop doing it?" I asked, needing, wanting, to understand.

"I can't speak for every man, Mi. I know with me, your mom's the only woman who will ever have my heart. She's the one I'm connected to. The one I'd bleed for. I'm not interested in having another family with another woman. All them other broads are strictly for sex. And not because I can't get it from home. I just get more of it out in the streets."

I frowned, not really wanting to hear about my dad's sex life, but he's always kept it real with me when it comes to boys, and dating, and sex.

"Baby girl, why do you think I school you the way I do? You're my daughter, but I talk to you like you were my son 'cause I want you to be up on what's up. I want you to always be on point. A man is only gonna do as much as a woman allows him to do, and I'm tellin' you this as man. You dig what I'm sayin'?"

I nodded.

"I don't want none of them lil knuckleheads out there ever breakin' ya heart, or playin' you to the left; otherwise, he's gonna have'ta answer to me."

I leaned forward in my chair, looking him dead in his eyes. "That's crazy, Daddy. You don't want anyone breaking my heart, yet you stay breaking Mom's heart."

Daddy looked at me kinda sad that night. Then shook his head. "I know. And she keeps lettin' me."

That was two weeks before everything fell apart and shit hit the fan—*this* time. And, the truth is, I miss our dates. It's something we've always done since I was two years old. Every Saturday. It would be just the two of us. Sometimes he would have Mom dress me up real in some cute little dress. And other times, he'd tell her to dress me in jeans and whatnot. Sometimes we'd go to Central Park. Other times we'd chill at Prospect Park, go to the zoo, then out for ice cream. There might be a movie and a day of him buying me anything I wanted. Then coming home to Mom snapping on him for spending a buncha paper on stuff I didn't even need. She stayed snapping on him. Sometimes I think she was kinda jealous of what Daddy and I shared together—without her. I don't think my mom has ever wanted to share my daddy with anyone. Not even me.

"This house is so empty without you and ya mom here," Daddy says, bringin' me back to our convo. "I miss you, baby girl. And I want you home, where you belong. You're my heart, Miesha."

I blink back the sting of tears. He knows just the right things to say. He knows how to manipulate me. But not this time. Nope, I'm not gonna fall for the okey-doke. I'm not gonna play the devoted fool, *again*. I'll save that slot for my mother. He's on his own!

I glance over at the clock. It's almost 9 PM. I can't believe I've let him beat me in the head for over thirty minutes.

"I'm gonna see if Mom will let me come for the weekend...."

"That's what I wanna hear, baby. You done put a smile on ya ol' man's face." He tells me to hold on while he takes another call.

I roll my eyes. *It's probably her calling him now*. Whatever. I know Daddy misses me. And I know he loves me. But I also know *this* is about Mom. And that's why I'ma run his pockets, just because. So no matter what Daddy's *real* agenda is, it's still a win-win situation for me. I get to shop, be in Brooklyn, *and* chill with my besties all weekend long.

"Sorry 'bout that," he says, returning to the line. "That was your mom on the other line." I fake a yawn. Tell him that it's getting late and I have homework to finish. "Okay, baby girl. Ya ol' man's gonna let you go. I'll see you Friday. Shoot me a text to let me know what time I need to pick you up at Penn Station, a'ight?"

"Ummm, I still know how to ride the subway, Daddy. It hasn't been that long, you know."

"Yeah, I know, Mi. But it seems like forever...." *Yeah, thanks to you and Mom!* "I thought since I was already in the city I'd just leave from work and meet you. Then we could go and have dinner in Times Square somewhere."

I sigh. "Okay. Sounds good," I say, glancing over at the clock again. "I'll text you to let you know what time I'll be at the train station." I end the call, then quickly log in to my laptop. I'm about to hit up my girls. Stacy and Tre are gonna be over at Jalanda's. And we agreed to FaceTime it up at ten. And that's what we're about to do in five, four, three, two, one...

"Heeeeeeeeeeeeey, hooker," Jalanda says, snapping her fingers up at the computer screen.

"Ooooh, you still ugly," Stacy says, laughing.

I laugh with her. "Bite me. You the ugly one, trick."

"Hahaha...you wish," she says back.

"Girl, move ya big bubblehead out the way," Jalanda

says to Stacy, pushing her outta the way, then pressing her face to the screen. "Kisses, babes. How's Jersey?"

"Busted," I say.

"Girl, boom," Tre says, pushing Jalanda outta the way. "I wanna know how them boys lookin'? Any cuties in the school?"

I shrug. "I guess there's a few. But I'm not thinkin' about none of them busters. I miss Brooklyn, girl."

"And Brooklyn misses you," they say in unison. "Do-or-Die Bed-Stuy, boo. You already know!" My girls are mad hyped and that gets me hyped, too.

"Ooh, I'm so hot with ya moms for snatchin' you up like that," Stacy says, swinging her fists into the air. "I wanna fight her."

I laugh. "Me too. She stays doin' dumbness."

"We should jump her," Jalanda says, laughing. "We could mask up and bring it to her real good for doin' you dirty, girl."

"Right, right," I say, getting more amped. "Hahahaha. Oooh, we could do her face real good, too. Oh my god, let me stop. Y'all sooo ain't right. You know I could never do my mom like that."

"Well, she lucky she's ya mom," Tre says, sparking a blunt. "Or we'd give her a lock in a sock." She takes two deep pulls, then passes it off to Jalanda. Now I don't mind getting my drink on—and, yessss, I take a few hits every now and then. Getting lifted off weed has never really been my thing though, especially on a school night. But my girls, they'll burn whenever.

"Then karate-chop her in her neck," Stacy adds, reaching for the blunt.

I crack up laughing, knowing they're both dead serious. "What. Ever. I'll be in Brooklyn this weekend so make sure y'all have ya stash up. 'Cause I'm tryna get right."

"Yesss, boo," Stacy says, snapping her fingers. "We gonna do it up, boo. 'Bout time ya corny behind gettin' wit' the program and smoke wit' ya girls. Make sure you come straight here as soon as you hit the block; then we can all meet up over here."

"Sounds like a plan," I say, excitedly. I'm sooo bored being here. I need some excitement in my life. I need fun. I need the heat from the streets. And going back to my hood to drink, smoke, and chill with my girls is just what I need. "I can't wait."

"Tramp, are you gonna smoke that, or eat it?" Stacy snaps at Jalanda. I bust out laughing 'cause Jalanda stays chewing the ends off a blunt, which always pisses Stacy off 'cause she hates when good smoke is wasted. Jalanda starts laughing and choking at the same time. I start laughing too.

"Oooh, hooker, you wrong for that," Tre says. "But it's soooo true. She does suck on it like it's a—"

"Eff both of you stank tramps," Jalanda says cutting her off, finally passing the blunt. "Y'all a buncha haters anyway."

I watch my girls go back and forth, passing around the blunt and dogging each other, popping mad ish—while I sit on the opposite side of the screen alone and feeling kinda sad that I'm not there live and direct, kicking it with them. And that only makes me more pissed at my mom. Me and my girls stay on the phone until way after midnight, laughing and bugging out, just like old times.

15

Antonio

"Yo, son, what's poppin' for tonight?" I ask Cease the minute he picks up his cell. It's Friday night, and I'm tryna get into somethin' real right. Sittin' up in the crib def ain't what I'ma be doin' tonight. I need'a get out 'n' do it up heavy. That ish wit' Tiffany had me buggin' for two days, yo. And I ain't even gonna front. That craziness she hit me wit' still has me feelin' some kinda way, for real for real. I'm still kinda jacked up 'bout it, yo. Then today she emailed me—since I done blocked her numbers from my phone, and blocked her from my Facebook and Twitter—a pic of a sonogram, talkin' 'bout, Meet your unborn child, Antonio Lopez, Jr. or Antoinette Selena Lopez. Hope you like, baby daddy. Then the broad had the nerve to have a buncha smiley faces next to it, like that ish is somethin' to be happy 'bout. Yo, eff what ya heard. There ain't jack to be smilin' 'bout. Not 'bout some young broad bein' knocked up. And, real ish, I don't even know what I'ma do if she's really carryin' my seed. I still ain't even tell my boy 'bout it 'cause I ain't really tryna hear what he gotta say. Not now anyway. Still, how effen triflin' can a broad be to do the kinda craziness Tiffany pulled, goin' through the trash 'n' squeezin' my jizz out a condom. That's some straight nastiness. I still can't believe it, yo. *That skeezer's really tryna trap me up.* I shake the thought.

That broad ain't pregnant. Not by me!

What I need is a good time to get my mind right.

"Yo, we still gettin' it in over at Luke's crib tonight?" I ask, tryna push back a headache.

"No doubt, fam. He just hit me up to let me know his parents are def gone for the weekend, so we 'bout to get it in real right, son." Luke's crib is the party spot anytime his parents dip outta town, which is like every other month 'cause they stay drivin' down to Atlanta to see his older sister, who just had twin girls like eight or nine months ago. And his brother, Lance, who's like two years older than him, goes to Morehouse. One of the five schools I'm applyin' to for next fall.

"A'ight, a'ight," I say, rubbin' my chin 'n' grinnin'. "That's wassup. And what the honeys lookin' like? They gonna be on deck?"

"Yo, you already know, bruh. Like whoa. I posted it up on the Book 'bout an hour ago, and mad broads hit me up for the addy, so it's gonna be hot like fiiiyah, son. Mad fluffy, puffy booty cheeks gonna be up in the spot, yo." He laughs. "I'm sayin', yo... it's gonna be like a night at Maggie Moo's." I start laughin' wit' this fool comparin' the party to this spot up at the mall where they make homemade ice cream.

"Yo, Cease, man. I ain't effen wit' you, yo. You shot out for real for real."

"Yo, I'm dead-azz, fam. We 'bout to turn up the heat wit' extra scoops of thick, delicious treats in skimpy lil outfits for all you horny mofos lookin' to lick up somethin' sweet."

"A'ight, a'ight. That's what I'm talkin' 'bout." Yeah, that's exactly what I need. Some new booty to get my mind right. I lie back on my bed wit' one hand in back of my head, imaginin' bein' all pressed up wit' some mad sexy cutie against the wall over in a corner somewhere, gettin' my grind on. "Yo, I should post somethin' up on my wall, too, and drop a tweet or two 'bout it so we can really get it cranked to twenty. The more the merrier, feel me?"

"No doubt. Make that ish pop, son." He laughs. "Wall-to-wall booty, just how I like it."

"Yeah, man," I say, slippin' a hand down into the waist of my basketball shorts, then rubbin' my stomach as it growls. *Damn, I need to eat somethin'.* "It better be, yo. 'Cause the last party he threw was mad whack."

He laughs. "I kinda thought it was a'ight. But, then again, I was twisted outta my head, too."

"Yeah, you definitely was, yo. You was so drunk I don't even think you noticed. But I did. There were a buncha mofos up in that piece and hardly any broads there. And the few broads that were there were either birds, or had wide backs. Real rap, yo. I ain't tryna be 'round a buncha dudes. Or a buncha chicks wit' raggedy weaves built like straight-up linebackers, yo. Not tonight."

He cracks up laughin'. "Nah, fam. Me either, yo. It's all covered. Word is bond. I got you. And Luke said one a his cuzzos bringin' a few of her girls wit' her, and they some real live firecrackers, yo. Always hot 'n' always ready to make it pop."

"Oh, word? That's what it is then. I'ma come through 'round eleven. E'erything should be in full swing by then."

"No doubt, no doubt. Yo, you think you can sneak a few bottles of ya pop's booze? We already got the brews covered. We just need a few bottles to top it off right." I tell him yeah. Tell him I'll swipe up a bottle of Pop's Henney and two bottles of Ciroc—coconut and peach. Pops has mad liquor in the bar downstairs in our basement so it's like havin' my own personal liquor store. Besides, he's not gonna beast if a few bottles are missin'. Well, uh, he might snap if I take that V. S.O.P Cognac up outta here. Now that might get me grounded. But e'erything else is all good. Pops knows I get my party 'n' drink on e'ery now and then. He just doesn't want me makin' it no habit. And I don't.

"Oh, a'ight," Cease says. "Cool-cool. Good lookin' out. And I'ma get this chick, Trisha, to bring a couple'a bottles of Hpnotiq so we can toss back them Incredible Hulks."

I laugh. "Nah, yo. I ain't effen wit' them joints, son. You ain't 'bout to have me twisted up tonight, yo."

He laughs wit' me. "Yeah, yadda, yadda, yadda. Ya biscuit head can have one drink wit' ya boy, yo."

"Yeah, a'ight. We'll see, yo."

"One drink. That's it, son."

"Yeah, whatever," I say, sittin' up. I have another call comin' in. "Yo, I gotta bounce, yo. I'll holla."

"A'ight, one."

I glance at the phone screen. It's LuAnna. "Yo, what's good?"

"You," she says, all sexy-like.

"Oh, word? How you know?"

"Uh, I don't. But it's what I heard."

I laugh, gettin' up from off the bed and walkin' into the bathroom. "Yo, maybe it's time you found out for ya'self, and stop frontin'." I handle my business, flush, then wash my hands. "I see how you be checkin' me on the low, yo."

"Boy, whatever. You're so conceited. Ain't nobody checkin' you."

"Yeah, whatever. Stop frontin', yo. You know you want it."

"Boy, please. Ain't nobody frontin'. Annnyway, why you do my girl, Chantel, like that?"

I frown. "Yo, eff her, yo. That bird stuck on kiddie games. She ain't ready for no real work. But wassup wit' you?"

She laughs. "Is that all you think about, boy? You know I gotta man."

"Yeah, whatever, yo. That's what ya mouth says. And no...that's not *all* I think about."

"Mmmph. Coulda fooled me. Annnyway. Ya girl stepped to Chantel after school today."

I frown. Ask her who she's talkin' 'bout. She tells me Quanda. Tells me she cornered Chantel in the stairwell after school today, got all up in her face and asked her if she was screwin' me. *WTF, yo?!* Then Quanda threatened her.

"That chick's psycho. And you need to handle her for real, Tone."

"Yo, she ain't my girl. And there's no handlin' her. She's gonna do what she does." I pause, sighin'. "I'm glad I stopped effen wit' her. But no lie, yo. Chantel shoulda took it to her head. Real rap. Quanda needs her sockets rocked one good time, for real for real. But, yo. I ain't tryna talk 'bout that silly broad. What's good wit' you, yo, wit' ya sexy self?"

She laughs, suckin' her teeth. "Oh, boy, puhleeze. Compliments will get you nowhere."

"Nah, I'm sayin, yo. What you gettin' into tonight?" She tells me she's not sure. That she's thinkin' 'bout goin' to the party tonight. I tell her she should. That she should come thru wit' some'a her girls. "But leave that bird Chantel home," I tell her, walkin' downstairs to the kitchen to find somethin' to grub on. "We don't need her droppin' a buncha feathers 'round the room."

"Don't be dissing my girl like that. And why she gotta be a bird, anyway? Because she didn't give you what you wanted?"

I open the fridge in search of somethin' to dead my growlin' stomach. "Nah, yo. She just is."

She laughs. "Whatever, boy. You just mad she didn't give you none."

I pull out two containers of leftover Chinese food—chicken 'n' broccoli and shrimp fried rice—from last night. I pull out a bottle of OJ, then shut the door. "Mad? Nah, never that, ma. I ain't that dude. I don't get mad. I get more booty."

I grab a plate and scoop out the containers onto it, then stick it in the microwave for three minutes. While I'm waitin' for my food, I crack open the OJ, then guzzle it down. When the microwave dings, I take out my plate and start grubbin'.

"Sounds like you eating," LuAnna says.

"Yeah."

"Oh, well. Let me let you go. Maybe I'll see you at the party if I decide to go."

"A'ight. Bet. But, yo. If you comin' through, you need to

be ready to come outta them panties 'cause you know I'm tryna hit that. Tonight, yo."

She starts laughin'. She don't say it's a go. But she don't say no, either. So I already know what it is.

The party's on full blast by the time I walk up in Luke's spot. It's a lil after eleven. Mad heads are down in his basement posted up against the walls, smokin' and holdin' forties. There's a buncha strobe lights swirlin' 'round the room. He even gotta fog machine goin'. And this time, there's mad chicks on deck.

I walk through the crowd tryna see what's really good. I grin when I see Cease pressed up against this thick biscuit wearin' a pair of booty shorts and some kinda halter-thingy. I mean, it's still kinda warm out, but it ain't hot enough for that ish. But whatever, yo. She's bent over wit' her hands on her knees grindin' her booty up on my boy. He's holdin' her by the hips like he's hittin' it from the back. I can tell they both diggin' what they feelin' 'cause they both goin' at it real hard.

"Yo, wassup, playa!" Luke yells in my ear over a Meek Mill joint. We give each other some dap. "It's 'bout time you got ya pickle head here." He's holdin' a cup in his hand, filled to rim. I can tell he's toasted.

"Yo, what you drinkin'?" I ask, lookin' over his shoulder, tryna scan the room. So far I don't see Quanda's crazy behind nowhere. And I don't see LuAnna, either. I zero in on a few honeys who look like they might have potential. But it's mad dark down here so I already know what that means. That most of these broads only look good in the dark.

"Got that Henney on the rocks, son. You drinkin', yo?" He hands me his cup. I shake my head. Tell 'im I'm good. I ain't tryna drink, not tonight. Besides, if I drink, I'ma hafta stay the night 'cause Pops don't play that drinkin' 'n' drivin' ish. So I ain't beat. "A'ight. Be on that corny ish. More for me," he says, gulpin' down his drink. I shake my head at 'im as he grabs up this light-skinned broad wit' green eyes. I ain't gonna front, she's kinda right.

"Yo baby, let me be yo' baby daddy. You sexy as hell. I wanna lick ya toes." He tries to lick the side of her face.

"*Illll*, boy," she snaps, jerkin' her head back, pushin' him away. "Get ya nasty tongue outta my face."

"Yo, baby. If you act right, I'ma show you how nasty my tongue gets." He starts flickin' it up 'n' down at 'er. I bust out laughin' at this fool. But she don't see nothin' funny. She's lookin' at 'im like he's extra special. And real rap. He is. This dude can't drink for nothin', yo. The last time he had a party at his spot, he got so drunk he ended up takin' off all his clothes and was dancin' butt-naked. Then he tossed up his guts in some girl's weave. Yo, real ish, that was some straight-up nastiness. Chick was so heated she was ready to fight 'im, for real for real. All he did was laugh. We had to carry his drunk, naked butt upstairs to his room.

"Yo, you stupid, fam. Chill, man." I pull him away from 'er. I look at 'er. "Yo, 'cuse my boy, cutie. As you can see, he's kinda twisted."

She frowns. "Yeah, he's all the way twisted, comin' at me all crazy like that."

"Yo, come upstairs," Luke says, lickin' his lips. "I got somethin' you can twist on. I can tell by the way you lookin' at me, you want it." She rolls her eyes, steppin' off.

We both watch her booty as it shakes in her black catsuit getup. "Yo, how much you wanna bet she ain't wearin' no panties?"

"Yo, you wildin', son. Leave that broad alone."

"Yo, eff her," he says, takin' a sip of his drink. "I ain't want none'a that anyway. Trick prolly gotta nasty yeast infection."

I laugh, shakin' my head. "Yo, man, you a fool, yo. Go take ya drunk azz somewhere and sit down." He laughs, wavin' me on as he walks through the crowd 'n' snatches up a brown-skinned honey wit' a long black weave. I don't know 'er personally, but I know she's a cheerleader over at Lincoln High—one of our rival schools 'cross town.

"Heeeeeeey, Tone!" a girl named Alicia shouts over Kanye West's joint, "Clique," as it pumps outta the speakers. She is manning the bar. She sits her cup down. And by the glaze in 'er eyes, I can tell she's tossed a few drinks back. "What can I get you, boo?"

Alicia's a real pretty chick. She has high cheekbones and a thin nose wit' long, jet-black hair. She looks...exotic! And as I'm standin' here lookin' at 'er, I wonder why I ain't ever hit that. Then it dawns on me, she ain't *always* look like this. She was mad chunky and wore thick glasses. Then her parents sent 'er away somewhere over the summer and this is what she came back lookin' like. Fine!

I grin. "Wassup, yo. Let me get a Sprite." *And a side order of you to go.*

"That's it? You not drinking like the rest of us?"

I tell 'er nah. Not tonight.

"That's good." She takes a sip from her cup, then hands me a cold can wit' a napkin. I pop the can, askin 'er what she's drinkin'.

"Vodka and pink lemonade," she tells me, handin' me her cup. "You wanna taste?"

Yeah, but not that. I wanna piece of that kit-kat. "Nah, I'm good." A Cassidy joint comes on and she starts dancin'. I stare at her boobs as they bounce up 'n' down. She asks me if I wanna dance. And, before you know it, we on the floor gettin' it in. She's dancin' all nasty. *Yeah, she's good 'n' roasted,* I think, movin' in closer. I didn't really come out tryna get some, but now I've changed my mind. I'm seein' an opportunity 'bout to pop off and I ain't tryna miss out.

Our hands touch. Our bodies touch. We hip to hip, bumpin' 'n' grindin'. My hand goes to her waist. I pull her in more. I feel somethin' shoot through me, like electricity or somethin'. But I know it ain't really no electrical current that got me feelin' excited. It's the way she's throwin' it at me. It's them boobs she got on display in that lil low-cut shirt. She must know it, too, 'cause she's eyeballin' me like she wants me to get at 'er. Like she ready to put in some work. So I go in for the kill.

"Yo, let's go outside or somethin'!" I holler over the music. "It's too loud in here!"

"What?!"

"Follow me!"

I grab her hand and lead her through the partygoers, catchin' Cease's eye as we make our way 'cross the room. He gives me a head nod, grinnin'. I grin back. He already knows what it is. I take her up to the third floor of Luke's crib. To his bedroom. I close the door behind us.

"Why you bring me up here, boy? I know you don't think you gonna get you some. I'm nice, boy. But I ain't drunk."

I sit at the foot of the bed, lean back on my forearm. I grin. "Nah, yo. I wanna chill, that's all."

She smirks, eyein' me over the rim of her cup. "Yeah, right." She takes a long sip, then holds her cup up to me. "I know how you do it, boy."

"Oh, word? How I do it, ma?" I pat the space next to me. "Why don't you c'mere and tell me. Or if you want, show me." She rolls her eyes up at the ceilin'. Tells me she knows how I stay tryna hump somethin' up. "Nah, I ain't even on it like that, ma. You know we always been cool." She gives me a "yeah right" look. I kinda laugh. And that makes her laugh too 'cause we both know it's a buncha bull I just spit. Still, she's here. And I'm here. And since she claims she knows how I do it, I wanna make sure she *really* know. "For real. C'mere."

She tilts her head, puts a hand up on her hip, then kinda stares at me like she's tryna decide if she should turn 'round 'n' run out the door, or get wit' the program. I flash 'er one'a my smiles. Tell 'er all we gonna do is talk. And even though she knows it's a lie, she finally comes over and sits next to me.

"See. Was that hard? I'm not gonna bite you, yo. Not unless you want me to."

She laughs. "Boy, you stupid. Where's ya lil crazy *girlfriend* at?"

I frown. Tell 'er I don't have one of them. "Yeah, right. Tell that to Quanda. That chick goin' up to all the girls at school telling them they better stay away from you."

"What? Man, she buggin' for real, yo. That girl needs to get over it. But, yo, I ain't tryna ruin my night talkin' 'bout her. What's good wit' you, yo? You lookin' mad sexy." She

grins. Thanks me. I sit up, then lean into her. "You smellin'
all good. Damn. You got me feelin' some kinda way, yo."

"Oh, boy, please. When I was all fat, you wasn't even
checkin' for me. But now that I done dropped all them
pounds, I got you feeling some kinda way."

I tell 'er when she was over two-hunnid pounds she
was too much woman for me. That I couldn't handle 'er.
She was a heavyweight. That I was scared she'd break my
back. But now that she's dropped down to the lightweight
division, it's all good. I can rock wit' 'er.

She laughs, shakin' her head. "You a mess, Tone. But
I've always liked you."

"Oh, word?" I stroke the side of her face. "You mad
pretty, yo." She blushes. I can tell she diggin' the attention.
"You got on a thong?" She grins. Nods her head. I ask her
what color it is. She tells me it's red. I lick my lips. Lean in
'n' start whisperin' that freaky ish in 'er ear. She squirms a
bit, but I got 'er blushin' hard. She gobbles up the rest of
'er drink. To relax 'er nerves, I bet. "Can I see it?"

"Can you see what?" I tell her I wanna see her in that lil
thing-thing she got on. She giggles, shakin' her head. "Un-
unh. I'm not lettin' you see me in my thong, boy." She eyes
me, then grins. "You probably couldn't handle seein' me
in my thong, anyway, boy."

"Oh, word? It's like that?"

"Maybe," she says, battin' her eyes. She's a cutie, yo.

I glance at my watch. It's close to midnight and we been
up in Luke's room for almost ten minutes. I wanna get wit'
'er, bad. And I can tell she wanna give it to me, too. But
she ain't comin' outta them jeans, yet. I lean in closer 'n'
sniff 'er neck again. Tell 'er she smells good enough to eat.

Let 'er know I'm ready to eat 'er up. She giggles. I lick her neck.

"Oooh, boy, don't do that. My neck is my spot. You'll mess around and have me outta my clothes."

I grin. "That's the plan, yo. Stop playin', ma…you already know what it is…." I go back to lickin' 'n' kissin' her neck 'til she leans back 'n' lets my hands roam 'er body. She keeps tryna kiss me 'n' I keep movin' my head, givin' her my cheek, my neck. She wants to know why I won't kiss 'er. I frown. *Is this effen broad serious?* I wanna spaz on 'er. Tell 'er I don't know where her mouth's been, but I'm mad excited 'n' wanna rock the springs so I don't snap on 'er. Instead, I hit 'er wit' some BS that I only kiss my girl. She kinda looks at me like I'm crazy for a minute, but I can tell the booze and the way my hands are all over 'er body got 'er hot 'n' bothered and she wanna get it in too, so she lets it go.

She lies back on the bed, lifts her hips up and lets me remove her skirt, then her thong. "I've always wanted to get with you, Tone," she whispers, starin' me in the eyes.

"Then tonight's ya lucky night, ma." And in a matter of moments, her moanin' starts to sound like music to my ears as I strap up 'n' give it to 'er just how she want it.

16

Miesha

I glance at my mom as I eat my cereal. She has a coffee cup in one hand and the latest issue of *Essence* in the other. We're sitting across from each other at the kitchen table. Alone. Every so often I eye her over the rim of my bowl as I bring it to my lips and sip down almond milk. She's acting like she's all wrapped up in whatever article she's reading. But I know better. She's crazy pissed at me for hanging out all weekend with my girls, instead of spending time with my dad, like they both *assumed* I would. Womp, womp, womp... epic fail!

I did it up with my girls in Brooklyn over the weekend and I'm good. So she can be pissed all she wants. I already knew I was gonna be in trouble when I decided to stay out Saturday night and part of Sunday. Oh, well. The fact is, I'ma do what I wanna do. And there's nothing she can say or do that's gonna stop me. She does her. So I'ma do me.

I try to hurry up and eat the rest of my breakfast, knowing she's going to try to bring it to me. But I'm too late.

She shuts her magazine, then looks up at me. "I'm still waiting for you to tell me what you were doing all weekend. And until you do, you're going to be grounded."

I tilt my head, looking at her like she's extra crazy. Because she has to be if she thinks I'm gonna be on anybody's punishment. Oh, noooo. I don't do punishments. And since she's never grounded me in the past, there's no need for her to try to get brand new now. "*Grounded? Who me?* Hahaha. Real funny, Ma."

"Yes, you! And I don't see anything funny about it."

"Well, I do. Since when you start tryna ground me?"

"Since you *lied* to me, and your father. That's when."

I huff. "I didn't *lie.* To you or Daddy. He wanted me to come to Brooklyn...."

"Yeah, so the two of you could spend time together."

"And we *did* spend time together. He took me shopping. And bought me mad stuff. Then I went to lunch with him yesterday before he put me on the train." I roll my eyes up in my head at the memory of him standing there waiting for me to catch the PATH train back to Jersey. How tired is that? I'm seventeen years old and he still treats me like I'm some little girl he has to protect. Give me a break! I still can't understand why I can't drive my car into the city. I know what they tell me. That they don't feel comfortable with me driving the streets of New York by myself, yet, since I just got my license over the summer. Whatever.

"And you were *supposed* to stay with *him*—all weekend. Not be gallivanting all over Brooklyn doing God knows what."

"Uh, *nooooo*. That was his plan. And *yours*. Not mine. And I wasn't wandering all over Brooklyn. I was at Tre's house." Well, uh, most of the time. There's no need for me

to tell her about the party we went to over in Crown
Heights—packed to the seams wit' mad cuties, drinks, and
weed—Saturday night. And she definitely doesn't need to
know that we didn't get back up into Tre's house until almost four in the morning, twisted outta our minds. Oh,
noooo. Those details I gotta keep tucked on the low. All
she needs to know is that I was chilling with my girls.

"Yeah," she snaps, slicing into the memory of my weekend as she gets up from her seat, "*without* my permission."

I frown. "Ma, stop. I didn't need *your* permission."

"Girl, you most certainly did."

"And how's that if I was staying with Daddy?"

"But you weren't with your father, so don't go there."

"Well, I don't know what the big deal is if Daddy said it
was okay."

She slams a hand up on her hip. "Oh, please, Miesha.
You left outta here with me thinking you were going to be
staying with your father. Of course he was going to tell you
you could stay out. He hates saying no to you. But that
didn't mean you could stay out for almost two days."

"I wasn't out for *two* days."

"Miesha, shut it. Up. You left your father Friday night at
ten o'clock and didn't walk back up into that house until
two o'clock Sunday afternoon."

I roll my eyes. "I don't know why you hate seeing me
have any fun."

"Miesha, don't try it, girl. You can have all the fun you
want as long as I *give* you permission. And I approve of it."

I pull in my bottom lip. "And you're not gonna sit there
and tell me you sat up in Tre's house all weekend, either."

"Okay, I wasn't. Big deal. I'm stuck in Jersey effen miserable, okay?"

"Don't you use that language with me, young lady! Who in the hell do you think you're talking to?"

I roll my eyes. "I didn't curse at you. The point is, I miss my friends. As long as Daddy was cool with it, why you care? I came back, didn't I? And don't *think* for one moment I wanted to. I hate it here."

She narrows her eyes at me. I can tell she's trying not to go off in Aunt Linda's house, but she's so ready to blow her wig. And I'm soooo not in the mood to get into it with her. She's staring me down so hard I feel like she's tryna burn a hole in me. I look up.

"What? Why are you standing there looking at me all hard and whatnot, like you ready to bring it?"

She huffs. "Miesha, you're testing my patience, girl. And I'm trying real hard not to jump on you. Now I wanna know what you were doing in Brooklyn *all* weekend. And I'm only gonna ask you one more time."

"Or what?" I say, setting my spoon down. "Mom, you need to chill. I wanted to chill with *my* friends. Not be all up under Daddy. You've been doing enough of that for the both of us, don't you think?"

She blinks. Slams her coffee mug down on the counter. "And what *exactly* is that slick comment you just made supposed to mean?"

I get up from the table and walk over to the sink to rinse out my dishes. I brush by her, deciding to ig her. But she grabs me by the arm.

I yank my arm away from her, then step back so that there's enough space between us in case she tries to lay hands on me. "It means I know you've been sneaking over to Brooklyn to be with Daddy, lying about having to stay in the city for work. So spare me about lies."

"*Whaaat?!* Miesha, you are really trying me, girl. I've been letting you get away with that slick mouth because I know this whole move thing has been hard, but now you're crossing the line and seem to be forgetting who the mother is around here. I don't answer to you. So you'd better get back in your lane real quick before you find yourself on the floor."

"No, you don't answer to me. But you don't get to pick and choose when you wanna play mother, and when you wanna be friends. It doesn't work like that. So if you want me to stay in my lane and be the child, then you need to stay in yours and stop..."

Aunt Linda comes stepping in, dressed for work, carrying a pile of newspapers. She frowns. "What's going on in here?"

"Nothing," I say, relieved she walked in when she did. I walk over and give her a kiss on the cheek.

She eyes me. "Uh-huh. Sounded like more than *nothing* to me."

I shrug. "I don't know what to tell you. Ask *her*. I gotta get to school before I'm late again." I walk outta the kitchen with my mom shooting me daggers. I hear her saying, "Linda, I swear. I'm two seconds from beating the snot outta that fresh-mouthed girl..."

What. Ever!

"Okay, class," Mrs. Sheldon says as she turns from the chalkboard and faces the class. As much as I like English and reading, I don't like this class. And I don't like this

chick. I think she's a rude teacher and her attitude stinks!
"Who can tell me the name of the main character in James
Baldwin's *Go Tell It on the Mountain*, along with the loca-
tion and year it is set in? Mr. Lopez?"

"Yo, what's good, Mrs. Sheldon?" he says. "You a'ight up
there? You know you my peoples, right?"

Mrs. Sheldon eyes him, raising a brow. But I can tell
she's tryna keep from getting all grins and giggles. If you
ask me, her old butt acts like she has a crush on him or
something. Ugh, how gross is that?

"A'ight, a'ight. My bad, Mrs. Sheldon. I got you. Dude's
name was James Grimes."

"Wrong answer, Mr. Lopez. Let me guess. You haven't
opened the book yet." He opens his mouth to say something else and she shuts him down. "I don't want to hear
it. Starting tomorrow, I expect to see you sitting"—she
points to the front row—"in one of these seats right here.
And if you are not, I will toss you up out of here. Do I
make myself clear?"

Someone says, "Yo, man, she's tryna play you, yo. Don't
let 'er clown you, fam."

"No, Mr. Benson. What I'm trying to do is keep Mr.
Lopez from flunking his first marking period. But since
you seem to know what's good for him, how about you
answer the question for him?"

"Nah, I'm good," he says. "I ain't study that part yet."

"Well, I don't know why not. You had a week to read
this book cover to cover."

"Nah, my bad, Mrs. Sheldon. I'm only messin' wit' you.
You know I've read it. But that part slipped my mind, for
real for real."

I sigh. Like c'mon already. Answer the dang question

and let's keep it moving. Geesh! "His name is John Grimes," I blurt out. "The story takes place in Harlem in nineteen thirty-five."

She eyes me. Tilts her head. "That is correct, Miss Wilson. However, in the future I ask that you raise your hand, and wait to be called on before blurting out answers."

I hear a few, "Ooohs" in back of me. But I ig 'em. I raise my eyebrow. Tilt my head. And eye her right back. This chick's been giving me her funky butt to kiss since I got here. I bite down on my bottom lip to keep from lighting this hag's fire.

"Okay, class. At the heart of the story, there are three main conflicts. Who can tell me what they are? Mr. Lopez?"

Mmmph...this trick must have a thing for him or something since that's who she keeps calling on. To my surprise, he actually *does* know. He tells her that the main conflicts are a coming-of-age struggle, a crisis around religion, and the conflict between the main character and his father. Now she wants to know what the conflict is/was between the father and son. "Real rap, dude doesn't understand why his pops hates 'im and favors his brother over 'im."

"That is correct, Mr. Lopez," she says, smiling at him like he's won the door prize or something. Give me a break! She continues, "John is torn between his desire to win his father's love and his hatred toward him." She writes this all down on the board, then turns back to the class. "Who can tell me where the title *Go Tell It on the Mountain* originates from?" Again, no one seems to know the answer. This time I turn in my seat and cross my legs, folding my arms across my chest. *I'll be damned if I'ma raise my hand in this stupid class.* And of course she calls on her pet, again. Mr. Lopez.

"From the Bible," he says.

I shake my head and grunt. "Mmmph."

"Umm, Miss Wilson is there something you'd like to say?"

I frown. "Oh, no, boo. Do what you do. It's obvious that the only person you seem to see in this room is your precious Mr. Lopez and he didn't get the answer right. Then you got the nerve to look over at me, and call on someone else. Like really? Who does that?" She puts a hand up on her hip. Tells me I'm outta line. Then threatens to throw me outta her class. I laugh. "Bit…chick, throw me out. I don't wanna be up in here anyway. Ever since I walked up in this classroom you've been shooting daggers at me, like you want it with me or something. And guess what, boo-boo? I'm not the one."

I snatch up my bags, and head for the door. I swing it open, then turn back to face her, pointing a finger at her. "And for the record, the title comes from a Negro spiritual." I walk out and slam the door behind me.

17

Antonio

"Yo, so wassup wit' you 'n' shorty?" I ask Justin the minute she shakes her stuck-up azz away from us. I ain't gonna front; I eyed her as she popped her booty down the hall. Real rap; she gotta real phatty and I swear she was swingin' that thing-thing extra hard for me. I couldn't help but lick my lips. But dig. I peeped how she tried to play me like she didn't know we were in the same English class. She's mad funny, for that—for real for real. "Y'all kickin' it now?" I ask, shiftin' my attention to him as we walk down the hall in the opposite direction. They been kinda chummy over the last few weeks so I'm tryna see what's really good before I go in and try to get at 'er.

"Yeah, somethin' like that," he says, cuttin' his eyes at me.

"Oh, a'ight."

"Why? You checkin' for her? Don't think I didn't peep how you were eyeballin' her walkin' down the hall."

I frown. "Nah, yo. Yeah, I was def checkin' that shake

out. But I def ain't checkin' for her. Not like that, yo. So you good."

"I'm *good?*" he laughs as we climb the stairs to the third floor. "Yo, you mad funny, dawg. I was gonna be good re-gardless, fam. You know how I do. But you sayin' that like there'd be some kinda comp *if* you were tryna check for her."

"Nah, fam," I say. "Handle ya handle, bruh. Ain't no comp. Not over here. "

"Oh, a'ight. That's what it is. Just checkin', yo." We pound fists, then head to our classes wit' plans to meet up at lunch. At lunch, I make plans to hit the court to shoot some hoops wit' the fellas right after school, flirt wit' a few chicks, then, drum roll please...argue wit' Quanda. And now I have a bangin' headache.

"Yo, son," Cease says, drapin' an arm over my shoulder, "effen wit' her is like havin' baby mama drama, just wit' out the baby, for real for real."

I shake my head. "Tell me 'bout it, yo." I sigh. "She stay goin' at it. For nothin', yo. Man, I'm 'bout ready to split her wig back. She's lucky she's a chick 'cause, real rap, yo, she woulda had these knuckles down her throat by now."

He laughs. "I feel you, yo. But it ain't even worth it."

"She's really pushin' it."

"So what you gonna do? Take her back? That seems to be the only thing that's gonna calm her down."

I frown. "Hell, nah. I'm not takin' that broad back. Are you serious, yo? Man, listen. I'm done wit' Quanda."

"I heard that, fam." He chuckles. "But don't look like she's tryna fall back anytime soon, yo. You musta really put that smackdown on 'er."

"Yeah, seems that way. Just like I'ma 'bout to do to you the minute we hit the courts. So D-up, mofo, 'cause I'm comin' for ya."

He laughs, hittin' me wit' a body shot. "You don't want it, yo." He makes an imaginary free-throw shot. "*Swoosh!* All net*," he says, holdin' one arm in the air.

"Nah, mofo. You don't want it. Lace up 'n' let's see what's really good," I challenge as we walk into the locker room to change.

"Yo, Pops," I say, walkin' through the front door. It's a lil after six. His car is in the driveway, but it's mad quiet in the crib. "Where you at, man?" Usually when Pops is home, he'll have the TV on in the livin' room even if he's not in here watchin' it and he'll have some of his old-school music playin' on his record player. I don't know why he won't toss all those old records out and buy CDs, like the rest of us. He says the music sounds better on vinyl. Whatever.

"Yo, Pops?" I call out again, walkin' into the kitchen. He's not there. I walk down into our basement to see if he's loungin' down there. We have it set up like a game room wit' a pool table, full bar, pinball machines, and mad games for the PS3 and Xbox joints. Sometimes Pops comes down here to have a few drinks and shoot a round of pool. But, not today. *He's prolly upstairs gettin' it in.*

I climb the stairs and head back into the kitchen. I grab a bag of Doritos and pour myself some apple juice from the fridge. There's a note on the counter from Pops. I straddle a stool at the counter and begin readin' it while chompin' on a handful of chips.

Tone,

I'm In Delaware With Marisol. Be Back Tomorrow Night. There's Money Up In My Top Drawer If You Need It. Hit Me On My Cell If Something Comes Up. Make Sure You Handle Ya Business Right While I'm Gone. Oh, Marisol Cooked You Some Food. It's In The Fridge.

Love,
Pops

I shake my head, smilin'. Marisol is one'a Pops's jump-offs. They been rockin' for a minute. He says he isn't really diggin' her like that. But if you ask me, yo, I think Pops is frontin' heavy, though, 'cause he stays chillin' wit' her more than the other four broads he's smashin'. Dude's diggin' her. I dig her too, real rap. She's mad sexy for an older chick. Anytime she comes over, she cleans the crib and cooks mad food for me and Pops. I can tell she's big on Pops.

I finish off the bag of Doritos, then get up and hit the fridge to see what Marisol cooked. My stomach growls as I pull out the six Tupperware containers. Marisol has hooked me up wit' yellow rice 'n' peas, fried plantains, empanaditas—turnovers stuffed wit' meat. She also made fish balls—one of me and Pops's favorite Dominican dishes—in tomato sauce wit' green peppers, pitted olives, and onions—another DR dish. Real rap, Marisol can cook her butt off. And she gets mad points for bein' able to cook bangin' Dominican dishes when she's Puerto Rican.

I grab a plate outta the cabinet, pile my plate up, then nuke it in the microwave. When the microwave beeps, I remove my plate and sit back at the counter. I guess I should be happy that I have the crib to myself, but I'm not. Not tonight. I was kinda hopin' Pops was gonna be here so we could chill. Maybe shoot some pool. Or, maybe, play a game of chess.

Oh, well. Pops is out doin' him. So I might as well do me tonight. While I'm housin' my plate of food, I'm thinkin' 'bout who I wanna do. I ain't really beat to be drivin' nowhere. And I'm not really feelin' company. But I don't wanna be alone, either. I decide to just kick back 'n' play a few rounds of *NBA 2K13*, then take it down for the night.

Fifteen minutes into my game, my cell rings. I reach over and grab it off the nightstand, then glance at the screen. It's Alicia. After she let me smash at the party, I ain't really been beat for her. And she knows this. But she keeps hittin' me up anyway. At school, she speaks 'n' keeps it movin', def not sweatin' my space. And I dig that. But the minute we get outta school, she's blowin' up my line, wantin' to chill again.

"Yo, what's goodie?"

"You, boy," she says, soundin' all grown. "I was callin' to see if you wanna go to the movies tonight."

"Oh, word? That's wassup. But, nah, yo...I'm kickin' back, chillin' tonight; feel me? But what you tryna go see?"

She tells me that new Denzel Washington joint. I glance over at the clock, again. It's still mad early 'n' it's not like I got any other plans. I could tap that up again, even though she was kinda lame.

"And I was thinkin' maybe we could grab something to eat before the movie started."

"Oh, word?" I grin. Yeah, she tryna get rocked again. "Then what?"

"I don't know. It's whatever."

"So you tryna let me get that?"

She laughs. "What you think?"

"I'm askin', yo. So if you wanna 'nother round, just say it. We ain't gotta hit no movie, yo—feel me? We can hit the sheets 'n' make our own movie, so if it's really whatever, come through and let's get it crackin'. But check it. I ain't tryna make you my girl so don't start tryna make this out to be nothin' more than what it could be."

"Boy, please. I already know how you get down. I already know tryna be your girl isn't gonna happen, so I'm good. I just wanna chill with you; that's it. I had fun with you the other night. And I wanna do it again."

I grin, rubbin' my chin 'n' goin' into Kevin Hart mode. "All right, all right, all right. That's what it is, ma. But check it. My paper's mad low right now. So if we gonna hit the movies, you gonna hafta spot me."

"It's cool. I got you. I was gonna treat anyway if you wanted to go."

I get up outta my seat, then walk over to my closet 'n' start tryna find somethin' to put on. "Yo, it's all good. You comin' through to scoop me, or you wanna link up at the movies?"

"Welllllll," she says all low into the phone. "I kinda like that idea of us making our own movie tonight. So if you down, how 'bout I just come there and we can chill." I hit 'er wit' the ground rules. Tell 'er it's strictly sex. That after we finish, she gotta bounce. There ain't gonna be no cuddlin' or any other kinda mushy ish. "Ohhhkay. And who said that's what I want? You don't gotta tell me the rules, boo. I already know how'ta play the game. All I want is for you to make me feel the way you did the other night. That's it."

"Yeah, a'ight. That's what your mouth says. But I don't think you really ready for it."

She laughs. "Oh, trust me, boo. I finally got a chance to see firsthand what all the other girls were talking about and I wanna keep gettin' it."

"Yo, check it. If I give you some, I don't want you gettin' all psycho on me 'cause you know how some'a you broads can get when the lovin's good."

She starts laughin' again. Tells me I'm buggin'. That she ain't weak. Yeah, whatever!

"A'ight. We'll see. So what time you comin' through to get this?"

"I'm on my way," she says, gigglin'.

"A'ight. Bet. See you when you get here."

For some reason that broad Miesha's booty pops in my head and I feel myself gettin' excited just thinkin' 'bout all the things I would do to 'er. Today she came to school in these tight beige leggin' thingys wit' a brown crochet blouse thingy that hung off her smooth shoulders. I ain't even gonna front. She was lookin' mad sexy.

18

Miesha

A month into the school year and I still can't find my groove up in this rathole. Truth is, I'm not even trying to. I still hate it! Most of these dizzy chicks are still ice-grillin' me, the dudes stay tryna sex me wit' they eyes and whatnot. And the only dude—well, uh, two dudes...okay, okay, three dudes—I'm even giving any airtime to is that boy Justin on the basketball team, this cutie Brent—he looks like he's mixed with Indian with his reddish-brown skin and wavy hair—who's one of the star players on the lacrosse team here. *Lacrosse? Like really?* What kinda dude plays that mess? A cornball, that's who! But, whatever. And, then there's Trevin, a big hunk of milk chocolate skin with slanty brown eyes, who plays on the football team. Outta the three guys, he drives the fliest car—a convertible Mustang. But, anyway, they all have nice bodies and they're cute enough. Okay, fine! But they still aren't my flavor. They dress nice and all. But that swag isn't on high the way I like it.

Anyway, boys aren't nothing but headaches. Still, they are a necessity, especially for a chick like me who likes to spend their paper. Forget tryna get ya hump on or getting all caught up in hot, steamy kisses. Feed me, boo. Take me shopping. Get my hair and nails done. That's right. Feed me. Finance me. And, *maybe*, as a reward for his generosity, I *might* let him press up on this big booty or squeeze my boobies. You best believe he's gonna have to earn a ride up on my goodies, or find himself standing on the sidelines. And, nope...I'm not a gold digger. I'm a chick who knows how boys move. They're sneaky, they're liars, and they're always looking for a girl to give up the goody-goody, then when you don't—or even if you do—they wanna run off with the next chick 'cause they're greedy dogs. Boys ain't *shhhhheeeeit!* So my motto is this: Let him chase, but don't ever let him catch. That drives 'em crazy. It makes 'em want you more. And, then...just when you have 'em right where you want 'em—and they *think* they got you, dump 'em. Yup! Play 'em, before they play you. Simple as that. Besides, the chase is always more fun—well, for me, anyway.

So I'm not shocked when the hottest boy in the school, Antonio Lopez, *finally* walks up on me. I feel his burning gaze on me before he ever opens his mouth. And why I am not surprised that he's finally got up the nerve to step to me is beyond me. Point is, he's here. And I'm bracing myself for, well, uh...I really don't know why or what I'm preparing for. All I know is, he's up on me. Live and direct. But I play it off like I don't know he's standing here. Like I don't smell his scent—a mix of fresh soap and cologne, swirling all around me.

He clears his throat. "So you just gonna act like you don't know I'm standin' here?"

I smirk behind the door of my locker, glancing at myself in the mirror before I decide to peer around the locker door. I look him up and down with as much stank as I can possibly dish up, which is almost kinda hard to do with him being so dang fine. Mmmph, he's rocking the new Jordans. "Can I help you?" I say, looking up into his eyes.

He leans against the lockers, eyeing me. "Yo, what's good wit' you?"

I frown, placing a hand up on my hip. "Excuse you?" I say wit' my 'tude still on ten.

He smirks. "Yo, you heard me. I asked you what's good wit' you. I mean. You sexy 'n' all, but you walk 'round here wit' ya head all stuck up in the air like you too good to speak when peeps holla at you. Wassup wit' that?"

"Ain't nothing up with it," I say, swiping a strand of hair outta my face. "Maybe I'm not beat to speak. Maybe I'm not beat for chitchat. Maybe..."

"Heeeeeey, Tone," this light-skinned chick with grayish-colored eyes says. She turns her nose up at me, flipping her hair as she walks by. I pay the ho dust. He gives her a head nod, never taking his eyes off me.

He narrows his eyes at me. "*Maybe* you need to be checked."

"*Checked?* Ha! Check me, boo-boo. That'll never pop off. Trust."

"Yeah, a'ight. Whatever, yo. Dump the attitude for real, yo. I ain't tryna come at ya neck; just tryna see what's good wit' you. But you wanna be all stank. How you expect to make friends here if you actin' all funny-style?"

"Uh, newsflash, boo-boo: I'm not running for a popularity contest. So be clear. I'm not interested in convo. I'm not interested in makin' friends. And I'm definitely not interested in *you* and your doggish self being all up in my face, so if you don't mind"—I slam my locker shut—"I have a class to get to. That's what's up with me." I walk off, and without even looking back I can feel the heat from his gaze on me. And there's something about knowing that he's staring me down that makes me feel, uh, nervous. No, light-headed.

He catches up to me. "Yo, you know you too pretty to be actin' all funky, right? All I'm tryna do is holla at you for a minute, nothin' serious, yo. But you actin' like I'm the one who broke ya heart."

I roll my eyes, stopping in my tracks. I stare at him. Shift my weight from one foot to the other, letting my handbag drop in the crook of my arm. "First of all, boo-boo, I don't give a mofo the chance to break my heart, trust." *I do the heartbreaking.* "Second, whatever it is you selling, I'm not buying. Third, I know ya kind. And, once again... I'm. Not. Interested. So step."

He grins. "Oh, word? That's what them pretty lips say."

I let out a disgusted grunt. "And that's what it is. Like I said, I know your kind."

"And what's that?"

"A dog. A player. Someone who's only out to get one thing..."

" How you gonna just pass up an opportunity to be wit' the most popular dude at this school?"

I frown. "Easily. I'm not interested."

He shakes his head, grinning. "I'm tellin' you, yo, you

'bout to give up the opportunity of a lifetime. Don't you know I'm the man who can make all your dreams come true?"

I twist my lips up. "Mmmph. Sounds more like a nightmare. I'll pass."

"Check this out, yo," he says, stepping in front of me. "I'ma follow you all 'round school 'til you holla at me, yo. And if I gotta stand outside e'ery one of ya classroom doors and wait for you after each class, I'ma do that. And if I gotta follow you home, then I'ma do that, too, 'til you give me them digits so I can get to know you better."

I almost smile. Almost. I take a deep breath. Stop walking. "Look," I say, staring up at him, this time *really* looking at him. Right into his... *Oh my god, his eyes are beautiful!* And he has skin most chicks would kill for, smooth and clear. No pimples, no blackheads, no splotches, no scars. Perfect. *Every*thing about this boy—his super straight, white teeth, his sexy grin, his broad shoulders and muscled arms and that thick curly hair—is hmmph... *perfect.* Too perfect! I can see why these silly girls fall all over him. But I'm not about to get caught up in the matrix. I'm not the one.

"You might as well skip on back over to them little hot-in-the-drawers hookers you got fighting over you 'cause you'll never be ready for a chick like me." And with that, I walk off, throwing a buncha shake in my hips. This time he doesn't follow me, but I can feel his eyes on my butt. *Damn him!*

As soon as I round the corner to get to my class, there's a posse of dudes hanging out in the hallway, clowning, popping jokes back 'n' forth. They all laugh. The minute they see me...silence! Out of the little circus crew, a brown-skinned boy rockin' cornrows with a zigzag design in his hair steps to me, all grins.

"Yo, ma, what's your name?" His voice is deep.

I tilt my head. "Why?"

Out of the corner of my eye, I peep them nudging each other, like they've never seen a hot chick before. Then again, maybe they haven't; at least not one as on fiyah as *me*.

He licks his lips and I frown. "Maybe I'm tryna take you out."

Little boy, puhleeze. You couldn't afford me. And even though I know this without having to look down at his sneaker game, I look down at his feet, anyway. I sigh. He has his long feet in a pair of black Nike slides with a pair of black socks on. Call me whatever you want, but I'm never gonna stop checking a dude's footwork before I look at anything else. I don't care what he looks like, or what kinda body he has, if his kick game is whack, then *womp, womp, womp*...I ain't got nothing for you. I toss my hair, then brush right by him, slipping into my Algebra III class just as the bell rings, with one of them saying behind me, "Yo, eff that stuck-up *beeeyotch!*"

I crack up laughing now when I hear that. Yeah, okay, I'm stuck up. Yeah, I'm conceited. Why shouldn't I be? I'm hot like fire. And can't none of these busters stand the heat. Obviously they know it too; otherwise they wouldn't stay sweatin' me. By sixth period, I'm staring at the clock counting down the minutes, the seconds, before next period. And the minute the last period bell finally rings, I'm amped to be gettin' outta this hellhole. All I can think is, *TGIF!* I can't wait for the weekend to pop. Mariah and I have plans to hit this club tonight in Bayonne—it's teen night so we're gonna turn it up. Then Saturday I'm goin' to Brooklyn until Sunday night. Yeah, I'm staying with my dad. But, my girls are crashing there with me. Oooh, I can't wait. I'm so psyched.

I race to my locker, grab the books I need to do my homework assignments, then head out the door. As I'm walkin' out to the parking lot toward my car, someone whistles in back of me. Of course, I pays it dust 'cause I ain't some trick you gonna whistle at, then expect me to turn around and be all grins and giggles. No, boo. You don't whistle at me. I'm not in heat.

I keep stepping.

"Yo, ma, let me get some fries wit' that thick shake."

I roll my eyes, knowing who it is. He catches up to me, his steps falling into place with mine. "Can I help you?" I say, keeping my face forward but checking him outta the corner of my eye. He has his book bag slung over his broad shoulder and I can feel he's looking at me as we're walking.

"Yeah, you can help me get to know you."

I stop dead in my tracks. Tilt my head. "And who are you again?"

He laughs. "Hahaha, you mad funny, yo. Don't front like you don't know who I am. I know you've *heard* who I am. And I know you've seen who I am."

"Uhhhh...not to bust ya bubble, boy. But...not!"

I try not to breathe in his cologne as he walks alongside of me. He smells...delicious! I'm tempted to ask him the name of the fragrance he's wearing. But I don't. I won't. He's conceited enough. And I'm definitely not about to let this boy think I'm checking for him. "Yo stop frontin' like you ain't checkin' me on the low. I see you lookin' at me outta the corner of ya eye."

Busted!

But before I can open my mouth to deny, to tell him some kinda fabulous lie, I spot Trouble storming across the parking lot. He spots her, too.

"Mmph," I grunt, raising my eyebrows. She's walking mad hard and has her face all frozen up into an ugly scowl, like she's ready to bring it. I already know if she comes at me swinging that I'ma have to put the drop on her. But I'm really not tryna fight this chick. I don't like the ho, true. But that's doesn't mean I wanna fight 'er either. I just want the trick to stay outta my face. Wishful thinking...

"Trick, I thought I told you to stay away from *my* man."

"Yo, Quanda, go 'head wit' that dumb shit, yo. I ain't ya man. So don't—"

I add, "You storming up over here like you tryna get it crackin'. I don't want *your* so-called man, boo-boo.... Now smack that, trick."

"I ain't her man," he snaps. "Yo, Quanda, bounce. For real yo. 'Fore I snap on ya dumb-azz."

"I'm not bouncing nowhere, boy! I told you what I'ma do every time I see you all up in some ho's face, so get used to it. Stay outta these"—she shoots a look over at me—"tricks' faces and you won't have to—"

"Listen, girlie. I don't know what kinda beef you *think* you got with me, but I'm *not* it. Now run along before you get ya feelings hurt. I don't want this boy, so have at 'im. But don't drag me into whatever problems y'all got going on."

"Ho, I'll drag you into whatever I want...." I take a deep breath. In five, four, three, two, one...this ghetto-bird is about to catch it Brooklyn-style real fast. "You better go bobble some other chick's man."

"Yo, Quanda, word up. You need to get the eff up outta here wit' that rah-rah; for real, yo," Antonio says.

I stop in my tracks. "Trick," I snap, dropping my book bag and purse down to the ground. "If you wanna fight, then let's bang it out and be done with it. But know this, I'm not gonna fight you over some boy that I *don't* even know or want. I already told you, you can have him." This crazy chick tries to lunge at me, but Tone steps in front of her and grabs her by the arm. She pushes him off of her, yelling and cursing. And of course there's an audience in the parking lot now.

I am straight disgusted with this whole scene. I feel like punching a hole in her forehead for being so dang stupid, but I'm determined not to hook off on her first.

As three dudes pull her away, I laugh, waving at her. "Bye, bye, sweetie. That's right, y'all, drag her ugly, clown azz on with her raggedy, nappy-azz weave."

"Don't let me catch you in the halls. I'ma beat your face in when I do," she hollers back.

"Catch me, boo." I walk off toward my car, deciding that Monday I'm coming to school rocking jeans and sneakers and wearing my hair in a tight ponytail pinned up and tucked under a hat 'cause the minute I see her coming in my direction, I'ma lay her out. Screw waiting for her to hook off first. That ghetto-trash trick gotta get stomped down real good—quick, fast, and in a hurry! I'm sick of her!

19

Antonio

The school is buzzin' 'bout what popped off in the parkin' lot Friday. And e'eryone's on alert 'pectin' somethin' to pop off between Miesha 'n' Quanda. I had'a try'n go into damage control mode 'n' try to get this chick to chill. And you wanna know what this broad effen said, yo? She hit me wit', "Come over and do it to me and I might let that ho live." I've had a buncha Facebook alerts from heads who are friends wit' Quanda 'n' me on the Book. Supposedly she was poppin' mad ish all last night 'bout how she's gonna take it to Miesha's face in school. How I ain't wanna hit it 'cause I'm switchin' teams. E'ery-time someone hit me up wit' the dumbness I told 'em I ain't wanna hear it. But, real rap. I don't care what kinda ish she pops about me 'cause it ain't true. But I wanted to get at Miesha to let 'er know to watch her back. A'ight, a'ight...I also wanted to holla at 'er so I could see what's really good wit' 'er. But since she's not cool wit' any heads from school, and I don't even know where she rests at, I

didn't know how to get at 'er. So I'ma slide past her locker
on my way to homeroom 'n' hopefully I can catch 'er before Quanda cranks it up. So far, I haven't seen or heard
Quanda's loud mouth. And I didn't peep her whip in the
lot when I came in so I'm hopin' she isn't in school today.

I pull out my cellie and start scrollin' through my news-
feed. I have a message in my inbox from this chick Allison
I used to rock wit' who goes to Lincoln High School wit'
Tiffany. She says Tiffany's poppin' her gums 'round the
school that she's carryin' my seed. *Like I really need this
BS, too*! I shake my head, glad I got her off of my Facebook
page when I did. And even more relieved her triflin' butt
doesn't go to school here. Otherwise her lies would be
spreadin' like a wildfire for real for real. I hit Allison back
real quick 'n' tell her that that broad's lyin'. That she's on
some real grimy type ish. I tell her what she told me she
did. She hits me back wit': GTFOH! That tramps mad nasty!
you want me to beat her up for you?

I respond back, telling her nah. But that don't mean
I'm not feelin' the idea of Allison rockin' her sockets for
tryna do me dirty. That broad ain't carryin' my baby, period, point blank. And I ain't gonna entertain any of her
lies or dumbness. I go back to scrollin' through the news-
feed, comment on a few posts, then post up on my wall.

YO, WATS GOODY MY NIGS. 'BOUT TO GET THIS EDUMACATION
REAL QUICK. HOLLA!

As I'm walkin' to my locker, I'm so caught up in my
thoughts and what's poppin' on Facebook that I'm not
payin' attention to where I'm goin' 'til I practically bump
smack-dead into my future wifey.

"'Sup?" I say as she glides her fine self right by me. She doesn't speak. This stuck-up broad doesn't open her mouth, or even look my way. Just sucks her teeth and frowns at me. She straight-up tries to play me like I'm some crab-type dude. And real ish, I'm not feelin' that. *Man, stop trippin'. She prolly didn't even hear you. Yeah, that had to be it. Nah, yo... she looked right at me and rolled her eyes!*

She fumbles wit' the lock, then swings her locker door open, almost hittin' me wit' it. I lean up against the lockers and fold my arms, starin' at this cutie as she snatches books outta her locker and stuffs them into her bag. She sighs. "What, so you just gonna stand there staring at me like some psycho?"

I grin. "If that's what it takes."

She slams her locker shut. "I'm not interested."

"Well, I am," I tell 'er. "So keep it gee, ma. You stay checkin' me on the low, don't you?"

She stops in her tracks. Frowns. "Checkin' you? Boy, please. You're delusional. You could never get this, hun. But what you better do is *check* ya girl..."

"She's not my girl, yo."

"Well, I don't care who or *what* she is. But you had better put a muzzle on her, before I yank her leash for you. And trust, it ain't gonna be cute. I don't know how these Jersey hoes do it, but I'm not with all the ying-yang. That chick's been tryna bring it to me from the gate, and I'm done. Today, I'm takin' it to her skull. And if her corny-azz groupies want it, they can get it, too."

I blink. Blink again. *Damn, I knew somethin' looked different wit' her.* She's not rockin' heels or some lil slinky jump-off. There are no big-hooped earrings hangin' from her ears. Her hair's pulled back. And she's laced up in a pair of white Nikes 'n' wearin' a pink Baby Phat sweat suit that hugs her hips real right. She looks like a straight-up 'round-the-way chick who came to put in some serious fist work. A part of me hopes Quanda isn't here today 'cause the way this cutie's goin' in, I can already tell she plans on rockin' Quanda's snotbox. No matter how much Quanda runs her mouth—and deserves a smackdown—I don't really wanna see this hottie snap her trap.

"Yo, dig…don't pay that broad no mind. She's just talkin', yo."

"Well, she's been talking to the wrong one because I'm not having it. So you can stand here and take up for her if you want. Stand by your girl, boo-boo. But don't beat me in the head about it."

"Yo, I ain't standin'…" My voice drifts off as Justin walks up on us. He's ice-grillin' me. "Yo, what's good?" I say, steppin' toward him to give him dap.

He steps back. Eyes me up 'n' down, then frowns like I'm a piece of gum stuck to the bottom of his crispy kicks. "Yo, you tell me, fam. What's good?" He looks over at Miesha. "Wassup, ma? You a'ight?"

She shifts her book bag from one shoulder to the other. "Yeah, I'm good. I'm tryna get to homeroom, though."

"I'll walk you," he says, bumpin' into me as he brushes by. He grabs her book bag, then shoots me a look over his shoulder.

I blink.

WTF?

This mofo's really gonna let a chick come between us.

"Oh, it's like that, yo?" I say, spreadin' my arms open.

"That's how you doin' it, fam?" He keeps walkin', leavin' me standin' in the middle of the hallway, feelin' some type'a way.

"Okay, class," Mrs. Sheldon says, turnin' from the chalkboard, "let's . . . Uh, Miss Wilson. You're *late*, again."

"And I have a note, *again*," she snaps back as she walks up toward the front of the class. It's mad obvious that they ain't feelin' each other. Mrs. Sheldon been hatin' on her from the rip. And that ish is crazy. I grin as she hands Mrs. Sheldon a note. Mrs. Sheldon glances at the slip of paper, then eyes her. Tells her to take a seat. I watch as Miesha drops her bag onto the floor, then slides onto the seat two rows to the left of me, six chairs up. Now I wish I was sittin' up in the front, right next to 'er. Nah, sittin' in back of 'er, I get a better view of that booty 'n' them hips.

Mrs. Sheldon shuffles through a stack of papers. "Okay, where was I before I was sidetracked? Yes. I was getting ready to pass out last week's essay. Then discuss your next reading assignment." She walks around the class, handin' out e'eryone's papers. We had to write an essay summary on *Go Tell It on the Mountain.* "Your next reading assignment will be a novel by Ishmael Beah titled *A Long Way Gone.* Everyone . . . Mr. Lopez," she says as she slides me my essay, "is expected to read it." I glance at my grade. C+. "It is a true story of Mr. Beah's life as a boy soldier in a civil war in Sierra Leone. Why are we reading it? Because it is a riveting and extremely compelling story worthy of discussion."

When she finishes handin' everyone's papers, she returns to the front of the class. "Mr. Lopez, please tell the class the name of the storefront church the Grimes family attended in *Go Tell It on the Mountain*."

I shift in my seat. "Uhh, umm"—I hit the center of my forehead with the palm of my hand—"it's on the tip of my tongue." I snap my fingers. "The Temple of Fire and Brimstone."

She folds her arms. "That is incorrect. Anyone else? How about you, *Miss* Wilson?" I shake my head, wonderin' what shorty did to Mrs. Sheldon other than come to her class late.

Shorty sucks her teeth. "Call on someone else."

"I called on *you*."

She huffs. "The Temple of the Fire Baptized."

"Correct. Now had Mr. Lopez and a few others read their books, all of you would have known that, wouldn't you? Then perhaps there would have been more A's instead of a room full of C's and D's. This is an advanced English class, people. You should not have to be reminded of that. *If* you are not going to take this class or your reading assignments seriously, then either withdraw or be prepared to fail. And we know some of you cannot afford not to graduate on time, or to have your GPAs drop. Isn't that right, Mr. Lopez?"

I shift in my seat. "I got you, Mrs. Sheldon." She starts to respond just as the bell rings. All I hear is her sayin' somethin' 'bout discussin' the rest of James Baldwin tomorrow. No one is tryna hear her, though. I eye Miesha as she walks by.

"Yo, what's good?"

The stuck-up broad keeps on walkin'. I follow out the door behind her.

"Oh a'ight. That's how you doin' it?"

"Is that how I'm doing *what?*" she asks, frownin' at me like I'ma piece of doo-doo she had'a step over.

"Frontin' like we ain't just kick it out in the parkin' lot yesterday. Now all of sudden you not beat to even speak. What's up wit' that, yo?"

She smirks. "First of all, we wasn't kickin' it. You talked. I half-listened. Second, I'm not interested. What part of that do you not get?"

"Yo, I ain't tryna hear all that. I tol' you, if I gotta wait for you after e'ery class, then that's what I'ma do 'til you stop frontin' on me."

She shakes her head. "That's on you, boo-boo. I'm still...not. Interested."

I'm walkin' alongside of her, eyein' her on the sly 'n' tryna slow down so she can walk ahead of me just enough for me to watch her booty shake 'n' bounce as she walks.

But she ain't havin' it. "And *stop* tryna look at my butt, boy."

I laugh. "Whatever, yo. I'ma man. That's what men do. We butt watch. And you gotta..." She straight-up dips on me into the girls' bathroom.

"So what's good, yo? We beefin' now?"

I eye Justin from 'cross the lunch table. He's been shootin' me bricks e'er since I walked up over here 'n' took a seat. And I ain't feelin' it. Real rap, he's my dawg. But I'll chip 'im up if he tries to come at me. There's mad chicks out here so there ain't no need for us to be beefin' over no broad, especially one he ain't even get it in wit'.

He frowns, slowly shakin' his head. "Nah, we ain't beefin'."

"Oh, word? Then what was that bull you pulled in the hallway, yo'? You brushed up on me like we had'a situation brewin'. If that's what it is, let me know, dawg."

"Yo, what kinda beef y'all talkin' 'bout?" Cease asks, lookin' from Justin to me.

I nod my head in Justin's direction. "Ask ya boy over there."

"Yo, whatever, man. You just need to fall back. Stay up outta shorty's face, yo. And we good."

I laugh. "Bruh, are *you* serious, yo? Really?"

"You know I'm tryna holla at shorty...."

"And so is *e'erybody* else at the school, bruh. So 'til someone snatches her up, it's open season; feel me? You should already know this."

"And *you* should know to fall back if you know one'a ya boys is tryna holla at someone. Why you always gotta try'n get at e'ery chick that comes through?"

"Yo, fam, y'all need'a chill," Cease says, "for real for real. Bros before hoes, you already know how we get down, yo."

"Yeah, tell that to this, mofo," I say, flickin' my thumb over at Justin, gettin' up from the table. "I'm out. This mofo think he can get wit' shorty, then have at it."

He smirks. "*Think?* Nah, dawg, I *know*. Get it right."

By the end of the day, I ain't beat for any extras. I head straight to my locker to grab my things so I can dip, but remember I have basketball practice today. A few chicks holla, and I give 'im head nods, or a quick hug. I peep Quanda comin' at me 'n' I straight spazz on 'er the minute she starts in wit' her BS.

"*Bit...*" I catch myself from callin' her the B-word. "Look, just stay away from me, yo. All you are is a buncha

trouble, yo. E'erything 'bout you makes me sick!" I slam
my locker shut, then walk off.

I make my way down to the boys' locker room, change
into my gym clothes, and hit the hoops. I get out on the
court before e'eryone else. Shootin' the ball helps me clear
my head. I stand on the free throw line, focused on nothin' but the rim. Playin' pro ball is all I think 'bout. I just
wanna get my diploma 'n' get away from all these crazy
girls. I take a deep breath, aimin' at the rim. I take another
deep breath. Release the ball...*swoosh!* I run after it, then
dribble it through my legs. I shoot it, again...*swoosh!* I
fake a few moves, do a few layups, then knock down a
hunnid free throws, sinkin' e'ery last one in wit' out a
miss. I keep goin' at it 'til the squad comes out on the
floor.

I peep Justin comin' outta the locker room, followed by
Cease 'n' Luke. Justin shoots a look at me. I can tell he's
still stuck in his feelin's. I ain't gonna press up on that
broad, so he needs to relax. A few secs later, the coach
comes out, blowin' his whistle.

"Lopez...Davis...partner up."

I frown. As captain of the team, I usually partner the
players up. But, whatever. I know not to come at Coach's
neck if I don't want the whole team to suffer for it.

Justin ain't too happy 'bout it 'n' neither am I. But it is
what it is. I glance over at Cease. The mofo gotta smirk on
his face so I already know what it is. I shoot him the finger,
then toss Justin a chest pass. It's time to make it pop. *D-
up, mofo! It's game time...*

20

Miesha

"Ummm, hey, girl," the Fiona chick says, walking up to me at my locker, "you think I can bum a ride home with you today...?" *Is this chick effen serious?* "My brother usually picks me up but can't today. And none of my friends' parents allow them to have passengers in their cars. I can give you gas money, if you want."

I look her up and down. She's all flossy-glossy in a fly sky-blue denim jumper. She has her boobs pumped up lovely, all perky and happy. The legs of her pants are tucked down into a bangin' pair of six-inch, wine-colored boots. Her Dooney & Bourke hangs in the crook of her arm. Yeah, I said this ho was messy. And I still believe it. But she stays runway ready. I immediately start taking her measurements in my head and thinking up designs for her. I do that sometimes. Imagine chicks wearing my collection.

"Yo, what's good, Fiona?" this medium-build, brown-skinned guy says to her. I've seen him in the halls, but he's one of the few who hasn't said anything extra to me. He just stares.

"Oh, hey, Benji. You know my girl Miesha, right?"

Your girl? Boo-boo, since when?

"Nah," he says, eyeing me, "I've seen her around though." He nods at me. "What's up?"

"Nothing much. Chillin'," I say, gathering my things from outta my locker, then shutting the door.

"I feel you." He looks over at Fiona. "You comin' through later?"

"I don't know. I might. It all depends on what my girl here wants to get into."

Oh, wait a minute! *My girl? Again? Really?* This broad is really reaching now.

He looks me over. "Yo, bring her, too. We can all get *into* somethin' together."

I frown.

She waves him on. "She ain't ready for that, boo. I'll text you later."

I ain't ready for what?

"Oh, a'ight. Bet." He pulls Fiona into him, then whispers something into her ear. She giggles. He steps back, looking over at me. "I'll see you around, ma. Nice meetin' you."

"Yeah, you too." I wait until he walks off and is almost down the hall before I turn to her and ask, "What was that all about?"

She waves me on. "Oh, that. Psst. Girl, it's nothing. Benji stays tryna hump, girl."

And I bet you stay letting him.

"He's another one of those boys you gotta be on watch for." Why I even bother asking her if she messes with

him—when I know she probably does or has—is beyond
me, but I do, anyway. "Well, I'm not one to gossip, girl,
'cause I can't stand hoes who kiss and tell, but yeah...he's
my BWB."

"Your what?"

"My boo with benefits, girl."

"Oh." She tells me they have a special understanding.
That they can chill with other people if they want as long
as the other is cool with it. "Wow, so y'all don't mind sharing, huh?"

"Not at all, girl." She runs her hand through her thick,
luscious hair, walking alongside me down the hall toward
the stairs. "It cuts down on all the drama. There's no
cheating. No lying. I'm not jealous. He's not jealous. And
we both stay very happy. Everything's right out in the
open."

She waits until we hit the bottom flight of stairs to hit
me with. "Benji thinks you're hot. And so do I, girl...."

I blink. *Uh, ohhhhkay...And?*

"We wanna have a threesome with you."

I stop in my tracks. "I don't know what kinda kinky
freak games y'all got going on up at this school, but I'm
not playing 'em. So you had better hop along and go find
yourself another participant."

She giggles, flipping her hair. "Oh, relax, boo. I know
you're not. *Didn't* you hear me tell him that you're *not*
ready for that? That's what I was talking about."

"Well, you got that right! I'm *not* ready. Nor will I ever
be." I shoulder my book bag and head toward the doors
that lead out into the parking lot. She's right behind me.

"Well, can I still get a ride...?"

"Yo, Miesha," I hear in back of me. I crane my neck to

see who's calling me. It's Brent. He's in his lacrosse practice uniform. The season doesn't start until the spring, but
he's in some kinda fall league. I stop and wait for him to
catch up. I take in his swag. The way his uniform shirt
hugs his arms and his chest and flat stomach. Whew, he
has a nice, toned body. It's hard not to keep staring.

"Hey," I say, shifting my eyes.

"Yo, wassup, Fiona?" he says, giving her a nod. She says
hi to him, then tells me she'll wait for me. Brent waits for
her to walk off. "Hey what are you doing later? You wanna
go grab something to eat?"

I tell him I'ma need a rain check. That I have a buncha
homework to do and a test to study for. I glance down at
his legs, again. Oooh, I just wanna run my hands all up
and down them. He has nice, brown, muscular legs. And
they're kinda hairy. Hairy legs on a guy is sexy to me. It's
soooo manly to me.

"Oh, a'ight. Then maybe this weekend we can do something."

"Yeah, maybe," I say. He asks if he can get my number.
"I guess." I reach into my bag and pull out a pen. I fish out
a scrap of paper, and write my number down for him.

"Okay, cool. I'll hit you up later." He walks off. I stare at
his heart-shaped calves for a hot sec, then quickly glance
around the parking lot, hoping that that Fiona chick is
ghost. When I don't see her anywhere in sight, I make a
sudden beeline to my car. But there she is, standing by my
car, waiting with a smile on her face.

"Girrrrl, I see you met Brent," Fiona says, looking over
at me. "Mmmph. Girrrrl, between me and you, he's the
only one who can *get* it unwrapped. All day, okay? Ooh, I

know he'll make some pretty babies with all that wavy hair and nice skin. That boy's too dang cute. And he's nice, too." She's so busy running her trap that I don't think she even realizes that I haven't said a word since we left the parking lot.

I take my eyes off the road real quick to look over at her. "Well, it does sound like you like to have sex, a lot of it."

She waves me on. "Girl, sex is good for the soul. And I only have sex with boys I really like. Or if I'm extra bored and don't have anything else better to do. I just like to have fun."

"Well, there are other ways to have fun. You do know that, right?"

She shrugs. "I guess."

"Ummm, how about taking up a hobby? Oh, wait. Sex *is* your hobby."

Now she shoots me a look.

"Well, from what it sounds like," I say, tryna clean it up. "I mean, look. I don't know you. But all you've talked about, since you introduced yourself, is boys or about something relating to sex. Isn't there anything *else* you like to talk about other than boys and sex?"

She frowns. "Well, no. I mean, yeah."

"Okay, good. Like what?" I ask, not that I'm really pressed to know. But since she's all up in my space, I'm tryna get inside this chick's head to see if she's more than just a walking sex ad. Anyway, Miss Messy Hot Box tells me she loves shopping and going into the city. Okay, so we have two things in common. "Where do you get all of your pocketbooks and belts and stuff? And I know it's all real 'cause I can tell."

She waves me on. "All of my stuff is from my older sisters. They have good jobs and can afford all this high-priced stuff, so I get all of their designer hand-me-downs."

I make a right onto Martin Luther King Boulevard, then stop at another light. She tells me to make a left onto Bergen, then go down and make a right onto Wilkerson. I can't wait to get this broad outta my car. She's givin' me a pounding headache. She tells me her house is the brown and beige one on the left. I stop in the middle of the street. I don't even give her a chance to shut the door good before I am pulling off. *My gawd, that ho's all over the place!*

By the time I shut off the engine and remove my key from the ignition, it's almost four o'clock. And school let out at 2:37 PM. I sigh, opening the car door. I swear I don't wanna be here by myself. My mom won't be home until after seven, maybe eight, depending on what PATH train she catches. And my aunt Linda probably won't get home until about six. So I'll have the whole place to myself. Alone. I take a deep breath, letting myself into the house. I head straight for the kitchen and grab a bottle of water from the fridge, then go upstairs to my room as my cell rings. I fish it outta my bag, walking and shutting the door behind me.

"Hello?"

"Hey, wassup? It's Brent."

"Oh, hey," I say, dropping my book bag and purse onto my bed, then kicking off my shoes. I look around my room. The one my aunt Linda has soooo graciously given me. I know I should be thankful. And I am. But I still don't have to be happy about it. We weren't homeless. No. My mom chose to move. She chose this. And it really pisses me off. So what if I have a nice full-size bed, and my own closet, and a flat-screen TV. I had those things in Brooklyn.

"Yo, you a'ight?' he asks, sounding concerned. "You sound kinda down."

"Yeah, I'm good," I lie, gazing down at my water, twisting the cap back and forth, forth and back. "Just getting home, that's all."

"Oh, a'ight. Do you want me to hit you later?"

"No, it's cool. We can talk now." I finally unscrew the cap and put the bottle to my lips, taking a long gulp of water. It goes down cold and refreshing, quenching my thirst. But it does nothing for my screwed-up mood. I need to get outta here.

"Listen, Miesha. I, uh, dig you. I know you prolly got a lotta guys at the school checkin' for you. And you prolly already messin' wit' someone, but if you not, then I wanna spend time with you."

I sigh. "Look, Brent. You seem like you might be a nice guy. But I'm not really interested in getting serious with anybody. I'm going back to Brooklyn the first chance I get so we should just keep things how they are."

"Oh, a'ight. When are you goin' back?"

I close my eyes. "Soon, I hope."

"Okay. Then for now, how about we chill? Let me get to know you. And you me."

"It sounds good, really. But I'm not beat for any boy drama or silly games 'cause you know how you boys can be."

He chuckles. "Correction. How *some* of us can be. I'm not any of them. All guys aren't about drama or playing games so you shouldn't categorize us all in one box."

"Well, all the ones I know are."

"Then maybe you should try spendin' some time with some of the good guys."

I get up from my bed and walk over to my mirror. I stare at myself. *Girl, you too dang fly to be lookin' all pitiful. Snap outta this funk and get yo' life, boo!*

"Umm, hmmm...maybe you're right. Maybe I *do* need to do just that. Chill with the good ones. You know any you can introduce me to?"

He laughs. "No doubt. You're talkin' to one, me."

"Oh, is that so? That's what ya mouth says."

He keeps laughing. "Oh, that's what it is, ma. I'm all that. Let me show you."

Oh, I know exactly what'll snap me outta this funky mood. I know I can't drive my car into New York. And no matter how much slickness I pop to my mom, or how much she pisses me off, I don't really ever break her or my dad's rules, especially when it comes to my car. But that doesn't mean I won't break a rule or two to get to Brooklyn to see my girls. I grin. "Hey, you still wanna hang out tonight?"

"No doubt," he says, try'n not to sound all hyped.

"Cool. And I know just the place we can go. But I gotta be home by eleven."

"A'ight, bet. I'll have you back way before then." He tells me he'll scoop me up at six. I give him the address, then end the call. *Oooh, I'm feeling better already!*

21

Antonio

Real rap, basketball is my first love. Heck, my *only* love. And I know I should be focused on perfectin' my dunks, 'n' layups, 'n' crossovers so I can get up in the NBA. And on some real ish, there really should be no time for chicks. But there always is. Even when I don't want there to be, they're in my face heavy on the regular, checkin' for a dude like me. And, yeah, some'a them broads don't even deserve to have me in their beds. I know it the minute they drop their clothes, that I ain't got no business givin' them a taste of this Lopez lovin'. But I do, anyway. And sometimes I end up kickin' myself, like I've been doin' wit' Quanda over the last few weeks. And now this...

"So, you wanna explain ya'self?" Pops says, eyein' me mad hard. The minute I step through the door. There's smoke comin' outta his ears, that's how heated he is right now. My stomach drops to my feet, along wit' the spinnin' ball I have up on one finger. This ain't what I expected to see—Tiffany 'n' her parents sittin' on the sofa. But here they are! And *this* is how my day ends. The minute I see their faces, I feel sick. They're starin' me down. Well, not Tiffany. She's lookin' down at her hands in her lap.

"I'm waitin'," Pops snaps. "Don't have me ask you again, boy."

"I-I...uh," I stutter, lookin' from him to trick-azz Tiffany to her suited-up pops to her Mary Kay-caked-faced moms.

"Don't stand there stutterin', boy. This girl's parents tell me you done got their daughter pregnant. Is it true?"

"No, it ain't true. Pops, you know me, dawg. I ain't go in raw, yo."

"You a lie!" Tiffany snaps, coverin' her face in her hands. "You told me you was gonna get me pregnant. You told me you wanted me to have your baby."

"You a damn lie," I snap back. "I ain't never wanna have no seed wit' you, yo. Yo, Pops, this skank broad's lyin'!"

"Now hold on a minute, son," her pops says, loosenin' the knot in his blue, pinstriped tie. He's already outta his suit jacket. His starched white shirt is buttoned up to his thick neck. "I'm not gonna let you stand there and talk disrespectful about my daughter. Now, did you and my daughter have sex?"

I nod. "Yessir. But we always used condoms."

"That's not what I asked you, son. I asked if the two of you were having sex. Now, I want to know where the two of you were *having* it."

"Daddy, I—"

"Not a word," he warns Tiffany, shootin' her a dirty look. "You're in enough trouble as it is, young lady, bringing shame to our name. I'm a deacon in a church for God's sake. This is not how your mother and I raised you."

He turns his attention back to me. And Pops is shootin' me mad rocks. I can tell he's ready to bring it to my head. I ain't seen him this heated at me in a minute. The last time musta been like six years ago, when I was eleven and I took his car keys, got behind the wheel of his whip, and took it for a spin, knockin' over mailboxes and sideswipin' other whips before hoppin' a curb 'n' runnin' into someone's fence. He tried to whoop the skin off 'a me, after he made sure I was a'ight. But the look in his eyes that day had me shook, like right now. "Where were you and my daughter having *sex*?"

"Mostly at your crib, sir. In her room. Down in your basement. Out in the garage. Or sometimes, she'd sneak outta Bible study on Wednesday nights 'n' we'd do it outside in my whip. But that was only twice we did that."

Her moms gasps, clutchin' her chest. Her pops's eyes almost pop outta his head from hearin' this. That his lil church girl is a freak. "On the church grounds?"

I nod.

"Daddy, that's not true! He's lying!"

"Girl, shut your mouth!" her pops snaps.

"Sir, I don't gotta lie. I admit I was smashin'—uh, havin' sex wit' Tiffany. But I ain't the only one. Tiffany's been mad loose for a minute."

"Oh my god!" she shouts. "I don't believe this. Don't even try'n play me like that, boy! You was the first boy I been with."

"Yeah, whatever, yo. I mighta been the first *that* night, but I def wasn't ya first, yo. You know it and I know it, yo. So save that BS for the next mofo."

"You're such a dog! I *was* a virgin!"

"Yeah, in ya dreams."

She starts cryin'. "Daddy, Mommy…you gotta believe me. He's lying on me!"

"I'm keepin' it a hunnid, yo. And you know it. But you sittin' here lyin' on me, like that's cool. That's some real savage ish, Tiff. You know that's not my seed, yo. But tell ya parents what you told me. How you was goin' into the bathroom pullin' the used condoms outta the trash."

"She did what?!" her moms snaps, her face all twisted up in disgust. "Oh, no. I know my child didn't do no nastiness like that. Girl, tell me this boy is making this mess up." Tiffany's skank-butt keeps up wit' the lies. Tells them I would put the condom on, then when she wasn't payin' attention, I'd take it off. And it just pisses me off more.

"Oh, word, Tiff? That's how you doin' it, yo? I ask, reachin' in my bag 'n' pullin' out my phone. I search through my files, then play the one I'm lookin' for. "Tell me if I'm lyin' now, yo."

Her face cracks the minute she hears her voice. *"Yeah, and I know you was dumb enough to let me take the condoms off of you, too. And why you think I'd go straight into the bathroom? So I could handle my business. All it takes is a turkey baster, and a few drops in the right spot…and bam!"*

Her moms gasps, again.

"Say what, yo? Tell me you didn't do no snake-azz shit like that, yo."

"Oh, believe it, baby daddy. Every condom you used, I used too. And, yeah, it took six tries to get it right. But it worked. I'm carrying your baby, Antonio Lopez. And I'm keeping it. So you might as well kiss your little basketball scholarship good-bye 'cause we're having a baby."

I stop it.

My pops is shakin' his head. He glares at me. I shift my eyes.

"Now," I say, frownin'. "I don't gotta lie 'bout jack. And, sir, no disrespect to you or ya wife, but your daughter's a ho."

"Now, you wait a minute, young man," he says, standin' up. "You're way out of line."

"No, Mr....uh—" Pops snaps his finger. "Wait, what did you say you last name was again?"

"Fitzgerald."

"Yeah, Mr. Fitzgerald. Sounds like your daughter is the one outta line here. Now, I'ma deal wit' Antonio. Best believe. But I suggest you and ya wife go on home and deal wit' your daughter. If my son says that baby ain't his, then it ain't his. But we gonna wait 'n' see for sure. If them test results come back that it's his, then he's gonna handle his responsibilities as a man." He shoots me a look. "Isn't that right, boy?" I peep the veins in his neck thumpin'. And that only means one thing.

I'm dead, yo!

I shift from one foot to another. My palms are sweaty. I nod, hangin' my head. "Yes, sir."

"Daddy, it is—"

He yanks her up by the arm. "I told you to shut your mouth. Now take your fresh tail on outside with your mother before I forget my religion up in here. Olivia, get this girl out of my sight before I do or say something I can't take back." Mrs. Fitzgerald snatches Tiffany by the arm 'n' drags her outta the crib, spewin' a buncha curse words at 'er. Tiffany's pops waits for them to walk out, and shut the door behind them.

"How old are you, son?" I tell him seventeen. He asks

when I'll be eighteen. I tell him in November. "Listen, son. I was your age once. And I know all about peer pressure. And I know all about raging hormones and having sex way before you're really ready, even when you think you are. I know you young kids all want to have sex and grow up fast, but all you're doing is messing your lives up. Now look." He pauses, shakin' his head. "The damage is already done. There's nothing we can do to undo what's already done. All I'm asking is that—*if* this baby is yours—you do *right* by my daughter."

I frown.

Pops frowns. "Now, Mr. Fitzgerald I done already told you if that baby your daughter's carryin' is his, Antonio's gonna take care of it. He's gonna be in that child's life, period."

"I trust you'll make sure he'll do right by his baby. But, he *needs* to do right by *my* daughter."

"Right by *your* daughter?" Pops says, tiltin' his head. "What exactly you tryna say here? I know you not suggestin' what I think..." He eyes him. "Are you?"

"I most certainly am. When this young man turns eighteen, I expect him to man up and marry her."

My mouth drops open. "*Marry her?*" My knees buckle. I feel sick!

"Yes," he says. "It's the right thing to do. She'll be seventeen by the time she has this baby. And I will sign consent for the two of them to be married."

I can't believe this! I swallow. "Sir, no disrespect, but I'm not about to marry that girl. I don't even like her. I'm goin' away to college."

"*Not* if that's your baby, you won't be," he says, raisin' a brow. "You may not *like* her. But if she was good enough to have sex with, then she's good enough for you to marry."

"Mr. Fitzgerald," Pops says, stormin' over to the front door 'n' swingin' it open. "It's time for you to bounce. Like I said, my son *will* handle his financial responsibilities. But he ain't about to wife no young trick."

Mr. Fitzgerald grabs up his suit jacket. And heads toward the door. "I can't blame the boy for bein' who he is. I had hoped we could all be men about this. But I see the apple don't fall too far from the tree."

"Yeah," Pops snaps. "And it's fruit ya daughter kept tryna eat. Now get the hell outta my house."

"We'll be in touch," he says, brushin' past Pops, walkin' out. Pops slams the door behind him.

I don't get my mouth open good to say a word, to try'n cool things down, before Pops is on me, snatchin' me by the throat 'n' slammin' me up against the wall, hard. "What I tell you 'bout handlin' ya business, huh?"

I gasp. "Y-y-you s-s-said...don't...be...sloppy."

He slams me into the wall again. "Then what the hell you got this lil ho comin' up in here wit' her folks for talkin' 'bout you got her knocked up, huh?" He slaps me upside the head. "And why you didn't mention this shit to me?" His face is all up in mine. His hot breath 'n' spit hits my face. I ain't ever disrespect my pops, and I ain't 'bout to start now, even though I feel like he real outta pocket for yokin' me up like this. My blood is boilin', but I know enough to keep my hands at my sides, palms open, 'cause if I close 'em into a fist, it'll be curtains...lights out for me. "Answer me, boy!"

"I-I-I c-c-can't..." I try to talk but he's really chokin' me up. And now I'm mad spooked that he might really crush my windpipe. He must see it in my eyes. Fear. He lets me go.

"Go up to ya room," he says. "I'ma deal wit' you later." He ain't yellin'. But I wish he was 'cause now I don't know what he's gonna do next.

"But, Pops—"

"I *said*. Go. Up. To. Ya. Room. And I'm not gonna tell you again." He says this, lips tight. Jaws clenched. I do as I'm told, takin' the stairs two at a time. I ain't even gonna front. Pops got me shook.

"I'm disappointed in you, son," Pops says, leanin' up against the doorframe. He's up in my room, holdin' a half-full beer in his hand. I'm lyin' on my back, starin' at the ceilin', listenin' to music. I sit up, grabbin' the remote to my stereo. I lower the volume. His face isn't all twisted up, like earlier. And I'm relieved, for real for real. He puts the bottle to his lips, takes a sip, then drops his hand down to his side. "You know the rules. Don't be sloppy. And you know what I expect of you. No cuttin' school or classes, no C's or D's on ya report cards, no drinkin' 'n' drivin', no lock-ups, 'n' no damn babies; period."

I lower my head. "I know." I look over at him. "And I'm doin' all that, Pops. Word is bond. I ain't get that lyin' trick pregnant."

He takes a deep sigh, walkin' into my room. He takes a seat on my bed. I scoot over some. He looks at me. "I believe you. And I was dead-wrong for puttin' my hands on you like that. But how you think I felt when the doorbell rings and I open the door and this girl 'n' her folks are standin' in front of me, talkin' 'bout 'we need to talk 'cause your son got my daughter pregnant and now doesn't want anything to do with her'? Then I find out you knew about this. How you think that made me feel?"

"I know, Pops. And I shoulda tol' you. But I ain't really think it was a big deal. I mean, I knew she was lyin', man. I didn't mean to keep it from you."

"I know you didn't. But we're supposed to be able to talk about e'erything. We don't keep secrets from each other."

"I wasn't tryna keep..."

He puts his hand up, stoppin' me. "Let me finish. The last thing I wanna hear is 'bout you havin' some young thing knocked up out there. That's not what I wanna hear, you feel me?"

I nod. "I got you, Pops."

"Now you see what I been tellin' you all these years 'bout how grimy broads are, don't you? I tol' you they can't be trusted. Didn't I tell you that?" I nod. "See. That's why you gotta always be three steps ahead of 'em. I tol' you, play smart. Be smart. You don't ever let a broad catch you slippin'. They'll screw you over e'ery time."

"Yeah, tell me 'bout it."

"And let this be a lesson to you. You don't ever toss ya condoms in the trash when you done spankin' it up. And you don't ever trust some hungry lil ho to handle it for ya. Those are ya lil soldiers stuck down in that wrapper. You take off ya own condom, then get up 'n' handle ya own business. You drop it in the toilet, flush, 'n' stand there 'n' wait 'til you see it go down. And if the lil broad want another round, you strap up again 'n' handle ya business. You hear me?"

"Yeah, yeah," I say, noddin', takin' it all in. "I got you, Pops."

He sighs, then takes another sip of his beer before handin' it to me. I tell 'im I'm good. Any other time, I woulda taken it 'n' tossed it back wit' 'im. But, I don't know, right now, it don't feel right, drinkin' wit' my Pops. I don't know why, though. Real rap. I def could use a drink, for real for real. Seein' that grimy broad Tiffany posted up in here wit' her parents really got me on edge, yo. Then her pops talkin' 'bout some marriage if she is carryin' my seed. Eff outta here wit' that dumbness! He done banged his dome talkin' that ying-yang.

Pops apologizes again for flippin' on me. I tell him it's all good. "All I want is for you to graduate high school wit' out becomin' another statistic."

"I don't wanna be a statistic either, Pops. I'm not tryna get locked up, or be a teen dad."

"Good. All I want is the best for you, son; that's it. Understand?"

I nod. "I know, Pops. And I 'preciate e'erything you do."

He balls his fist, holds it out to me. "We cool?"

I nod, givin' him a pound. "No doubt."

He smiles at me, gettin' up from the bed. "That's what I wanna hear. Listen, son . . ." He pauses. Runs his hand over his face. "I don't tell you this much. But so far you've done me real proud. You gotta good head on ya shoulders. I don't wanna see you get all twisted up in the game. Play or get played. You know how we do."

Now it's my turn to smile. "I got you, Pops. Playa for life, man. You already know."

22

Miesha

"Unh-uh, Miss Honey-Boo," Mariah says, walking into my bedroom. I'm lying across my bed listening to Elle Varner's CD and reading over my notes for my English test. It's a sunny Saturday afternoon and I'm holed up here. Yippee. I couldn't go to Brooklyn this weekend 'cause my dad had to fly out to California to check on my granny. And my mom wouldn't let me stay at Tre's. She feels her mother lets her have too much freedom, and that there's not enough parental supervision going on. Oh, puhleeeze! She thinks I'ma get in a buncha trouble hanging out over there. Like, really? Whatever. Anyway, two days ago I spoke with my dad about living with him instead of here and he said he would talk to my mom about it. Well...surprise, surprise. I can't! She told him we're a package deal and if she's not going to live with him, neither am I. Are you serious? Who does that? When I heard she told him that mess I almost took it to her throat.

"And *why* would you tell him some dumb mess like that?!" I snapped, shooting her daggers. "I wanna go *home.*"

"*This* is your home. And this is where you're gonna stay. With me. So you might as well get over it now and get used to it."

"*No*, this is not my home. And this is *not* where I wanna be. And I will *never* get used to being here. If you wanna stay here, then stay. But let me go back to Brooklyn. Let me live with Daddy. *That's* where I wanna be."

She huffed. "Absolutely not! You're my child and—"

"I'm *his* too," I said, cutting her off. "And I'm old enough to decide where I wanna live and who I wanna live with. And if I have to start running away for you to get it, then I will."

"And where *exactly* do you think you're gonna run to, huh? Your father's? Your little girlfriends'? Please. You know all your father's going to do is send you right back here with me. And them little friends of yours' parents are not going to want any parts of harboring a minor, a runaway at that. So don't you dare try'n blackmail me with that mess, girl."

She was right. Daddy might let me stay for a few nights; then again...if it was a school night, he'd drive me right back. And Tre's mom...mmmph, she isn't really even beat to have Tre in the house, let alone letting me stay there for any extended period of time. And as far as Stacy and Jalanda, well...those are my girls and all, but staying with them is definitely outta the question. Stacy's mom is mad cool...when she's sober, that is. But once she gets liquored, all hell breaks loose and she turns into a drunken beast. And Jalanda's mom keeps a real nasty spot.

Dishes stay piled up in the sink, dirty clothes are all over the place, and they act like they allergic to taking the trash out. So, no thanks, boo-boo. Staying there is a definite no-no. I don't do filth.

"I'm not tryna blackmail you," I told her, tryna convince her to let me move back home with my dad. But she wasn't tryna cooperate. "It's my life! And I should be allowed to do what I want with it. What gives you the right to think you can control it, or me?"

"You listen here, little girl. I gave birth to you. And I am responsible for you. So until you turn eighteen, you will do as *I* say. And this is where you're going to stay, whether you like it or not—end of discussion!"

Whatever! I'll be eighteen in three months, then I'm outta here. And there's nothing she'll be able to do or say to stop me. I made sure I told her that, too.

"And if that's what you still want to do when that day comes, then I'll be glad to help you pack."

Soooooooo, needless to stay, I'm marking the days on the calendar while I do my bid here in Jersey. Stuck and disgusted!

"C'mon, hooker," Mariah says, snapping me outta my thoughts. She claps her hands. "Chop, chop! Let's get it crackin', boo."

I roll my eyes in up in my head, glancing up from my notebook. "Excuse you?"

"*Whoop-whoop!* Wrong answer," she says, strutting across the room wearing a sexy pair of ripped-up faded jeans cuffed with a matching jacket over a red cami and a pair of black pointy-toed ankle boots. "There's no excuse, hun. It's time we get out and breathe in some fresh air. It's nice out. And you need a man in ya life, boo. And today is the day to make it pop. I know just the place for you to bag one."

I laugh getting up. "Girl, you stooopid. Let me find something to wear, then hop in the shower."

She grunts. "And don't even think I forgot to ask how your lil date with that lil chocolate hunk on the lacrosse team went. I was waiting to see how long it would take before you told me. But as usual, you fail miserably. You stay withholding juicy details."

I wave her on, standing in front of my packed-tight closet overflowing with a buncha clothes—some still with tags on them, mad boxes of shoes, and handbags. "Puh-leeze. There's nothing to tell. And it wasn't a date. We went to Brooklyn for a while, then got something to eat in the city. Brent's a nice guy, but not my type. So that's about as juicy as it gets."

"Oh, well. So much for a love connection," she says.

"Exactly. Now where are we going? I need to know how to dress."

"Cute. That's all you need to know. Dress real cute."

I step outta my jeans. I scoop them up, and toss them into the hamper. Since it's still kinda warm out, I decide I'ma rock a faded, short jean skirt, a cute lil black stretch top with the words TEMPT ME scrawled across the front in red glitter.

Mariah screeches, causing me to look over at her. "What?"

"Oh my god! You are so wrong for"—she points at my pink granny panties—"havin' that big, bouncy booty of yours stuffed in them big, ole nasty drawers. Please tell me you do not wear them ugly things to school. It's no wonder you're man-less." I crack up laughing, giving her the middle finger and telling her to kiss my big, ole bouncy behind. She shakes her head at me. "Girl, if you wore some sexy drawers, you might have you a man kissing *it* for you."

She rummages through my underwear drawer, pulling out a red thong and matching bra, then tossing it over on the bed. "Wear this."

"Yes, mother," I say, sarcastically walking off to take my shower. Twenty minutes later, I step back into my room with a big, fluffy towel wrapped around me. Mariah has her butt perched up on top of my dresser, flipping through a Ni-Ni Simone book. She grunts and hisses every so often as she thumbs through it.

"What in the world? Why you making all those crazy-azz sounds?"

" 'Cause this chick is a trip. Oh my god, what the hell is an Uncle Shake?" She tosses the book over to the side. "I can't."

"Well, I like her books. They're entertaining and have some real-life lessons in them."

"Whatever." She huffs, glancing at the time. "Umm, will you hurry up, please? I wanna get to the courts before all the birds start flockin' in." I slip into my wears, then slide my feet into a sexy pair of red heels.

I twirl in front of my mirror. "*Boom*, boo, *boom!* Oooh, I'd be scared of all this fierceness if I wasn't me." I shake my hair out, run my hands through it, and let it hang off my shoulders, wild and carefree...like how I wanna be.

"You doin' it, boo," Mariah says, hopping off the dresser and snapping her fingers. "Now let's do this out the door. Please, and thank you!"

"Okay, okay. One sec," I say as I glide a coat of lip gloss

over my lips. I grab my purse, stuff my lip gloss, keys, cell, and ink pen inside, and slip my shades on. "Let's roll, boo." We head for the door. "Umm, you're driving."

"Of course I am." She disarms the alarm. "Now get in."

O-M-G! Lincoln Park is hot and poppin'! And I can feel myself getting caught up in its heat. There's mad heads out, flossing it up in their wears. And the cluckers are out in full force, shaking their tail feathers every which way, tryna snag the attention of a cutie or buffed boo. I can't even front. My cutie meter is on high. The energy and excitement is enough to get me outta my funk—for the moment, anyway. Me and Mariah strut through the crowd snapping mad necks. All kinda cuties keep tryna check for us.

"Yo, ma, what's goodie?"

"Damn, let me get them digits, yo..."

"Yo, Mariah, who's shorty you wit'? Let me holla at 'er..."

"Yo, let me bounce up on them cakes you shakin'..."

Mariah waves 'em on, though. "Girl, these fools extra thirsty out here. But they lucky I'm taken 'cause I'd be out here quenching their thirsts." A group of chicks grill us, rolling their eyes as we strut our sexiness. "Bonita, girl," Mariah says, stopping in front of one of the chicks. She's a cute brown-skinned girl with long, thick lashes. "I know you not even tryna serve up the stank 'cause you out here with your girls, ho. You know I will do you, girl."

"Oh my god, Mariaaaaaah?!" she yells, running up and giving her a hug. "Girl, I ain't seen you in like forever. Where you been, boo?"

"Off these streets, hun. You know how I do. Anyway, I peeped how you and ya girls were grillin' my cuz. Not cute, boo. Not cute at all. She's my baby cousin."

I eye the chick, then cut my eyes over at her crew. They're all cute chicks, but they still ain't bringing it like me. But whatever . . .

"Ooh, girl," she says, glancing over at me. "We ain't know. It's all love, though. You know how I do it, boo."

"Uh-huh. I sure do. And you make sure you and ya girls get a good look at"—she pulls me into her, draping her arm around me—"this pretty face. Anyone out here effs with her, they gonna catch it from me. And you *know* how I do. So, keep it cute, boo. And bring it to someone else." Mariah tilts her head. She straight punks this chick.

The chick chuckles. "Girl, you still crazy. I miss seein' you around the way, boo." She looks over at me again. Tells me her name is Adrina. Then introduces her crew. I give 'em all phony smiles and half-waves 'cause I already know what it is. These broads would try to bring it to me if they could. Hatin'-azz tricks. I kinda laugh to myself.

"We need to chill, girl. Smoke a blunt and get drunk like old times," Adrina says.

Mariah tells her she'll hit her up, then steps. We make our way through the crowd over to the bleachers, then take a seat three rows up.

"Girl, will you look at them hard-body boos," Mariah says, fanning herself. "Whew, lawd have mercy. I feel hot all over. I think I need a doctor. Makes no sense."

"What? A doctor? What's wrong with you?"

She rolls her eyes, pointing toward the court. "Girl, you sure know how to screw up a wet dream. I was talking about all of that fineness out there on the court."

I give her the finger. "Oh, hush. How I know that's what you meant?"

"Pay attention and follow the yellow brick road, boo. Now look on the court."

I laugh. "Whatever, tramp." I take in the two teams on the court. One team is rocking wife beaters. The other players are all bare-chested and sweaty. I blink. *Oh my god, they go to my school.* I peep Justin as he calls a time out. I gotta admit, he's a cutie-pie. I watch as the team swaggers over toward the sidelines, huddling up. Their shorts hang low, showing off their different color boxers. And, yes, oh yes...they are all looking finger-lickin' good! But of course the one who stands out the most is the one and only, drum roll puuuuhleeze...Antonio Lopez. Of course I keep my thoughts to myself. Not. A. Word!

Mariah leans into me, then whispers, "Soooo, has Tone tried to holla at you, yet?"

"Who?" I ask, feigning stupid.

She rolls her eyes. "Tone, girl."

I frown, leaning away from her. "*Ewwww...*no thank you! I mean, yeah, he's tried to speak, but nothing major. I pays him dust."

She twists her lips. "Uh-huh. You think he's cute, don't you?"

I shrug. But I don't stop looking at him. As Antonio dribbles the ball down the court, he takes it up in the air. *Swish!* The ball goes in, smooth. Just like him. Ugh! "He's okay. I guess."

She playfully pushes me. "Mmmhmm. Yeah, yeah, yeah. You *guess?* Ha! You stay stylin', boo. You know that ninja's more than just some *okay.* But whatever. Trust. If I wasn't in love and didn't believe in monogamy, Tone could get it. Mmmph. They all could."

I laugh. "That's 'cause you're a ho on the low."

She laughs with me. "You already know." She stops laughing. "Great," she hisses, elbowing me. "Here comes this dirty *beeeyotch!*"

Quanda! *Oh lawd! Why this ghetto trick gotta show up here?* I think, eyeing her as she shakes her hips all fast, hard and nasty over toward the bleachers. I narrow my eyes. Open and close my fists. And outta all the places to sit out here, this messy broad just has to squeeze her stank butt in a space next to these dudes two rows down. Dead-smack in front'a me. She glances over her shoulder, cutting her eye at me. The heifer just wants to make sure I see her. *Oh, I see you, boo; trust.*

"I can't stand that ratchet *beeeeoytch*..."

"Girl, ignore her dumb azz. We here to chill and have a good time. Unless her sister's out here with her, she doesn't want it. Trust. That ho's all talk. Is she still poppin' her gums at you in school?"

"Every chance she gets. But I keeps her on ghost. Make her invisible, all day."

"Good. But, I'm tellin' you. You might have to do her face the next time she comes at you. Tricks like her never learn unless you learn 'em real good."

I shake my head. "I already know. And trust. If she even looks at me wrong, I'ma snap her head back."

Both teams are going at it hard, but Antonio and his boys murder them. They shoot jump shots from every angle of the court, shutting the game *down!* Mad heads are going wild, popping mad junk. I'm not even gonna hate. I'm impressed with his skills.

Ghetto Tramp jumps up and yells through cupped hands. "Get it, Daddy! Do that shit, boo! Oooh, my baby knows he can play some ball. Y'all don't want it with him.

Whoop, there it is!" The chick really turns it up, knowing I'm sitting in back of her.

These dudes in back of me start goin' in on her. "Yo, Quanda, sit ya ugly, ho azz down, yo," one of them says this while the others start making clucking noises. His boys start laughing.

Middle finger up, she turns around and starts going off. When she finally shuts her trap and sits back down, somebody throws an empty soda can and it hits her in the back of the head. Of course, I laugh because it's mad funny to me. But that's all it takes to set it off.

"Trick-ho, I know you not sitting there laughing at me."

"Quanda, girl, boom," Mariah warns, eyeing her. "Take a seat, boo. You don't really want it. Not today. So fall back, sweetie. Before you get knocked back."

"Nah, don't tell her nothing. Let her bring it," I say, getting up from my seat. I place a hand up on my hip. "Yeah, I'm laughing. Hahahahaha! Now what you wanna do about it? Where's ya little fan club at now?"

"I don't need no fan club. Trust. I handles mine, solo. So it's whatever. Believe that." I hear a buncha oohs and aaaahs. Eyes are on us, like they watching a tennis match with all the back and forth going on between us. Finally I'm sick of it. I'm ready to go with the fists.

"You know what, ho. I'm done with all this talking." I excuse myself, squeezing through people as I step down from the bleachers. I wait until I hit the ground, then spread open my arms. "Let's do this. From day one you've been tryna bring it to me. So bring it, boo-boo!"

"Whoop her tail, Mi," Mariah says, hyping me up. "Stomp that ho for old and new. And nobody better even think about tryna jump in it."

I don't even wait for her to swing first. I just take it to her face the minute she comes at me. We go at it hard, too, swinging fists like we in the boxing ring. But my hands are quicker. My punches are harder. I have a buncha adrenaline pumping through my veins. I'm so amped up I might really break all of the teeth in her mouth. Blood gushes out. I'm stinging her face up.

She swings one good right hook that lands on the side of my head. But it's not enough to take me down. I got too much fight in me. She screams when I wrap my hands up in her weave, then swing her. It's quick. And it's hard when she hits the ground. I rep for Brooklyn. I rep for the chicks who stay mindin' their business. I give her a beatdown she won't ever forget. And if she does, she'll get another one to refresh her memory. I go hard, tryna snap her neck.

"I'ma kill you!" she yells, swinging wildly. But I'm not pressed or stressed about it 'cause I *know* I can fight. And I know without a doubt that this ghetto-trick can't beat me.

I punch her upside the head and all in her face. I take all of the bottled-up anger I have about moving to Jersey, about being at a school I hate, about my mom ruining my life, and all of Quanda's slick talking me from day one out on her face. Finally someone tries to break us up. But I hear someone else saying, "Nah, let them hoes fight. Somebody needs to beat Quanda down for once."

I hear loud voices yelling. And then I feel a set of big hands around my waist, yanking me up off 'a her. I kick, and thrash about tryna break free so I can finish punching that ho's lights out.

"This ain't over, *trick!* I promise you. You better watch ya back and ya front 'cause this ain't over!" she screams.

I laugh. "Whatever, ho. It was over the minute you hit the ground! And that boo you think you have? You know the man you keep claiming as yours? Well, guess what? He's gonna be mine now, trick! I'ma show you who the real chick in charge is!" All eyes are locked on me, but I don't care. I'm soo pumped right now, ready to fight whoever wants it. I hate when I get like this 'cause once I do, it's hard for me to reel it back in.

Three dudes drag her away, still yelling and screaming, threatening to have me bodied. But I'm not fazed. That ho got what she deserved. And I'm ready to give it to her again. I blink, looking around, wondering why all these dudes are gawking at me with they mouths all open. It's not until Mariah comes over to me that I realize why these fools are all on me. My shirt is torn open and my boobs are hanging out for all to see. I'm so worked up that I don't even try to cover them. They can look all they want.

Mariah pulls me to her, tryna cover me up. "Girl, let's get outta here. You whooped that trick down, boo. You did me proud. Now let her run home and tell her skank sister that. I'ma..."

I tune Mariah out. The only thing I'm thinking about is getting to school on Monday. To get to *him*, Antonio Lopez, right in front of *her*. Truth is, I don't even want that boy. So this isn't about him. Oh, no. This is about showing that ho what I'm capable of. She forced my hand.

Later on in the evening, I'm in my room, listening to music. My right hand is swollen so I have it wrapped in an ACE bandage with an ice pack up on it. Aunt Linda and my mom are out shopping or whatever it is they do on Saturdays together. I'm just glad neither of them were home when we walked back up in here. Hearing my mom's mouth is the last thing I'm in the mood for. I've texted, Skyped, and talked to my girls about what popped off since I got in. And now I'm up on Facebook.

I post: STOOPID CHICK AT MY SCHOOL TRIED TO CLOWN ME, AGAIN. AND I TOOK IT TO HER HEAD DOWN AT THE COURTS. SHE DON'T KNOW ABOUT ME. I COLD CRUSH HOES. I'M THE CHIN CHECKER. THE MAN SNATCHER. SHE WANTED IT, NOW SHE GOT IT. SHE COME AT ME AGAIN N I'MA ROCK HER JAW, AGAIN! THAT'S Y I'M TAKIN HER SO CALLED MAN! Y? CAUSE I'M THAT CHICK!

Funny thing, that boy, Antonio, hasn't opened his mouth to say not one word to me over the last few days. Not even in English class. Usually he has some kinda slickness to say when I walk by his desk to get to my seat, but nope...he doesn't even follow me around the school now, or stop past my locker. He just keeps it moving. Oh, wait. Don't get it twisted, boo. Not that I care. I'm just sharing; that's all. But anyway...

As soon as my status hits my Timeline, I get mad likes and then comments.

THAT'S RIGHT GURRL. LEARN THAT TRICK!
SHOW HER HOW WE DO IT, BOO!
BK, STAND UP!
DO DAT HOE DURTY, HUN! BROOKLYN, BABEEEE!
DO OR DIE BED-STUY!

I grin. Then comment back: YOU ALREADY KNOW WAT IT IS! 2MORROW IT'S ON!

Mmmmph! Play with me if you want!

23

Antonio

Yo, it's all over the school how Quanda got her top rocked by the new hottie. And how the hottie's shirt was tore open and her boobs were outta her bra. I look over at Justin, who ain't diggin' how dudes are talkin'. I gotta laugh to myself, though. She ain't even thinkin' 'bout him. In fact, I doubt she thinkin' 'bout any'a these clowns. But they all think they got the magic plan to wife her. A'ight, a'ight, includin' me. But, difference is, I know I can bag 'er *if* I really wanted 'er. But after Justin got all sensitive on me, I fell back. It's not worth the effort or the aggravation. I get enough of that from Quanda. Maybe now that she done got her sockets rocked, she'll fall back 'n' leave me the hell alone.

"Yo, chill, how you speak about her, dawg," Justin says to Leon, foldin' his arms across his chest. His face is all scowled up. "A'ight cool. You saw her boobs. But you ain't gotta be all disrespectful about it."

Leon grills him back. "I talk 'bout her, or any broad,

how I want. What, you bonin' that or somethin'? She ain't nothin' special, yo. She a trick, just like all the rest of the hoes up in here. The only difference is, she just ain't been had, yet."

"Yo, dawg," Justin says, droppin' his arms. "I know you don't want it, bruh. But if so, then it's whatever, yo. But you need'a chill wit' ya mouth, yo."

"Or *what*, bruh?" They're in each other's face now, chests heavin' all fast 'n' hard like they both ready to lock horns. Both of their jaw muscles are clenchin'.

"Hol'up, hol'up," I say, steppin' in between them. "Are y'all mofos serious right now? That broad ain't thinkin' 'bout neither one of you. And y'all standin' here gettin' ready to go at it." I shake my head. "Man, listen…y'all really 'bout to clown ya'selves over some chick." Leon narrows his eyes, stares Justin down. Neither wants to be the one to back down first. But I can see it in Leon's eyes that he really don't wanna get into it.

"Yo, c'mon, Just, man. Let it go, yo." I look over Justin's shoulder and peep one'a the security dudes—the one we call Batman 'cause he's always somewhere tryna rescue someone—is comin' down the hall toward us. I pull him by the arm. "Yo, chill, fam. We got company comin'."

Justin snatches his arm away. "Yo, I'm out." He walks off down the hall, headin' toward his homeroom. I turn to Leon, tell him it really wasn't worth it.

"Yo, eff that punk-azz dude," he says, walkin' off in the opposite direction. I shake my head, goin' over to my locker to get my books for my first three periods. *Man, that chick ain't even been here but a minute 'n' she got mofos fightin' over her. And not one'a 'em got them cookies, yet. I knew she was def gonna be a problem!* I slam my locker shut, headin' down the hall. There are mad heads in the halls tryna scramble to homeroom before the bell rings. I holla at peeps as I walk by. Give a few chicks hugs, then press on.

"Heeeey, Tone," I hear in back of me.

I glance over my shoulder. It's Fiona. Real rap, this broad got some real juicy fruit. But she done let most of the school chomp all up on it. "Oh, wassup, girl? How you?"

"I'm delicious, as always, boo. Thought you knew."

I grin. "Yeah, I do."

"And you know you can always get another taste."

I laugh. "Yo, you stay tryna freak off." Fiona's most def a ho, and she knows it. But she's so cool you can't help but respect 'er, which is why she's prolly one'a the few girls none'a the dudes go in on. "Well, you know I have my favorites. And you can always get it."

"Yeah, I know that, too."

"Just making sure, boo. But, annnyway, I heard ya girl got her face beat in by the new cutie-boo, Miesha."

"That ain't my girl, yo."

She laughs. "Whatever. Tell that to Quanda. Annnyway, you know her jaw is all wired up, and her nose is broken, too."

"Oh, word?" I say, turnin' the corner and walkin' down the East Wing toward my homeroom. Damn, she did her dirty like that? Wow. "Nah, I ain't hear all that."

"Well, that's what they were sayin' at first. But then I heard that her nose isn't really broke; she just got lumped up real good. You know I'm not one for a buncha gossip, but that's the word on the streets. And on Facebook." I tell 'er I haven't really been playin' the Book too tough lately.

I laugh, though, at her always sayin' how she ain't beat for gossip, but she stay gossipin'. This broad got the 411 on e'eryone. Sometimes she knows ish that's poppin' off wit' peeps before they do. I shake my head. *This broad's nosey as hell.* She walks 'n' talks 'n' flirts wit' me to my class, then tells me she'll catch me later. I ain't gonna front, I watch her walk off. She gotta nice shake 'n' it's thick, so hey…what can I say?

I get through my next two periods, wonderin' why I haven't seen Miesha, yet. She wasn't in English second period 'n' I haven't seen her in the halls. I even went past her locker, but she wasn't there. And since she don't really eff wit' anyone here at the school, I can't even holla at 'em to see what's good wit' 'er. I bump into Chantel 'n' LuAnna as I'm walkin' outta the bathroom.

"Aye, wassup, LuLu, baby?"

"Nothing much," she says, eyein' me all sexy-like. "What's up with you?"

I grin. "You already know." I glance over at Chantel. She standin' here wit' her eyes all rolled up in her head, lookin' in the other direction, like she ain't beat. "Yo, what's goodie, Chantel?" She sucks her teeth, iggin' me. I laugh. "Oh, it's like that? You still ain't speakin', yo?"

"LuAnna, girl, I'll meet you in the cafeteria," she says, walkin' off. I keep laughin'. "Screw you, Tone," she snaps over her shoulder.

After walking LuAnna to her locker, I say, "You stay stylin'. You know you wanna give me that goody."

She slams her locker shut. "Yeah, I do. But that doesn't mean I will."

I press up on 'er, grabbin' her 'round the waist. "Yo, stop frontin' 'n' come slide through…"

"Heeeey, boo," someone says in back of me. I glance over my shoulder. It's Alicia.

"Oh, wassup, Alicia?"

"You, punk." She laughs as LuAnna pushes my hand off 'a her. "Call me when you get a chance. I need you to help me with something."

I grin, knowin' she wanna 'nother round wit' the kid. "Oh, a'ight. I got you."

She looks over at LuAnna. "Hey, girl."

"Hey," she says back, cuttin' her eyes at me. They exchange a few more words, then Alicia dips. I tell 'er I'ma hit 'er up later. LuAnna smirks. "Did you get *that*, too?"

"See? There you go tryna be all up in grown-folk business. Stay in a child's place."

I crack up laughin', spinnin' off in the opposite direction toward the cafeteria to meet up wit' the fellas.

Hol'up, hol'up...what the...Wait. What just happened here? She *kissed me!* Nah, yo. Tongued me down. And... the crazy thing is, I tongued her back! Me! Mr. I Ain't Wit' The Lip Service! Yo, real rap. I'm buggin' for real for real. This broad actually walked up on me, tapped me on the shoulder, and when I turned to look up at her, she grabbed me by the back of my neck, leaned in, and kissed me on the mouth. Not one'a those quickies, either. The kiss seemed like it went on forever, yo. It happened so fast. But, then before I knew it, my mouth slipped open, her tongue slipped in, and we were goin' at it. Right in the middle of the lunchroom, right in front of my boys, me 'n' shorty got it in. Then she pulled back 'n' spun off, not sayin' a word. Nothin'. But, yo, I ain't even gonna sit here 'n' front, she had me dazed for real for real. And now my head's spinnin'. I was in shock for like, five minutes, before I realized what had just popped off.

I blink.

"Oh snap!" Cease says, hoppin' up outta his seat. "You see that? Shorty just tongued you down outta nowhere, yoooooo, son.... Damn, she wildin' for real...."

"Yo, mofo, you a real savage for that, yo," Justin says, pushin' up from the table.

I blink. "What just happened?" I manage to ask after a few moments. I look up at him. Then over at Cease 'n' Luke, who are sittin' here wit' their mouths dropped open. They are just as much in shock as I am. But Justin ain't diggin' it. He's evil-eyein' me, hard.

"Yo, you tell us, dawg," he sneers. "Obviously you got somethin' goin' on you ain't been tellin' us. I knew ya lyin' azz wasn't gonna fall back. You a real grimy mofo, yo."

"Word is bond, yo. I ain't said two words to that broad since I tol' you I wasn't beat. I put that on e'erything, yo. I ain't know she was gonna come up in here 'n' kiss me. All y'all mofos know I *don't* kiss a broad."

"Mmmph. I can't tell. You coulda fooled me the way y'all were goin' at it." He waves me on. "Whatever, yo. Once again, Antonio gets the girl he knows one'a his boys is diggin'. That's real effed up, yo."

"Yo, chill, J," Luke says, tryna reason wit' him. "You can tell what shorty did was straight-up outta left field. Tone def didn't know that was gonna go down."

"Yeah, whatever. Maybe the muhfuggah didn't know it was gonna pop off right here in the lunchroom. But I ain't tryna hear he wasn't hollerin' at 'er on the low. We all know how this mofo move. He stay creepin'."

"Yo, hol'up, dawg. What is you tryna say? I don't gotta

creep. I do my dirt out in the open, yo. You got me effed up wit' someone else, bruh. And I don't 'preciate you comin' at my neck all crazy."

"Whatever, man. I don't 'preciate you snakin' me for someone you know I'm tryna get wit'."

I frown. "Yo, is you muthafu..." I pause, shakin' my head. I don't wanna go at him, but he's really pressin' it, yo. "Look, man. I ain't 'bout to beef wit' you over some broad who I wasn't even tryna get at, yo. Did you not see *her* come up over here? Did you not see *her* kiss me? I was sittin' here, mindin' mine, chillin' wit' you mofos."

"Yeah, muhfuggah, I saw all that. And I saw you kiss her back!"

"Yo, man," Luke says, shakin' his head. "He gotta point there. I peeped that, too. So it does look kinda suspect."

"Man, shut yo' face," I snap. "You suspect, yo. And whose side are you tryna be on, anyway?"

"Right now, neither," he says back. "But I know what I saw." Cease shoots him a look, elbowin' him. "Nah, man... I'm jussayin'. It looked kinda crazy that's all. I mean, like, yo. Y'all were goin' at it like y'all were ready to take it to the sheets, word is bond, yo."

Cease and I just stare at him. Luke don't never know when to keep his trash can shut.

Justin grabs his book bag and slings it over his shoulder. Tells me I ain't shit. Tells me he knew I wanted her from the rip. This dude musta really been diggin' her. But, she couldna been diggin' him back 'cause otherwise she wouldna been all up on *me*.

I shift in my chair. "Yo, dawg. Think what you want. I'm not 'bout to sit here and explain myself to you. I already tol' you what it was. And you still wanna think what you want. So have at it, fam. Like I said, I had nothin' to do wit' what she did."

"Yeah, okay. Then riddle me this, if not feelin' her, then why'd *you* kiss her back? You had'a be tellin' us one thing, then goin' behind my back snakin' me."

"Yo, eff outta here. I ain't kiss that broad back 'cause I'm diggin' her, or because I been on some snake ish. It was just reflex." I say that ish to him, but even I don't believe how it sounds. It was more than just reflex. I know I coulda pushed her up off'a me. But I didn't. Yeah, I coulda snapped on her, too. But I didn't do that, either. Truth is, I liked it. Nah...*really* liked it.

Her lips were soft.

Juicy.

They felt good.

Tasted even better.

And, yeah...I want more.

24

Miesha

"Ooooh, you dirty skank. You did *whaaat?!*" Tre asks, pressing her face all up into the computer screen. I'm in my room with the door shut and the stereo on low. My future husband, Trey Songz, is playing in the background while me and Tre FaceTime it up. It's just she and I tonight. Stacy couldn't log on to her computer for whatever reason. And Jalanda's on punishment for the next two weeks for sneaking some boy into her bedroom. Her mom caught them in bed together. They weren't *doing it-doing it*, but they were doing enough for her moms to go off. And the fact that they were both only in their underwear didn't help matters any. So she's on lockdown.

"Hello? Hello?" Tre says, snapping her fingers. "Don't keep me waitin'."

"Oh, whatever. You heard me, boo. I walked up on him and tongued him down right in the middle of the lunchroom."

"Oh my god! What did he do?"

"At first, nothing. I think I shocked him." I start laughing. "But then, after he realized what was happening, he kissed me back. And when I tried to walk off, he pulled me back and starting kissing *me*, again."

"OMG! *Whaaaat?!* He kissed you back? Like with tongue?"

"Mmmph. Did he. And lots of it."

"Boom, boom, boom! Ring the alarm!" She starts clapping and jumping up in her seat. "You done set it off, boo! You know how we do it. Snatch a ho's man. I want details! Details, boo!"

I wave her on. "Girl, please. There's nothing more to tell. I kissed him. He kissed me back. It was just a kiss. Besides, he didn't even know what he was doing." I tell her this. But, the truth is, it wasn't just a kiss. It was a *kiss-kiss*. The kinda kiss that makes your knees buckle. The kinda kiss that has you seeing fireworks. The kinda kiss that makes your heart skip three beats, then start racing fast and hard. And, yeah, I could tell that he didn't really know what he was doing—which, by the way, kinda surprised me since he's the school's little Stud-Daddy. But whatever. The point is, Antonio Lopez has some nice, sexy lips.

"Oh my god, this is some juicy juice-juice, boo. Wait 'til Jalanda and Stacy hear about this. Oooh, them hookers make me sick for not being online right now." I agree. "So where was the chick you had'a beat down at? Was she right there when you kissed her man?"

"He's *not* her man." I state this with a pinch of stank, causing Tre to raise her brow and give me one of her oh-wait-a-minute-let-me-find-out looks. "Well, *not* anymore he isn't," I quickly say.

"Mmmph. I know that's right. Not after the way you

smacked them lips up on him. Oooh, I woulda been like,
Bam! Take that, trick! If that was ya boo, he ain't no more.
Now hit the floor, whore."

I laugh. "She wasn't even in school when I kissed him.
But her dog-faced groupies were. And that's exactly why I
waited 'til lunch period to do it. I wanted all'a them
heifers to see it go down so they could run back and tell it.
And I'm sure they were blowing up her phone, and flood-
ing up her Facebook wall with the news."

"Oooh, and I'm sure someone took pics and got them
up on Instagram by now."

"Mmmph. You're probably right. Whatever. All I know is
that ho brought it all on herself. I warned her. And she still
wanted to pop her lips, so she got 'em popped."

"And then got dropped," Tre adds, laughing. "Ooooh, I
wish I coulda been there. Why you ain't have someone
video that for you? I know you gave it to her Brooklyn-
style. Fast and furious, boo. Fists stay on ready."

I laugh. "Yup. And if she comes back on that rah-rah ish,
she'll get it again."

"That's right. Let that ho know. We go in. We go hard.
Wait. What's your new boo's name again?"

"He's *not* my new boo."

"Not yet he's not."

I roll my eyes. "Trust. I'm not thinking about that boy.
And his name is Antonio."

"Ooooh, Antonio. Is he Spanish or something? 'Cause
ain't no Black boy named Antonio unless he gotta lil Puerto
Rican in him." She laughs. " 'Cause you know them Black
boys' mommas stay givin' them those ugly-ghetto names,
like Kavonte Al'Sadeeki Brown, Nyquil Nighty-Nite Tyson
Abdul Jones."

I chuckle. "Girl, you stupid. I don't know what he is. I mean, he looks mixed with something, but it's kinda hard to tell since I really don't pay him any mind."

"Girl, *boom*. Lies. So, save it. You mighta not been letting him think you wasn't payin' him any attention. But I know you, boo. You stay on cutie alert. And I know you woulda never kissed no dog-faced boy, boo." Ooh, she's so right. I crack up laughing. "Now, what does this Mr. Antonio look like?

Tall. Fine. And sexy! "He looks a'ight. I mean, he's cute and all. And he has a nice body. But he knows it."

"Oh, like you. Conceited or convinced?"

"Oh shut up. I'm convinced. *He's* conceited." She cracks up. "Whatever." I glance over at the clock. It's almost eight o'clock. And I still have to finish up two reading assignments, one for English and the other for my Afro Studies class.

"Oh my god, girl, wait. Speakin' of ghetto. Guess who I saw, lookin' gooder than a Snickers bar ridin' the number four train?"

"Who?"

"Your old boo, Dynamite. And guess who he was with? And guess what they were carrying?" Ugh! I messed with that boy for like three weeks until this girl Shaneeta with a head like a horse texted me and told me he was at her house over in Clinton Hill and had just got done doing it to her. Then she sent me a picture of him in her bed, naked, to prove it. Messy trick! I was through. Then the stupid boy tried to lie and say it was Photoshopped. That he ain't never sleep with her. Like, really? Where they do that at? I wasn't tryna hear it. I pulled the alarm on that real quick.

I roll my eyes. "Girl, I don't care about that boy. And I'm not in the mood for no guessing games. So just tell me. Geesh."

"Girl, whatever. He was with that girl Tay-Tay and..."

"*Eww*, yuck! Tay-Tay with them big teeth and black gums?"

"Yup. And he was holding their baby."

"Their *baby*? Ugh. That boy don't care who he do it to. What the little thing look like?"

She smacks her lips. "Girrrl, I don't know all that. All I know is after she told me she named her baby Obamalee-sha, I was done. I didn't even wanna see it."

"She did what?"

"You heard me. Obama. Leesha. A hot ghetto mess! Who does that to their baby? But annnyway...back to you and your soap opera. Now what? Are you gonna fall back, or are you gonna take this all the way to the sheets?"

"Oh, no, boo. I'm not sleeping with that dog. He does enough humping around for the both of us. I'ma stick to the script. You know how we do it. If a trick wanna pop slick over a boy, we turn it up, snatch him up, then drop him, boo. You know the drill. That delusional ho stayed threatening me to stay away from her man. Now I'ma make him mine."

"That's right, hun. Snatch him up; snatch him up! She shoulda kept her trap shut and stayed in her lane. But don't you wanna sample them goodies?"

"Ugh! Are you for real? No thank you. Not interested. Kissing him was as far as it's gonna go. I'll string him along for a few weeks just to eff with that skank he used to mess with; then it's curtains. Anyway, you know dumb hoes stay testin' us. I don't know what it is. Is it the pretty face or this tiny waist that gets 'em all twisted up?"

"Boo, it's the hair. They stay rockin' them two-for one packs, and we keepin' it track free. Them bald-headed hoes can't stand the heat, boo." Tre starts gettin' all amped. "Girl, just talkin' 'bout it is makin' me wanna take it to a ho's face. I need a blunt to calm me down. Ooh, I wish you were here. Turn it up; turn it up! Learn that ho! Ooh, I know you beat her down, lovely. But I wanna jump on her neck myself."

"Trust me. After I'm done havin' her so-called man, if she still wanna pop off, she can get it."

"Oooh, yessssssss, boo, straight to the skull. And the next time you gotta take it to her, snatch her scalp off her head. Matter of fact, let me know when you wanna get her, and I'ma hop the PATH train over there so we can tag team that ho's face up."

I laugh. Tre stays ready for a fight. And loves when we snatch up a ho's man, just to prove a point. That we them hot chicks. The man snatchers. The heartbreakers. The Love 'Em 'n' Leave 'Em clique. Although she and Stacy likes to hump 'em 'n' dump 'em, I don't go that far. I just run they pockets, then toss 'em to the side once I'm done with 'em. Or once their chick finally gets the hint that he really wasn't hers from the rip, then I dismiss 'em. And that's exactly what I'm about to do to her. Teach her. I don't get played. I get even. Boom!

"Yo, I've been lookin' for you all mornin'," Antonio says real low as he slips into the seat right next to me seconds after the bell rings. It's second-period English and Mrs.

Sheldon is five minutes late. I can't stand that woman. She still be tryna do me in class with the attitudes and whatnot. And I stay giving it right back to her. At the end of the day, I'ma get an A outta this class whether she likes it or not. "We need to talk."

I lift my eyes up from my sketchbook and glance at him. "About what?"

"Yo, c'mon, ma. Don't front. You know 'bout what. About what popped off in the lunchroom yesterday, yo. About that kiss."

I tilt my head. I'm tryna sit here and be nonchalant about it, but inside I'm quickly melting like a double-dipped ice cream cone dropped on a fire. This boy never comes up to the front of the class. But here he is. I try to keep from sniffing in his cologne, but it isn't easy not to. Hmmm, he smells...mmph! I'm not even going there.

"Okay. I kissed you. What about it?"

He frowns. "What you mean, yo? I wanna know what was up wit' that. You came way outta left field wit' that ish."

I smirk. "What, you didn't like it or something?"

"Nah, I mean, yeah. I mean..."

"Okay, which is it?"

"Both, yo. I don't be kissin' chicks."

"Oh, that's interesting. 'Cause if my memory serves me correctly. And it does. You *didn't* stop me. And, *you* kissed me back."

He glances over his shoulder, then scoots his desk closer to me. He lowers his voice to almost a whisper. "That's just it. I didn't stop you. And I kissed you back. I need to know why you did it."

'Cause that ho Quanda tried to bring it to me. I shrug. "I felt like giving out kisses yesterday. And you happened to be the lucky recipient of these soft lips. You can thank your little girlfriend for that."

He frowns. "She's not my girl."

"That's not my problem."

"So, what, I'm some kinda pawn in ya lil game to get at her?"

I tilt my head. "Maybe. Anything else?"

He eyes me, licking his lips. Those lips. The ones I wanna lean over and nibble on. I shift in my seat. Blink my stare from his mouth. "I want them digits, yo."

"We don't always get what we want, now do we?"

He grins. "Yeah, but I do."

"Ha. We'll see."

"Stop playin', yo. Come up off'a them digits so we..."

"Okay, class," Mrs. Sheldon says, whisking through the door, all outta breath. "Sorry I'm late." She opens her desk drawer, drops her bag in, then shuts it.

I whisper. "Oh, well. Bad timing for you, perfect timing for me."

"Whatever, yo. You need a..."

Mrs. Sheldon looks from Antonio to me, then back at him. "Mr. Lopez. Isn't *this* cozy...you up in the front row." She shoots me another look. I roll my eyes, scooting my desk over a pinch, then closing my sketchbook. "Let me guess. The two of you are going over notes for class."

Antonio smirks. "Yeah, somethin' like that." He gets up to move.

"Oh, no, no...don't move on my account. Stay right there, please. As a matter of fact, I prefer you to sit there for the rest of the quarter. But perhaps not so close to Miss Wilson." He grumbles, but sits back in his seat. "Now scoot your desk back over in its proper row." She waits for him to fix his seat, then continues. "Okay, let's get started. Everyone should have finished reading *A Long Way Gone* by now. Am I correct?" Everyone tells her yes. "Good. Mr. Lopez, how about you tell us a little about the main character in the book. What did you think of his story?"

This chick really got it for this boy bad. He shifts in his seat, stretching his long legs out. I glance down at his feet. He has on a pair of Lebrons. His sneaker game is sick. I shift my eyes.

"It was deep. I mean for him to go through all he went through, and still come out on top...his fam bein' slaughtered, his village bein' attacked, havin' to wander from village to village to steal from other kids just so he 'n' his brother 'n' friends could eat. Then bein' snatched up to fight in a war 'n' forced to use drugs." He shakes his head. "Yo, them mo..." Mrs. Sheldon shoots him a look, raising her brows. "Uh, my bad. Them dudes were savages for that. Turnin' them kids into junkies like that. That dude really got put through it. That whole book was crazy."

"Yes, he did," she says, all grins and giggles. Sickening.

"I'm not gonna front. I started feelin' some kinda way how they was treatin' him. What they were doin' to all those kids. What they went through was torture."

"And still he survived," she says. "His story is a testament to us all that no matter what you're going through, or have gone through, you can come through it. It's a horrifying first-person account of life as a child soldier, but resilience rings loud throughout the book." She walks over to the board and starts writing as she discusses more about the book. The two of them go back and forth like they the only two in the room. Until a few other kids chime in. And that's fine by me. I glance at my watch. I have fifteen more minutes until next period, until I'm away from *him*. Sitting this close to him is making me...dizzy.

I take in his profile. He could definitely be a model. He catches me staring at him. He winks. I roll my eyes, shifting in my seat. He opens his notebook, tears a piece of paper out and scribbles something down. He folds it, then slides it over on my desk.

"Open it," he whispers, nudging it closer to me. For some reason, I feel like the whole class is looking at me, like everyone was this morning when I walked into the building. Girls who never spoke to me before are all of a sudden speaking, like it's all good. Oh, no, boo-boo. Boom! Not. They get the ig button, okay. I'm not with that phony ish. Yeah, most of them heard I stomped Quanda out down at the courts, but the fact that I boldly walked up and lip-locked it up with *her* ex-boo yesterday was worthy of keeping my name coming outta their mouths.

I open the note.

WHY YOU PLAYIN' GAMES?

I smirk, shaking my head. "I'm not," I say, sliding the note back to him.

Mrs. Sheldon glances over her shoulder. "What was that, Miss Wilson? Since you wanna talk in my class, tell us what the army brainwashed Ishmael into thinking."

I sigh. "That each rebel killing may avenge the murder of his family."

"That's correct. Now talk in my class again, and you'll be serving detention."

Antonio tries to keep from laughing. "Get away from me, boy," I mumble under my breath.

"Nah, you started it," he mumbles back. "Now it is what it is, yo. You stuck wit' me, baby. Now give me ya number so we can proceed."

"I'll think about it," I say as the bell rings. I stand up and grab my things with him hot on my heels, heading out the door.

"Yeah, a'ight. Let me give you somethin' else to think 'bout..." Before I know what's happening, he reaches for my hand. Then the next thing I know, his head is leaning toward mine; he's cupping my chin with his hand, and his lips...ohgodohgod. He kisses *me*! And, this time, it is *me* kissing *him* back. When he finally pulls his lips from mine, he steps back, grinning. I'm stunned. I blink.

"Yeah, that was nice. Now we're even." He walks off, leaving me standing in the middle of the hallway with kids walking by staring at me all crazy, feeling like I've just been swept up in a tornado.

Oh, no. This is not *how this game is supposed to get played.*

25

Antonio

Yo, what the heck is wrong wit' chicks? They stay on their bullshit, yo. I mean, like what's really good with the games they stay playin'? It's been two days since I kissed Miesha in the hallway 'n' she still ain't hit me wit' them digits. And, yeah...a'ight, I know what her mouth says. That she only kissed me from the rip to eff with Quanda. Okay, that might be true. But she ain't 'bout to have me believin' she ain't diggin' me. Nah, I ain't buyin' it. I know she felt what I felt when we kissed, *both* times. I can't explain it. It was like a rush of heat shootin' through my body; word is bond. I ain't never feel no ish like that before. Not even when I'm gettin' it in wit' a chick. Nah, if she can make me feel like that just kissin' her, I can only imagine what it's gonna feel like when we rock them springs.

Damn. I want them lips again.

Her lips.

Booty.

Boobs.

I want all of her.

And now I wish I shared more than one class wit' her. I can't believe this chick really got me buggin' like this. I walk past her locker and slip a note inside, then head down the hall to sixth-period French, replayin' those kisses in my head over and over.

"Um, hel-*lo,* Earth to Tone!"

I shake my head and squint, bringin' Quanda into focus. She's standin' in front of me wearin' a dark pair of shades wit' a hand up on her hip, her head tilted, attitude on ten.

"I *asked* you is this how you doin' it now?"

I sigh. "What are you talkin' 'bout, yo?"

"You screwin' that *bitch*, now?"

I blink. This is the first time I've seen her since the fight down at the courts. I heard she was back in school today, but didn't see her this mornin' at her locker, or in the halls in between classes.

"Yeah, muhfuggah, I heard all about how she kissed you in the cafeteria. And I heard how *you* had your tongue all down that whore's throat the other day in the hall. I *thought* you didn't kiss. All the times I tried to kiss you and you'd turn ya head tellin' me to *get that neck.* Like really? Where they do that at? But you kissin' all up on that ho." She bites her bottom lip. The right side of her face is still kinda puffy and her lip is still swollen.

I sigh. "Yo, on some real ish, let's not do this, a'ight? I mean, c'mon. How many times I gotta keep tellin' you it's over between us, yo? Why can't you get it through ya head. It's over."

"Why?" she asks, poutin'. "We were so good together,

Tone. We can still be if you'd just stop chasin' behind all these skeezers. You know them hoes can't handle you like I do." I walk off, not even botherin' to waste breath. "I'm not gonna stop loving you, Antonio Lopez!" she yells down the hall at me. "And I'm *not* lettin' you go without a fight. So tell that *slut*, she'd better buckle up and get ready to knuckle up."

All during French class, my mind is stuck on tryna figure out what class Miesha's in this period, and if she'll go to her locker afterward 'n' see the folded note I slipped through the slits for her. If she'll run into Quanda's dumb behind, and what'll pop off if she does. Fifty-seven minutes of wonderin', that's what I'll be doin' 'til the bell rings. I stare over at the door, then back toward the blackboard where Mrs. Duvet is writin' the lesson in French. I pull out my cell and text Luke. Yo wat class u hv wit' Miesha?

A few minutes later, Luke hits me back. afro history 5th period y?

I don't respond back. He askin' me why like he's her keeper or somethin'. These mofos kill me. As soon as the bell rings, I snatch up my things 'n' jet outta class.

I eye Miesha comin' down the hall wit' some mofo from the lacrosse team all up on her. "So, we still on for tomorrow night?" I overhear dude sayin' as I walk up on them at her locker. He's leanin up against the locker next to hers, wit' his arm up on her locker door all comfy while she's pullin' books outta her locker. I try 'n' keep myself in check as I approach them, but on the inside I feel like chippin' dude up, for real for real.

"Wassup?" I say.

"Yeah, we're still on," she says, iggin' me. "What time

you picking me up?" she finishes before lookin' over at me. "Oh, hey."

"What's up?" dude says, givin' me a lopsided head nod. Yo real rap, I feel like punchin' the smirk off 'a his face. I give him a head nod back.

"You two know each other?" she asks.

"Nah, not really. I've seen him around," dude says, eyein' me. "You on the basketball team, right?"

"Yeah."

"Brent, this is Antonio. Antonio, Brent."

He extends his hand. I wanna spit in it, for real for real. But I know I'm thinkin' real crazy 'cause the dude ain't never did or said nothin' sideways to me. I shake his hand.

"A'ight, so I'll talk to you tonight, cool?" dude says.

She grins. "Cool. Talk to you tonight."

"A'ight, later," he says and walks off.

I wait for him to be outta earshot, then say, "So, what's good? You still tryna be on ya BS, I see."

She smirks. "What BS are you talkin' about, boy?"

"I want them digits, yo. And you still frontin' on me. But I see ol' boy got ya number. What's good wit' that?"

"What, you jealous?"

I laugh it off. "Jealous? Ha! Never that, ma."

"Yeah, whatever." The bell rings. "See, now you've made me late for class."

I lean in close. "Yeah, a'ight. Tell ya teacher I held you up."

She rolls her eyes.

"Yo, keep it a hunnid, ma. Why you stuntin' on me, huh?"

She smirks. "Boy, please. I'm not hardly stuntin' on you."

"Oh, word? You not?" I say, kissin' her cheek.

"No, I'm not." She looks into my eyes, then shifts her stare at somethin' or someone comin' down the hall.

"Then stop playin' games wit' me, ma."

"Kiss me," she says outta the blue.

"Huh?"

"I said, kiss me."

"Give me them digits, first." She huffs. Pulls me to her by the neck, then whispers her number in my ear. I grin. "See? Was that so..." Her lips are on mine again.

"Trick-ho," Quanda snaps, walkin' up on us. I break from her kiss. Now I see why Miesha was so quick to wanna give me her number 'n' kiss me. She still tryna get at Quanda.

Quanda looks mad hurt. But that's not my problem. It's over. "You might *think* you got him for today, but trust. Tone knows"—she pats her crotch—"where his home is. So enjoy him while you can 'cause he'll be back."

Miesha laughs, shuttin' her locker. "Sweetie, boom! If you know like I do, you'll keep walking before you hit the floor again."

"Oh, I'ma keep walkin', ho. But I ain't hittin' no floor this time. So you better watch ya back, slut!"

Miesha waves at her. "Bye, hater."

I sigh, hopin' like hell these two don't start brawlin'. I ain't beat to be gettin' all up in the middle of a cat fight. "Yo, c'mon," I say, grabbin' Miesha by the arm. "She ain't worth it, yo."

"Well, you're worth it, Tone!" Quanda snaps, pointin' a finger at me. "But since you wanna take up for this stuck-up ho, you might as well watch ya back, too." I ig her. She's not even 'bout to drag me into her nuttiness. Quanda al-

ready knows I ain't no punk, so all that yip-yap she poppin' don't mean ish to me.

Miesha keeps laughin' at her. I shake my head. *This
chick hella fine, but damn she's a real problem.* I recite
her number in my head over 'n' over 'til I have it memo-
rized. I pull out my phone, decidin' to put her digits in my
contacts just in case I forget them. Yeah, I'ma most def hit
her up, but not today. At least that is the plan. *Yeah, I'ma
make her wait for me, even if it kills me.*

26

Miesha

Grabbing my iPhone from off the nightstand, I look at the screen. No calls. Why hasn't *he* called, yet? *I gave that boy my number like five hours ago. Mmmph.* He probably forgot it as soon as I whispered it into his ear. Boys! I shoulda never given it to him!

I click onto the last episode of *Project Runway* then pull out my sketchbook, grab four colored pencils, and start sketching a design that I've had on the brain for a few days. It's a sheer, ankle-length dress with a thigh-high split on the right side. Yeah, it's probably a little too grown, but it's sexy. I have mad sketches of all types of dresses and gowns that I hope to one day design. I remind myself to ask Daddy to buy me a sewing machine for Christmas. I'm gonna need to step up my game and learn how to make my own patterns and sew my own garments if I really wanna make it in the fashion industry. All I think about is getting into Parsons, and one day studying or interning in Milan.

I continue sketching my design. When I am done, thirty minutes later, it is a flowy, asymmetrical gown with a plunging neckline and low back. I smile. There's a knock on my door.

"Come in," I say, closing my book. It's my aunt Linda.

"Hey, sweetheart," she says, walking into my room. "I fixed dinner. Are you hungry?"

"Hey," I say back. "A little. Is my mom here yet?" She tells me no. I glance over at the clock. It's almost eight o'-clock at night. *Mmmph. She coulda at least sent me a text or called to let me know whether or not she was working late.* I ask her what she cooked. She tells me baked tilapia, broccoli, and wild rice. *Oh, no thanks!*

"Sounds good," I lie. "I'll be out in a sec to eat."

She smiles, walking out. "Okay. Take your time. You want your door closed?"

"That's okay. You can leave it open." I stop her before she leaves. "Um, Aunt Linda, can I ask you something?"

"Sure, sweetheart. What is it?"

"How did you know you loved Uncle Frankie?"

She smiles. "When all I could do is think about him and smile. When I couldn't imagine ever being with someone else. That's when I knew." Her face seems to light up talking about it.

"Do you still feel that way about him now? I mean after everything y'all have been through, like do you have any regrets?"

"No, I don't. I loved your uncle. And no matter what has happened between us over the years, I still do." Oh my god, she sounds so much like my mom. I swear if I closed my eyes right now, I'd think it was her standing here instead of my aunt. She eyes me. "Why?"

"Just curious."

She wants to know if I'm dating someone. I shake my head.

"No. Not since we've moved out here."

"Well, is there anyone from your school you like?"

I shrug. "Not really. I mean, there are a few guys there that are tryna talk to me, but I don't really like them like that. They seem nice as friends."

"Have you told them that?"

"Well, no. Not really."

"Maybe you should let them know how you feel before they get too wrapped up into you."

"I guess. It's not like I'm leading them on or anything. They know I'm not looking for anything serious. I just want to hang out. You know, have some fun."

She gives me a thoughtful look. "I know. Just make sure you're very clear on what your intentions are. Don't mislead anyone. That's never a nice feeling. I'll let you get back to what you were doing. Don't forget to come get something to eat."

"Thanks, Aunt Linda. I won't." I wait for her to walk out, then snatch up my phone. "Where are you?" I ask as soon as my mom answers.

"I'm still in the city," she says, sounding all giddy and free. I hear noise in the background, like a buncha chatter and music.

I frown. "Are you still at work?"

"No. I'm out having dinner with your father."

She's out having dinner and laughs with Daddy and I'm stuck here. Now I'm pissed. She gets to spend as much time as she wants with him. But she wants to limit when I can spend time with him. Until my birthday in January. I'm sooo outta here. "So, are you coming back here tonight?" She tells me no. Tells me she's staying in the city 'cause she has an early training. But I know she's lying. Always know when she's lying.

"Oh my god. You're such a liar."

"Miesha, don't you call me a liar, girl."

"Well, you are. You're out having dinner with Daddy. We both know you plan on going back to Brooklyn with him, so just say it. Stop acting like I'm some dumb little girl who doesn't know what time it is. I know you and Daddy are still sleeping together. And, before you go saying that's none of my business, I'll say it for you. I know it's none of my business. Still, you coulda at least sent a text saying you weren't coming here. Geesh."

"Miesha, I'm not doing this with you tonight. Yes, I should have let you know that I'm not coming home. I apologize. It wasn't my intention to not come home. But then your father called and asked me to meet him for dinner. By the way, he says hi...."

"Whatever," I say, rolling my eyes up in my head. "Look, since you're not gonna be home tonight, I'm going out. And I'm not coming home, either."

"Miesha, don't start. You had better be home by your curfew or—"

"Or what?" I snap. "You're gonna beat me? Hahaha. Picture that. Oh, wait. Threaten to take my car away. Whatever. Do what you gotta do. I'm outta here." I disconnect, tossing my phone over onto the bed. What really has me heated is the fact that I could *still* be in Brooklyn. She did all this moving and snatching me away from my life for what? So she can go out on dinner dates and sneak over afterward to sleep with Daddy? That makes no sense to me. *I gotta get outta here.* I reach for my phone.

"Hey. It's me," I say the minute Brent answers. "You busy?"

"Nah, just kicked back chillin'. Wassup?"

"I'm bored. Come get me."

"What time you gotta be back?"

I glance over at the clock. It's a quarter to nine. "Whenever I want."

"Bet. Let me throw on some clothes. I'll be there in thirty."

"See you when you get here." I disconnect the call, then head out into the kitchen to pick over the food aunt Linda cooked, then hop in the shower. My mom is busy living her life. Now it's time I start living mine!

By the time I get to school, I make it to homeroom less than a minute before the bell rings. I didn't get home until almost four in the morning. Purposefully. Aunt Linda was still in bed, but I'm sure she heard the alarm chirp when I walked in. I wanted her to. I want her to tell my mom exactly what time I got home. As far as I'm concerned, it isn't my aunt's job to watch me—not that I need watching. But still...she shouldn't have to be the one worrying about what I'm doing. My mom should! Anyway, I let Brent drive me into Brooklyn and we hung out over at Tre's house until like eleven-thirty. We woulda stayed out longer, but her mom started beastin' about her having company over so late on a school night so we bounced and went to Junior's to get something to eat since they don't close until midnight. After that, we just drove around Brooklyn, then over into Manhattan, then zipped back over across the water.

I can't even lie. Brent is a really nice guy in a nerdy kinda way. He's real smart, funny, and very thoughtful. I had to remind him that I only want to be friends. He says he's cool with that. But then he leaned over and kissed me. And, yes, I let him. It was okay, I guess. I mean he has nice lips. And they were soft. But, I didn't feel anything afterward. Not like I did with...ooh, there he goes now coming down the hall.

"Hey, what's up, Miesha?" this guy from my chemistry class says, walking by my locker. He sits a few seats over from me in class and every so often I catch him looking over at me. *Ooh good, just the distraction I need.*

"Hey," I say back. "You ready for that chemistry test next week?"

He stops, shifting his stack of books from one arm to the other, then smiles. "Nah, not yet. But I will be. What about you?"

"Ugh. I wish."

"Well, if you'd like, we could study together."

I smile all wide and extra. "Ohhh, for real? I'd love that."

He grins. "Cool. Do you want my number?"

Oh my god, boy, boom! He's all thirsty for my attention. "No. I don't need your number." He looks at me all pitiful and whatnot, like his puppy done pissed in his cereal. Geesh.

He places his hand up over his heart. "Dang, you just shot my dreams down. Can't knock a guy for trying. But I was definitely kinda hoping you would have said yes."

I eye Antonio as I'm standing here with this buster. He's all tore up in his plaid shirt buttoned all the way up to his neck. He's wearing a pair of jeans with...oh my god, *creases!* Creases?! Where they do that? That's soooo late and wrong. He has on a pair of Crocs. What Black boy you know wearing *Crocs*?

I start cracking up.

27

Antonio

By the time I get to my locker, I'm mad nervous, hyped, 'n' all sweaty palmed, thinkin' 'bout seein' Miesha. I ain't gonna even front, I hardly slept last night. I tossed 'n' turned. I don't know what it is 'bout her kisses, them lips, that got me goin' through it. E'ery time I think 'bout her, I get mad excited. And it's like nothin' I do cools me down. I was gonna hit her up last night when I got home from practice, but decided to fall back. But, man, listen. It was hard not hittin' her up just so I could hear her voice. So I hit up Shania instead and tried to rock out wit' her, but Miesha kept poppin' up in my head. And I got so caught up in my thoughts 'n' the moment that I accidentally called out her name. That set Shania off. She pushed me off 'a her, then started cussin' me out sayin' I disrespected her. Then she got up and started throwin' my clothes at me and told me to bounce. Like, whatever, yo. I don't know why broads gotta be all extra wit' the theatrics. She'll get over it. If not, eff 'er. I wasn't gonna ever wife 'er anyway.

So it is what it is. But, word is bond. I ain't never call a chick I was gettin' it in wit' another chick's name. Not even when I've been twisted from smoke 'n' drinks. Real rap, Miesha got me slippin', yo.

I gotta holla at 'er, today. I gotta see what's really good wit' her. But when I see some dude who I ain't really all that cool wit' standin' by her locker, all grins 'n' giggles, like that dude from the lacrosse team was yesterday, I start feelin' some kinda way. Yeah, I know she ain't my girl *yet*, but damn, this corny mofo is practically all up on 'er. These thirsty mofos stay tryna get at her. But they don't know. I'ma 'bout to shut ish down.

She sees me walkin' toward them, then starts laughin' mad hard at somethin' dude says. Whatever.

"Yo, what's good?" I say as I approach them.

"Wassup?" dude says, givin' me a head nod. He looks kinda shook 'bout somethin', but whatever.

Miesha shuts her locker. Tells dude she has seventh-period study hall—that's good to know. And she'll meet him in the library so they can study.

"A'ight. Cool." He looks over at me. "A'ight, man. Peace."

"Yeah, a'ight. No doubt," I say back. I'm kinda surprised she didn't introduce the dude like she did with dude from the lacrosse team. "So who's ya lil boyfriend?"

She flicks her wrist at me. "Boy, boom! Don't question me."

I grin. "Yeah, a'ight. I'll question you all I want. Who-ever that corny dude is, he looks like he's tryna be ya boyfriend."

She shoots me a look. "Why you care?"

"I don't."

She laughs. "Lies."

"Yeah, a'ight. Whatever. Yo, did you get my note?"

She frowns. "What note?"

"Yo, don't front. The one I left for you in ya locker yesterday."

"I didn't see it," she says, turning back to open her locker. She opens the door, then looks down, pullin' out the note folded into a rectangle. "Ohh, this note?"

"Yeah, that note. Don't open it 'til you get to class."

She laughs. "Boy, boom. Who says I'm gonna open it?"

I grab for her. "Yo, don't have me chip ya lil sexy azz up."

She pushes me off 'a her. "Yeah, picture that."

I peep Luke 'n' Justin comin' down the hall. "Yo, what's goodie, playboy?" Luke says, grinnin' as he walks up on us. He gives me dap.

"Yo, wassup, man," I say over to Justin. He's still actin' kinda funny-style since that whole kissin' scene popped off. But whatever. He gives me a head nod.

"What's good?" he looks over at Miesha. "Wassup, Miesha?"

"Hey, Justin," she says, smilin'. Damn, she gotta pretty smile. "I've been meaning to call you, but..."

He shifts his eyes. "Nah, it's all good. I've been mad busy with school and work and now practices."

"Okay," she says. "That's good." I introduce her to Luke. They speak; then she tells me she's gotta get to homeroom before the bell rings. I tell her I'll catch up wit' her later.

"Yo, we still chillin' tonight?" Luke asks, try'n not to stare at Miesha's booty. But you can't help but stare at it. There's so much of it to look at. "Party at my crib."

I laugh. "Man, you stay partyin'. Ya parents gonna flip if they ever catch you."

He laughs wit' me. "Man, they stay on the move too much to ever catch me."

"Yeah, a'ight. But, nah, I'ma lay low tonight."

I give Justin a pound. "Yo, we good?"

"Yeah, we a'ight," he says. But I can tell he don't really mean it. We all head to our homerooms just as the bell rings.

"Lopez," Mr. Watkins says as I walk through the door. "You're late. That'll be two days' detention."

I sigh, shakin' my head.

The rest of the day goes by kinda fast. Quanda is still up to her dumbness. And somebody wrote the word SLUT in red lipstick across Miesha's locker door. But, of course, no one peeped who did it. I already know it was Quanda. That's how she gets down. I'm just glad I got to Miesha's locker and peeped it before she did. I hit up the boys' bathroom and snatched up some paper towels and scrubbed it off real quick, then waited for her. But we could only talk for a few minutes 'cause I had'a get to practice. And Coach don't play that late ish.

"Yo, I'ma need you to scoop me up in the mornin'," Luke says, unfastenin' his seat belt as I pull up into his driveway. We just left the school from practice. I'm sore 'n' mad tired from all the drills. All I wanna do is get home, take a shower, then hit the sheets.

"Man, when you gettin' ya whip back?"

"Man, who knows....I told you my pops be on his BS."

I ask when they comin' home.

"My mom'll be home Saturday night. And my pops

won't be home 'til the end of the month. He's in China on some business trip."

"Man, ya pops stay on the move. That's wassup. I can't wait 'til I can travel like that."

He shrugs. "Yeah, I guess. I'd rather he be home more. But I know he gotta make that paper. I just wish he didn't have to travel so much. He'll probably miss most of my games this year."

"Hopefully not. But at least you got ya moms 'n' you already know ya pops is always gonna come through when he's home."

"Yeah, true. But now that my sister had the babies, that's all my mom thinks about."

"Yo, she just excited 'bout bein' a grandma," I say, tryna keep it light so he don't go gettin' all depressed 'n' ish.

"Yo, so what's good wit' you and shorty?"

"Who, Miesha?"

"Yeah. Yo, hands down, she's bad."

I grin. "Most def, yo. I don't know. I dig her, but she be on some extra ish."

"Oh, word? Like what?"

"I don't know, man. I know she only really got at me to get at Quanda...."

He looks over at me, shakin' his head. "Damn, that's crazy, yo. So why you even effen wit' that broad if you already know what it is wit' her?"

"Man, I don't know. It was somethin' 'bout that first kiss, yo."

"First kiss? What, you've gotten more?"

I grin. "Yeah, man. I had'a get another round of that."

"Yo, hol'up...get the eff outta here, son. *You* tonguin'

down a chick. Damn, son. Sounds like she's 'bout to put the whammy on you, bruh."

I shake my head. "Tell me 'bout it, yo."

He opens the door 'n' gets out. "Yeah, okay. She already got you kissin'. We'll see, yo."

"Yeah, whatever. Shut my door wit' ya ugly azz."

He shuts the door, givin' me the finger. I laugh, backin' out, headin' home so I can hit the shower, eat, then relax.

Around nine o'clock, I'm lyin' in bed, tryna watch the latest episode of *Criminal Minds* online, but my mind keeps wanderin'. I can't stop thinkin' 'bout her. Miesha. *Man, this is crazy,* I think, hoppin' outta bed. *This chick ain't even ya girl 'n' she got you buggin', yo.* Wonderin' what she's up to. Wonderin' if she's off somewhere laughin' it up 'n' chillin' wit' some other dude. Wonderin' if she's even wonderin' 'bout me. This ish is crazy!

I pick up my phone 'n' hit her up. "Yo, what's good?"

"Who's this?"

"It's Tone."

"Sorry, wrong number. I don't know a Tone."

I scoff. "Yeah, whatever. You know who this is, girl. Stop frontin' like you don't know my voice."

"Oh my god! Cecil, is that you, boo? Oh my god! The last I heard you ran off with some cross-eyed chick with two missing front teeth. Boy, how you been?"

I start laughin'. "Oh, you got jokes."

She laughs. "Well, who is this, again?"

I lower my voice, grinnin'. "Yo, why don't you quit playin'? It's Antonio."

"Ohhhhhh, Antonio. Mmmph. Why you just didn't say that in the first place? Anyway, how can I help you?"

"Yeah, a'ight. When we gonna chill, yo?"

"Who says I wanna chill with you?"

"I know you do, yo. But you stay frontin'."

"Boy, please. Frontin' about what?"

I stare up at the ceilin'. I peep a cobweb up over in the corner. "C'mon, yo. What you think? 'Bout that kiss. And the one after that. I know you felt it, too."

"You know I *felt* what?"

"Heat," I tell her. "It shot all through ya body, makin' you dizzy. You felt ya knees buckle."

"Ha! Boy, you're delusional."

"Yeah, a'ight. But tell me I'm lyin'."

"Bye, Antonio. I gotta go."

I grin. "Yeah, a'ight, sexy." I have another call comin' in. It's Luke. "Yo, I'll holla." The call drops 'n' I click over. "Yo, what it do, son?"

"Chillin', yo. You stoppin' through tonight?"

"Nah, yo. I'm beat. Practice whipped my tail, yo. I'ma take it down in a minute. And you should be doin' the same thing, yo."

He laughs. "I'ma take it down a'ight. Take them panties down. Them Spanish broads, Rosa 'n' Carmela, comin' through to chill, again, so you already know how it's goin' down. And I gotta few fellas comin' through wit' a few chicks."

"Oh, word? Cease stoppin' through?"

"Nah, he on some corny-ish like ya punk azz."

I laugh. "Whatever, yo. Get it in for me, bruh. I'ma 'bout to hit these sheets."

"A'ight. Make sure you come scoop me. Last time you forgot and I had'a catch a cab. Matter of fact, you owe me ten bucks for that, yo."

"Haha. You must be on that molly, yo. But I'ma be there in the mornin'. And make sure you ready, yo. I ain't tryna be late effen wit' you."

"Yo, Luke?" I call out, walkin' through the kitchen. I had'a walk 'round back of the house 'n' use the key he keeps hidden in a small box behind a buncha shrubs to get in his crib 'cause the mofo ain't answer the doorbell. I was outside leanin' on the buzzer and bangin' on the front door for almost five minutes. I shake my head at the mess in the sink, and all over the counters. There's mad Papa John's pizza boxes, KFC boxes, 'n' White Castle burger cartons along wit' half-empty liters of Pepsi, Sprite, 'n' orange sodas. There are empty bottles 'n' cans of beer e'erywhere. They were def havin' a feast up in here last night. I go down into the basement. There's bodies stretched out all over the place, passed out. On the floor, 'cross the sofa. There's a naked chick balled up, sleepin' on the makeshift bar table. I step over several peeps I know from school, makin' my way back up the stairs. *His parents are gonna snap for real if they walk up in here 'n' see this ish.* I glance at my watch. I have only thirty minutes to get to school before the first-period bell rings. *I'ma be mad late if I don't hurry up outta here.*

I shoot up the stairs, two steps at'a time, then tap on Luke's door. "Yo, Luke, man...you up?" No response. I turn the knob, walkin' into his room. I frown. It smells like hot funk 'n' feet. "Luke, man, wake ya drunk-butt up, yo." He's lyin' facedown, naked, on top of the covers between two other bodies. I walk over and grab his foot and shake him. "Luke, wake the eff up, yo!" He stirs, rolls over on his back, wipin' drool from the corner of his mouth. "Yo, I

ain't tryna see all that, fam," I say, tossin' him his drawers.
"Cover ya'self, man."

He blinks, bringin' me into focus. "What time is it?"

"Time for you to get up 'n' wash ya stankin' azz. You
ugly as hell in the mornin', yo."

"Man, eff you." He scoots down to the edge of the bed
and slips on his boxers. He starts scratchin' his crotch.

"Yo, ninja. You need'a go handle that itch. I know you
ain't go raw up in them hoes, did you?" I ask, noddin' my
head over at the bed.

"Who you callin' a ho?" one of the girls says groggily,
poppin' her head up from beneath the covers. She cranes
her neck to look at me. It's one of the Spanish broads
from over the summer. *I bet you he tryna wife that. Dumb
mofo stays tryna wife hoes.* She smiles when she sees it's
me. "Oh, hey, boo. You shoulda came through last night.
Why you stop callin' me?" She sits up, lettin' the covers fall
to her waist. She don't even try to cover her boobs up. I
stare at 'em and she don't seem to mind.

"Yeah, I guess I shoulda," I say. "Maybe next time." I hit
'er wit' some lame excuse—a'ight, lie—'bout not callin'
'er 'cause I lost all'a my contacts in my phone, and shift my
attention to Luke. She plops back into the pillow. "Yo,
man, you need to let me know what you tryna do, yo. You
goin' to school or what?"

"Nah, man. My stomach's all effed up."

"That's what you get effen wit' that White Castle, mofo.
I tol' you before that ain't real meat they servin'."

He laughs. "Yeah, whatever. But, nah, that ain't got my
stomach all jacked. It's that One-Fifty-One, yo. We was
takin' it to the head, no chaser. Got my stomach on fire."
He swings open his bedroom door, and rushes out into

the hall into the bathroom. I follow out behind him. He's down on his knees, clutchin' the toilet, tossin' up his guts.

I shake my head. "Yo, on some real ish. You effen up, fam. On a school night, yo? I mean, you really couldn't wait to go in hard 'til the weekend?"

He coughs 'n' gags, heavin'. "Yo, not right now, son. My head's spinnin', yo."

I stare at his back. He has scratches all down his spine from bein' clawed up from one'a them broads stretched out in his room. "Yo, I'm out. You can eff around if you want. But I gotta get to school."

Deuces! I spin off. Head down the stairs and out the door to my car. I back out just as Luke's moms is pullin' in. *Oh snap! It's 'bout to be on 'n' poppin' now. His moms is gonna flip her wig when she walks up in there.* She waves at me, gettin' outta her car. Damn! I stop, rollin' my window down.

"Hey, Mrs. Emmerson. How was your trip?"

"Hey, Antonio. The trip was good, thanks. I decided to get back a few days early." *And you're in for a real surprise.* "How's your father doing?"

"He's good."

"Good. Tell him I asked about him."

"Okay, I will." I reach for my phone 'n' try'n text Luke on the low to give him a heads up. Yo mofo ya moms is outside

"You here to pick up Luke?"

911 nucca ya moms outside

"Uh, yeah. But, uh, he didn't answer the door." I don't know what else to tell her. It's true. He didn't. I don't even know why I'm textin' him. It's not like he can swoop through the crib 'n' clean up 'n' get all them heads outta there before his moms hits the door. So, he's gonna hafta wear this one.

She glances at her watch. "Ummph. I hope that boy isn't still up there in bed. You boys weren't hanging out last night, were you?"

"Uh, nah, I was home last night."

She smiles. "Well, let me get in here and see about this child of mine. You'd better get going before you're late for school. Drive safe."

"I will. Thanks." She waves, and I wave back, backin' out, glad I ain't the one getting' caught up wit' a buncha nude chicks 'n' hungover dudes stretched out all over the place. *It's a wrap. Luke's dead!*

28

Miesha

"Ooh, girl, them jeans are so cute," Fiona says walking up to me at my locker. She pats my butt. "And your booty looks so big 'n' juicy in them."

I snap my neck in her direction. Narrow my eyes. "Girl, you must want your jaw cracked. I don't know what kinda tricks you into, but I don't play those kinda games. Now touch me like that again, and see what I do to you."

She giggles. "Girl, please," she says, dismissin' me. "I like what I like."

"Well, I don't *like* being touched, especially by a chick." I slam my locker shut. "Do it again, and I'ma break your arm."

She laughs. "Girl, ooh, I love it rough. But, relax. I'm not into girls like that."

Ugh! This chick is so annoying. "Fiona, what can I do for you?"

"What's up with you and Tone? Seems like there's something brewing between the two of you."

I cut my eyes at her. I don't trust a chick who stays tryna grin up in my face. "I'm just having fun," I tell her.

"I heard that. And you're having fun with the right ones, too. Brent, Trevin, and Tone. Oooh, all the hot jocks at the school. Mmph, you know how to pick 'em, boo. Wait, what happened with Tone's boy, Justin?" She pulls her hair behind her right ear. I catch the sparkle of a diamond stud.

"What about him? I wasn't messing with him, if *that's* what you're getting at. Matter of fact, I'm not *messing* with any of those boys."

"Girl, no judgment here. Do you. 'Cause I know I do me. But, annnnyway, back to you and Mr. Fine-Fine-Fine. Girl, Tone is a catch. Good luck with snagging that one." She looks over her shoulder. "I'm not one to gossip, but, girl, whatever you do, be careful."

I frown. "Be careful? Of what?"

"Well, you didn't hear this from me. But Tone doesn't care about no one but himself. All he's gonna do is use you up, then dismiss you when he's gotten all he can, or when the next hot chick comes along."

"Mmmph, that sounds personal. Trust me, hun. I don't have that worry. Can't no boy use what I don't give him. So it is what it is. Now tell me this, since you handing out advice tips, have you slept with him?"

"Have I slept with who? Tone?" We round the corner and there's Quanda and that big linebacker girl, Sam the Man. "Mmmph, here goes trouble. Girl, whatever you do, just ignore those two. They're gonna talk slick to get you to go back at them so they can jump you."

I laugh. "Oh, trust, I stay ready."

We walk by Quanda and Sam the Man. They eye us. "I

should punch her in the back of the head," I hear Quanda say.

I look over at her and laugh. "And get ya face dropped, okay. Just because you gotcha bodyguard with you, don't think that'll save you from another beatdown, ho."

She starts getting all loud and extra with it, drawing a buncha unnecessary attention. Sam the Man says something slick, but I'm not really checking for her, so I'm not hearing jack she's saying. The only one I want is Quanda. Fiona tells Sam to mind her business. I'm surprised when big girl doesn't jump bad with her.

"You got lucky that day, trick," Quanda says. "But trust. There won't be a second time. You better watch ya face."

I'm not even about to go with the back and forth. I drop my book bag and get ready to charge her when someone snatches me from behind. It's Antonio.

"Get your hands offa me," I snap. "This dirty roach wanna stay popping her gums, so let me stomp her out."

"Nah, yo. You ain't fightin' her." He starts pulling me away. "Quanda, you crazy, yo. You need to chill for real. She done beat you down once already. What more is it gonna take?"

"I told you, Tone. If I can't have you, I'ma make it hell for anyone else to have you."

"Well, guess what, ho?" I snap without thinking. "I got him. I'm everything you'll never be. And now I got the one thing you'll never get back. Your man! Boom! Come see me, boo." Her face is cracked. She tries to run at me, but two security guards snatch her up. They drag her down to the vice principal's office.

"All right, ladies and gentlemen, get to class. The show's over," one of the teachers says, telling everyone to clear the halls. He looks over at Antonio. "Mr. Lopez, please tell me you're not the cause of this commotion."

"Nah, not at all," he says, flashing the teacher a smile. "You know I'm all about world peace, Mr. D."

"Good. And I expect that you will come in peace and ace your Economics test third period."

"I got you, Mr. Dangerfield."

Fiona walks over with my book bag. "Girrrrl, I thought I was gonna hafta peel back these press-ons and punch a ho up."

"Thanks for having my back," I say, taking my bag from her.

"Girl, please. It's what I do. Ain't that right, Tone?"

He laughs. "No doubt, baby." I shoot him a look. *How he gonna call this chick baby right here in front of me when he claims he's tryna get with me?* He winks at me. I roll my eyes.

"I don't know about y'all two lovebirds. And don't even act like y'all don't have *something* going on," she says, walking off. "But I'm going to hang out in metal shop with my boo Mr. Lester until the next period bell rings." I tell her I'll meet up with her later. Okay, *maaaaybe*, I might be wrong about her. Well, not about her being sluttish. But, about her not being someone I can hang out with. Maybe she's not just a pretty face after all.

"Yo, you know we mad late for homeroom," Antonio says, leading me by the arm down the hall, "so we might as well skip it and just wait for next period. The bell should be ringing in another"—he looks at his watch—"ten minutes. Let's go down to the library. I can get Mrs. Barney to hook us up with a pass."

I smirk. "Oh, really? So you just got all kinda hookups, huh?"

He grins. "Nah, not really. The only hookup I'm tryna get is wit' you."

"Yeah, whatever."

He waits until we get through the doors and down the first flight of stairs before he has me up against the wall, kissing me again. Ohgodohgodohgod. I can't do this with him. But his lips, his tongue. Everything in my body is on fire. I push him back.

"Boy, are you crazy? Tryna attack me in the stairwell like that."

He laughs. "Ain't nobody attack nothin', yo. Now tell me you didn't feel what I felt. That heat."

"I don't know what you're talking about, boy."

"Yeah, a'ight. So, what's up wit' you tellin' Quanda you got me, that I'm yours?"

"I just told her that to piss her off. I don't know what you did to that chick, but she's a real nut over you."

He sighs, opening the door for me when we finally get down to the first floor. "Yo, I don't know what she is. All I know is, *I'm* over her. I got my eye on someone else."

Before we even make it to the library, the second-period bell rings and kids start pouring outta classrooms into the halls.

I smirk. "Oh, really? And who might that be?"

"I'll tell you...."

"What's up, Tone? What it do, baby?" this extra-tall boy says, giving him dap. "You ready for practice today? Ya jump shot was kinda whack yesterday."

"Yeah, whatever, man," Tone says, laughing. "Get ya

footwork up first, son. You know I'm big daddy out on that court, yo."

He walks off.

"Now back to…"

Another interruption.

"Heyyyy, Tone," a voice calls out in back of me. I swivel my neck around to see who it is, then turn back to eye him. It's a dark-chocolate chick rocking orange leggings and a brown blouse that hangs off her smooth shoulders.

"Yo, what's up, Peaches?" he says, looking over my head to greet her.

I can tell just by the sound of her voice that she's all grins and giggles. "You, boo," she says, brushing past me. I let it slide. Hatin'-azz tricks 'n' hoes will always see me as a threat. Antonio peeps what she does and drapes his arm around me.

"Yo, you know my *girl?*"

I blink. His girl?

"Your girl?" the hatin' trick says.

Now I look at her. *"Yeah,* his girl."

"Oh, I know who you are," she says, fronting like she didn't know who I was from the dip. "You're that girl who beat up Quanda down at the park." She laughs. "Good for messy azz." She says something else to Antonio, then walks off.

"Oh, so you my girl now," he says, grinning as he holds the door back open so we can go back up the four flights of stairs.

"Well, obviously that's what *you* think. And stop looking at my butt."

He laughs. A group of dudes come running down the stairs. He pulls me into him. "Yo, what's goodie, Tone?"

one of the boys says, eyeing me. "We still hittin' the gym this weekend?"

"No doubt. I'ma hit you later."

"A'ight, bet."

This goes on all the way up to the fourth floor, one interruption after another. Seems like everyone knows this boy. Teachers stay speaking and smiling at him. Chicks stay waving and grinning. Dudes stay dapping him up. He waits until we turn the down the west wing hall toward English, then says, "So you mine, right?"

I laugh in his face. "Boy, boom. I'm just tryna piss off your girlfriend."

"Yeah, whatever, yo. That's not my girl."

"And neither am I," I say, walking into the room with him right on my heels, just as the bell rings.

"Oh, Miss Wilson, Mr. Lopez," Mrs. Sheldon says, eyeing us both, "isn't this special. So glad the two of you could make it on time."

I roll my eyes, taking my seat. *Old ratchet heifer!*

29

Antonio

"Yo, Pops," I say, walkin' into the livin' room. He hasn't been home in almost four days, and I'm glad to see him. He's kicked back drinkin' a Heineken, watchin' *NCIS*. "Can I holla at you for a minute, man?"

He reaches for the remote and lowers the volume on the flat screen. "Yeah, wassup?"

I take a deep breath, tryna steady my nerves. Pops 'n' I talk 'bout mad things, but there's always been one topic that never comes up. That whole thing 'bout love. I mean, like, does it really exist? I know it does 'cause I got mad love for my pops. But can a guy really love a girl? I ain't never been in love, or felt anything other than horny when I'm wit' a chick—or thinkin' 'bout her. But that's not what it is wit' Miesha. She's different, yo. And I'm not sure how or why. All I know is, I'm feelin' some kinda way and it's makin' me crazy. She's makin' me crazy.

I slip my hands into the waistband of my sweats. All of

sudden I'm feelin' mad nervous wit' him starin' at me. "What's on ya mind?"

I shrug. "Nah, it's nothin', man. Forget it."

He frowns. "Now how you gonna BS me, son? You think I don't know when something's wrong with my own flesh? You my seed, boy. You forget I've been takin' care of you since you were six years old."

I shift my weight from one foot to the other. "You right, man."

"Then what is it? No beatin' around the bush, either. You a man, so come at me like a man and tell me what's on ya mind?"

"Have you ever been in love?"

He makes a face that lets me know I've kinda caught him off guard wit' the question. Real rap. I know I'm comin' at 'im from outta left field askin' him this, but it is what it is. I need to know. And he's the only one I've ever gone to 'bout any-and-e'erything. He's the only person I've ever trusted to keep it a hunnid wit' me.

"Yeah," he says, chucklin'. "Wit' good lovin', boy. That's the best kinda love. And I've been in love wit' some fine women who had that good whammie-jammie. Had me all twisted up in the head every time I gotta taste."

I shake my head. "Nah, Pops. I'm not talkin' 'bout bein' in love wit' sex. I'm talkin' 'bout bein' *in love* wit' some-one."

He takes a swig of his beer, then sets it down on the cof-fee table. "Yeah, I've been in—what I *thought* was—love, twice."

"And how did you know you were in love?"

"You too young to be thinkin' 'bout love, boy. All love's

gonna do is kick you in the sack and have you all screwed up in the head. Take it from me, son. Stay away from it."

"But what if you can't? What if no matter how hard you try to avoid it, it sneaks up on you and finds its way into ya heart?"

"You don't let it. You know the rule. Real men don't get caught up in love, and especially not wit' one broad."

I walk over and sit on the arm of the chair across from 'im. "I know, Pops. You've drilled it into my head for mad long. But what if it just happens? What if you wake up and realize you feel something you've never felt for anyone else before?"

He shakes his head. "Then get ready for a buncha sleepless nights. Love ain't nothin' but a buncha heartache and pain. Who you goin' soft for?"

"It ain't that. I'm just askin'," I say, all of a sudden feelin' mad uncomfortable knowin' how he feels about catchin' feelin's for chicks.

"You askin' a buncha questions for someone who says he ain't in love. All you need to be concentratin' on is finishin' high school and not gettin' any of them hot-in-the-tail broads you got runnin' in and outta here all hours of the night knocked up. You have a bright future ahead of you, Tone. Don't eff it up. You hear me?"

"I got you, Pops," I say, walkin' over and givin' him daps. I feel more confused now than I did before I came down to holla at 'im. "Thanks for the talk, yo."

"That's what I'm here for," he says, reachin' for the bottle opener, then pullin' back the cap on another beer. He extends it to me. "You want one?"

I shake my head. "Nah, I'm good. I better head back up

and finish the rest of my homework." For some reason, I wanna hear her voice. I can't front. I can't stop thinkin' 'bout her. I reach for my cell, then dial her number.

"Yesssss," she answers—nah...hisses. And it sounds mad sexy, even if it is wit' a buncha attitude.

I sit back on my bed, restin' against the headboard. "Yo, wassup? It's Tone."

"Come again. You got the wrong number. I don't know no boy named *Tone*."

I shake my head, smilin'. "It's Antonio."

"Okay. How can I help you?"

"Aye, yo, why you always tryna play me?"

"*Play* you? Boy, puhleeze. I got better things to do than spend my time *playing* with you."

I grin, lookin' over at the poster of Beyoncé. I ain't gonna front. Bey has been wifey in my fantasies for a minute. But now Miesha has kinda taken up space in my head, replacin' whatever thoughts I mighta had 'bout snatchin' Bey up from HOV. Real rap, yo. I gotta have her.

"Yeah, a'ight, yo. That's what ya mouth says."

"And that's what it is. Now how can I help you?"

"I wanna see you, yo."

"Not gonna happen. I'm booked."

Hearin' her voice got me wantin' to light some candles, turn on some slow jams, then spark a blunt 'n' zone. She's really got me goin' through it. I squeeze my legs shut, then try'n take my mind off havin' her up in here stretched out in my bed, butt-naked.

"Yo, stop frontin' and let's go somewhere this weekend 'n' chill."

"I already told you. I'm booked."

"Then get *un*booked. I wanna chill wit' you."

It gets quiet on the other end. And for a minute I think she done banged on me. "Yo, you still there?"

"Yeah. I'm still here. My bad, I was doing something."

"A'ight. So wassup? We chillin' or what?"

"Well, I guess I can pencil you in," she says, teasin'ly.

"Nah, eff that, yo. Ink me in. I'm tryna be permanent. Better yet, yo. Put me in bright red marker."

"Uh-huh. Annnyway, if you wanna come by and watch *The Notebook, Dear John,* or *Titanic* with me, then maybe."

I frown. What the heck is *The Notebook?* Or *Dear John?* I know what *Titanic* is. Some old flick 'bout a poor dude who falls in love wit' some mad rich chick 'n' the boat sinks or somethin' like that. So I guess those other two flicks gotta be some kinda chick flick wit' a buncha love ish up in it for her to be bringin' them up 'cause that's the only kinda movies chicks stay watchin'.

"Nah, I'm good, yo. I'm not wit' them chick flicks."

She starts laughin'. "Relax, boy. I'm only messing with you. Those kinda movies I'd only watch with my man. Something you'll *never* be."

"Then what was all that slickness you was talkin' at school in front of Quanda?"

"Boy, that was jus talk."

"Yeah, whatever. Let's chill this weekend."

She gets quiet and I can tell she's thinkin' 'bout it. I ain't gonna front, yo. She's the first chick I've ever asked to take out somewhere. I mean *really* take out, like scoopin' 'em up 'n' kickin' out bread. Usually, broads take *me* out. I might meet a broad up at the mall and take her up to the food court to get a Happy Meal or a two-for-one combo, but to actually take her to a nice spot—to impress 'er. Nah, that's not how I do mine. But Miesha got me steppin' outta my box. There's somethin' 'bout her. Maybe I wanna taste them lips again. Nah, ain't no *maybe*. I want it, yo! And I want her.

"Yo, so wassup...we chillin' or what?"

"Not."

"You can front if you want, but I know you feel what I feel every time we kiss. I see it in ya eyes, yo. And I feel it in ya kisses."

"Boy, lies. I don't know what it is *you* feel or felt. But all I *felt* is you tryna shove ya tongue down my throat, tryna choke me. Not once, twice, but three times. Annnnnyway, why you calling me, again?"

I lower my voice. "I wanted to hear ya voice, yo."

"Oh, really? Why?"

I shake my head, realizin' this girl's not gonna make it easy for me. "Look, check it, ma. I don't know what it is 'bout you. But I'm tryna find out. I ain't tryna wife you up...*yet*. I know that ish you stay poppin' in school ain't 'bout nothin', *yet*. But, I'm def tryna see what's good wit' you. All I'm askin' is for one night of ya time. Then if you not beat, cool. If nothin' pops off, then it is what it is. No pressure, no worry."

"Mmmhmm. It sounds good. Oh, and don't think I didn't catch those *yets*, either. I keep telling you, you can't do *nothing* I don't let you, so all that wifing mess, save it."

"A'ight, a'ight. I got you. So, I'm sayin'...you gonna let me scoop you up this weekend or not? I'm tryna chill wit' you, yo."

"I don't know. Ask me again tomorrow."

"And if you say no, then what?"

She laughs. "Then, duh, keep asking. I gotta go."

"Yo, a'ight, but..."

"*But* nothing. Good night." And with that said, she hangs up. I plop back on my bed, starin' up at the ceilin' grinnin', hard. *She must not know who I am, yo....*

30

Miesha

"Hi, Daddy," I say the minute he picks up. I'm in my car on my way to school. Um, actually, I'm on my way to pick up Fiona first; then I'm heading to school. She texted me last night asking if she could catch a ride to school with me. I told her yeah. Whatever. I'm not sure what that chick's agenda is, but she stays pressing me to hang out, so I'm probably going to hang out with her one day after school—for a test run—to see how she really moves before I start making plans to doing anything else with her. She's cute and all. And she dresses fly. And she acted like she can go with the hands when Quanda and the Bodyguard tried to serve me. But I still don't know until I see her actually hook off. Like I said, being a pretty girl don't mean jack if you can't rock if some hatin' ho tries to bring it to you. And I ain't about to be fighting some other chick's battles. Oh, no, boo-boo. That's not what I do.

"Hey, baby cakes," Daddy says. "Is everything okay? I

don't have to come through the tunnel and yoke none'a them little jokers up, do I?"

I smile. "No, Daddy. I just wanted to hear your voice. And I wanted to ask you something. Are you busy?"

"I'm never too busy for my favorite girl. Hang on. Let me finish up this last entry. It'll take a sec."

"Okay." I glance at the flashing red light on my phone alerting me that I have a new message, either email or text. I switch screens while I wait for my dad to finish up whatever it is he's doing. It's a text.

Gm sexy. I'm askn again, yo. Let me take u out

I smirk, deciding to make him wait. I already know I'm going out with the boy, but shoot. A hot chick never comes off thirsty for a boy. Oh, no. We make them sweat it out. And if he can't wait it out, then *poof*...on to the next! He wasn't worth the time. But, okay, okay...I'm gonna keep it real. The only reason I really haven't told him yes yet is because I want to talk to my dad, first. Being around Antonio makes me nervous. He's too much like my dad. And I'm so afraid of getting all caught in him and his BS that I might start becoming a mini-version of my mom. And I can't have that. I *won't* have that.

"Baby cakes, you there?"

"Yes," I say, stopping at a light. I dig in my bag for my lip gloss, but come up empty. *Dang, I left it on the counter in the bathroom.* I stumble on the note Antonio slipped in my locker. I had forgotten about it. I finger the folded piece of paper.

"Sorry about that. Now, you have my undivided attention. What's on your mind?"

"Well, Daddy, I wanna ask your opinion on something."

"Okay, baby, I'm listening. Shoot."

"What if, hypothetically, you kinda like somebody, and you purposefully try to avoid them, but they keep coming around and pressing you? And the more they press you, the more you find yourself liking them and wanting to be around them even though you know they have a reputation of messing around with a lotta different people." Someone in back of me blows their car horn when the light turns green. I roll my eyes, blowing my horn back as I drive off.

"Well, that depends," he says. "Does this person have anything to do with you?"

"What if it's not me?"

"Then I'd say go for it, but proceed with caution. You know, keep your eyes open. And if something doesn't feel right, then cut it off."

"Okay, but what if there's something about this person that still makes you want to give them a chance. Do you follow your heart, or follow what's in your head?"

"Again, if this is about you and some knucklehead playboy, then you follow what you already know."

I laugh. "Daddy, he's not a knucklehead. At least I don't think he is. He's actually in all honor classes and plays on the basketball team."

He chuckles. "Oh, is that right? And he just happens to have a harem of girls chasing behind him?"

"Yeah, something like that." I sigh.

"Okay, and you still want to spend time with him?"

"I guess. I mean, yes. I just don't wanna play myself out either, you know? I mean, I know how he moves. And I swore I wasn't gonna be beat for any more boys like him. But there's something different about him, Daddy. I don't know what it is, but deep down, I think he has a good heart. I don't know. But I wanna find out if I'm right or wrong about him."

"So you really like him?"

I smile, stopping at another light. "Yeah, I do. But I haven't told him that I do. Or anybody else." I tell him about the fight with Quanda and what I told her I was gonna do. I stare at the note. *To Sexy You,* the front of the note says.

"So, basically it's really about you tryna piss another girl off because you know she doesn't like you, is that right?"

"Well, at first, yes. But now…" I shake my head as if he can see me through the phone. "I'm not so sure."

"Then what is your heart telling you to do?"

I open the note.

YO, STOP PLAYIN' GAMES!!!!! YOU KNOW YOU WANT ME. YES OR NO?!

I sigh. "To give him a chance."

"Then there's ya answer."

"Okay, thank you, Daddy." I turn down Bergen, then down Wilkerson. "I gotta go."

He laughs. "Oh, so that's how you do ya old man now. Pump me for advice, then dump me."

I laugh with him. "No, silly. I'm picking up this girl from school and don't want her all in my business. You know I love talking to you."

"I know you do, baby cakes. Are you coming to spend the weekend with me this weekend?"

"Umm, I think I might have a date this weekend. But definitely next weekend, okay?"

He laughs. "Okay, baby. So, does this knucklehead gotta name?"

"Daddy, he's really not a knucklehead. And his name's Antonio."

"Oh, a'ight. Well, you tell Antonio that if he steps outta pocket with you that I'ma be at his doorstep, ya hear?"

"Okay, Daddy," I say as I pull up in front of Fiona's house. I blow the horn. "I love you."

"I love you, too. And remember what I said. Don't do nothing that doesn't feel right."

"I won't," I promise, disconnecting just as Fiona opens the car door and gets in.

"Girrrrrrl, I'm so glad you pulled up when you did," she says, strapping herself in with the seat belt. "I thought I was gonna hafta go off. My mother was just about to take me there with her early morning BS. I mean, c'mon. She snapping over dishes in the sink from last night. Uh, *hell-looo,* boo-boo. If I washed up all the dishes before I went to bed and *you* wake up to find dirty dishes in the sink, whose fault is that? I mean really. What, I look like the dish patrol to her? I swear that woman stays PMSing year round. I told her she needs to get that situation checked. It makes no sense for her to be that dang evil all the time."

I sigh. *First thing in the morning and this chick is at it with the drama.* I'm relieved when she pulls out her Galaxy S3 and starts clicking away on the keys. "Oh my god, Bennnnnnji has. Got. To. Be. Kidding. Me. If he thinks I'm going to be okay with him inviting some skank he met on Facebook to the motel this weekend when she doesn't even have a face pic up on her profile or any other pics posted up on her Timeline or in her photo album.

OMG, who does that? And then she doesn't even have Instagram. Is he serious? What kinda dinosaur is this chick? Who doesn't have pics up of themselves on Facebook or an Instagram account unless they some kinda atrocious."

She waits until I stop at a light about five blocks away from the school. "Would you look at this?" She shoves her phone up in my face. "Look at that old raggedy avi on her Twitter page. Oh, she's definitely some kinda natural disaster." She quickly yanks the phone back before I can glance at the screen to see the chick's default display picture. Her fingernails rapidly click against the keys. "Girl, I'ma gonna use that phrase *boom* you say. Boy, boom!" she says, typing. "Wait until I get to school. Oh, I'm about to shut it down on his head."

I wish she'd shut up!

She rambles on the whole car ride, talking to herself or to her phone or maybe to the voices in her head because I haven't opened my mouth to say a word. The only thing on my mind is getting to school and seeing Antonio Lopez.

I pull out my phone when we get to another light. I text: U can take me out fri. pick me up @ 6 sharp!

By the time we get to the school, park, then get outta my car and start walking toward the building, Antonio's outside standing by the gate waiting for me.

"Awww, there goes ya boo," Fiona says, taking her eyes off her phone for half a sec to look around the parking lot.

I roll my eyes. "He's not my *boo*," I say, holding back a smile. *But he will be.* "We're just talking."

She cuts her eyes over at me. "Yeah, ohhhkay, if you say so. I see the way the two of you look at each other and so does everyone else."

"Excuse *you?* And what is it you and the rest of this nosey school *think* you see?"

She drops her phone into her bag, then takes a deep breath. "You smell that?"

"Smell what?"

"Love, boo. That's what I see. That's what everyone else sees." She looks toward where Antonio is standing. "That boy right there is in love, hun. Trust me. And you know I ain't one to gossip. But let me tell you. He has never, and I do mean *never*, stood by that gate waiting for anyone. Not even any of his boys."

"Yo, Fiona," Crispy Critter from my math class calls out. "Why you ain't hit me up last night, yo? You stay frontin'."

"Travis, *boom*. And you stay ugly, but you don't see me throwin' that up in your face, now do you?"

I have to laugh. She's extra with it, but she's a cool chick. And yeah, someone I think I can hang with. Maybe even bring her out to Brooklyn. Uhh, on second thought, nah, I better not. I think she'd wear Tre and them's nerves down. They'd be ready to rock her top.

Antonio grins. "So, it's official. Me 'n' you."

I roll my eyes. "Me and you going out, chilling. That's it."

He laughs. "Yeah, a'ight." He holds the door open for me. "You smell good, yo." He tries to grab me. "I just wanna eat you up, yo."

I slap his hands off me, laughing. "Boy, please. Hands off! You can look, you can sniff, but you can't touch."

He grins. "Oh, word? I can look 'n' sniff. Then let me see."

"Ugh. You're so disgusting," I say, heading for my locker as he walks alongside me. I glance down at his feet. He's rocking a fresh pair of wheat-colored Timbs.

"So, what you doin' tonight? You wanna chill?"

"Nope," I say, spinning my combination lock, feeling his eyes on me. "I'm busy." He puts his hand up on the door of my locker when I open it.

"Yeah, a'ight. Busy doin' what?"

Just as I'm about to reply, I see Quanda coming down the hall, eyeballing me hard. I decide to give her something to feel sick about. I grab Antonio's hand, slipping my small hand into his.

"Yo, you need'a stop."

I smirk. "Stop what?"

"Yeah, a'ight. Let me get a kiss."

Oh, this boy thinks he's slick. But anything I can do to rub salt in that trick's face is fine with me. I stop in the middle of the hall, cutting my eyes over at her as he leans in and kisses me on the lips.

31

Antonio

"**M**an, I asked Miesha out, yo."
I'm at Cease's crib, up in his room, playin' PS3.
We're in a serious battle, blowin' up buildings and bodyin'
mofos. Blood 'n' guts splatterin' e'erywhere. Cease's all
amped, yellin' out commands like he's in real combat or
somethin'. And it's kinda funny to watch. He just starts
zonin' out, like he got mofos really takin' orders from 'im.

"Say what? You did what?" Cease asks, pausin' the game
and peelin' his eyes away from the screen and lookin' over
at me. I repeat myself. "Oh, word? What'd she say, yo?"

"She said *yeah,* man. You know the honeys can't resist
me for long." I kinda laugh, half jokin', half serious. She
got me wantin' to put in a buncha work I ain't used to. But
somethin' tells me she's worth it. Still...it feels a lil crazy.

He gives me a look that I can't figure out. Like he's jud-
gin' me or somethin'. Or maybe it's shock. Not that it
should be 'cause he already knows how I do it.

"Daaaaayumn, son," he says, rubbin' his chin, "you ain't

waste no time tryna snatch that thing-thing up. So y'all kickin' it now? That tongue work musta been real right, for real for real, yo."

I grin, thinkin' back to how her lips felt. The warmth of her tongue. The way her soft hand felt on the back of my neck as she pulled me in to get more of me. How I grabbed her up when she tried to walk away and started tonguin' her down. Whew, feel myself startin' to sweat a lil. I gotta shift gears real quick to keep myself from gettin' all excited. The only chick I'm tryna check for at the moment is her.

Damn, that girl got me all twisted up.

"Yeah, man. It was a'ight." I don't tell him more 'cause I don't want him gettin' any ideas for himself. I mean, he's my boy 'n' all, but still... he don't need to know all the details. Not 'bout her. He looks at me like I'm two scoops from crazy. "Yo, get the eff outta here! Are you serious, yo? *You* asked *her* out. The dude whose idea of a date is a box of popcorn and a pack of Twizzlers followed by sex."

I chuckle, shakin' my head. "Yeah, man. Go figure, yo."

"Hol' up, yo. Have you ever really been on a date, *date?* Like actually pickin' up a girl at her crib, walkin' in and meetin' her parents, then bringin' her back before her curfew?" Of course he already knows the answer, but he ask it anyway. I tell 'im, "Nah." He plops back in his chair, droppin' his controls in his lap. "Damn." He shakes his head, rubbin' his chin. "This is big, son. You sure you know what you doin', yo?"

I laugh. "Yeah.

"One kiss and that girl got you wantin' to peel paper off on 'er. Man, she must have some sweet tastin' lips fo' sho. You must be really diggin' her."

"Man, real rap. I think she might be the one, yo." He stares at me wit' his mouth open, but he ain't sayin' nothin' 'cause he's waitin' for me to finish. "I can't explain it, yo. It's like when I see 'er at school I get this crazy feelin', fam. Like drums beatin' in my chest or somethin'. And when I hit 'er up and we're on the phone vibin', it's like I can't get enough of 'er. Time just flies, man...."

Cease busts out laughin'. And I can't help but to laugh too 'cause I'm soundin' mad sappy 'n' the shit comin' outta my mouth ain't even me. It sounds mad crazy.

Cease shakes his head. "Man, listen. Don't do it, yo. That broad's gonna rape ya pockets fo' sho. And you know you can't take her to no crazy spot, like Popeyes, either. She's sexy as hell, fam. And I can see why you snaked Justin to get at 'er..."

"Yo, hol' up, hol' up," I say, puttin' my hands up. "Pump ya brakes, fam. I ain't snake Justin, yo. I wouldn't do him or any of my boys like that."

"Uh-huh. But you did. Or at least that's how he sees it."

I frown. "Man, go 'head wit' that. I can't help how he sees it. I ain't snake him, yo. But is that how you see it? Keep it a hunnid, yo." I eye him, hard. I got mad luv for my boy. And I'd like to think he *knows* that that's not how I get down. I've never got at any chick he or any of my boys were rockin' wit', even the ones who were tryna throw me them panties behind their backs on the low.

"They weren't even really kickin' it like that."

"Yeah, but you knew he was diggin' 'er."

"Yo, c'mon, Cease. You already know, yo. If I *knew* they were really vibin' like that I woulda fell back, word is bond. And I did. But, yo, she came at me. I wasn't even thinkin' 'bout her like that. You saw how she tongued me

down all up in the cafeteria two weeks ago. I was chillin'
wit' y'all, yo. You think I knew that was gonna pop off? I
was caught off guard wit' that, yo. But I ain't gonna front
like I ain't glad it happened 'cause them lips were right.
Hands down, she's bad as hell."

"Yeah, man," he agrees. "But you know all that sexiness
comes wit' a price tag, yo. And it ain't cheap, feel me?"

I laugh. "I know I'ma hafta put some work in, and
spend a few dollars...."

"A few?" he laughs. "Good luck wit' that, yo. You better
try'a stack, yo. Or damn near close to it. She def doesn't
seem like the kinda chick who's gonna be cool wit' a meal
at the food court."

"Nah, yo. I've gotta 'nother spot in mind. But, yeah, you
right, man. I'ma def hafta spend some bread."

He nods. "So when you doin' this?"

"Friday night."

Now I'm feelin' like a chump for admittin' that ish. I
mean, Cease's my boy 'n' all, but tellin' him that she might
be the one, or that I'm really feelin' her, isn't how a player
like me gets down.

"Let me know how you make out wit' that, fam. Now
let's get back to the game so I can finish slaughterin' ya
men. Talkin' 'bout you only tryna hit that. Ha, yeah right!
Hit this, ninja!" He goes back to blowin' ish up, hollerin'
out commands. All I can do is shake my head 'n' laugh.

32

Miesha

At exactly six o'clock, I hear the doorbell ring. I'm standing in front of the full-length mirror checking myself out for the fifth time since I put on this outfit—a pair of black skinny jeans, a red blouse that crisscrosses in the front and ties in the back, and a pair of black six-inch wedge heels—ten minutes ago. It's my third time changing already. And I still can't get it right—my look, that is. Why going out with this boy has me so nervous is beyond me. It's not like he's the only fine boy I've ever gone out with. Still, there's something about him that has butterflies beating all through my stomach. Truth is, I've been half-nervous, half-excited about going out with him since he asked me out a few days ago. And it seems like the last two days just dragged by. But, still...I played it cute and acted like I wasn't beat for him, even when he tried to holla at me after class or if I saw him in the halls. I gave him minimal convo and kept it moving.

I turn sideways, stare at the way my jeans are hugging my butt, then smile. Boys love a girl with booty. And I know I have lots of it. I run my hands along the sides of my head, smoothing out my already perfect hair. I have it pulled back into a sleek ponytail. *Oh my god! I hate my forehead. I shoulda wore my bangs out.* My mom comes to my bedroom door just as I'm thinking about undoing my hair and letting my bangs sweep across this big forehead of mine.

"Miesha, there's a Tone here for you."

I glance over at her. "Okay. I'll be out in a minute."

"I didn't know you were going out with a boy tonight."

I shoot her a look. "Uh, yes you did. I told you two days ago that I was going out."

That's the problem. You never listen to me.

"I assumed you meant out with Mariah. Not out, like on a date."

"It's *not* a date."

She tilts her head. "Then what would you call it? You're standing in the mirror primping"—she glances around at all the clothes tossed around the room—"and changing clothes until you get the right look you want. That sounds like a date to me."

I shrug. "Well, it's not." She wants to know who Tone is. "Some boy from school. Why?"

"I'd just like to know whom my daughter's going out with, that's why.

"What grade is he in?"

I sigh. "Dang, Mom. He's a senior. And he's on the basketball team. Anything else you wanna know, go ask him yourself."

She lets my attitude go over her head, like most times.

"Well, date or not, from what little he's said, he seems like a nice enough young man."

"Yeah, I guess." I slide on a coat of cherry lip gloss, then pucker my lips, pleased with my finished look. My mom is still standing in the doorway, staring at me. "What?" I ask, peeling my eyes away from my reflection.

She smiles. "Nothing. I just can't get over how you're growing up. I can still remember the day I brought you home from the hospital like it was yesterday. You were the prettiest baby a mother could ever hope for."

She walks over to me. Turns me to face her with her hands up on my shoulders, looking me dead in the eyes. "I know we don't always see eye to eye. And I know I'm your least favorite person at times. But I love you. And you are so very beautiful. Don't ever forget that." She gives me a hug. And I hug her back. She takes a step back. Takes in my wears. "You look perfect. Don't change a thing."

I smile. "Thank you." I feel myself getting emotional. It's been a minute since she's said anything nice to me, or since we've gotten along. Lately, all we do is stay at each other's throats. I decide I had better enjoy it while it lasts.

"So where are the two of you going?" she asks, taking this lil powwow of ours to the left. I tell her I have no clue. "Well, wherever it is, I'm just glad to see you're getting out and finally making some friends here. I'll let you finish getting ready. Call it what you want, but I'll tell your *date* you'll be out in a minute."

She heads toward the door, then stops and turns around. "By the way, he's real cute. There's something about him that reminds me of your father." And with that, she's out the door, leaving me standing here with my mouth dropped open.

"So, where are we going?" I ask, sliding into the passenger seat of his Acura, then fastening my seat belt.

He grins, flipping through his CD collection. "You'll see when we get there. Tonight, I'm in charge. So sit back, relax 'n' let a man be a man. I got this."

I laugh. "Boy, boom. You only in charge 'cause I'm letting you *think* you are."

He turns his head in my direction. "Yeah, a'ight. Like I said, I'm in charge." I turn my head, looking outta the window, acting like I'm not tryna hear him. "What, you gotta attitude now?" He backs outta the driveway and heads for the highway.

I glance over at him. "Trust. If I had an attitude, you'd know it. I'm chillin'."

"Cool. That's what it is, baby. Daddy's got you."

I frown. "I'm not *your* baby, number one. And, number two, I already have a *daddy*. Thank you and good day."

He laughs, lickin' his lips all sexy-like. "You mad funny, yo. I dig that. But, yo, chill. Maybe I'm tryna make you my baby if you act right."

"Hahahaha, picture that. Now who's the funny one? I told you before you can't make me nothing I'm not tryna be. So you might as well..." My voice drifts as Trey Songz starts playing through the speakers. He's singing "Playin' Hard." I snap my fingers. "Oooh, this is my jam. Turn this up." I lift both arms up, snapping my fingers with my eyes closed. I sing along. "Yesssss..." He allows me to do my thing for the next two tracks.

When "Pretty Girl's Lie" stops playing, he looks over at me and grins. "Do you know how to love a man?"

I raise a brow. Tilt my head. My father is the only man I

love. Boys aren't worthy of my love. Well, I haven't met one who was. They've either lied or cheated or played games. So no. If a boy wants me to love *him*, then he had better *know* how to love me as well. But I don't tell him this. "I've never had any reason to."

He looks over at me. "I feel you. So what kinda dudes you into?"

I frown. "Why, you putting in an application or something?"

He smirks. "Nah. I already got the position. I'm just waitin' on you to recognize I'm as good as it gets."

"OMG, you are so full of yourself."

"Nah, I'm confident," he says quickly taking his eyes off the road. I stare at him. He's all dipped out in a black, long-sleeved Polo shirt, a pair of baggy jeans, and black and white Lebrons. A thick stainless steel chain with a single diamond in the center of a cross hangs from his neck. His black Brooklyn Nets fitted is cocked to the side, just right. Whew, his swag's on ten. He's too dang sexy for his own good. *But he's a dog*, I remind myself. I shake my head, igging his comment. He laughs. "What, cat got ya tongue?"

For the rest of the ride, we kinda let the music take us through it. I'm not sure where his mind is. And I don't care. But mine is up on the stage with Trey Songz being pulled into him, hip to hip. Another song finishes. I turn my head and stare outta the window, taking the ride in. He takes the Triboro to Bruckner Expressway and it's not until he gets off on exit 8-B that I realize where he's taking me—Sammy's Fish Box on City Island in the Bronx. My mouth waters.

"Umm, what you know about Sammy's, boy? This is my

spot!" I say excitedly, remembering how me and my girls would catch the number six train, then transfer to the B-29 bus to come out here and chill. Every Saturday we'd be out here popping mad ish to the cuties and getting our grub on.

He grins. "C'mon now. Don't sleep on me, ma. There's mad ish I know. Stick 'round 'n' I might show you a thing or two."

"Oh, puhleeeeze." I say, waving him on. He parks, then gets out and opens my car door. I am surprised when he reaches for my hand and holds it as we walk up to the restaurant. And I'm even more surprised when I let him. He opens the door for me. I have to admit he's being a real gentleman, even though I know he's looking at my butt as I walk ahead of him. I know he can't help himself. It's part of who he is, doggish. Once we're seated, he tells me to order whatever I want. Boom, boo, boom! You don't have to tell me twice. I order the Maryland Lump Crab Cakes for my appetizer, then the Tender Jumbo Shrimp stuffed with King Crabmeat. "And can I have a lemonade, please?"

Antonio stares at me. I ask him if he's okay. He nods. Tells me he's good, then orders the spicy buffalo wings for his appetizer, the Chicken Parmigiana for his meal and a Sprite to drink. I frown.

"What?"

I shake my head. "Umm, how you gonna come to a seafood spot and not order seafood?" He tells me he's not big on seafood like that. I shrug. "Mmmph. You don't know what you're missing, boy. They have the best seafood around, boo-boo."

He smiles. "Do you, ma. Eat up." While we wait for the

waiter to return with our drinks, we start talking about our plans after we graduate. I tell him I wanna be a fashion designer. That I'm applying to F.I.T., but really wanna go to Parsons. He smiles. "Yo, that's wassup. I can see you being the next *America's Top Model*, for real for real."

I laugh. "Oh, nooo. I'm not tryna model on anybody's runway. I plan on making the clothes to be *worn* on the runway."

"Oh, a'ight. That's wassup."

"What about you? What are you gonna do when you graduate?" He grins. Tells me he's gonna be a professional playboy, or try out for the Chippendales and be one of their dancers. I laugh. "So typical. I can see you doing that, too."

He laughs with me. "Right, right. But, nah. I'm only effen wit' you. I have a few schools looking at me for their basketball teams."

"Oh, for real?" He nods. Tells me Rutgers, Syracuse, Penn State, and Duke really want him. "Oh, wow," I say, impressed. "That's great!"

He nods. "Yeah. But I really wanna go to Morehouse in Atlanta."

"Then why don't you?"

"Can't afford it. My pops told me from the rip if I wanna go away to school outta state I'd have to get either a full academic or athletic scholarship. Otherwise, I'd hafta stay in state. I have a three-point-three grade point, and I scored an eleven-hundred on the SATs, but I don't think it's gonna be enough for a full academic scholarship, so I'm hafta ride it out playin' ball."

Oh my god. This boy's fine and *smart. Who woulda thunk it?* "Wow. So you're not a dumb jock who sits in the back of the class and has his groupies doing his homework for him after all," I tease.

He laughs. "Oh so that's what you thought I was? Some dumbo?"

I shrug, feeling kinda ashamed and silly for assuming. "Yes, I mean, no. I, uh..."

He keeps laughing, clearly amused at watching me fumble over my words. "Yeah, you all tongue-tied now. Admit it, yo. You *assumed* I was ridin' the short bus on four flats."

I lower my head. Embarrassed. "Oops. My bad."

He grins. "It's cool. Most peeps seem to think that 'cause I sit in back of the class 'n' goof off. But why you think all the teachers, especially Mrs. Sheldon, dig me?"

I shrug. "Let me guess. 'Cause you're conceited."

He laughs. "Nah, yo. Because I'm talented on and off the court. And that's fact. Not conceit."

I wave him on. "Whatever, boy."

"So, why'd ya parents move to Jersey?"

"Long story," I tell him, shifting in my seat. "But they split up."

"Oh, damn..."

"Yeah, tell me about it. But, it's whatever. They'll be back together." I say this, but the longer the clock ticks and the longer my mom stays away, the more I'm starting to think that this time she's not gonna go back to him. And I'm not really sure how I feel about it, yet. "So, what about your parents? They still together?" He shakes his head. Tells me it's just him and his dad. "Oh, wow. Where's your mom?"

"Dead."

I gasp. As much as my mom works my nerves, I can't

imagine not having her in my life. "Oh my god! I'm sorry to hear that. How old were you when she died?"

"Six."

Without much thought, I reach over and place my hand over his. The gesture is innocent enough, but feels...I don't know. Weird. I pull my hand back. "I'm so sorry. I can't imagine not having my mom around. It must be real hard growing up without yours."

He shrugs. "Nah. I'm good." He says this without blinking, without showing any kinda emotion. The way his brown eyes darken makes me think he's not as good as he says. But I know enough to not press it. He ain't my man. It's not my problem. And I ain't interested in turning this into a teary-eyed Lifetime series. So moving on. My stomach growls as the waiter returns to our table with a basket of bread. Enough of the chitchat. Right now, all I wanna do is eat.

33

Antonio

Yo word is bond, Cease wasn't lyin' when he said shorty was gonna run a hole through my pockets. I mean. Damn. I know I told her to order what she wanted, but shit...I ain't mean order the most expensive dishes up in this piece. She's killin' me, yo! The whole time we talkin' 'n laughin', I'm startin' to get mad nervous as I hear the lil cash register in my head goin' off. Real rap, the only thing I see is me comin' up short and havin' to spend the rest of the night scrubbin' pots 'n' pans 'n' mad dishes to settle the bill. And at the rate we goin', if I'ma bag 'er, I'ma hafta get me a job after school 'cause my allowance definitely ain't gonna be enough to cover e'erything. I only have a hunnid and twenty-eight dollars left and so far—wit' her appetizer and meal, she done already ordered close to sixty-five bucks. But I'm tryna play it cool, front like I drop this kinda paper winin' 'n' dinin' it up all the time. I know I ain't 'bout to let her know that she's the first chick I've ever dropped this kinda paper on. But inside, I'm like,

Who the hell spends almost twenty-two dollars on two lil ol' crab cakes? I thought chicks s'posed to order salad and water and front like they ain't really hungry. But, nah. Not Miesha, yo. She's tryna eat up e'erything in sight. But damn. She's sittin' 'cross from me lookin' mad sexy and I'm diggin' e'erything about her, so I'm just hopin' she leaves me at least enough paper for tolls to get us back home.

A few minutes later, the waiter brings us a dish of mixed olives and a fresh basket of bread, somethin' they call their famous white Crusty Mountain Bread, wit' some corn-bread and a wedge of cheese. I ain't ever had cornbread served wit' cheese and I'm thinkin' I'm not 'bout to try it now. I'ma wait for my wings 'n' chicken parm to come through. So I sit back and watch Miesha grab some bread, then bite into it.

Real rap, I'm glad she's preoccupied wit' stuffin' her face instead of pressin' me 'bout my moms bein' dead. That's a subject I don't like to think, or even talk, about. She's gone, period. So there's nothin' sittin' 'round talkin' 'bout it can do to change that. And I ain't beat for thinkin' 'bout what-ifs either. Wonderin' 'bout what if she was still here ain't gonna do nothin' for me now. She ain't ever gonna come back and that's that.

"Antonio, sweetheart. Mommy loves you so very much. You are my pride and joy....No matter what, Mommy will always love her little handsome prince...."

I blink. Bring my attention back to this cutie in front of me. Her mouth is stuffed wit' bread. I stare as she chews, imaginin' what her mouth would feel like on my...

"So, is this s'posed to be a date or something?" she finally asks, stompin' out my freaky thoughts.

"Nah," I say, smirkin', "it's a mad cool dude chillin' wit' a hella sexy dime-piece, gettin' our grub on 'n' gettin' to know one another. Why, you want it to be?"

She smirks back, slowly shakin' her head. "Nope, not at all."

"Cool. Then we good," I say, shiftin' in my seat. For some reason I feel mad nervous bein' 'round her. I feel like I gotta think before I open my mouth to speak in case I say some off-the-wall ish. This ain't me, yo. I always know how'ta flow wit' the ladies, but she got me feelin' like a straight-up square. I lick my lips watchin' her lick her fingers. I wanna tongue 'er down 'n' sex 'er up, but I know comin' at 'er all sideways 'n' crazy ain't gonna cut it. Real rap, shorty got me all off my game. I swallow. The waiter returns wit' our drinks, and appetizers, then bounces. "So what time's ya curfew?" I ask, hopin' we ain't gotta gobble up our food, then run up outta here all fast 'n' crazy. Truth is, I don't wanna rush the night.

"I don't have a curfew," she tells me, placin' a crab cake on her plate. She cuts into it wit' her knife. "I can stay out as long as I want."

"Oh, word?"

She places a forkful of her crab cake into her mouth, slowly chews, then says, "Yeah. I do what I want. I'm grown."

"Yeah, a'ight. That's what ya mouth says." I rip into my spicy wings. And they got the nerve to be good as hell. Word is bond! "You prolly still get beatin's."

She laughs. "Ha! Never that. You the one probably still getting whooped up on." I laugh. Tell 'er I've only been beat twice that I can remember. She tells me her moms stayed beatin' her butt 'til she turned ten.

"Oh, word? Why'd she stop?"

"'Cause she got tired of chasing me around the house and hurting herself in the process. I wasn't the type to just stand there and get whooped. If she wanted to get it in, she had to work for it." She starts laughin'. "By the time she would catch me, she'd be all banged up from tripping and falling, and too tired to do anything but sit her butt down somewhere."

I laugh, shakin' my head. "So you like bein' chased, huh?"

She takes me in. Damn, she's so effen sexy, yo. The way she's starin' at me got my thermostat on high. She's got me on fire. "I like not getting caught," she says, runnin' her fingers through her hair, then tossin' her head.

We both just kinda stare at each other, then get mad quiet. We start eatin', smackin' our lips, 'n' lickin' our fingers. Not sayin' jack. E'ery so often she's eyein' me and I'm eyein' her back. I can tell she's feelin' me, too, by the way she's checkin' me. Even if she is frontin' like it ain't no biggie, I know she's diggin' me. All I gotta do is play it cool 'til I get her to fall, then it's game on. I lick my lips. I gotta go to the bathroom, but I can't get up 'til I can calm myself so I don't have her and e'eryone else lookin' at me mad crazy when I stand up. But I know it's gonna be hard—uh, no pun intended—to be 'round her the rest of the night and *not* be excited.

"So why you ain't got a man?" I ask, shiftin' in my seat, tryna shake all the freaky images runnin' through my head. I take a sip of my soda.

"Uhhh, same reason why *you* don't have one. I don't want one." She raises her brow, pointin' her fork at me. "Uhh, unless you already have one."

She says this as I'm takin' another sip of my drink, causin' it to go down the wrong pipe. I start coughin' 'n' chokin'. Soda gushes outta my nose and burns my nostrils. She got me chokin' hard. My eyes start waterin' from all the coughin'. She starts laughin', then asks if I'm okay. When I nod that I am, she patiently waits for me to pull myself together, then asks, again, if I'm all right.

"Yeah, I'm good," I say, wipin' my nose wit' a napkin. I grab two more napkins and wipe my eyes. "Damn, you tryna kill a mofo. But to answer ya question..."

"It wasn't a question. It was a statement."

"Well, to comment on your statement. *Hell naw*, yo. I don't want no dude, or have one! That ain't my flavor. I don't knock anyone else's flow, but that ain't me."

She smirks. "If you say so."

I frown. "Yo, what's that s'posed to mean? If I say so? That's what it is, yo. Don't clown me."

She rolls her eyes up in her head. "Whatever. I was only playing with you. Loosen up."

"Nah, don't play like that. If you wanna *play* with me, I can give you a *whole* lot more of somethin' to play wit' and can loosen *you* up and put a smile on both our faces."

She balls up a napkin and hits me in the chest wit' it. "You're so disgusting. Is sex all you think about?"

Oh, boy. Here we go, again, wit' this question. I don't know why chicks stay askin' me this when they should already know the answer. I'm a dude. Of course I always think about it! "Sometimes it is," I say, grinnin'. "Other times, I only think 'bout it once or twice a day."

She wants to know how many chicks I've smashed and if I use condoms.

"My numbers are up," I tell 'er, not to go into specifics. "And, no doubt. I stay strapped."

She raises her arched brow. "How many baby mamas you have?"

I frown. Shift in my seat. I tell her none. Tell her that I'm not beat for kids. Not now anyway. "So you've never gotten a girl pregnant or had an STD from all the sexing you do?"

Tiffany's voice plays in my head. *"I'm pregnant. And I'm keeping it."*

"Nope," I push out, pickin' up the last wing on my plate and cleanin' it down to the bone. She eyes me like she half-believes me, but I don't say nothin' more since it's the truth. "No diseases, and no babies, yo. I told you, I stay wrapped. Well, except when I'm gettin' topped off. And she can't get pregnant doin' that."

She frowns. "Umm, newsflash, boo-boo: She may not get pregnant, but *you* can *still* catch a disease from her doing *that*."

I know this broad ain't tryna sit here 'n' hit me wit' no sex-ed crap, like I don't know that. But I ain't 'bout to wrap up for that. Brain 'n' condoms just don't mix for me. It's not the same. "Yeah, I know. But I don't mess wit' no dirty broads, yo. I'm mad selective."

"Mmmph. Selective or not. She doesn't have to be *dirty* to have a disease, and give it to you. If you gonna play, then you need to stay safe. I'm just saying. But, hey, do you."

"No doubt. What about you? You always play safe? Who you toppin' off?"

She sets her fork down on her plate. "First of all, I'm

not toppin' *any*one. Second of all, not that it's any of your business, but *when* I play I *always* play safe."

I grin. "Oh, a'ight. That's wassup. So I ain't gotta worry 'bout no crazy baby daddy tryna come at my neck then."

"Not hardly," she says, grabbin' another biscuit, then bitin' into it. She gotta few crumbs on her lips and I ain't gonna front. I wanna lean over and lick 'em off. I gotta pump the brakes before I start gettin' myself all worked up again. I ask her if she's ever been seeded up.

She frowns. "What in the world? *Seeded up*? Ugh! That sounds disgusting. Never that. For one, I'm not tryna have nobody's kids. And, two, I'm not tryna have my body all jacked up. Anything else you wanna know."

"Yeah. When's the last time you had *some*?"

"Had some *what?*"

"You know, good lovin'?"

"Okay, I'm done." She raises her hand up, flaggin' the waiter. "Check, please. It's time to go."

I laugh. "Nah, nah. C'mon, chill. I'm just tryna get to know you, that's all."

She narrows her eyes. "No, what you wanna know is if I'ma let *you* get *some*. That's what you fishing for. Keep it real."

"Nah, I ain't on it like that, yo. I'm just askin'...."

"Asking *what*, if I'm a slut-bucket?"

I laugh. "Nah. You mad funny, yo. I know you ain't doin' it like that."

"Uh-huh. How you know?"

"I don't."

"Exactly. You don't. But I'm not. Now, *chaaaaanging* the subject. What kinda TV shows you watch?"

I shake my head, laughin'. I dig 'er style. I ain't even gonna front.

"Well? I'm waiting."

I tell 'er I'm big on shows like, *NCIS, Criminal Minds, Law & Order: Special Victims Unit, Nikita, Dexter, The Amazing Race*, and *Survivor*. She tells me she's big on them whack reality shows like *The Housewives of ATL*, that Keisha Cole joint, and *Basketball Wives*.

"And I stay clicked on *Project Runway, America's Next Top Model*, and *Scandal* with Kerry Washington. That's my girl."

"Yeah, she can get it," I say.

"Annnyway. I looooove Kerry's character, Olivia Pope. She's strong, determined and knows how to handle her scandal."

I smile.

"What?"

"You mad pretty, yo." She blushes, smiles back. "Thanks. Now finish your food so I can order dessert."

I blink, hopin' she's playin', but she isn't. And I hope like hell she don't order the most expensive thing on the menu. But when we finish our meal and the waiter finally comes through, she does just that. Almost eight dollars for a slice of red velvet cake! What kinda ish is that?! *Man, this chick's tryna drain me. And I ain't even gonna get to hit it. Broads!*

34

Miesha

"Yo, I had'a real nice time wit' you tonight," Antonio tells me as he's pullin' up in my driveway.

"Yeah, I had an *okay* time with you, too. I didn't have to cut you," I say jokingly. Truth is, I really, really, really had a nice time. Even though I feel kinda bad for ordering up all that stuff and spending his money like that. And, yeah, I was doing it tryna be funny. Heck, I didn't even eat all of it. But he didn't flinch or complain, so I guess it was all good. Well, he paid the bill without breaking a sweat so it must'a been. Anyway . . . He's not as conceited as I thought he was. I mean, yeah, he's cocky with it. But it's more like he has a buncha confidence. Like me. *But he's still a dog!*

He laughs, putting the car in park. He shifts his body toward me. "Oh, word? Just *okay*, huh?"

I keep from grinning. "Yup. But you're not as bad as I *thought* you were, either."

"Oh a'ight. That's wassup. So that means we can chill again tomorrow night, then."

"I'm booked," I lie.

"Yeah, a'ight. What about next weekend? Friday, Saturday, *and* Sunday?"

I eye him. Sweet Lawdy, he's too effen cute! *But he's no good, girl.* Like my granny would say, "He's rotten right down to the core. Even the worm don't want 'im, chile." I almost laugh at the thought of her saying that about him.

"I don't think so," I say, shifting in my seat. He wants to know why. "'Cause I still think you're mad trouble."

He places his hand up over his heart like he's been crushed. "Ouch, girl. Cut me deep, why don't you?"

I shrug. "I'm just saying. Like I told you before, I know your kind. And I'm not interested."

He sighs. "Damn, yo. We still on that? I thought we moved past that already."

"No, *you* moved past it. *I* never left it. I think you got too much going on. And I don't need the trouble, or the headache."

He grins. "Nah, yo. I'm good trouble. Good lookin', good body, good lover...I'm all 'round good, ma—true story. And I got somethin' for ya headache, too."

"Ohhhhhmiiiiiigod, you are so full of ya'self, boy." I open the car door. "Thanks for the meal. It's been real. But I'm out." He jumps outta his side of the car coming over to me.

"Ninja, *boom!* What you doing?" I ask, stepping back, placing a hand on my hip.

He shakes his head. "Chill, ma. Put the claws in. I'm tryna be a gentleman, that's all. I'm only walkin' you to the door."

I roll my eyes, laughing. "Boy," I say, pointing toward the house, "the door's right here in front of us." I reach inside my bag for the keys. The house is dark. Not one light on. A mess. I already know Mariah went to Connecticut for the weekend with her boyfriend so she wouldn't be here. And I know my aunt is in Atlantic City. But I kinda thought my mom would be here. *Mmmph. I bet she ran off to Brooklyn. She wouldn't let me go, but I'll bet you that's where she is. All pressed up, lip-locking it up with Daddy.* Now I'm kinda pissed that I'ma have to stay pressed up in this hellhole, alone.

Antonio grins, placing his hand on the small of my back as we walk up the driveway. "Maybe a brotha's really diggin' you and ain't tryna see the night end."

I remove his hand. "Well, *maybe*, all good things gotta come to an end." *I can't believe she's not even home! She coulda at least sent me a text or called to let me know she wasn't gonna be here.*

"Yo, not *all* good things gotta end," he says, stepping up into my space. I step back, backing into the door. He looks down at me, slowly pulling in his bottom lip. I try not to look too long at him. But it's real hard not to when he's practically all up on me. "Yo, real rap, ma. You sexy as hell. I don't know what it is 'bout you, but I ain't gonna rest 'til I figure it out, yo." He leans in to kiss me, but I shut it down. *Don't do it, boo! Stick to the script!*

"Oh, really?" I stop him with the palm of my hand pressed up on his chest to hold him back. "Well, the only thing you should be tryna figure out is your way back home. So good night, boo."

He starts laughing. "Yo, you got that. I'ma bounce. But I'm sayin'." He makes this cute little sad face, poking his bottom lip out. "You really want me to dip?"

"Yes, Antonio."

"Can I come in, yo?" he whispers, tempting me with his lips as they glide their way down my ear, my neck, and all along my collarbone. He's driving me...wild.

But I'm not goin' there with him, not tonight. I push him away, shaking my head. Not because I don't wanna let him in, but because I need to let him know he can't manipulate me with his sexy grin and those lips that are practically causin' me to melt.

"Good night, Antonio," I say, quickly pushing open the door and slamming it in his face, before he can change my mind.

He groans on the other side of the door. "Ugh! You killin' me, yo. This ain't over, yo. I'ma be back tomorrow for you. Be ready by three, yo."

I press my back up against the door, holding back a giggle.

O-M-G, I can't believe this is the first weekend that I've been in Jersey and I haven't wanted to be in Brooklyn and hang out with my crew. I've had so much fun it's insane. I've been out with him *all* day. He came at the time he said he would and we drove allllllll the way down to Pier Point—this South Jersey beachfront town that has a strip of casinos, shops and restaurants—where we walked along the boardwalk, laughing and talking, then finally taking off our shoes and going down onto the sand and walking along the edge of the water, letting it splash up against our feet. I couldn't believe how cold the water was, even though it was warm out today. But it felt good. So did being with him.

We walked through some of the casinos, and watched all these fools gamble up their money, probably their life savings tryna hit it big. Then we played a buncha games at the arcade before going out one of the piers where they have a buncha amusement park rides. We rode the Ferris wheel and a few other rides, and I watched Antonio shoot hoops and win me two cute, cuddly teddy bears. "Now you have something to cuddle when I'm not around," he said, his lips on my ear as he squeezed my hand.

I rolled my eyes at him, but inside I was cheesing, hard. Then we went into Ripley's Believe It or Not and took a buncha pictures, goofing off. And finally, we walked to Trump Plaza and ate at Rainforest Café. That was kinda cool since I had never eaten there before. And seeing all the live tropical fish, all the animated wildlife, and hearing the cascading waterfalls made it feel like you were really in a jungle. I can't lie. Going to Pier Point was really fun. I mean, it's not like being on Coney Island, but it was still fun. Different.

I glance at my watch as we finally pull up into my driveway. It's only midnight. The ride home seemed so much quicker than the ride going down, maybe because there wasn't as much traffic coming back. I kinda wish we were still on the Parkway stuck in traffic. Crazy, right? At least then, the night wouldn't have to end.

"So does *this* count as a date?" Antonio asks, shuttin' off the engine. He leans in toward me, his hand on my thigh.

I smirk. "Maybe."

He laughs. "Yeah, a'ight. Why you stay stylin', yo? Keep it a hunnid. You dig givin' me a hard time, don't you?"

"Lies," I say, smiling. "I do no such thing."

"Yeah, a'ight. Yes, you do. I bet you get off on it, too."

He leans in closer. "Can I get some'a them sexy lips?"

"Good night, Antonio," I say, climbing outta his car.

"Thanks for the...*date*. I had a lotta fun." I smile at him when I tell him this.

He quickly gets outta the car. "C'mon, yo. It's mad early. I don't wanna go home, yet. Let's chill some more."

I eye him. "Well, you ain't gotta go home, boo-boo, but you can't get up in here. Not tonight."

He looks up at the house. "I'm sayin', though. It's lookin' mad dark up in there. Don't look like anybody's home. I think maybe you should let me go in wit' you so I can make sure e'erything's good. Or you can just come back to my crib 'n' chill wit' me."

I raise my brow. Narrow my eyes.

"Nah, I ain't tryna be on no freaky trip wit' you, real rap." He grins. Crosses his heart. "Scout's honor, yo. I told you last night, I'm bein' a gentleman. *All* weekend, even if it kills me, yo."

I laugh. *Girl, just go on and chill with this boy. It's not like you have anything else better to do.* "Then it should be a very sloooow death. 'Cause trust and believe, if I let you up in here you're *not* getting any."

He grins, rubbing his chin. He steps up into me. "Can I at least get a kiss?"

I push him back. "Nope."

"A'ight, a'ight. How 'bout some milk 'n' *cookies*? I'm hungry."

I laugh. "Oh, you think you slick. You won't be getting any cookies from me, boy."

He laughs with me. "Nah, I'm sayin'. I'm hungry. *Real* hungry."

The way he says that makes me think he's talking about more than just food. I smirk. "Uh-huh. I bet you are."

He licks his lips. "C'mon, yo. I know you got some

warm cookies up in there I can nibble on." Oooh, he's so dang sexy!

I grin. I can feel him practically all up on my booty as I slip the key into the lock and open the door. "Can you dance?" I ask over my shoulder. I decide to have some fun with Mr. Antonio Lopez.

He gives me a confused look. "Huh?"

"Can you dance?" I repeat, stepping through the door. He's right in back of me, pushing the door shut as I spin around to face him. He tells me, "Yeah, I can dance. Why you ask me that?"

"Beat me in a round of *Dance Central*, and you can have all the milk *and* cookies you can handle."

He laughs. "Oh, word? *Dance Central*? You think you want it wit' me?" he busts a move, pumping his hips. "Yo, this is gonna be like snatchin' candy from a baby. Don't you know I'm the king of dance moves? *Dance Central* is my ish, yo. But if you tell anyone, I'ma hafta snap ya neck, for real for real."

I laugh with him. "Uh-huh. That's what your mouth says. We'll see." I tell him to follow me. We walk through the living room, through the kitchen, then down the stairs into the basement where Aunt Linda's family room is. She has a sofa, entertainment center, and flat-screen TV, along with an Xbox and PS3 game stations. He wants to know what happens *if* by some chance he loses. "Oh, you will lose, boo-boo. And when you do, you'll be tossed up outta here with *no* milk…and definitely no warm *cookies*."

"A'ight, yo," he says, pulling off his shirt, and kicking off his kicks. "That's what it is." I try not to stare at his chest or his arms, or the way his wife beater wraps around the ripples of his abs. I look down at his long, socked feet, and back up at him as he rubs his hands together. "Let's do this. Let me see what you got for me, ma?"

I click on the TV, turn on the Xbox... and let the games begin!

"Nah, you cheated, yo," he says after I rip the dance routine to 50 Cent's "In Da Club." We're both sweating and outta breath from dancing all hard, tryna keep up with the graphics. I can't even front on this boy; he got moves... along with his game. But I still slayed 'im.

"Cheated nothing. I stomped you out fair and square, boo-boo. You saw it. Flawless, boo. Face it. I won. You lost. And it was a song *you* picked. Hahaha."

"Nah, I wanna 'nother round, yo."

I laugh. "OMG! I can't believe I have the one and only, Mr. Antonio Lopez, school playboy, up in here begging for me to whoop him in *Dance Central*. Oooh, I wish I could get this on video. I'd have it all up on Facebook, YouTube, and Instagram."

"Oh, word? So you'd really do me dirty like that?"

I crack up inside at the thought of seeing this sexy hunk on video. "Yup. I sure would. And I got just the song for you." I select "Cupid Shuffle" by Cupid. "It's all you, boo-boo."

"A'ight. Get ready to feed me that milk 'n' them cookies, yo, 'cause I'ma 'bout to do my thing...." I bust out laughing at him walking it out, then right kicking it up. He's killing it. But I ain't gonna tell him that. "Oh, you think this is funny, huh? I'm the king of the shuffle, yo." Who woulda thunk Mr. Smooth was mad cool and fun? *Mmmph.* Definitely not me.

The next round, he tries to be funny and picks some

old dusty eighties song, "Let the Music Play." "Oh, see. You tryna be funny."

He laughs. "Nah, yo. Do you."

"Whatever, boy," I say, flipping him the finger. "It's all good. I'm still gonna kill it." As soon as the music starts playing, I go into my routine. "Ha! Flawless! You see that? You ain't ready, boy!"

"Nah, eff that, yo," he says, blocking the screen. "Yo stay tryna cheat."

I laugh. "You stupid. How am I cheating? All I'm doing is keeping up with the dance moves, and serving it up. Bam! *Flawless!* Ha! *Flawless!*"

He jumps in front of the TV, blocking my view.

I push him outta the way. "Move, boy. Let me finish, so I can toss you outta here...."

He laughs. "Nah. I ain't leavin' 'til I get them cookies, yo." He grabs me, then starts dancing, shimmying his shoulders and we both start acting a fool. Dancing and laughing. I bump him outta the way with my hip; he grabs me and starts tickling me. Then something changes. We start wrestling around. I hook my foot around his ankle, knocking him off balance. He hits the floor, pulling me down with him. We start rolling around on the carpet. Both laughing and tryna catch our breaths. I am on top of him. Then I don't know what happens. I mean, maybe I do. No, I do know what happened. He's looking at me. His hands are on my waist, then my butt. He squeezes. And before I can stop myself, I am kissing him. And he is kissing me back. I feel his hand under my shirt. I can't remember when he slides it up there, his hand on my boob. His lips pressed against mine.

Oh god! What in the heck am I doing? What if this boy tries to go all the way? Oh my god! And what if I let him? It's been soooo long since I've made out with a boy. And the heat from his hands and his kisses is burning me up. I'm on fire. I try to pull away. Try to get up off him. But he has the nerve to pull me back into him and kiss *me*. And I kiss him back. And flashes of that first kiss, where our tongues danced and swirled right there in front of the whole lunchroom, flood my mind. Everything inside of me started to tingle that day. I almost lost myself in that kiss, like now, in his strong, muscular arms. There's no telling what I would have done if I hadn't pulled away and run up outta there, fast. I've tried to not think about that day, or the other times he's kissed me. I try not to think about him. But I do. And here we are, again.

Lip-locking it up.

Me on top of him.

His hands all over me.

And like that day in the cafeteria where it was like neither of us cared who was looking or what they were thinking, I am feeling things about this boy that I've never felt for any other boy. And that scares me. Making out with Antonio feels...good. No, great!

He's no good.

He's a player.

He's only out for one thing.

I know all of this, but I don't care. I want more. I want him.

His eyes have become dreamy slits of dangerous what-ifs. What if I let him? What if I want it? What if I can't stop myself?

"Wait, wait...I-I...w-we..." I'm panting. He's panting. "...gotta stop..."

"Nah, yo," he pushes out, his hands still places I know they shouldn't be. "Let me get them cookies."

We keep kissing.

35

Antonio

"How come you don't ever talk about your mom?" Miesha wants to know, lifting her head up from my chest. We're lyin' up in my room, listenin' to one'a Pops's old-school mix tapes wit' different love songs on it. This dude Lenny Williams is singin' 'bout how much how he loves some chick. I played this CD wit' other girls in my bed, but ain't never really listen to the words. But, tonight ...lyin' here wit' Miesha in my arms, I really hear the lyrics. I *really* feel his pain. And I'm like, *Wow. He really poured his heart 'n' soul out to her. He really loves her.* And I realize, that's the kinda love I want. That's the kinda love I think I can have wit' Miesha. Real rap.

It's been two weeks, three days, and fifty-five minutes since our first date, even if that's not what she wanted to call it. That's what it was for me. That's when somethin' changed for me. But whatever. We've been spendin' mad time together, for real for real. And I ain't bored wit' her, yet. Real rap, I don't even think I can ever get bored wit' her even if I tried. She checks me real quick. And keeps me on my toes. And she doesn't let me have my way when I want it. I ain't gonna front. Sometimes it's kinda frustratin' like when I'm tryna get some from her 'n' she keeps puttin' me off. Yo, I ain't used to not havin' some kinda sex on the regular. At least three times a week, even when I want it e'eryday. But she's makin' me wait. I mean. Damn. She ain't passin' off on nothin'. And it's slooowly killin' me, yo.

"Boy, be clear," she snapped last night when I was hoverin' up over her tryna undo her pants. She kept pushin' my hand away and finally told me to get off 'a her. And I did. "I'm not gonna be some easy lay for you. Oh, no, hun. You got the wrong one."

"A'ight, Miesha. I got you," I said, sighin' in frustration. I stood up. "You see what you got me goin' through, yo? You really tryna give a brotha blue balls."

"Well, be glad you not getting you a batch of blue waffles."

I frowned. "Oh, you got jokes. That's some nasty ish, yo. Let me get ya waffles, yo." I grabbed her, tryna press up into her. "I'm achin' for you."

She laughed, spinnin' outta my arms. She glanced down, then back up at me, tryna keep her eyes off my, uh, excitement. Real rap. She really makes it hard to stay focused. "And you gonna keep on aching, boy." She walked over and picked up her lace bra on the floor, then put it on. "If what we do isn't enough for you, then maybe this isn't for you."

"Yo, c'mon, why you buggin'? Take that off," I coaxed, pullin' at it. "I'm cool wit' what we do. But, I'm sayin', yo. It's hard." I glanced down. "Really, really hard."

She rolled her eyes. "You stupid, boy."

"C'mere, girl." I pulled her in my arms and started kissin' her. "Where you think you goin', yo?"

"Home. I'm not..." I covered her mouth with mine. I wasn't tryna hear it.

"You ain't goin' nowhere, yo. It's mad early." She stood there staring at me all sexy 'n' whatnot, then gave in after a few more kisses. Word is bond, yo. I ain't ever think kissin' a girl could have me feelin' some kinda way. I never thought just lyin' up in bed, holdin' a girl could feel so good. Right. Perfect. But it does. All of it, with Miesha.

It's like ish is too good to be true. That I really met a girl I'm diggin'. Not for what I can get outta her, or for what I think she can do for me, but for *who* she is. And, yeah, I ain't gonna front. I wanna tap that, bad. But, it ain't the only thing I want from her. I want her love, yo. And I wanna love her back.

I haven't loved any other female since...

"Or have any pictures of her in your room," she continues. Her eyes are locked onto mine. *Because my pops said she was dead, so we had to leave any memories of her behind. We had to bury them. And bury her.* Of course I ain't gonna tell her all that. But I feel like I gotta tell her somethin'. She's like the first girl who really even asked me 'bout her. That woman. The one who walked outta me 'n' Pops's life.

"We don't ever mention her again, you understand? Anyone asks, you tell 'em she's dead...."

I take a deep breath, shifting my eyes from her gaze. "There's nothin' to talk about."

She rubs my chest. Then turns my head back to her.

She's lookin' at me in a way no other girl has. Wit' care. "What was she like? You know, before she died?"

"I really don't wanna talk 'bout her," I say, feelin' myself startin' to drown in things I'm not tryna remember. My past. My fears. I shift my body so she's no longer lying on me so I can sit up. "Can we talk 'bout somethin' else, yo?"

"I don't mean to pry," she says, all soft 'n' sexy. And the way she says it as she's lookin' at me wit' them dreamy eyes is makin' me feel...I don't know—weak, like I'ma 'bout to crumble or some ish. Miesha's really tryna pull me back to someplace I ain't tryna go. Someplace dark. And lonely. She leans over and kisses me on the cheek, then lightly on the lips. "I just wanna know everything about you."

I smile, leanin' in 'n' kissin' her. I just wanna block it all out. Push back the thoughts. Push back the pain 'n' anger, yo. Her kisses help, a lot. We kiss for a long minute 'n' when I pull back, she got my head spinnin'. "I know you do. It's just hard for me to talk 'bout that part of my life— about her."

She touches the side of my face wit' her soft hand. No girl has ever touched me like this. I don't ever remember feelin' like this except when I was a lil boy. When I felt loved. And wanted. And special. That's what *she* made me feel like. That's what *she* told me I was. That's what *she* made me believe. And then *she* snatched it all away from me, just like that. My whole world turned upside down. And now I've let this girl into my heart, get all up in my head 'n' open myself for...I don't know. For her to do somethin' to hurt me, too, just like *she* did.

"Never let a woman into your heart...."

I wanna tell him it's a lil too late now. But I know Pops'll be lookin' at me some kinda way, like I'm soft or somethin'. But I'm startin' to think that openin' ya'self to care 'bout someone or love 'em doesn't make you soft. It makes you...vulnerable. That's how I feel wit' Miesha, yo. Like I'm all out in the open. Like I'm transparent. And she's here, lookin' through me, in me, at me 'cause I let her, 'cause I want her to see me in a way no one else has.

I take a deep breath. I try to swallow back a lump of emotions. But e'erything kinda pushes its way outta me and before I know it, e'erything I thought I'd never say, or think, or feel, comes rushin' outta me. "She bounced on me, yo."

Miesha blinks. "Who? Your mom?"

I turn my head to avoid her eyes. "Yeah. She didn't die. I lied. I've always lied about it because the lie never hurt as much as the truth. That one day I woke up and my moms was gone. She walked outta my life, yo." I turn to look at her. "What kinda woman does that, yo? Leaves their kid 'n' never comes back? How you think that made me feel, knowin' she wasn't ever comin' back?"

"Oh my god, Antonio," she says, huggin' me. "I'm sorry. I can't imagine how that was for you. I know my mom pisses me off, but..."

"Yo real shit, I'd give anything to have a mom to piss me off. But I don't. Mine bounced. She ain't want me."

She climbs up into my lap 'n' wraps her arms 'round me 'n' kinda just rocks back 'n' forth, rubbin' my back. And it kinda calms me. "I'm sure she loved you; maybe something happened for her to leave. Did you ever ask your dad? Maybe something happened between them."

I nod, chokin' back hurt. "Yeah."

She keeps rubbin' my back 'n' rockin' me. "What did he say?"

"She stopped lovin' us...."

I blow out a long breath. "That she didn't want us anymore. She abandoned me, yo."

Miesha cups my face, lookin' at me all teary-eyed 'n' ish. "I'm so sorry she did that to you." She plants kisses all over my face, sayin' over 'n' over, "I'm so sorry." We start kissin' 'n' this time they feelin' kinda different. Intense. This time it's *her* hands all over me. This time, she's tuggin' at my shirt, my shorts, my underwear, strippin' off e'erything. And I let her. Crazy thing is, I already felt naked long before she ever took my clothes off.

36

Miesha

"Oooh, you scandalous tramp," Mariah says, barging into my room. She plops down on my bed. "You better tell me everything! And I do mean *everything*! Start to finish. I want all the dirty details; leave nothing out!"

"Girl, *boom*!" I say, putting a hand up in her face. "What are you talking about?"

"Don't you sit here and play Miss Innocent with me, hooker. I saw Antonio Lopez drop you off late—very *late*—last night, then tongue you down in the driveway."

"Oh my god," I say, hopping off the bed. "I don't believe you. What in the world are you doing spying on me?"

"*Spying* on you? Girl, quit! You were right out in the open. Y'all were going at it so hot and heavy I had to turn on my fan, okay? Now divulge, little Miss Hooker. I want to know, are the rumors true? Is he swinging low and heavy, boo? Give it to me raw and uncut. Chop, chop!"

"I don't know what you're talking about," I say, tryna figure out a way to tell her enough to shut her up, but not enough to have her looking at him, too. I mean, I know she gotta man whom she is madly in love with. And, yeah, we're real close. But, *boom-boom!* Tre thought she could trust her own sister with her juicy sex saga and the trick did her in. Her own sister slept with her boyfriend. Then Tre and her sister got into a big nasty fight, clawing each other's faces up and yanking out weave tracks. Oh, it got real messy. Yeah, he was grimy for doing it to her, but she was dead wrong for pushing up on him in the first place. Sooo, no. Mariah can't get too much of the details. I'm not gonna tempt her to ever do me in.

She's staring at me, brows raised, lips smirked in suspicion. "Okay fine, we kissed. And made out some." She narrows her eyes. "Okay, we made out a lot."

"Fine, be like that," she pouts, grabbing one of my pillows from off the bed and throwing it at me. I sidestep it, then pick it up and throw it back at her. "But tell me this. Did. *You.* Sleep. With him?" I bite down on my bottom lip, tryna hold back a grin. "Oooh, you nasty ho. I knew it!"

"Oh my god, will you be quiet? I don't want my business all over the house. Geesh."

She dismisses me with a wave. "Please. It's not like Aunt Rhonda was home when you got here. Besides, she didn't crawl up in here until three o'clock this morning. Thirty minutes after you, *okay?*"

"OMG, who are you the door patrol? What were you doing up that time of night anyway?"

She laughs. "I had just snuck Brian up outta here a few minutes before you came home."

Now it's my turn to ride her. "Oooh, and you talk about me. Who's the real tramp in the room? You, boo."

"Girl, *boom!* Brian is my man. Now, what's Antonio to

you? Last I heard you was only going to get with him to get at that loudmouth Quanda, not sleeping with him in the process."

I shrug. "It just happened."

She raises her eyebrow. "What just happened? *You* sleeping with him, or you *falling* for him?"

Both.

But I don't get a chance to say it 'cause there is a knock at the door. And it's my mom. "Ooh, you lucky," she whispers, getting up from the bed. "But we will finish this conversation. Trust." I laugh as she opens the door and lets my mom in.

"What time did you get home last night?" she wants to know, standing there looking all wild and crazy in a flimsy robe. Her hair's all over her head. Black liner all smeared up under her eyes.

"Why? What time did *you* get home?"

"Miesha, don't play with me, girl. I'm grown. You're not. Now what time did you—"

I press my lips together and shake my head. Just because she's the adult and can come and go as she pleases, that doesn't mean I want to hear it. So I cut her off when I say, "When are *we* moving back to Brooklyn? Because it seems like you spend more time there than you do here, where you claim is home now. But it's mighty funny I'm the only one stuck here."

She puts a hand up. "Miesha, don't."

I put a hand up on my hip. "Don't what, Mom? Don't question you? You leave up outta here to go to work on a Monday and don't step back up in here until two and three days later. And don't even say you have trainings. 'Cause guess what? I called your job two days ago. And they said you were off. And I called Daddy's job, and ding, ding, ding…he was off too. So what's really going on here?"

She blinks.

"It's not right that you dump me off on Aunt Linda like I'm *her* responsibility. You wanted to move us here. But you're hardly ever here. Yeah, I'm seventeen, about to be eighteen. And, yeah, I can take care of myself. But I keep telling you, you don't get to pick and choose when *you* wanna play mommy. And, yes, I'm counting down 'til my birthday; then I'm going back to Brooklyn with or without your consent. And I mean it."

She sighs. "You know what, Miesha? I'm tired. Do whatever you want. You're right, you'll be eighteen soon, so do what you're gonna do."

I shake my head at her. "Oh my god, so now once again, you're the victim here." I laugh. "What a joke!"

She narrows her eyes to icy slits. "I'm warning you, girl. You're really pushing it, Miesha."

"Mom, don't you get it? I. Don't. Care. I'm pissed at you, okay? And you don't seem to care about it."

"What the hell are you pissed about, huh, Miesha?" she snaps, walking over and slamming my bedroom door shut. "You wanna have it out, then let's! Let's get it all out in the open once and for all!"

I yell back at her, "Why the eff do you keep going back with Daddy if all he's gonna do is keep hurting you, huh?! I'm pissed that you get to go back to Brooklyn to lay up in our house with a man you left because you said you couldn't take him hurting you anymore. But here you go, again, right back to the same place you swore you wasn't gonna ever be back in!" I stamp my foot, pointing at her. "And I'm stuck here!"

"What do you want from me, huh?! I love your father, okay?! I'm weak for him. I know he's a cheater. And I know he's a liar. But he's mine! And I know that man loves me. He loves both of us. But right now, I want him to myself. I don't wanna share none of his other women. And I don't wanna share him with *you . . . !*"

Oh my god! I feel like I've been punched in the gut. Everything in me hurts. And before I know it, I am bending over clutching my stomach, crying my eyes out.

She doesn't want to share her husband, my father, with his own daughter. Is that what she thinks she's been doing all these years, *sharing* him with me, like I'm the one who's taken him away from her? Oh my god. I'm hyperventilating. "I-I-I don't b-b-b-believe this! Y-y-you're j-j-jealous of m-m-m-my relationship with m-m-my d-d-d-dad-d-ddy. Ohmygodohmygod." I plop on my bed and curl up in a ball. "Get outta my room!" I can't stop crying.

"Miesha, I didn't mean it like that," she says. She's sitting on the bed, next to me, rubbing my back. "I-I-I'm sorry. That didn't come out right."

"Get away from me! You said exactly what you meant. And you said it just *how* you meant it!"

"I only meant we need time to ourselves, alone time, to work on us."

"Yeah, without meeeee! Like I'm the problem!" She tries to explain herself, but I'm not hearing her. My own mother is jealous of my relationship with my father. I feel like she's stabbed me. And I can't stop bleeding. I can't stop crying. "Just get out! And leave me alone!"

"Miesha, I'm sorry. I really didn't mean to say it that way. I would never do anything to come between your relationship with you and your father. I know how much you mean to him. And I know how much you love him."

"Then let me go live with him! Let me go back home where I wanna be! It's not like you want me, anyway! I hate you! I hate you! Just leave me alone!"

She gets up from my bed, and walks out, closing the door behind her. I cry so hard that I start coughing and gagging. *I gotta get outta here!* But I can't move. Mariah comes into my room. Tries to talk to me, to see what happened. But I can't talk. I just keep crying. I wanna go home! I hate it here! I try to open my mouth to say something, but the words are stuck in the back of my throat. *I gotta get outta here!*

37

Antonio

Yo, word is bond. Miesha got my head spinnin'. I don't know what she did to me, but last night she put it on me. Had me curlin' my toes 'n' singing out Drake's "Best I Ever Had." And real rap, I wanted her to stay the night, ya heard? I wanted to wake up to her in bed wit' me. Heck, I mighta even got outta bed 'n' fixed her some breakfast, for real for real. That's how good she put it on me. She had'a go home. But, man. I ain't wanna stop holdin' her. And I definitely didn't wanna stop doin' what she was doin' to me.

She rocked me so good, all'a brotha could do today is lay in bed 'n' think 'bout the work she put in. I'm drained, yo. I yawn 'n' stretch as my cell rings. I glance at the screen. It's Alicia. "Yo, what's good?"

"You," she says all low 'n' sexy. "You wanna chill today?"

Now I ain't gonna front, I'm kinda thinkin' 'bout it, but only for a minute, though. "Nah, yo. I'm good," I say, lookin' over at the poster of Beyoncé.

"Oh, okay. But if you change your mind, hit me back."

"No doubt," I say, glancin' over at the clock. It's almost one o'clock. *I wonder what Miesha's doin'*. "Listen, yo. I gotta go. I'll holla at ya later."

"Okay, bye."

I place my cell back on the nightstand, gettin' up to use the bathroom, then headin' downstairs to raid the fridge. I grab an apple 'n' chomp into it while I nuke the rest of some Popeyes chicken. When I finish eatin', I wash it all down wit' a tall glass of Sprite, then head back upstairs. *Damn, shorty did me in*, I think, ploppin' back on my bed. I grin, replayin' our night over in my head. But my cell disrupts my thoughts. I reach over on the nightstand for it, and grin when I see that it's Miesha. "Yo, what's good, sexy? I was just layin' here thinkin' 'bout you, yo."

"Are y-y-you home?" she asks, soundin' all muffled, like somethin' done happened to her.

I sit up in bed. *WTF?!* "Yo, what's wrong? You a'ight? What happened?"

"I just gotta get outta here. Are you home?"

"Yeah, yeah. I'm here."

"Can I come over?"

"No doubt. Do you want me to come scoop you? You sound outta it, yo."

"No. I can drive. I'm gonna get in the shower. I'll be over in a few."

"A'ight. Be safe drivin' over here, a'ight?"

She sniffs. "I-I-I will."

"A'ight, cool. I'll see you when you get here."

I end the call, wonderin' what done popped off that got my baby upset. Now I'm ready to go in someone's mouth for comin' at her all crazy 'n' makin' her cry. I pace my room, tryna calm it down 'n' wait for her to get here before I start jumpin' to conclusions. I pick up the clothes tossed 'round the room from last night, change my sheets, then hop in the shower.

Twenty minutes later, I'm downstairs in the kitchen gettin' somethin' else to drink when the doorbell rings. *Good, she made it.* I don't look through the peephole or outta the window 'cause she's the only one I'm expectin'. But when I swing the door open, it ain't Miesha. It's Quanda.

I look over her head out toward the driveway. "Yo, Quanda, what the eff you doin' here?"

"Tone, please," she says, lookin' all pitiful 'n' whatnot. She stares at my bare chest. "I really need to talk to you."

I shake my head. "No, you gotta bounce, yo. We ain't got nothin' to talk about, yo. I'm not beat for the drama. I tol' you all I'ma say."

"Im not tryna bring you any drama. I just need to talk to you, and I'll leave. Ten minutes, that's all I'm asking for, please."

Now my gut is tellin' me to slam the door in her face, but somethin' in my head is sayin' to just listen to what she gotta say, that maybe if I just listen to her, she'll finally see that it's over between us. I tell her to wait a minute, then shut the door in her face, goin' back into the kitchen to get my phone. I text Miesha, walkin' back to the door. U left yet?

I open the door again. "Talk. But make it quick."

She blinks.

No not yet. Still gettn dressed

k, I text back, decidin' in my head that I have 'bout fifteen, twenty, minutes before she gets here—enough time
for Quanda to say what she gotta say, then dip.

"Can I please come in?"

Don't do it, yo!

*Nah, she's only gettin' ten minutes, then I'ma put her
out.*

I step back, pullin' the door open wider. "A'ight. I let
you in. Now what you wanna talk to me about?"

She sighs. "First, I wanna apologize to you."

"For what?"

"For everything. I was wrong for going through your
phone and for acting all crazy when you slept with other
girls. I know you always kept it real with me. And I know
you told me from the gate that you were gonna sex other
girls from time to time. I just couldn't handle that. I
thought I could. But it was hard for me because I really
started catchin' feelings for you, Tone."

I glance at the time on my phone. "Look, can you speed
this up? What you gotta say, Quanda? 'Cause so far I'm not
hearin' jack that's keepin' my attention."

She blinks back tears. "Tone, why are you treating me
so mean and nasty? All I ever did was love you."

I gotta laugh to that. This chick ain't love me. She loved
the sex. She loved bein' able to sport me around as her
man. That's it.

"What's so funny?"

"You, yo. You standin' here talkin' 'bout you loved me.
Why'd you love me, yo? Answer me that." She hits me wit'
some BS 'bout knowin' how'ta make her feel, that I made
her feel loved. I shake my head. This broad's confused.
"Quanda, all we ever had was good sex. There was no

love, yo. Not by me. I mean, yeah. I *liked* you. But *love?* Nah. I ain't tryna be mean, yo. But the only thing I loved from you was the sex. That's it. And then when I tol' you it was a wrap between us, you wanna start buggin', actin' all reckless 'n' whatnot. For what, yo?"

I don't wanna go in on her, but damn. She needs to hear it once and for all that I'm done. That there is never gonna be *us* or *we*. I want her to hear it loud 'n' clear. It's. Over. "I want—nah, I need—for you to fall back, Quanda. Like for real for real. Let this crazy ish you got goin' on in ya head go, yo."

She swipes at her face, wipin' tears. "You really like *her*, don't you?"

"This has nothin' to do wit' Miesha, yo. This is 'bout you. I don't want you, yo. Why can't you just accept that?"

"I know you don't want me. B-but...it's been hard for me to let go of you. I mean, in my head I know it's over. In school, I see you with *her*. And I know it's over. But, it h-hurts. It hurts seeing you with *her*. When you were just having sex with other girls it bothered me, and I was mad, but it didn't hurt—not like this. I *know* you like that girl. I can tell by the way you look at her. It hurts knowing you never looked at me like that. It hurts knowing you don't want me. I know, I know...I finally get it. It's over. And I know *she* didn't do this to us. I did. But my heart won't let me let you go, Tone. I know I need to. But it's hard." Her shoulders start to shake. "I-I-I know I messed up things with us. And I know I can't do anything to change it. And it...hurts."

Quanda buries her face in her hands, then falls to her knees and bursts into tears.

I ain't never see her like this. All broken up 'n' ish.

"C'mon, Quanda, yo," I say, walkin' over 'n' tryna help her up. "You gotta pull ya'self together. You gotta let me go, feel me? This ain't good, you know what I'm sayin'? I'm not gonna ever be wit' you, yo."

"I know, I know, I know," she says wrappin' her arms around my neck 'n' holdin' on wit' all her strength. I try to pry her arms from around me, but she won't let go. "I won't ever bother you or her, again. I promise, Tone. Just kiss me, please. Let me feel what you give *her*, please. Kiss me and do it to me one last time, please."

"C'mon, yo," I say, tryna push her off me wit' out man-handlin' her. "You wildin'. I ain't kissin' you, yo. And I ain't 'bout to sex you. How that sound? That's crazy, yo. Like, you buggin', for real for real. It's over." She starts tryna wrap her legs 'round me 'n' the next thing I know she's kissin' me on the mouth 'n' I'm tryna get her off'a me, movin' my head outta the way. I'm wrestlin' wit' her to get her off'a me. But she won't let go. She keeps pleadin' 'n' beggin' me to get wit' her. She's not hearin' nothin' I'm sayin'. Her legs, her arms, she's wrapped all tight 'round me like an octopus. "Yo, Quanda, for real, get the hell up off'a me, yo. C'mon. I'm not playin'." I trip on somethin', maybe she tripped; all I know is I fall back over the arm of the sofa 'n' she falls on top of me.

"I love you so much, Tone. Just do it to me. I wanna make a baby with you...."

"Oh my god! What the hell?!"

I jump, pushin' Quanda off'a me. She hits the floor. I left the front door open. Forgot to close it. Nah, I ain't wanna close it 'cause Quanda wasn't s'posed to be here long. "Yo, Miesha, hol'up...it's not what you think. I, I mean she was, um..."

"Kissing *you!*" she snaps, backin' outta the door. Quanda gets up from the floor. And the next thing I know Miesha bum-rushes her 'n' they start goin' at it. "You skank-azz ho! You didn't get enough of me beatin' ya face in the last time, did you?" Miesha is hookin' off on her, like a dude. Real rap, I ain't never see a chick rock like this. And I'm kinda shook that she's gonna crack Quanda's neck back.

"Ho, he ain't ever gonna be yours!" Quanda yells, swingin' her arms around like a windmill all fast 'n' hard. "You're not enough woman for him, trick."

Miesha swings her into the coffee table. And things start smashin' to the carpet. I'm tryna break them up, but they fightin' like they tryna kill each other 'n' all I keep thinkin' is they gonna eff up my crib 'n' Pops is gonna flip.

"Yo, y'all chill. You can't be fightin' up in here. C'mon, Miesha, get off 'a her."

Quanda's screamin' now at the top 'a her lungs, like she's bein' tortured. "Get off my hair, slut! Aaah! Get your crazy whore off 'a me!"

I get in back of Miesha 'n' hook my arms up under her arms and yank her up, while tryna hold back Quanda. But Miesha still got Quanda's weave all wrapped up in her hand, while she's swingin' punches wit' her other. And now she socks me in the mouth. And now I gotta manhandle at least one 'a them to get them calm down. I ain't into puttin' my hands on females, but I can't let them tear up my crib.

"C'mon, Miesha, let go of her hair, yo." I pry her fingers loose. She punches me again. This time in the chest. I tell Quanda to bounce. "Get out, yo! Just get the eff outta here, yo!"

Quanda hits the door, fast.

Finally I let Miesha go 'n' she starts pacin' 'n' cursin', goin' off like a wild woman. "I knew I shoulda never effed wit' you! I knew you were an effen dog! That's why you sent me that text wanting to know where I was, so you could screw that rusty skank-trick-ho!"

"I swear—"

"Shut ya face!" she snaps, glarin' at me. The look on her face effs me up, yo.

"Please, yo. Let me explain. It's not what it looks like." She's lookin' at me like I'm the no-good, cheatin' dude she thought I was from the rip. But I gotta let her know that I'm not that dude, that I'm all about her. But how am I gonna say anything that she's gonna believe when she walks in 'n' finds my ex on top of me, wit' her lips on me. And I'm standin' here in only my boxers?

38

Miesha

It's been a whole week since that incident at his house. A whole, loooong, excruciating week since I've stopped taking his calls. Stopped responding to his texts. Stopped talking to him in the halls. Stopped looking at him. It's been a week since I've told him to leave me alone, told him that I wanted nothing to do with him. But it's killing me! I am *not* supposed to be thinking about *him*. But I am. Antonio Lopez. As bad as he hurt me, I can't stop thinking about him. His name scrawled across the top of my sketchbook. His lips, his hands, his body, all etched into my head. *This* is not supposed to be happening. *Me* feeling some kinda way about that boy. He's a player! A dirty, panty hound! This is not a part of the script—me thinking about *him*, me wanting *him*. But those kisses. Oh, and those lips. And his hands. The way they felt on my body.

They were soft.

Warm.

Oh so sweet.

I can't stop thinking about his kisses. The way his hands felt on my body.

But he hurt me!

I can't stop thinking about how he told me about his mother and cried in front of me.

But he's a liar!

The way we made love.

It didn't mean anything to him!

What the heck was I thinking? I shoulda never messed with that boy. I shoulda stayed away from him. Why didn't I just beat that crazy ho up and be done with it? I didn't have to walk up on that boy and kiss him like that. And I didn't have to ever go out with him, or let him into my house, or make out with him. And I didn't have to start spending so much time with him, either. And I didn't have to give myself to him. But I did. I wanted to. I wanted him. And now I can't stop thinking about him. Can't stop playing his kisses over and over in my head. Can't stop wondering if he's thinking about me, our kisses, our touching, too. Is he missing me, too? Is he hurting the way I am? Probably not. He's probably already laid up with some stank skeezer skank right now.

Okay, so maybe I was playing him. So what? He doesn't know that for sure. Okay, okay, he *does* know. But, that's not the point. The point is, Antonio Lopez is a capital D-O-G. Plain and simple. And, yeah, I kinda did like him. Okay, okay…I still do like him. Okay, I *really* do like him. But whatever! I don't like him enough to put up with all of the crazy drama he has going on. I'm not that kinda chick. And I'm not beat to have to keep going upside some chick's head because she can't get over him. That Quanda chick ain't tryna go down. And I'm sick of her. So, no. Let someone else have at it. I'm done.

I knew it was all too good to be true. Once a cheater, always a cheater, right? Cheaters don't change. They just stop what they do until they think you done forgot about it then go right back to doing the same mess. Just like Antonio. Just like my own dad! So why am I acting all surprised?

Why am I holed up in my room crying over him every day after school?

Why am I tripping?

Because I really like him!

Because I really care about him!

This is horrible! Falling for him was *not* the plan. No, the plan was to teach that Quanda a lesson. To take her *man,* toy with him, then toss him back. Ha! The joke's on me. I'm the fool. And now I'm sure that ghetto hyena is laughing it up at my expense.

And yeah, I know what he *claims* happened. But I know what I *saw.* That slut on top of him with her lips on him. Okay, maybe he was tryna get her off of him. Maybe he did trip and she fell on top of him. But none of that woulda happened if he hadn't let her in the house in the first place. I'm so pissed at myself for liking that boy. I really wanted to be wrong about him. I mean, I wanted to be right that underneath all that playboy swag was a really nice, sweet guy who wanted to settle down with the right kinda girl. And I thought that girl was me. I felt it was. Even when I didn't tell him that. When I didn't admit it. I felt it. I felt what he felt. Heat. If I close my eyes and think hard enough, I can still feel it.

He's trouble. I know he is. Everything about that boy is wrong. But those kisses, the way his tongue touched mine, the way his arms wrapped around me, all felt...right. Like we're a perfect fit. Like two juicy strawberries dipped in sweet milk chocolate. That's what his kisses tasted like. That's what he felt like.

Girl, snap outta it. You're buggin' for real. Stick to the script, I think. *You proved ya point. And now it backfired on you.*

It's hard seeing him in the halls. It's hard sitting up in English class with him staring at me. I can't concentrate. I sigh, shutting my locker, relieved that he isn't here today. All seeing him does is remind me of him up in his house in his boxers with that skank. And all that does is make me wanna fight him. So, yes, I'm glad I don't have to look at him.

Girl, boom! You'll get over him. You only have two more months until you turn eighteen; then you'll be going to Brooklyn. I've decided that I am not staying here. As soon as I turn eighteen, I'm signing myself out of this school and going back to Fashion High, and there's nothing my mom can do to stop me. *That's exactly what I'll do. Then I'll never have to see him again.* Yeah, that's it. Good-bye. Good riddance! I sigh, feeling all mixed up and confused. I rush into the girls' bathroom and try to pull myself together. I can't let these hatin' tricks see me all tore up. I'll never give any of them the satisfaction of knowing he hurt me.

I shut myself in one of the stalls and pull out my compact case, flipping it open then dabbing my eyes with this hard-azz toilet paper in here. I blow my nose, then toss the paper into the toilet and flush, walking out. I stop dead in my tracks when Quanda walks in. I drop my bag, close my fists, ready to bring it to her.

"I don't wanna fight you," she says, putting her hand up. "I didn't even know you were in this bathroom."

I narrow my eyes at her. I pick my bag up and head for the row of sinks to wash my hands. She goes into one of the stalls. I pull my brush outta my bag, then brush my wrap. Yeah, I know I should probably leave before she gets done, but I don't. A part of me wants to fight, but I know it's not worth it. I already beat her up twice. And getting suspended isn't an option. Not when I'm so close to getting accepted into Parsons or F.I.T.

I can't mess that up over no boy, or behind some ratchetness. I pull out my lip gloss and slide it over my lips, waiting. For what, I don't know. Outta habit, I still check my phone, expecting to see a text message from Tone, or to see his picture pop up on the screen when he calls and Trey Songz's "Inside Interlude" plays as he rings through. But that was then. And this is now. And now, I have a new number. I had to change it. It was the only way I could keep myself from answering his calls, or responding to his texts. It's the only way I could get through the night. And keep myself from wanting to believe his lies.

I walk in the back to where the stalls are. She's on the toilet. The old me would kick in the door and drag her off the toilet, but...I bang on the door.

"I don't wanna fight you, Miesha. I'm done. You can have Tone."

"I don't want him," I say. But I'm not sure how true that is. I just know I can't mess with him. "I just need to know why'd you go over to his house that day? Were you tryna get him back?"

"No. I wanted to talk to him."

I frown. "About what?"

"I went there to apologize to him."

"Did he know you were going over there?"

She passes gas. And I curl my nose up. *Ugh, she stinks!* "Listen, can we talk about this when I'm done? I'm tryna use the bathroom."

"Well, too bad. We're gonna get this out in the open right here and right now. So answer the question. Did he know you were going over there?"

She sighs. "As bad as I wanna lie to you and add some extra ish into the mix, I can't, because I know he doesn't want me. So no. He didn't know I was coming there. When he opened the door, I could tell he was expecting it to be you. He didn't even wanna let me in. But I begged him to give me a few minutes of his time. I love him. But I know he wants you. Not me. And I can't keep playing myself like this. Do you know how many girls I've fought over him in the last four months? At least ten."

"And that just goes to show how stupid you are."

"Don't you think I know that? And I still kept playing myself. I'm done. I apologized to him. And now I'ma apologize to you. I shoulda never started with you. All you were was the new girl at the school. The fly chick all the boys were talking about. And all I was worried about was Tone wanting you, even though he had already dumped me. I didn't wanna see him with anyone else. But I know that no matter how many girls I fight, he's not gonna come back to me."

She flushes the toilet. I step back from the door just in case she comes out slinging a handful of her poop at me. She opens the door, looking at me. I take another two steps back. She goes over to the sinks and washes her hands. I watch her watching me through the mirrors.

"I'ma stay away from you, and you just stay away from me. Deal?" she says.

"*And* stay away from Antonio."

"Deal."

I walk outta the bathroom, letting out a sigh of relief. Okay, so he didn't know she was coming over there. But he still had no business letting her in, and definitely not while he was half-naked.

"Oops, hey, boo," Fiona says, walking into me as I round the corner to get to the stairs. It's fourth-period lunch and I wanna go out to my car. "Where you on your way to?"

"My car."

"Oh, good. I'll walk with you," she says, her heels clicking alongside of me. "How you holding up?"

I blink. "I'm good," I say with a buncha sass. Even if it's a lie, never let a ho see you down. "Why wouldn't I be?"

"Girl, I just figured you'd still be goin' through it over Tone, that's all." She shrugs. "Guess I was wrong."

"Dead wrong. Girl, I'm onto the next." I snap my fingers. "You miss a minute, you miss a lot, hun. Here today, gone tomorrow, that's my motto."

"Ohhhhhkay," she says, flipping her hand open. I slap her five. "Out with the old, in with new. Good for you, boo. Tone was up to no-good, anyway. Not that I'm tryna kick his back in."

I frown. "Oh, really? Well, it's over between us, so I'm not pressed. I couldn't care less what kinda no-good mess he was into."

"I knnnnnnow that's right. You didn't need the stress anyway, especially with him having a baby on the way."

I blink, stopping in my tracks. "Say *whaaaat?* Baby?"

My heart drops! Everything stops! If I had any doubts before, I definitely don't now. Baby daddy and BM drama is a no-no for me. Antonio Lopez is dead to me!

"Girrrrl, you didn't hear this from me, 'cause you know I'm not one for a buncha gossip." I roll my eyes up in my head. "But some chick from over on the West Side—" I give her a blank look. "Oh, that's right. You're not from here. It's another section of JC, boo. Annnnyway, Miss Chickie-Boo has it all up on her Facebook and Instagram page pics of her sonogram, saying it's Tone's."

I swallow. "Well good for her, and congrats to him. I wish them both well."

"Girrrrl, you good. 'Cause if it was me, I'd be ready to set it off. Tone is so dang messy. He didn't even tell you about this chick, did he? Mmmph. He knew this chick was with his child for at least two months."

"Who is she?" I ask before I can stop the question from spilling outta my mouth.

"Some church skank who was doin' it to him down in the church basement or some nasty mess like that."

What?! O-M-G! He is outta control! What and who won't *that boy do?*

"How long have *you* known about this?" I ask, eyeing her. The moment of truth has come.

"I found out about it a few weeks ago when I was across town at my cousin, TastyCakes'—one word—house." *TastyCakes? What the hell?!* "She goes to Lincoln High with his BM. So when Tasty asked me if I knew Tone, you know I had to get the four-one-one, then do a lil more re-search before I said anything. One thing I don't like to do is spread gossip that ain't true."

Ugh, this dumb trick is a mess! But she's given me all I need to stay the hell away from the likes of Antonio Lopez. If I never see him again, it's fine by me!

39

Antonio

"Awww, damn," Pops says, standin' at the foot of my bed, shakin' his head. "I knew somethin' had'a be serious when the school called 'n' said you been absent for *four* days 'n' you didn't answer ya phone when I was callin' you. I thought you was in here dead. Look at you. I knew somethin' like this was gonna eventually happen. I told you what happens when you open up ya heart..."

I open my eyes.

Stare at him.

I haven't left the crib in four and a half days. I haven't bathed. I haven't eaten. I haven't done jack 'cept lie in bed, playin' this Lenny Williams joint over and over and over. I thought listenin' to Trey Songz would do it for me. Thought maybe I could drown my sorrows listenin' to Jaheim. But, nah... "'Cause I Love You" says how I feel. It speaks what's in my head. It screams what's in my heart. I'm all effed up, yo. I know e'ery word to the song. Feel e'ery inch of his pain. My whole body aches. I'm sick. I haven't felt this effed up since I was six years old—when my moms bounced. For the first time in my life, I trusted myself enough to trust someone else, somethin' I didn't think I'd ever be able to do. Miesha did that to me. Made it easy to talk. Made it easy for me to trust—*her*. And now she's gone!

She won't even talk to me. She stopped takin' my calls, stopped talkin' to me, stopped wantin' me. I can't even call her now 'cause her number's changed. "Stay the HELL away from me!" That's what she tol' me the last time I walked up on her at her locker, tryna get her to just listen to me, to let me explain. I begged her. *Me,* yo! Beggin' a girl to talk to me. That's not what I do. That's not who I am. Or who I was. But, in that effen moment, that's who I became. Desperate. All needy 'n' shit.

I still am.

And the crazy thing is, I don't feel like a punk, or weak. I feel effed up. I feel lonely, like before. When my moms left 'n' didn't come back. And like then...I'm desperate. I'm sad.

I'm desperate to hear her voice. See her face. Hold her in my arms.

I am connected to her, yo. When I'm wit' her, when I *was* wit' her...I didn't feel empty, like I did wit' all them other females. I smashed them broads 'cause I could. I didn't wanna be tied to any of 'em 'cause I when I looked in their eyes, I couldn't see anything other than sex. That's all I wanted from them. That's all they were good for.

But Miesha...she's different. Special.

E'erything 'bout her—her slick mouth, the way she smiles, her walk, the way she dresses 'n' doesn't care 'bout what other peeps think 'bout her, the way she looks at me,

the way she feels in my arms, the way she makes me feel—
is perfect...for *me*!

I want her back, yo. I need her back. I want another
chance. Nah, I *need* another chance. But she ain't beat.

"It's over between us! I don't ever wanna talk to you,
again! I *hate* you! You're just like all the rest of the boys,
no-effen-good! Just stay outta my life!"

Those were her words to me. And they cut me inside-
out.

The one time when I'm not gassin' a girl's head up, or
tryna do her best friend, or press up on her older sister—
the one time I'm bein' straight-up, puttin' e'erything on
the line, I get dumped over some BS, for somethin' that I
wasn't even doin'. I never get dumped! I don't get dismissed! But Miesha dismissed me. Told me I was invisible
to her. That nothin' I said mattered to her.

And now I have all'a these emotions, all'a these
thoughts, swirlin' 'round in me. It's like a switch clicked
on 'n' now I can't stop thinkin'. Can't stop wonderin'.
About my moms. About Miesha.

Why my moms bounced on me.

Why she didn't want me.

Why Miesha won't talk to me.

Why she can't believe me.

Why, why, why...over and over, I play the ish in my
head. I tried to forget 'bout my moms. I can't forget 'bout
Miesha. I don't wanna forget 'bout her. But I don't know
what else I can do.

"What's her name?"

I blink.

Pops is now standin' on the side of the bed lookin'
down at me. "You gotta snap outta this, you hear me? You

lyin' 'round lookin' all pitiful, feelin' sorry for ya'self ain't gonna bring her back. This ain't what a man does. She's gone. Let her go...."

I don't wanna let her go!

"There's too many other woman out there for you to be lyin' up in here wit' the shades down, playin' depressin' music...."

I don't want anyone else!

"Listen, son, you gotta get ya mind right. You gotta get up 'n' handle ya business, you hear me? Call up one'a them other lil girls you got sniffin' behind you. Let them help you get over her...."

I don't wanna get over her!

"How many times I tell you, keep you a string of women on your team? How many times I tell you, they can't be trusted wit' ya heart, huh? You get 'em in ya bed. You don't let 'em get up in ya head."

I don't wanna string of girls! I want Miesha!

I know what he's beat me in the head wit' since I was six years old. I know some girls can't be trusted. But I don't wanna believe all can't be. Miesha *can* be. And I wanna believe, I gotta believe, that there are more girls like her. Yeah, I know what Pops tol' me. But I'm old enough to make my own decisions. And I don't gotta believe him. I don't gotta think his way is the right way for me.

"I'm not you," I push out. "Why I gotta be angry 'cause you are?"

"What?"

I look up at Pops. "Why'd *she* leave me?"

He shakes his head. "That's what women do when they don't want you. They leave."

I keep my eyes on him. They burn from holdin' back tears. "But I was her kid."

He kinda looks at me, and now he gets it. He blinks. Rubs his hands over his head. "I thought we promised never to mention her again."

"No, Pops. You did. You tol' me that's what we were gonna do. And I haven't. But now I am. I wanna know. Why?"

He sighs. "Damn. I hoped we would never hafta have this conversation." He starts pacin' the room. He stops 'n' looks at me. "I loved ya moms, son. But I loved the streets 'n' the pretty women more. She got fed up 'n' wanted to leave me. I tol' her she could go, but she couldn't take you. Not my firstborn son. I tol' her I would hunt her down 'n' kill 'er if she did....She knew the kinda man I was in the streets. She knew that violent side of me. And believed me."

I blink.

He hangs his head. "It hurt me that she wanted to leave me. And it hurt even more when she tol' me she had met someone else. I tol' her I wasn't lettin' another man raise my son. Tol' her if she ever came near us again, I'd put a bullet in her head...."

I blink. E'erything comes back to me. My mom's face, her smile, the tears in her eyes, all pop into my head. "Why are you cryin', Mommy?"

"Because Mommy loves you so much."

"I love you too, Mommy."

"Listen, sweetheart. Mommy has to go away for a while, sweetie? But I promise I'm gonna come back for you real soon, okay?"

"Don't leave, Mommy."

"Honey, I have to. Only for a while." I remember now…
noddin' my head, 'n' her leanin' in 'n' kissin' me on the
forehead. "Mommy's gonna come back for you."

"You promise?"

"I promise. Now promise me you'll be a good boy for
Mommy. You'll do good in school and make Mommy real
proud, promise?"

"I promise, Mommy."

She kissed me, again. Waited for me to fall asleep.
And then… she was gone

I swallow back a ball of emotions. "So all this time you
effen had me thinkin' she didn't want me, yo? You had me
thinkin' she didn't love me! Pops, do you know what that
did to me, yo?" I shake my head. "I can't believe this. *You*
did this to me, yo. Effed my head all up. Got me thinkin' I
gotta dog girls out. You brainwashed me. Why, huh?"

"I'm sorry, son."

I frown. " 'I'm sorry'? Is that all you gotta say?"

He tells me he doesn't know what else to say. Word? He
tells me he didn't wanna see me hurt. Really?

"And you didn't think tellin' me that crap 'bout her not
wantin' me was gonna hurt, huh? You made her out to be
the bad guy. Made you look like you were there to save the
day. That was real foul, for real for real. You're all I've ever
had in my life, Pops. And I've always looked up to you, yo.
But this…" I shake my head. "This is some straight-up
bullshit, yo. E'erything I've believed has been 'cause it's
what you believed, yo. And you wanna know why I believed it? 'Cause I believed in you! I trusted you!

"And now look at me. All screwed up 'cause of you! All
that crap 'bout women bein' no good, all that did was
make *me* be no good. Like *you*, Pops!" I say all'a this to my

pops and he stands there 'n' lets me get it off. He ain't tryna flex on me, ain't tryna shut it down. He lets me get it out, prolly 'cause he feels guilty. I don't know. All I know, he really effed me up wit' this.

"I thought I was protectin' you," he says.

I stare at him. I can feel the muscles in my jaw tightenin'. "Nah, you *thought* you was protectin' ya'self. I trusted you." I shake my head. "I don't even know what to think anymore. If I can't trust you, then who can I trust?"

"Listen, Tone. I know I screwed up. I didn't wanna hurt you. But I was hurtin'. When ya moms tol' me she didn't love me anymore, that she was in love wit' someone else, that tore me up. I lied to you because I wanted you to hate her as much as I hated myself for losin' her. I knew it was wrong, but once I said it, I didn't know how to undo it. A few months after ya moms left, I tried lookin' for her, but she was gone. Her sister, ya aunt Christina, wouldn't give me her contact info. The last I heard she was somewhere on the West Coast. Hol' on a sec...." Pops walks outta my room.

My aunt Christina? I try to remember who she is, try to picture her face. But it's all a blank. I don't remember anything 'bout her. All I know—from what Pops tells me—is that she's my moms' only sister. She was the only livin' link to my moms—since my moms' parents died when I was mad young—and Pops took that away from me. All 'cause he didn't want me to have any kinda relationship wit' my moms 'cause he couldn't have one wit' her. I can feel my heart poundin' through my chest. She's a piece of a puzzle that opens up more questions for me. Questions that I am hopin' she'll be able to one day answer.

Pops comes back into the room, carryin' a shoebox.

"I've been holdin' on to this," he says, handin' it to me. "I know it can't undo what I've done, but maybe it'll help."

I look at Pops, mad nervous—my hands all shaky 'n' ish. I open the box 'n' inside there's a buncha pics of me 'n' Pops 'n' my...moms. There's one wit' her holdin' me in her arms when I was mad little. There's another of her breast-feedin' me. Another wit' her 'n' Pops. He has his hand on her stomach. Her stomach's mad big like she's ready to pop. Seein' these pictures of my moms, I don't know. I feel all kinda choked up. "I miss her, yo," I say real low, lettin' a tear slide down my face.

"I miss her, too," Pops says, soundin' all sad. "I still love her. I shoulda never let her get away from me. I shoulda been a better husband to her. I pushed her into another man's arms, son." He shakes his head. "I haven't been able to forgive myself for that. I know I've disappointed you, Antonio. There's a card on the bottom off all those pictures. On the back of it, there's an address for ya aunt Chrissy in the Bronx. It's over ten years old, but maybe..." He wipes his eyes. Oh, damn. Pops got tears in his eyes. "Aaah, damn." Turns from me for a few secs, turns back, then continues, "Maybe she's still there or someone else in the family is. Maybe they can help you get in contact wit' ya moms....It's time."

I sift through all the photos 'til I locate the card he's talkin' 'bout. It's a postcard of Las Vegas. On the back is an address in the Bronx.

"I'm sorry, son. I know that won't be enough for me to right the wrong, but hopefully it's a start. Hopefully, you won't hate me as much for lyin' to you all these years."

I swallow back the lump I feel formin' in my throat, starin' at my moms' face in one'a the pictures. Her brown skin, big brown eyes, her thick hair pulled back, her wide smile. She was beautiful. I hold my head down for a minute, shut my eyes real tight 'n' try to keep from breakin' down. All'a this is too much for me. Losin' Miesha, but gainin' memories of my moms.

I look up at Pops. "I'm pissed at you. But I don't hate you, Pops. I could never hate you. I just don't wanna be another you."

"Then don't be. Ya moms was one'a the good girls, son. She was a good woman who got caught up wit' a man who turned her heart cold. I pushed her away with my running the streets and chasing other women. I don't want you to be me. It's not too late for you to be a better man than I could ever be. Listen to ya heart, son. If you love that girl, then fight for her. Go get her."

Wipin' my nose wit' the palm of my hand, I nod. "Her name's Miesha."

"Then go get Miesha."

40

Miesha

"**M**iesha," my mom says, walkin' into my room *without* knocking. Ever since our last big blow-up she's been tryna be extra nice to me. But I'm not buying it. The guilt of her saying what she said to me is eating her up. Good. "There's someone standing outside to see you."

I've been in my room the whole weekend, OD'ing on reality TV. And I stayed up all last night watching the first two seasons of *Dexter* on Netflix. He's one sick, twisted character, but I'm hooked. Now today, all I wanna do is watch the rest of *Project Runway*, then curl up under the covers and sleep the rest of the day away. I just wanna go to sleep and *not* wake up again until my eighteenth birthday when I can get outta Jersey City and as far away from McPherson High as I possibly can. I don't wanna have any reminders of Antonio Lopez or his drama. And to think I was ready to give him another chance after I had that little chat in the girls' bathroom with Quanda. Oh my god, I woulda looked like such a fool going back to him, then finding out that some chick was having his baby. Thank goodness for gossiping-azz chicks like Fiona. Otherwise, I woulda been looking like Boo-Boo the damn Fool.

I roll my eyes, clicking the remote. "Whoever it is, tell them to go away. I'm not interested."

"You don't even know who it is."

I shoot her a look. "And I don't wanna know. Now can you leave my room? And shut the door behind you. Please and thank you." I go back to clicking the remote.

She walks all the way into my room, yanks the remote outta my hand, then shuts off the TV. "What the—"

"Listen here, Miesha. You can be mad at me all you want. And all that attitude is fine and good. But you sitting around here moping is not gonna change the fact that *you* miss him, okay?"

I blink. "I don't know what you're talking about. There is no *him*, okay?"

"Oh yes, there is a *him*. And *he's* standing outside, looking all lost and pitiful, wanting to talk to *you*. *He's* the reason you've been coming straight home from school, and locking yourself away in this room. Look at you. You're not even eating."

I sigh. "I haven't been hungry, okay? And I just don't feel like being bothered with anyone. So, please, can you drop it?"

She narrows her eyes. "Don't give me that. And no, I won't drop it. That boy came over here three, maybe four, times last week. And all you did was scream at him, then slam the door in his face. Well, what do you think screaming accomplished? Did it make you feel better? Did it solve whatever problems the two of you are having, huh?"

"*We* don't have any problems. He does. And no, screaming at him didn't solve anything. There's nothing to solve. He's a cheater. And I'm not beat."

"And you know this to be fact, how? Has he cheated on you?"

I huff, folding my arms. "Well, no. Not exactly—not that I know. But a buncha chicks stay sweating him, and I know it's only a matter of time before he cheats, so I'm not gonna sit around investing a buncha time and energy into a boy who I know is only gonna dog me out in the end."

"So you're not even willing to give this young man the benefit of the doubt?"

"It doesn't matter 'cause I'm not messing with him. Not after finding out that he has some girl pregnant. I don't do baby daddies and I'm not about to play stepmommy to some other girl's baby. Oh, no. I'm not that chick."

She shakes her head. "I think you should talk to him before you start jumping to conclusions. Hear him out, first."

I frown. "And what's it to you? Why do you care whether or not I talk to him? You don't even know who *he* is."

"I know he's that same young man who picked you up and took you out on a date. I saw how excited you were. I saw it in your eyes. And besides, your father told me he'd spoken to you about him."

What a big mouth!

"And I also know he's the same young man who you were staying out past curfew with on more than one occasion. He made you smile, Miesha. You think I didn't notice? You're my daughter. I know when you're hurting or sad. And I know when you *like* someone. But this time, it's more than like. You've never moped around before, looking all miserable, over a boy...."

"Exactly," I say, eyeing her. "I dismiss 'em, then *boom*...

on to the next! I'm not *you*. I don't sit around crying over no boy. And I'm not about to spend my life running behind some boy who wants to be all up in a buncha other girls' faces. All that sleeping around with a buncha different girls…mmmph, no thank you. He's too much like Daddy, and I don't wanna end up like *you*."

She blinks. Pulls in her bottom lip. Then takes a deep breath. "Don't compare what I've gone through with your father to what you may or may not end up going through. I made choices. And so did your father. I chose to run behind him because *he's* who I chose to be with. But you don't have to make that choice unless *you* want to. If you don't wanna end up like me, then don't. But don't throw away what could possibly be a good relationship with a good guy who *maybe* has had some troubles trusting. At least talk to him."

"I have nothing to say to him."

She shakes her head. "Girl, you are about as stubborn and bullheaded as your father."

I roll my eyes. "Are you taking him back?"

"Don't try and change the subject, Miesha. This isn't about me and your father. This is about *you*."

"And *that* is about me, too. So are you going back to Daddy, *again*?"

She sighs. "Miesha, I don't know what I'm doing. I love your father, period. But, I no longer love him enough to settle. I'm not willing to share him with other women, not this time. So if I decide to go back to him, *again*, it will be on *my* terms. Not his. But for right now, your father and I are talking. We are communicating. I am listening to him. Something he says I never did. Something you need to learn to do. Listen. Stop flying off the handle. You go from zero to one hundred for no rhyme or reason, like I do. If you don't wanna be like me, then don't be like me. Listen. Go out there and hear what that young man has to say. And then decide what's gonna work for you. You owe yourself, and him, at least that. Now take a few minutes to get yourself together. Then go out there and look that boy in the eyes and *listen* to him. I'll tell him you'll be out in a minute." She walks toward the door, looks over at me, then shakes her head. "Stop being so stubborn." She shuts the door behind her, leaving me feeling more confused than ever.

41

Antonio

I've been outside pacin' back 'n' forth, waitin', tryna play out in my head what I wanna say. But e'erything in my head is all jumbled up. I'm still tryna sort through the bomb Pops dropped on me yesterday. After he left my room, I spent the rest of the night lookin' at all'a those pictures Pops had stuffed in that shoebox. There were eighty-seven flicks all together of my mom, of me, of Pops, of all three of us together, of me 'n' my moms, and of me 'n' Pops. Flicks of my first six birthdays wit' birthday hats on 'n' cakes wit' candles on 'em. And in e'ery flick, I was all smiles, lookin' mad happy. The happiest I had ever been 'til Miesha came into my life.

I'm all effed up inside, yo. This girl got me feelin' ish I didn't know I could feel. She got me thinkin' ish I never thought I'd be thinkin' 'n' now I'm standin' here 'bout to say some ish I never thought I'd say.

My heart leaps in my chest the minute she comes to the door. She opens it, and steps out on the porch. All I keep thinkin' 'bout as she's ice-grillin' me is how beautiful 'n' sexy she is. How badly I wanna reach out 'n' touch her, pull her into my arms 'n' never let her go.

"How can I help you?"

I walk up the stairs, but she puts a hand up to stop me.

"No, don't come up here. Now, what do you want?"

"I just wanna talk," I say, tryna keep calm. But inside, I'm mad nervous. And now I wish I woulda smoked before comin' over here.

"I want you to stay away from me, Antonio," she says, slammin' a hand against her curvy hip. I try not to remember how my hands felt up on her hips. I don't wanna let my thoughts take me there. But, the way them yellow sweats are huggin' her hips isn't makin' it easy not to go there.

"I can't, yo."

"I'm not playing with you, Antonio. I mean it. I'm done with you."

I know she's pissed, but I'm not 'bout to throw in the towel wit' out goin' down wit' a bang. "I miss you."

Her eyes narrow to slits. "Well that's too bad 'cause I don't miss you. As a matter of fact, the sight of you is making me sick."

"You don't mean that, yo. That's anger talkin', yo. C'mon, you can't give me another chance?" I'm tryin' like hell to keep from scoopin' her up in my arms 'n' kissin' her. Even though her face is lookin' extra tight, frownin' at me, she looks mad sexy standin' here wit' her arms folded.

"Nope," she says. "I'm not in the habit of giving out second chances. You had your first and only chance. And you blew it, boy. I don't do playboys. Been there, done that. Now bounce. We ain't got nothing else to say to each other. When you see me in the halls, just keep it moving. Don't look my way 'cause I'm definitely not gonna be looking yours."

I can tell she's hurt. And I feel really bad. Real talk. She goes to walk back into the crib 'n' shut the door in my face. "Yo, Miesha, wait! *Please!*" Yes, I'm goin' out like a sucker, beggin'—again.

"Beat it!" She goes to shut the door, but I call out to her, again. "What?" she snaps, her 'tude still on ten. She folds her arms. "Well…"

"Listen. I, uh…I know you think I ain't shit. And I'ma keep it a hunnid. I haven't always been, yo. I've smashed mad girls. And all it was was a buncha empty sex, yo. I've dogged mad girls 'cause they'd let me. And I've gassed a buncha broads' heads up, tellin' 'em all what they wanna hear. But I ain't never front on you, yo. From the rip, I've kept it straight-laced wit' you. I dig you, Miesha. Real ish, yo. I've never felt 'bout any other female the way I feel 'bout you. I can't eat. I can't sleep. I can't even think straight wit' out seein' you. I miss you, Miesha. I put that on e'ery-thing. I'm all effed up, yo. I'm empty."

She narrows her eyes. "Then why the heck did you let her in your house with only your boxers on?"

"I thought it was you. When I heard the doorbell ring, I just opened the door. If I woulda knew it was her, I woulda never opened it, yo."

"Yeah right, but you still let her in, *after* you knew it was her."

"She begged me to let her talk, like I'm doin'. I'm beggin' you, yo. Just give me another chance."

"Well, *maybe* you wasn't tryna get with her. And *maybe* you are telling the truth about that. But I'm still not beat for you, boy. So don't come over here anymore. I'm not ever gonna be some silly chick who puts up with her man cheating and lying to her. And I'm definitely *not* about to do no boy with babies. Oh, no, boo-boo. I ain't signing up for that."

I blink. *How'd she find out 'bout that?*

"Yeah, that's right, *baby*. You didn't think I would find out, huh? Well, yeah. I heard all about the baby you got on the way with the little church mouse. I asked you when we were out having dinner if you had kids and you told me *no*."

"I don't," I say, runnin' my hand over my face, then head.

"Yeah, whatever. Save your lies. I'm done."

I swallow. I try to keep my voice from crackin'. But she's killin' me. "Will you just listen to me? Please. It's *not* my baby. That broad lied on me, yo."

She frowns. "What?"

"It was all a lie. She only said it to get back at me for tellin' her I wasn't beat for her. She felt like I was playin' 'er. She had her parents all up in my crib believin' that BS. But it's not true. My pops told me this morning before coming here that her pops called him to apologize, yo. She admitted to her parents it's not mine."

"Well, good for you. That doesn't change the fact that you didn't mention it."

"I didn't say anything, not because I was tryna hide something, but because I knew that girl was lying on me."

She twists her lips up. "And how many other chicks you got out here *claiming* to be knocked up by you?"

"None, yo."

"Good for you. I'm still not interested. I'm never gonna

be the kinda chick you gonna try'n run game on, boy. I'm not gonna let you hurt me. That's not what I'ma 'bout to let *you* or any other boy do."

I feel myself gettin' all choked up 'n' ish. "I'm not tryna hurt you," I say, tryna keep my voice from crackin'.

She eyes me all crazy-like, but at least she ain't tellin' me to go screw off. Her arms are still folded, but her face ain't all tight like it was. "Then *what* are you tryna do?"

"Love you." It comes out in almost a whisper. Those are words I've never said to—or felt for—any other female, 'cept to my moms.

She blinks. "What did you say?"

I repeat myself. This time it comes out clear 'n' steady. "I'm tryna love you, yo. If you'd let me. That's it. I ain't perfect, yo. And I don't know what might pop off tomorrow or the day after that. But what I do know is, nothin's been right wit' out you. I want you back in my life, Miesha. I got it bad for you, yo." I keep my eyes focused on her when I say this, but I can't read her expression. I can't tell what she's thinkin', but I'm still hopeful. The door hasn't slammed in my face, so I know I still gotta shot.

She grunts. "Mmph. That's what your mouth says. And how do I know you won't get tempted and start creeping with them chickenheads you got clucking around you all the time?"

"Because, on e'erything, I won't. I'm not beat for none of them broads, yo. That's my word. On some real ish, the first time I peeped you walkin' into the cafeteria, I knew I had to get at you. At first, I ain't gonna front, it was on some real hit-it-'n'-quit-it type stuff, but then...I don't know. I peeped how you moved and I knew you were the kinda girl I could fall for. And that's on e'erything, yo.

Even when you was playin' me to the left, that only made me wanna get at you more."

"Then you're a damn fool."

I shake my head. "Nah...that makes me—for the first time in my life, yo—someone who finally knows what he wants. And the moment you kissed me, I knew what I already felt—that you were the one for me."

She stares at me, and shifts her eyes. I can tell she's tryna not to cry 'n' that effs me up even more. I don't wanna ever see her hurtin'. I pull her into my arms, relieved she doesn't push me away. I know she's angry 'n' hurt, but I see more, I feel more. E'erything in my heart aches for her. And I know she wants me, needs me, as badly as I want 'n' need her.

"I love you, Miesha," I whisper, pullin' her in closer. I lift her chin. "I love you," I say again, leanin' in to kiss her. She moves her head away, but I don't stop. I keep sayin' it over 'n' over 'til she finally hears it, 'til it finally sinks in, that I am in love wit' her. I lean in again, brushin' my lips against her wet cheek. "I love you."

"I don't believe you, Antonio." She says this, but that's not what I see in her eyes. She sees what I feel for her. And she feels it.

"Real rap, yo. All I wanna do is hold you in my arms, 'n' watch those flicks *Dear John* 'n' *The Notebook* wit'—"

"And *Titanic*," she cuts in, raisin' an eyebrow.

I grin. "Yeah, that one, too. Or any other love flick that makes you smile." She looks me in my eyes, intensely. "Let me be ya man, Miesha. I've never wanted to be wit' anyone the way I wanna be wit' you. I trust you wit' my heart. And, now..." I swallow back my emotions. "All I'm askin' is for you to trust me wit' yours."

I kiss her on the lips 'n' this time she doesn't pull away. She cups me on the back of the neck 'n' pulls me forward, kissin' me back—deep. The kiss is fast 'n' intense, before she pulls away. Before she allows me or herself to get caught up in it, lost in the moment.

"And *why* should I do that? Why should I trust you with anything of mine, huh, Antonio? Especially my heart."

I look into her beautiful brown eyes, knowin' that wit' out a doubt I am turnin' in my player's card to be true to her. I'm done wit' runnin' game 'n' tryna have more than one girl. I smile. Real rap, Miesha Wilson is all I need, yo. All I wanna need. "Because," I say, kissin' her on the lips again, "you're the girl of my dreams."

THE GIRL OF HIS DREAMS

Amir Abrams

ABOUT THIS GUIDE

The following questions are intended to
enhance your group's reading of
THE GIRL OF HIS DREAMS.

Discussion Questions

Wassup, my peeps, it's ya boy Amir coming at ya with some discussion questions for my joint, *The Girl of His Dreams*. Definitely hope you enjoyed the read as much as I enjoyed writing it. A'ight, with that being said, here goes:

1. What did you think of Antonio's character? Do you know anyone like him?

2. Have you ever dated someone who you knew was a player? If so, why did you date them? And how was that experience for you?

3. What did you think of Miesha's character? Do you think she should have perhaps gotten to know either Brent or Justin more before getting caught up in Antonio?

4. Do you think guys like Antonio can ever really give up their "player's card" to be faithful to one girl? Why?

5. What is your view on relationships and cheating? Do you think all boys creep in their relationships? If so, why? And would you tolerate it? If you have accepted it in your relationships, why?

Don't miss Amir Abrams's debut novel,

Crazy Love.

In stores now!

"Giiiiiiiirrrrrrl, this party is fiiiiyah," Zahara shouted over the beats of a Rick Ross joint.

"I told y'all it would be," Brittani said, swaying her hips and popping her fingers. Brittani's sister, Briana, had the hookup for us because her boo-of-the-month was one of the frat boys whose fraternity was hosting the party. So she invited us to get our party on. Brittani's sister is mad cool like that. She's always getting us into all the hot spots.

"I'ma get my queen-diva on tonight!" Ameerah exclaimed excitedly as she popped her hips. We laughed at her as she flicked her tongue at this cutie who eased by eyeing her.

Anywaaayz, it was the weekend after Fourth of July and we were at an off-campus house party packed with mostly college heads. Mad cuties and thirsty chicks were every-where, sweating it out on the dance floor. Fraternities and sororities represented, hard-rocking their colors and em-blems. Hot beats were blaring through the speakers as dudes danced and grinded up on chicks who were booty-popping it all up on them.

"Ooooh, I wanna dance," Zahara said, snapping her fingers and bopping her head. She did a two-step, dropped down low, then popped it back up. She danced and twirled until she got the attention she wanted. Zahara loves attention!

Anywaaayz, Zahara, Brittani, Ameerah, and I had just finished our dance-through, where we dance in a line through a party, all sexy-like, to peep what's what and who's who before we find a spot to post up—and be cute!—when I spotted him. He was standing over in a corner with three other guys. And they were all fine, *but*... not as fine as him. I acted like I didn't see him. But the truth is, how could you *not* see him? All eyes were already on him. He was rocking a red and white Polo button-up with a pair of designer jeans and a pair of white, crispy Jordans and a red and white Yankees fitted. Tall and built, with skin the color of milk chocolate. Whew... he looked... *delicious!* Even in the dimly lit room, I knew he was fine.

And the minute I was certain he'd seen me, I stepped, making sure to throw an extra shake in my hips as we strutted off. As soon as we made it to the other side of the room, these dudes came over to where we were standing and asked each of us to dance. Zahara, Brittani, and Ameerah said yes to the dudes who asked them, and bounced their booties toward the dance floor, leaving me standing there with this tall, light-skinned guy with really big teeth and gums, grinning at me and licking his lips. He reminded me of a big yellow crayon.

"You sure you don't wanna dance?" he asked again, slowly looking me up and down, dragging his tongue across his lips. I blinked, blinked again, hoping I could erase him from my view. No luck. He was still there, staring down at me, looking like a glow-in-the-dark wand as he bobbed his head to the beats. Truth is, I did want to dance. Just not with *him*. Not that he was busted or anything. He was just too bright and his teeth were too big for me to have to look in his face. I would either have to keep my eyes shut and zone out on the music, or keep my back to him. Lucky for me, I didn't have to do either.

This brown-skinned chick with a long black weave, wearing a skintight pair of jeans and a teeny-weeny shirt, was on the dance floor near us, dancing all fast and nasty by herself. That caught his attention and he bounced on over to her. *Yuck*, I thought, shifting my eyes around the room to see where my girls were.

I glanced around the party and peeped Briana walking toward the stairs with her boo in tow. *Mmmph*, I thought, curling my lips up as she climbed the stairs. *Miss Hot-Box probably going upstairs to get her back blown out.*

I shook the thought from my head and shifted my attention toward the dance floor, watching my girls act a fool. Every so often, I glanced over in his direction and would see a buncha birds flocked around him, and he'd lean into their ears and say something to them, then they'd start smiling or giggling like real dizzy chicks before walking off. I caught him staring over in my direction a few times, trying to make eye contact with me. But I kept it fly. And, when I finally let him catch my eye, he grinned. I wanted him. Knew I had to have him. And I was going to make it my business to bag him quick, fast, and in a hurry without making myself look like a straight-up bird. Fly girls never look thirsty. They keep it cute, okay! Well, um, that's until they reel their catch-of-the-moment in. Then you can't be too proud to beg, or too scared to beat a trick down, to keep him.

As soon as Young Jeezy's "I Do" started playing, I started swaying to the beats, popping my hips just enough to prove a point. That I was the hottest chick in the room; that I could bag any of these boys up in there if I really wanted. A few seconds later, I heard him. And right then I knew my point was made.

"Wassup," I heard someone behind me say in my ear. Even over the music, the voice was mad sexy. And I knew who it was without even looking over my shoulder.

"Wassup," I coolly said back, eyeing him real slow and sexy.

"Looks like ya boy did me a favor," he said, grinning at me.

I raised my brow. "Excuse you. He did you a favor how?"

"Ole boy made it easy for me not to have to tell him to step off."

"Oh, really?"

He smirked. "Yeah, really. You know you wanna be mine."

"How you know that?"

"You been wanting me to notice you from the moment you stepped through the door with your girls."

I smiled, twirling the ends of my hair. "Obviously it worked. So you wanna dance or what?"

"No doubt."

"Then follow me and take notes," I said, taking him by the hand and leading him onto the dance floor. He laughed, letting me lead the way. We started moving to Drake's "Miss Me." He stepped in closer to me, staring at me as he moved. I stared back, lifting my arms up over my head and matching his rhythm. Each time he stepped in closer, I stepped back. When he stepped back, I stepped in. I twirled my hips a taste. Let him see what I was working with, but didn't let him grind up on me.

I spotted Ameerah, Zahara, and Brittani dancing with the same guys, laughing and switching partners every so often. I smiled, then returned my attention back to the fine catch in front of me. We danced for three songs until some whack song came on. I grabbed his hand and led him off the floor, like he was already my man.

"Yo, so what's your name?" he yelled over the music.

"What?" I yelled back.

"What's your name?"

Just as I was about to open my mouth to tell him, this Spanish-looking chick with wavy black hair walked over to us and rudely pulled him away by the arm.

"Yo, I'll be right back," he said to me in my ear over the music. "Don't go no where. Let me get this one dance in with my homegirl real quick. I'll be right back."

"Don't keep me waiting too long," I said all sweet and sexy, eyeing him and licking my lips. But inside I was screaming, "*Oh no the hell she didn't just step up and disrupt my groove!*" But I kept it real cute as they walked off toward the dance floor 'cause that's how I do it. Still, every so often I shot her daggers on the low as she popped her booty up and down on the front of my future man's crotch. *That ho musta got the news feeds mixed up. I'm the wrong chick. I will spin her clock back.* I stared her down for a quick moment, then caught myself before I turned the party out. I wasn't about to let Mr. Fine and

Sexy see the other side of me, so I popped my hips over to where my girls were, keeping an eye on the object of my desires from afar. Oooh, he was so sexy. And I wanted him.

Zahara walked up on me, looping her arm through mine, pulling me toward the door. "Girl," she screamed over the music, "it's hot and loud in here. I need some fresh air. Let's go outside for a minute."

"Yeah, let's," I said. Brittani and Ameerah were behind her.

"Whew, I need me a cigarette," Zahara stated the minute we got out into the night air. "Did y'all see how fine my future baby fahver was? And he could dance, too!"

I laughed at her silly butt. "Girl, you don't even smoke."

"Well, not yet, I don't. But let me get a few rounds in with him and I will be."

"Mmmph…these college boys are too fine for their own good," Brittani agreed. She wiped sweat from her face with a napkin. "But what was up with that broad with the big pumpkin head on the dance floor?"

"Oh, that ho tried to play me, but I had to show her what's what."

"I know that's right," Brittani said. "I thought we were gonna hafta bring it to her face real quick."

I laughed. "Oh, trust. She didn't want it. You see she stepped."

"She better had," Ameerah stated, pulling her braids up and wiping sweat from around the back of her neck.

"Wait, what happened?" Zahara asked. "Who was tryna set it off up in there?"

"This nobody," I said. "Don't even sweat it."

"Have any of you seen my sister?" Brittani asked, pulling her hair back from her face. We all told her no. Shoot, it wasn't my place to tell her I saw her sister sneak off up the stairs with her man. Brittani rolled her eyes knowingly. "She's probably somewhere pinned up against a wall with her boo."

"Hold up, let's rewind," Ameerah said, planting a hand up on her hip. "Speaking of boos, who was the tall glass of dreamy, sweet chocolate you were dancing with? Don't think we didn't see you serving it up."

I shrugged. "Some guy who asked me to dance; that's all."

"That's *all*?!" Zahara screeched. "Girl, that chocolate-drop cutie was all that and a bag of M&M'S, okay? Melt all up in ya mouth; not in ya hands."

Ameerah and Brittani laughed. I rolled my eyes, trying to keep from laughing with them. I played it off instead. "He was all right, I guess."

"Well, you guessed wrong," Brittani said, placing a hand up on her hip. "So run along. Girl, do you need ya eyes checked? That boy is more than *all right*. Hon, he's super-duper, capital F-I-N-E. Did you at least get his name?"

I shook my head.

"*Whaaat?*" they snapped in unison, not believing me.

I shrugged. "It wasn't that serious," I stated, shifting my eyes from their stares. Truth is, it was! I needed to reel him in, and quick. "C'mon, let's go back in."

"Yeah, let's," Zahara agreed, pulling me by the arm. "If I'm lucky, I might be able to get me another dance in with that cutie, and bounce all this booty up on him again."

I laughed, shaking my head.

Once we got back inside, I glanced around the dimly lit party to see if I could spot him and that Latina hooker dancing again. But neither were anywhere in sight. I watched my girls on the dance floor, getting it in with the guys they had danced with earlier. Glow Worm found his way back over to me, grinning. "You ready to dance?"

I stared at him for a long minute, then decided he wasn't *that* bad to look at. Besides, I had finally spotted my future boo, dancing it up with some other chick. So I told Glow Worm yes, and dragged him over to where Mr. Milk Chocolate was and started dancing with him. My boo eyed me. And I eyed him back. I dropped it, popped it, locked it, then spun it around. Shaking everything my momma gave me: hair, hips, and booty. And Glow Worm had the nerve to be able to groove and keep up.

Three hours later, it was already time to go because Ameerah and I had two o'clock curfews—well, mine was really one, but I begged my dad to let me stay out an hour later. Anywaaayz, we all wanted to hit up the twenty-four-hour IHOP over in Irvington before we had to be in. I caught Briana's boo coming down the stairs, then a few minutes afterward she did, too.

We all stared at her. Her hair was all over her head and her lipstick was smeared all around her lips. She looked a hot, greasy mess!

She blinked. "What?"

"Uh, hellooo," Brittani said, rolling her eyes. "You might wanna go fix your situation 'cause you are looking real tore up right now."

"And extra funky," Ameerah added, holding her nose.

"Like a real circus clown," I stated, adding my two cents in.

We burst out laughing as Briana spun off to go to the bathroom.

Brittani huffed. "I swear I love my sister, but sometimes she acts like a real bird. And I bet she spent the whole dang night rolling around upstairs on some nasty sheets. Ugh! Let's wait for her outside."

And just as we were walking toward the door, out of nowhere Milk Chocolate appeared, stepping in front of me. "Yo, where you going, beautiful? You still owe me another dance."

I playfully rolled my eyes. "Mmmph. Oh, really? Now you want another dance *after* you dissed me for some other chick. No, thank you. I don't do sloppy seconds."

He laughed. "Nah, it wasn't even like that. That's my homegirl. I kept promising her a dance; my bad."

I smirked. "Uh-huh. It sure is. And it's your loss, too. So go on back and get the rest of the cooties."

He laughed. "Oh, damn. I don't have cooties."

"I don't know that," I teased.

"Well, come dance with me and find out."

He grinned, licking his lips. And right there, I wanted to kiss him. I stared at him, trying to act uninterested. "Not tonight, playboy. I'm leaving."

He smiled. "Playboy? Nah, that's not me."

"Mmmph, yeah right. I can't tell. All night all I saw were a buncha chicks clucking around you."

He laughed. "Yo, you real funny, for real. Wasn't none of 'em checkin' for me like that."

I waved him on. "Oh, puhleeeze. That's what your mouth says. But I know what I saw."

He laughed. "Oh, damn. It's like that? Let me find out you tryna put a claim on me."

I tilted my head, sweeping my bang over my forehead. "Maybe I am. Maybe I'm not."

He stared at me real hard, then broke into a wide smile. "You real feisty."

I smiled back. "Yup. And don't forget it."

Briana walked over with her hair pulled back in a pony-tail and her lipstick wiped off from around her mouth, asking me if I was ready. She told me she'd bring the car around and pick me up out front. I waited for her to walk off, then said, "Look, it's been real. I gotta go."

"A'ight, let me walk out with you."

"Suit yourself," I said, trying to act like I wasn't pressed.

"So, what's good with you? Where you from?" I tell him I'm from South Orange. "Oh, a'iiight. That's wassup. You a freshman?"

I shook my head. "No, I'm a senior."

"A senior, daaaaamn. That's wassup. What's your major?"

"Dance."

He smiled. "A'ight, a'ight. That's wassup. I've never seen you on campus before. You go to Seton Hall?"

I shook my head again. "No, South Orange Performing Arts Academy."

He frowned, repeated what he heard. "*South Orange Performing Arts?* Wait, you're a *senior* in high school?"

"Yup."

"Damn. That's a good school. You gotta be on top of ya game to get up in there."

I shrugged. "Something like that." But he was right. South Orange Performing Arts Academy is one of the hottest schools in Jersey. Shoot...in the country! And it's one of the hardest to get into. The only way you getting in is through an examination and application process. And then you better be bringing it in the classroom, or you'll end up on probation, then tossed out if you don't step it up.

He smiled. "I'm impressed."

I smiled back. "Thanks."

"So, how old are you?"

"Seventeen... well, I will be in two months. What about you?"

"I just turned eighteen."

I smiled. "So, I guess you're too old for someone like me."

He laughed. "Nah, you good. You seem chill."

Briana pulled up, blowing the horn as if I couldn't see her. I shook my head. "Well, I gotta bounce. Nice talking to you."

"Yeah, you too. But I didn't get your name."

"That's because I didn't give it. It's Kamiyah. And yours?"

"Sincere."

I smiled. "Nice to meet you."

Briana blew her horn again. "Girl, will you hurry up already," Brittani yelled out of the passenger-side window. "We're starving."

"Yo, I'ma let you go. Can I get your number?"

I smiled, eyeing him real sexy-like. "Are you going to use it?"

He eyed me back. "No doubt. I wouldn't ask for it if I wasn't."

I motioned him with my finger to come in closer, and when he leaned his head in toward me, I whispered it, grazing my lips against his ear. He grinned.

"Yo, I'ma hit you up tomorrow, a'ight?"

"If you do, cool. If you don't, oh well. It's your loss."

He laughed, walking backward toward the house. "A'ight, hold that thought. Make sure you pick up."

I opened the car door. "You just make sure you call."

"I got you."

I slid into the backseat, then rolled the window down as Briana pulled off, and yelled out, "If you don't call me by eight o'clock tomorrow night, lose my number."